A Splinter, in the Night's Sky

# Table of Contents

*Book 5:* ........................................................................... 7

*Dedication:* ..................................................................... 7

*Quotes:* .......................................................................... 8

*Copyright:* ...................................................................... 9

*Disclaimer:* ................................................................... 10

*Dramatis personae.* ..................................................... 11

*Timeline.* ...................................................................... 15

**A Splinter, in the Night's Sky.** ...................................... **17**

*Their terrible purpose.* ................................................. 17

*A Beginning.* ................................................................. 18

**After.** ......................................................................... **20**

*Earth's Orbit. July 26th, 2024.* ..................................... 20

**Their terrible purpose.** .............................................. **30**

**Kate.** .......................................................................... **31**

**Mission Date: Day 1** .................................................... **34**

*Emergence.* .................................................................. 34

**Mission Date: Day 23** .................................................. **43**

1

A Splinter, in the Night's Sky.          Book 5:

*An unbalanced force.............................................................43*

*Capability Brown. ...............................................................50*

***Mission Date: Day 60. ...................................................53***

*The old man and the sea. ....................................................53*

***Mission Date: Day 61. ...................................................62***

*Battle ready. ........................................................................62*

***Mission Date: Day 73 ....................................................70***

*Awake. .................................................................................70*

*Perhaps we are not alone.....................................................73*

*Sendler: The handshake protocol. .......................................76*

***Mission Date: Day 75. ...................................................79***

*Mission. ...............................................................................79*

*Revolver. ..............................................................................92*

***Mission Date 79. ...........................................................95***

*Living in the now..................................................................95*

***Mission Date: Day 81. .................................................102***

*Exercise..............................................................................102*

*Hacker................................................................................105*

***Mission Date: Day 83. .................................................111***

*Prepare. .............................................................................111*

A Splinter, in the Night's Sky.          Book 5:

*Awake.* ........................................................................... *115*

## *Mission Date: Day 84.* ...................................... ***117***

*Piano man.* ..................................................................... *117*

*Cook off.* ........................................................................ *119*

## *Mission Date: Day 85.* ...................................... ***122***

*Heading back.* ................................................................ *122*

## *Mission Date: Day 92.* ...................................... ***128***

*Catch.* ............................................................................. *128*

*Elite-Recon.* .................................................................... *131*

## *Mission Date: Day 103.* .................................... ***133***

*Finding balance.* ............................................................. *133*

## *Mission Date: Day 120.* .................................... ***139***

*Lessons learned.* ............................................................. *139*

*Friends.* .......................................................................... *141*

*Evening.* ......................................................................... *143*

## *Mission Date: Day 134.* .................................... ***144***

*Clear.* ............................................................................. *144*

## *Mission Date: Day 151.* .................................... ***147***

*Sword.* ........................................................................... *147*

A Splinter, in the Night's Sky.            Book 5:

## ***Mission Date: Day 180.*** .................................................**149**
*Survey.* .................................................................................... 149

## ***Mission Date: Day 212.*** .................................................**152**
*Alone.* ..................................................................................... 152
*Perhaps there is proof in the pudding.* ................................... 155

## ***Mission Date: Day 231.*** .................................................**158**
*Rudely interrupted.* ................................................................ 158

## ***Mission Date: Day 297.*** .................................................**164**
*Frontier planet: Corkier-Shay.* ................................................ 164

## ***Mission date: Day 335.*** ..................................................**185**
*Rebellion.* ............................................................................... 185
*Open space.* ........................................................................... 194
*Phase two.* ............................................................................. 198
*Not quite as smoothly.* ........................................................... 203
*In the dirt.* .............................................................................. 205

## ***Misson Date: Day 336.*** ...................................................**210**
*The next step.* ........................................................................ 210

## ***Mission date: Day 341.*** ..................................................**217**
*Teghra-Dorne: Planet fall.* ...................................................... 217
*Running and gunning.* ............................................................ 231

A Splinter, in the Night's Sky.    Book 5:

*Fight and flight.* ............................................................................ 248

*Capture* ............................................................................................ 256

## **Mission Date: Day 342.** .......................................... **266**

*Transit.* ............................................................................................. 266

## **Mission Date: Day 346.** .......................................... **269**

*Conversation.* ................................................................................ 269

## **Mission Date: Day 348.** .......................................... **276**

*We must hurry.* ............................................................................. 276

## **Mission Date: Day 374.** .......................................... **281**

*Forbidden.* ...................................................................................... 281

*Sneaking in.* ................................................................................... 285

*Warning.* ......................................................................................... 294

*The planet.* ..................................................................................... 297

*The Last day on Earth.* ............................................................... 303

*The Pequod.* ................................................................................... 316

*The Thunder-Child.* ..................................................................... 319

*Aftermath.* ..................................................................................... 334

*Anger.* .............................................................................................. 338

## **THE END!** ................................................................... **342**

*For now.* .......................................................................................... 342

A Splinter, in the Night's Sky.                Book 5:

## ***Authors Note.*** ..................................................***343***

*Book Five: Their terrible purpose.* ......................................................*343*

*Originally, 'The longest patrol.'* ........................................................*343*

## Book 5:

## Dedication:

It's hard to always write here. After enough books, and it seems to be that it could too easily seem to be little more than platitudes. They are not that.

To my wife. Louise. My love. My everything.

To Colin, a man who helps another man who rarely leaves an infinitive, unsplit. Or a comma, correctly used.

To my mum and my dad. As always, thank you. My sister, too.

But also, to my brother. I wish sometimes things could be a little less bumpy here.

To all those I love, you all know how much you mean to me.

Also, to whoever reads this and finds enjoyment. As always, that means the world to me.

\*     \*     \*

## Quotes:

"Never have I had such a strong fish - or one that acted so strangely. Maybe he's too wise to jump. He could ruin me with a jump. Or one quick rush." The old man and the sea. Hemmingway.

"If anybody ever tells you anything about an aeroplane which is so bloody complicated you can't understand it, take it from me: it's all balls." R. J. Mitchell.

"No man ever steps in the same river twice, for it's not the same river and he's not the same man." Heraclitus.

\*    \*    \*

A Splinter, in the Night's Sky.          Copyright:

## Copyright:

© This work is protected under UK copyright and (by extension) protected internationally under the Berne Convention.

All rights are reserved and this document, or any part of the document, cannot be shared or distributed without the prior agreement of the author.

*    *    *

A Splinter, in the Night's Sky.              Disclaimer:

# Disclaimer:

This is a work of fiction. Names, characters, businesses, events, and incidents are the products of the author's imagination. Any resemblance to actual persons, living or dead, or actual events, is purely coincidental. Some real persons, and organisations, will be mentioned; however, these are done so to enable the story to exist within the real world and are not included to draw any reference or conclusion as to the character, or conduct, of those persons or organisations.

*   *   *

A Splinter, in the Night's Sky.  Dramatis personae.

## Dramatis personae.

Note: For reference only. Some characters will be returning, but many are new. This should help.

Spoilers are possible.

| Name | Background | Origin Story |
|---|---|---|
| The Thunder-Child | The Elite-Recon Starship | Book 2: Something old and something entirely new. |
| The Pequod | A ship of exploration. Now of war. | Book 2: Something old and something entirely new. |
| BOB | A sentient machine, from a race only known as 'the benefactors' | Book 2: Something old and something entirely new. |
| Orac | Sentient AI, running the Ark | Book 2: Something old and something entirely new. |
| The Ark | The benefactor's starship | Book 2: Something old and something entirely new. |
| **Elite Recon** | **Epsilon Marine Force.** | |
| Captain Jason/Michael Young. | Captain of Elite Recon. Purestrain. | Book 1: Watching the sea. |
| Alistair Connaught. | Soul attached to Jason. | Book 1: Watching the sea. |
| Billie, TT, Callan | Marine, sniper. Asian descent. | Book 3: A confounding mess. |
| Leftenant Dani. | Second in charge. Elite Recon. | Book 1: Watching the sea. |
| Neil. | TANK Driver. Elite Recon. | Book 1: Watching the sea. |
| Colonel Colm Carter | (Retired). President's husband. | Book 2: Something old and something entirely new. |
| **Epsilon Colonists** | | |
| President Jennifer Carter | Epsilon's President. Wolf. | Book 2: Something old and something entirely new. |

# A Splinter, in the Night's Sky.    Dramatis personae.

| | | |
|---|---|---|
| Clare Carter | President's Daughter. Purestrain. | Book 2: Something old and something entirely new. |
| Lieutenant Commander Dr Katherine Harper | Science lead, and Captain of the Pequod. | Book 1: Watching the sea. |
| Dr Jansen | A member of Katherine's original team. | Book 2: Something old and something entirely new. |
| Dr Summers | Katherine's oldest colleague | Book 3: A confounding mess. |
| Admiral Kate Harris. | Daniel's daughter. Purestrain. | Book 1: Watching the sea. |
| **Hermentia Survivors** | | |
| Daniel Longbridge | Purestrain. Kate's father. | Book 1: Watching the sea. |
| Natalie Clearwater/Bridgewater | Mission lead. | Book 3; A night ride. |
| Julien Dench | Retired Mi28 agent and copper. | Book 1: Watching the sea. |
| Dr, Thomas 'Capability' Brown | Mi28 Scientist and Historian. | Book 4: Fracture |
| Tyler Herricks | Delta. Master Sergeant. Retired. | Book 3: Patrol. |
| Antony (Tony) Flaherty | Lance Corporal 42 Commando | Book 4: Fracture |
| Ben 'Crater' Tatler | Retired Navy SEAL | Book 4: Fracture |
| Peter 'Impact' Cole | Retired Navy SEAL (wolf) | Mention: Book 3: Patrol. |
| Lance Corporal Coltheart. Cleo. | British Navy Apache Gunner. | Book 4: Fracture |
| Alice Cuomo. | American child. Rescued. | Book 4: Fracture |
| Steven (Steve) Hacker. | British Solicitor. Rescued. | Book 4: Fracture |
| **Aliens met.** | | |
| Babalich-ThrunderArch | The rebel leader. | Book 5: The longest patrol. |
| Orga-Loathe'clichemere. | The race hunting the rebels. | Book 5: The longest patrol. |
| Captain Redroot-Tessera'd | Boylston Armada | Book 5: The longest patrol. |
| Boylston Armada | We learn little so far. | Book 5: The longest patrol. |
| Teghra-Dorne empire | The Orga-Loathe'clichemere empire. | Book 5: The longest patrol. |
| Darla | The Orga- | Book 5: The |

# A Splinter, in the Night's Sky.

## Dramatis personae.

|  | Loathe'clichemere home planet. | longest patrol. |
|---|---|---|
| Captea D'Laghas | Darla's capital city. | Book 5: The longest patrol. |
| Strenuous. | Teghra-Dorne flagship | Book 5: The longest patrol. |
| Corkier-Shay | First planet to meet with rebel contact. | Book 5: The longest patrol. |
| Cordax | First rebel contact. | Book 5: The longest patrol. |
| Karma-Yermic-Tata. | A Tarka-Jebshate. Rebel agent. | Book 5: The longest patrol. |
| Karma-Tata-Ye | Tata's son. | Book 5: The longest patrol. |

A Splinter, in the Night's Sky.    Timeline.

## Timeline.

| Event: | Date: | Book. |
|---|---|---|
| Daniel found Lord Strynthorpe killed. | 1920. | Book 1: Watching the Sea. |
| Julien finds Daniel's diary. | July 1988 | Book 1: Watching the Sea. |
| Kate is spotted by the organisation. | Sep 26th, 1997 | Book 1: Watching the Sea. |
| Daniel encounters Tobias Hawker. | Oct 15th, 1997 | Book 1: Watching the Sea. |
| Ambush at the university. | Oct 30th,1997 | Book 1: Watching the Sea. |
| The battle at the manor house. | Nov 6th, 1997 | Book 1: Watching the Sea. |
| The terrorist attack on London. | Dec 11th, 1996 | Book 2: Something old… |
| The council. | Sep 11th, 2001 | Book 3: Songs to dance to. |
| Beach. | Apr, 2002 | Book 3: Songs to dance to. |
| The Magic Men. Training in Kent. | Jan 2003 | Book 3: Songs to dance to. |
| Monster. Tobias Hawker, London. | Feb 2003 | Book 3: Songs to dance to. |
| Piano man. Jason's apartment. | April 2004 | Book 3: Songs to dance to. |
| Patriarch. London, serial killer. | Sep 2005 | Book 3: Songs to dance to. |
| Patrol. Jason, Afghanistan. | July 2006 | Book 3: Songs to dance to. |
| Tokyo. Kate working with Mi6. | August 2010 | Book 3: Songs to dance to. |
| FOB. Jason, Afghanistan. | September 2010 | Book 3: Songs to dance to. |
| Just being. Jason returns to London. | Feb 2011 | Book 3: Songs to dance to. |
| Taskin. Kate breaks the rules. | April 2011 | Book 3: Songs to dance to. |
| Hobby. Jason, the Kings Road. London. | Aug 22nd, 2011 | Book 3: Songs to dance to. |
| A wedding. Julien's son. | Jul 6th, 2017 | Book 3: Songs to dance to. |

# A Splinter, in the Night's Sky.    Timeline.

| | | |
|---|---|---|
| A night ride. Jason; Billings Hawkswood. | March 2018 | Book 3: Songs to dance to. |
| New Blood. Kate, Oxford. | Sep 2020 | Book 3: Songs to dance to. |
| Louder. Kate, a terrorist attack in Paris. | Jul 4th, 2022 | Book 3: Songs to dance to. |
| Bordeaux. Jason approached by… | Apr 11th, 2023 | Book 3: Songs to dance to. |
| Hermentia. Earthquake. | Mar 28th, 2024 | Book 4: Fracture. |
| Hermentia. Natalie arrives. | Jun 17th, 2024 | Book 4: Fracture. |
| Hermentia. Last day. | July 9th, 2024 | Book 4: Fracture. |
| Jason prepares for the mission. Epsilon. | Nov 22nd, 2408 | Watching the Sea. |
| The ambush at the comet. Epsilon. | Jan 12th, 2412 | Watching the Sea. |
| Preparing to return. Epsilon. | Mar 22nd, 2412 | Book 2: Something old… |
| Return to Epsilon. | June 14th, 2412 | Book 2: Something old… |
| A confounding mess. Epsilon. | Aug 22nd, 2412 | Book 3: Songs to dance to. |
| The first time around. Progenitor home. | 2537 | Book 3: Songs to dance to. |
| Their terrible purpose. | -443,033,012 BC | Book 5: Their terrible purpose. |

# A Splinter, in the Night's Sky.

Book 5:

## Their terrible purpose.


Original title (as referenced in book 4): The longest patrol.

They had fled the chaos at Hermentia. Ripped away from the doomed island, rescued from what should have been their last day.

Which had been, the first time around.

Pulled into a very different world. One which existed far beyond the scope of their imaginations. With some finding versions of their friends, who were now impossibly separated from them by centuries.

Friends who had mourned for them. Friends, who had forgotten some of them.

Joining the crews of the Thunder-Child, and the Pequod, as they head off on a terrible mission into the impossible past.

Entering worlds of starships, of faster than light travel, and also time travel. Miraculous things. Unlikely things.

Dangerous things.

But they had prepared as best they could. They had, at least, done that.

It just had to be enough.

It's unlikely that it is going to be.

## A Beginning.

There is always a beginning to every story, only you will not find it in this book.

This is the fifth in the series.

This is 'Their terrible purpose.' The first novel in the series to be entirely based off-Earth. This is my first truly science-fiction based novel. Apart from the magic stuff and werewolves. Science-Fiction-Fantasy. I fear I might be a gentle google away from coming up with a better answer than simply calling it 'science fiction'... I have no idea why I don't.

Hell, Star Wars has space wizards and few of my generation easily see criticism against the great George Lucas.

So here we are. Jason will now have to take a role he might rather not: mission lead.

He will have to lead a team into the impossible past and face a galaxy they are ill-prepared to even understand.

# A Splinter, in the Night's Sky.    A Beginning.

Book 1:           A splinter in the night's sky;   Watching the sea.

Book 2:           A splinter in the night's sky;   Something old and something entirely new.

- Story 1:        2412: Prelude: Epsilon.
- Story 2:        1997: A rainy day in London.
- Story 3:        2412: Return to Epsilon.

Book 3:           A splinter in the night's sky;   Songs to dance to.

- Story 1:        The first time around.
- Story 2:        The council.
- Story 3:        Beach.
- Story 4:        The Magic Men.
- Story 5:        Monster.
- Story 6:        Piano man.
- Story 7:        Patriarch.
- Story 8:        Patrol.
- Story 9:        Hong Kong.
- Story 10:       FOB.
- Story 11:       Just being.
- Story 12:       Taskin.
- Story 13:       Hobby.
- Story 14:       A wedding.
- Story 15:       A night ride.
- Story 16:       New blood.
- Story 17:       Louder.
- Story 18:       Bordeaux.
- Story 19:       A confounding mess.

Book 4:           A splinter in the night's sky;   Fracture.

Book 5:           A splinter in the night's sky;   Their terrible purpose.

## After.

## Earth's Orbit. July 26th, 2024.

Just over three weeks after the rescue of the team from Hermentia.

\*   \*   \*

After.     Earth's Orbit. July 26th, 2024.

"So, genocide it is then?" Daniel asked.

Jason shrugged. Allowing his friend to pursue his train of thought to wherever it might lead him.

"It should not be an easy thing, this thing you are planning to do."

"It isn't. We did not come to this point lightly, or even easily." Jason replied.

"It is justified?" Daniel asked.

"It is necessary. That is the most we can ask for."

"Such things, such terrible things... they should never be considered necessary." Daniel mused.

"No, they really should not."

Silence. For perhaps five minutes, neither man spoke further. But they were friends, and as such, such moments would only ever be fleeting.

"So, this whisky... we should perhaps talk about this instead. It was made where exactly?" Daniel inspected the amber liquid in the glass before him. Holding it up to the incredibly beautiful star-scape, which was painted across the transparent ceiling above him, in order to better do so. Sniffing it carefully just a moment later.

"Originally, it was made on Epsilon... this is a copy. A copy which is exact down to the molecular level." Jason replied, leaning back on the padded seat in the intimate booth. The table between them was littered with the remnants of what had become a long session. Eating, smoking, drinking. They had been at it for hours now. Talking of many things. Inconsequential things. Both skirting the more important things.

Mostly.

"Alcohol is alcohol, and this was made from the purest... that I can smell, that I can taste... but it was aged in wood, not from the Earth. You have been busy, across these last few centuries of yours... you have had quite the adventure."

After.        Earth's Orbit. July 26th, 2024.

Jason seeing a wonder written large across a face he had missed for far too long.

"BOB, the machines here which are capable of such wonders... he is working on what we pulled out of London... we will have more familiar things soon. Some of the wine we liberated... the cigars." Jason said. "Food, too... proper cheese... Christ, I found chorizo sausage... Potatoes, butter... Can you imagine what it is like to dream of such simple things as mashed potatoes?... chocolate Hobnobs, and pasta... I had forgotten about pasta,"

He didn't realise it, but a few tears ran down his face.

"We have chocolate hobnobs... Not the dark-chocolate ones? those are a travesty." Daniel asked.

"We do. You have always been wrong about that, but we have the ones you always preferred."

"I should not make light of this. Not so casually. Such things, I can barely imagine what they mean to you... The paradigm shift of looking at a man I have known for years... For you, it has been centuries... for me it was only weeks since we were last together in London... Also, remember that just days ago I was staring into a portal from hell and praying that I was killed first by a nuclear strike before the vampire god killed me... Now I am drinking whisky which was aged in a cask made from trees which grew on a planet on the other side of this galaxy... Doing so, whilst sitting onboard a starship capable of crossing that galaxy. I am struggling with this new world. But the wonder I find in this drink, alone, it is more than I have felt in as long as I can remember."

"À ta santé, my friend," Jason raised his glass.

"To your health, too." Daniel replied to Jason's toast.

"You are not getting any younger. But you don't seem to be getting older, not anymore. Have you stopped aging?" Jason enquired. Looking at his friend's white hair, his white beard. The lines deepened on a face which had always been a little craggier than it should have been. A strong face, one wearing dignity and power. The years, they suited the man.

After.        Earth's Orbit. July 26th, 2024.

"I don't feel like I am aging, not anymore... I stared into hell itself, and it took a toll on me that I struggled with. What worries me a little more, is your man in the metal suit... he has been augmented by science, got just as close, and shrugged the whole thing off."

"Neil, and his suit is something we call a Tank. It's not metal..."

"I know, my friend... it is your magical material, which is harder than diamond." Daniel replied. "What I don't understand, though. Is why you don't all use those things... That vampire god, he threw Kate and I around like we were toys... your man Hulk-smashed him, with ease."

"There are few gods out here. Sometimes being a bigger target... Okay, good question. We should circle back to it. Here is another one of mine. Could you roll back the years?"

"I could, but I am enjoying the look. I never allowed myself to age this far before."

Jason watched as his old friend traced the lines on his own face. Intrigued by the fascination he saw, written upon that same face. "It suits you very well, my friend. You might even be considered looking distinguished." Jason laughed. "Alistair agrees with me."

"As well, he should. That man had many flaws. But good taste." Daniel paused. Changing tack. "So, right now we are hanging directly above the North Pole... you said that it is not as straightforward as simply ignoring gravity?"

They were sitting in a booth in the magnificent observation room on the dorsal surface of the Pequod. The room's roof was a domed expanse of transparent carbyne, over thirty-metres in diameter. A more comfortable room than had been originally designed, with the recent additions of a bar, and also a small stage where a fabulous Steinway piano now rested. Beside it was a drum kit, one which Alistair had played touring with a rock band in the early eighties. Both of which had been liberated from Jason's old apartment just off the King's Road in Chelsea. Along with many other things.

The room had always meant to have been a place for the crew of either starship to meet, to relax. A social area which now, and quite deliberately,

After.       Earth's Orbit. July 26th, 2024.

looked very much like a jazz-club from the 1950s. One with perhaps the best view of any jazz club, yet. The sky was filled with stars, and the only other thing that was otherwise visible was the prow of the docked Thunder-Child, which was currently awaiting her next mission. Whilst her captain drank himself insensible.

But Daniel was not looking at the view above, not now. He was looking at the display, which was imbedded in the wall just to the side of the booth. It showed the Pequod's position above the Earth's north pole. It had prompted his drunken question.

"Gravity, it is more complicated than just bypassing Earth's. Gravity, it is also what drags the Earth around in its orbit of the Sun. It is what holds the moon close. It is also what holds our solar system in position as we orbit the centre of our galaxy... and as the galaxy hammers through the void, she is governed by every other body in the universe... The most distant galaxies, they affect those closest to them... each of which passes on their own effect... and so on... We hang here because we asked the ship to do so. We are not ignoring all gravity, we are being very selective about what gravity we still obey... the complexity of which is exceptional, and it needs to be driven by machines, not by humans." Jason expanded.

"Right... Okay, that I now understand. So, help me understand a little about these challenges to navigation. Those that you expect to face out there." Daniel asked. "Or back then..."

"Okay, so things not being as simple as they might otherwise seem to be... we can travel, and forget the time-stuff, for now, far faster than light... but, when we look at the sky, we see things as they were a long time ago."

"I think I get it... Actually, scrub that. Explain?"

"Right, so... we spoke about this a lot when Kate and I were first studying... I mean, a lot a lot... She ran a college in Oxford that spent most of its time staring into the heavens... considering these exact questions. Granted, against amongst many others. Were you just pretending to listen?" Jason asked. More than a little horrified.

After.    Earth's Orbit. July 26th, 2024.

"Not every time," Daniel replied. Somewhat sheepishly. Raising both of his hands to mime pistols, shooting Jason with his extended fingers, and winking in what he was clearly hoping was a winning way.

"Okay, right..." Jason sighed. "Light is fast. It is energy without mass, and it travels at the speed limit of the universe... the fastest thing is energy without mass. But Proxima Centauri is around four-point-two light years from Earth. When we look at it from Earth. We are seeing it where it was, how it was, four-point-two years ago... Now imagine a galaxy which is over one-hundred and twenty thousand light years across. Where every object has been in constant motion throughout those millennia and each one being affected by the gravity we just discussed. By every other body close to it..."

"Okay, that makes sense..."

"We have moderately solid maps of the galaxy for right now. But most of those came from the first team who fought the Progenitors with the remnant fleet. Built up over centuries of fighting across much of the galaxy. We are planning on travelling back hundreds of thousands of years. Those maps will not be without value. But they will be horrendously out of date." Jason took a drink. "Honestly, when we were sending the first probes. Once we finally understood how to cheat that universal speed-limit, our next biggest challenge was navigation. It was perhaps the larger challenge." Jason replied.

"So, the plans, trust them and don't ask too many questions?" Daniel laughed.

"As many questions as you ever have, always feel free to ask any of them that come to mind. The key is to eventually spot the questions that you still need to ask," Jason replied. Laughing too.

For a while, both men sat together and drank, neither talking much. Just enjoying good whisky and each other's company. There were several others in the room. Hacker was there with Alice and Clare, attempting to show the children how to play a simplified version of Gin-Rummy. Jason eavesdropped just briefly. The man had left a family behind. An estranged one, but he had children only a little older than the two on the ship. It gladdened his heart to see Flaherty enter the room, the young Royal Marine joining his countryman to join in with the game. Flaherty had spoken of a younger brother and sister he had left behind. Jason's attention drifted away from that group, seeing

After.        Earth's Orbit. July 26th, 2024.

Colm with Jennifer, enjoying a date-night. Able to do so, even with their daughter so close. It was good to see them happy. Jennifer noticed his attention and smiled over at him. A smile he returned to his great-granddaughter. Distracted by it all, it took him a moment to spot that Daniel was offering him a cigar. He took it and gladly accepted the light. Noticing afterwards that Daniel had retrieved the amulet. The ornate necklace with a green-stone in its middle, and with two golden dragons encircling it. That he had placed it on the table between them.

The elephant in the room. The object which had brought the team back to Earth, to snatch it from the last moments of the Fracture.

"When you gave me this... When you asked me to wear it..." Daniel started.

"So, you have found at least one question you do still need to ask?" Jason asked.

Daniel nodded slowly.

"I was approached by a woman I had once known, albeit years earlier, and then only briefly. One with a message from another woman you had met once yourself, apparently... It was all very cryptic. But she said I would need it one day. But that you should have it first. That you would need it for the Fracture, and that I could get it from you, then... She called it the Fracture. A year, perhaps a little more, before the Fracture happened, and she called it that. I took a lot of crazy, basically on faith back then." Jason paused. "I knew you had it. But then I saw that woman. I met her myself just a few years later... in Monaco. She was wearing the thing and thought I was a mad bastard when I said she shouldn't be. As I have said, I was exposed to a hell of a lot of crazy back then, and much of it, I took entirely on bizarrely inappropriate amounts of faith. But it has been that sort of life."

"So did I... and yet, it is here with us... it was always with me after you gave it to me... and although we might always keep saying that it has been that sort of life, we both know that is too often has been exactly that... But it has power. Power which it turned out we very much needed. It stopped the ancients from being able to work that mind-voodoo on me... so there was that... I heard that the female made you her own personal flying monkey

After.        Earth's Orbit. July 26th, 2024.

there for a little while?" He laughed. Jason didn't. Not at that, not yet. "… but you are right, it was a lot of crazy to take on faith." Daniel finished.

Daniel was enjoying his own cigar and studying the smoke that was trailing from its tip. Thoughtful… reflective of things he hadn't questioned. Not just this thing. But a lifetime of…

"Centuries later, and I still agree…" Jason said. "Then you died, which hit us all like a train, and for years, centuries, I practically forgot about the thing… You know that we can't truly forget anything, not our kind. But we might forget to think about a thing. You have always been a bit of a dick, but Alistair and I have always been fond of you. We always missed you." Jason leant forward. "But then there was always the other thing… The woman had also said something about the Thunder-Child, and that made no sense… not then… claiming that the Thunder-Child would help me get that thing back…" Jason indicated the amulet on the table between them. "Then, after over a century stranded across the galaxy, soon after I should have died for the umpteenth time, we met the benefactors, and to make a long story, short… I made the ship there…" Jason nodded slightly, indicating the starship, the nose of which was visible just over his left shoulder. "I called her the Thunder-Child."

"Then my daughter came to you with stories about time-travel…" Daniel replied.

"Honestly, it has been that sort of life." Jason replied. Repeating their mantra. Resting his cigar on the ashtray, he downed what was a healthy amount of whisky and, leaning over, he filled both his glass and Daniel's.

"To be honest, you were always going to call a ship, literally any ship, the 'Thunder-Child'. I was just surprised it took you so long," Kate said, gliding into the empty spot beside Jason, the one he had slid away from when he noticed her approach, and nudging him until he filled the glass she had brought with her.

"Hey, I was a rich man, and I spent some time with a fascinating shipbroker in Monaco… If you want to make a rich man, poor… sell the bugger a yacht… It was never going to be a boat. Our dream, to reach the stars… One day… It was always going to be a starship."

After.            Earth's Orbit. July 26th, 2024.

"So, do we know what this thing is?" Katherine asked, moving to sit beside Daniel with her own glass. Jason looked at her, an unspoken question in his eyes. "Trust me, my micro-bots will stop me from doing too much damage, so will my new metabolism."

"Okay, old-girl. I trust you..." Jason grinned.

"... and Daniel... I don't know you well, not yet. Although Jason has spoken of you often. But when we first discussed that we might need that thing, it became hard for many of us to focus always on things so huge as changing the fate of galaxies. We moved away from the big picture, and we focussed instead on coming for you. They might not tell you that, but it's true." She smiled, looking down at the amulet. "But we do still need to know what this thing is."

"It is from Theia, a remnant of that planetoid which should never have been... But where the rock gives us potential... I am afraid that this brings with it intent." Kate replied. Swinging the focus fully back onto the amulet before them all on the table. "It will take us to when we are needed... It will tell us where we need to go. That side of me that came from mum, it is aligned with this stone... I know this stone, who owned it... but she had it later. Perhaps there were two..." Kate said. Her voice fading. Her face was thoughtful. "Hell, I could be wrong. It was all centuries ago."

"Oh, great. Witch stuff... that never goes well... and now we have a magic-eight ball, that only speaks to you..." Jason ran his hand through his long blond hair and took a long drag from his cigar.

"Witch stuff?" Daniel asked.

Because that had all come later. After the Fracture.

\*     \*     \*

After.    Earth's Orbit. July 26th, 2024.

The world would not see it. The vessel was hidden behind cloaking technology that the world would not even understand could exist, not for centuries yet. It had remained locked in place, in its impossible position above the outer-edge of Earth's atmosphere, whilst the crew, both new and old, prepared for what needed to happen next. It had remained there also to await the return of the small shuttle-craft, which had made its way to the Earth's moon. Staying there whilst equipment, originally designed to aid in the galaxy's exploration, was used instead to mine for something they would need for the next stage of the mission.

So, it was weeks later before the ship left its stationary position above the planet's north pole and gently made its way out of the system.

It passed through the orbital plane of each of the planets. They would not see them all. No practical course could make that possible. But they deliberately chose one close enough to that of Jupiter to visit.

This was an indulgence. Almost unique in the known galaxy, Jupiter was a planet of such size, such enormous importance, that it was impossible to ignore what might be their only opportunity. The two starships split, for the first time since they had entered the solar system. It was the Pequod, the larger and arguably more ungainly ship, which made its way carefully into the planet's upper atmosphere. Doing something that it had been built for. Doing so, to satiate the unquenchable thirst of the scientists onboard. Both human, and also the sentient machine. The alien intelligence who had become their friend. Whose charity had allowed for any of this... all of this.

The other, the warship, which was called the Thunder-Child; she remained patiently in orbit. The warriors there, they were held in almost equal awe to their scientist brethren.

So it was that it took weeks of delay before the starships left the birthplace of humanity and started upon the next step of their terrible purpose.

\*    \*    \*

Their terrible purpose.         Earth's Orbit. July 26th, 2024.

## Their terrible purpose.

They moved outside of Earth's solar-system. Navigating past the dense Öpik–Oort cloud, and travelling onward toward its theoretical edge. Doing so, until the space around them emptied enough to take that next step.

In the end, they moved clear of the sun for almost half a light year. Taking weeks to do so, even with the immense speeds the starships were capable of, outside of FTL.

Delaying the next steps. Working to prepare the vessels for the challenge of the journey into the past.

Their terrible purpose.

The genocidal killing of every member of the furious alien species who were humanity's greatest enemy. The enemy of every sentient life-form in the galaxy.

Moving into history, to hunt down, and turn that species home world into a cinder. Millennia, before they would erupt into the heavens with their own terrible purpose.

To see if they were quite the same threat whilst they were still shitting in caves.

Sometimes, although thankfully rarely, the right thing to do, it was also the dreadful thing.

*   *   *

Kate.                Earth's Orbit. July 26th, 2024.

# Kate.

She was running, yet something was holding her back. All she was aware of was that she was running for as long as she had been aware that she was...

Where was she?

It was dark, but her eyes should have let her still see... not unless there was no light at all. There was always some. She was never... never unable to see.

Her feet thudded across the floor... but whilst she had once known that she was moving, she now knew that she wasn't. There was no wind on her face, her hair was not flowing behind her. Had it done so before? When she had been moving?

She didn't know.

So where was she? And what was holding her back?

Because something was.

Pushing onward, she threw everything into movement... and now, were even her arms moving?

Was she anything else but thought?

... and there, out of the darkness, she saw a flicker. Something was out there... At first, it was almost entirely indistinct. Barely there. So far away. Little more than a feeling... but it was that. It was a feeling... she felt afraid.

It was calling to her from somewhere else.

It moved through the black, brief, fast movement, which was a darker black, or... it might have been lighter. For a little while, it was impossible to tell. She was standing still now. Had she been before? But her head was darting around to track the thing, which was now...

Was it circling her?

Kate.     Earth's Orbit. July 26th, 2024.

Was it getting closer?

Then she saw something other than just shades of black… it was the hint of another colour, or perhaps just light. A light which resolved itself as two distinct, as the… They were green lights, the impossible eyes of a dragon. Eyes, which she knew were emeralds, glowing with such ferocity as the creature surged toward her. A golden dragon and one which was ferociously hungry.

With hypnotic eyes.

She was no longer a nebulous thing; she was Kate. She was standing, frozen in place, as the creature hammered toward her. Its eyes burning with such fire… Its mouth opening and…

\*     \*     \*

Kate.  　　　　Earth's Orbit. July 26th, 2024.

Kate awoke to find herself standing on bare feet. Her duvet puddled around her feet, and her vest top and light leggings drenched in sweat. She had awoken just in time to stop herself from screaming… The dream was lost for a second, but as she looked down, as she saw the amulet clasped in her right hand, the dream came crashing back to her.

Her arse hit the side of the high-bed in her quarters as she staggered backwards, and she hopped a little to sit upon the bed. Bringing her breathing and her heart-rate back under control. Before her, the wall of softly textured cabinets was in chaotic disarray. Many of the draws were pulled open, and much of her clothing had been pulled free and now lay scattered about the floor, tangled with her duvet. Even her deployable desk was out, the chair lying on its side and her scroll computer open to a search window.

She didn't remember using that last night. So why was it turned on now? Anxiously, she stepped toward it, pulling her chair upright, and sitting at her desk. Laying the amulet beside it, forgotten for a moment. She looked through her search-history, through the machine's logs… navigating an interface now intimately familiar to her. She worked for perhaps half an hour before she was satisfied that she had learned what she could. Staring nervously at the amulet again, she ran her hand through her long, tangled hair. Looking toward the far end of the small room, she considered her general condition. Standing and finding her legs to be uncharacteristically unsteady, she made her way to the small bathroom. She stayed under the hot shower for perhaps half an hour.

This was not normal. This was the sodding witchy stuff. The amulet was going to be a pain in her arse.

The beep on her door was unexpected. Checking the ship-time, she saw that it was a little after four-am. She pulled on a towelling robe and answered it.

Before her was her father. As dishevelled as she had been before her shower. He looked past her, to her desk. Staring at the amulet.

"Funky dreams?" she asked.

"Funky dreams." He confirmed.

Kate.  Earth's Orbit. July 26th, 2024.

    \*　　\*　　\*

## Mission Date: Day 1

### Emergence.

"... and in three, two-one and go. We are back in real-space." BOB's disembodied voice came over the bridge's audio system. The living machine was physically with the wolves, who were all in the Pequod's medical bay. If intervention was needed, it had been agreed that it would be better for him to be there, rather than here.

Katherine processed that they were finally done. She forced herself to count slowly and up to ten. Trusting BOB, but giving just a little time to verify. Far more than long enough for a corrupted universe, one that they might have inadvertently torn into existence, to dissipate. To have killed them all as it ceased to be.

She processed that she was still alive. Which was something, at least. So, they were somewhere. She had a job to do.

"BOB, when you can," Katherine ordered. "We need to know exactly what happened."

"Working on it Katherine,"

"How are the wolves?" She asked.

"They are all conscious. They are all suffering the after-effects of the jump. They will need a few minutes."

"BOB, thank you. Jansen, Summers, have you been able to break down where the errors crept in?'

"Not yet. I can see the ship ignoring the planned exit. But I cannot see any of the controls failing. The relativity bubble simply failed to dissipate." Jansen replied. Shock still written across his face.

Mission Date: Day 1                Emergence.

"Katherine, I concur with Dr Jansen. We will need longer to review everything. However, regarding our current location, I can report that I am detecting nothing of concern in our immediate vicinity. Radiation levels are within acceptable, if still chaotic, parameters. There do not seem to be any objects of significant mass out there. We are cloaked... effective... now. Although, to be fair, our entrance was less than subtle, and if anyone was watching, they would have seen us the moment we got here. But for now, passive scans only, we are only listening..." there was a pause. "But we appear to be alone."

"Hold for further status," He added, only seconds later.

Which was better than it might have been.

"BOB, thank you. If you can update with both when and where we are. That would be splendid." Katherine asked. Tension in her voice.

"As soon as I know more, you will know more, too, Katherine." BOB responded. "It is still messy out there. We can see enough, but there is still the vestigial footprint from the collapsing time-fields. It should dissipate in the next few minutes."

"Thank you. Jansen, Summers, I want you both working on the problem. If you require any assistance, call anyone in. Anyone. Including me."

"Boss, we are on it." Summers called back. Already standing beside Jansen, leaning in to share his monitor.

She had time to kill. Katherine stood from her chair and strolled forward towards the curved opaque wall that dominated the bridge. Oppressive, it left her feeling claustrophobic when it was like this. But it was rare that it was like this.

The rainbow, the scrolling colours of the electromagnetic spectrum, which would surround the two ships as they cut through space in FTL, were only noticeable by their absence during time travel. Replaced by a haunting nothingness, which had unsettled everyone. Even the most rational amongst them. Including BOB. After the first jump, back to Earth's past, Katherine had made it standard operating procedure to render the carbyne dome opaque during time-travel.

Mission Date: Day 1                Emergence.

Out there, there may be answers... There would need to be. She would have to be patient. Her team had jobs to do. She needed to let them do those jobs. This was the first time an error had crept into a time-jump. Internally, she reviewed the variables, the differences. It was the third jump made by the combined Pequod and Thunder-Child. It was, by far, the furthest of any jump attempted. It was the first jump made with Kate's magic-bloody-eight-ball, contributing to what bloody witchy stuff it was that it did.

Perhaps one, perhaps all, or perhaps any combination. She was a little twitchy, realising that she would be very surprised if the amulet were not a part of the explanation. Kate had said it had an intent.

They had missed their exit. So, where had they exited?

Her hand reached out to touch the surface of the dome. Imagining what was out there. Not wanting to sneak a look, not just yet. The original crew, those who were entirely human, they had all received enough of the bio-tech augmentations now, to tap into the exterior sensors of the combined starships should they want to.

The others, the wolves, the new team. Unless they had strayed too close to a window...

Katherine was giving the wolves time. They would need it, after what they had just been put through. She was eager to speak to them. Jason first, and Kate. Even the president. Those she trusted. The new ones. The huge 'American' who was apparently a retired member of an elite team called 'SEALs'... and Daniel.

They had risked stopping on their journey into the past, at first doing so for only for one thing. But also, later, it had become more important for Kate's father. A man whose story she had heard told many times since Jason had come clean on that first day. Even if she had been too injured to hear it for herself, certainly that first time. Telling them of a man sitting on a beach, and just happy to watch the sea. Jason's story, when he told it, he often started there.

A terrifying man. One who had always followed his own star. Capable of shocking levels of both violence and kindness. Unpredictable, and almost

Mission Date: Day 1        Emergence.

singularly powerful. Chaos personified, within the soul of a somewhat gentler man.

A man who had meant a great deal to the woman who had sacrificed so much to set them all on this path.

A man who would have just felt himself torn to pieces as the wolves used their combined magic to lock them all into this reality. Something which would have, which should have, only lasted an hour.

Only, this time-jump had not taken an hour. The other jumps, all the other jumps, those which were travelling more than an hour into the past, they would always take almost exactly an hour. A shade over, but only a fraction of a second over. A wild coincidence, but it seemed to be locked into some universal constant they were yet to identify.

For every jump undertaken, either by the first crew of the first Thunder-Child, or the first two jumps of the new team, it had always been the same.

But not this last one. They had hit the hour, the exit parameters coinciding with exactly then... and they had sailed right on past. Continuing on their merry way for a shade over forty-minutes longer, unable to influence it at all. Forty minutes, before they had been spat out. Back into real space.

Katherine's mind drifted briefly to Hipparchus, the ancient Greek astronomer whose work had defined the precise split of the day into equal parts. Twelve hours for daylight, twelve for night, at the point of the equinox. Creating the hour. What would he have thought of the coincidence?

She meditated about this, about everything, until her internal bio-augmentations clicked past the ten-minutes she had allocated. Ten minutes where the chaotic energies of their emergence from a time-jump would need to disperse, anyway.

It was time now to be the captain again.

"Team... I am ordering the canopy clear. I want a full situational report from all sensor stations. We need to know everything we can about what is immediately around us. BOB, tell me when you're confident enough from us to go from passive to active scans. First, though, before that step, I want to

Mission Date: Day 1                Emergence.

know the condition of the ship and all her systems. That we are ready to respond if there is anything out there which might be listening... anything that might react to our arrival." Katherine ordered. "BOB, if you would please tell us what you know so far about how far we have travelled."

Then, at that moment, the wall before her switched from opaque, to a clarity which was so close to being optically perfect, that it was reasonable to consider it so. Staring into the heavens before her, Katherine was immediately lost for words.

"Well, that is a hell of a thing... Beautiful, but it is certainly also a hell of a thing." Dani spoke up from the helm.

Because it was.

All of that.

And so much more.

BOB had said something. She was horrified that she seemed to be unable to focus on it. Her brain ran into a wall as she tried to.

She heard herself asking him to repeat what he had said. Almost in a daze. Staring at something through the huge, transparent dome which dominated the bridge. Something she had never expected to look at from this perspective.

BOB's words... his repeated answer.

Disquieting.

\*        \*        \*

Mission Date: Day 1                    Emergence.

"So, that was truly sodding awful." Daniel looked white as a sheet to anyone who might glance in his direction. Few did. Most there had their own problems.

"I know you warned us... but Jesus Christ, that was..." Impact paused, leant over and threw up again. His black face, ashen. The sick-bag beginning to look worryingly full. "Exactly the worst thing I have ever experienced." He finally finished. "... and I was at Crater's first and third bachelor's party..." he hadn't finished.

"Not the second?" Jennifer asked. Barely able to get the words out.

"Actually, funny story..." Impact said.

"To be fair, it was a lot punchier than the first time-jump. But that was a few centuries. This was... Okay, it was a lot further..." Jason replied. "How did everyone else fare?"

"Clare, she is okay. She will be." Jennifer was holding her daughter in her arms. The young purestrain was in tears. Being part of the process. It was not optional for any of the wolves. "But the ship's time... this went on far longer than it should have. What happened?"

"We do not know yet what happened. But the ship is safe." BOB answered.

Daniel looked over at the machine. His head feeling like it was filled instead with storm clouds. His focus ruined. His whole-body aching.

To hold themselves into the universe proper, to break the causality lock and to prevent the time-travellers from appearing again in a broken, tiny fragment of a copy of their own universe, only to die there a heartbeat later... it was not a free ride. The moon-rock. Tonnes of it, newly mined before they had set themselves on this path. It was the anchor.

But they were the chain.

He felt like he had been pulled apart by the bloody universe.

He saw that Alice, the young-girl he had rescued from Drogger-Drift as they had made their way to Cramer's compound. She was sitting beside Clare and was looking with concern at her friend. The two having become almost

Mission Date: Day 1                    Emergence.

inseparable since she had come onboard. Their friendship meant a lot to Daniel. He focused instead on that. Fighting through the fog.

"BOB, do we know what happened? What caused this?" Jason asked.

"The operational teams are all still at their stations and are working to answer a lot of the questions we all inevitably have. But whilst we are always right to be careful to have ourselves ready to respond to any possible threat, when we emerge, it takes the brunt of their focus for the first few minutes." BOB replied.

"If we spent longer in the relativity bubble than we expected. What does that mean about where we emerged?" Kate asked. Her face, as white as a sheet.

Daniel looked across at his daughter. She held the necklace in her right hand. The amulet painful against her palm as she gripped it so hard. He could see the discomfort registering in her face, the tremors in her right arm. He knew his daughter more than well enough to understand she was hurting herself. He remembered that she had been wearing it, and not holding it, before the time-jump had begun.

"Did anyone else feel the amulet pull us out of that time-stream, or whatever we're calling that dreadful place, now? Kate asked. Finally, putting it back around her neck and fastening it there. Daniel spotted that there were wounds which were closing on her palm.

"I don't know... I thought there was something that released us..." Capability Brown said. "I thought that it might also have been holding us there..."

"Same here." Jennifer added. Jason just nodded in confirmation.

"Balls, okay... That is a concern. BOB, where are we and when are we?" Kate asked.

"We are checking against the cosmic-background-radiation. We do not know for sure, we can't, not until we also have our exact position. But we can estimate. We are pretty sure that we travelled between perhaps around four hundred and twenty, to four-fifty, million years back in time." BOB

Mission Date: Day 1                    Emergence.

responded. "Although it will take days, perhaps weeks, to better refine the answer."

"Okay, well, that is substantially further back than we meant to." Jason said. Surprise and fear written across his face. Staring at the amulet in Kate's hand. Daniel could hear Jason's heart suddenly thudding in his chest. "This changes quite a lot. Do we know where we are?"

"Other members of the crew have found this equally unsettling. However, I believe that it is like a band-aid... one best ripped free quickly. We are in open space, around forty-three thousand light years away from the outermost halo of a nearby galaxy we are currently hoping is the Milky Way." BOB answered. His pixilated face portraying a wide, reassuring smile. "A distance, almost a third of the width of the galaxy itself. The view is rather spectacular."

"Kate, we have discussed that amulet. You have suggested its intent. Did you feel any of that during our journey here?"

"I think so. Although I was being pulled apart... my focus... sorry Jason, I can't say for certain."

"I didn't think that we were moving during the jump." Hacker said. "... and what do you mean about hoping it is the Milky Way?"

The man had sat with the wolves during the jump. Effectively a spare wheel during the process, he had put himself where he might at least help a little. He was bringing water to those still unable to move far.

"We don't move. We do, but not in the way you might be thinking. Everything moves through time. The Earth spins on its axis, the Earth orbits the sun, the sun orbits the... and so on." BOB replied.

"So, Marty McFly should have appeared floating in space with the Earth, not even a dot in his sky... nowhere even close to the Twin Pines Mall?"

"Yes, essentially. Unless the DeLorean could also travel through space, as well as time. We can't, though. We can do one, or the other, but never both, not at the same time. Every position in space only exists in relation to everything else and nothing exists that remains stationary in relation to anything else... interestingly, that is apart from us, when we move backward through time...

41

# Mission Date: Day 1          Emergence.

Our position is locked, and what was there when we left hasn't arrived here yet," BOB replied.

"Locked, relative to what exactly?" Hacker asked.

"We don't know, we have never known... we always move... even if we only travel a few centuries, we have popped out light years away from where we started. Measurements suggest that whatever it is that anchors us, it could be moving, too. But again, everything is relative. So, whilst we are locked to something... to what is still unknown." Kate said this, stopping only to shrug.

"So, where we are exactly, it is not a straightforward question. Hence BOB's ambiguous answer..." Hacker mused.

"It is not an immediate thing to easily understand our position by the celestial bodies we can see. Even more so as we have travelled through time... I imagine that if we are staring at the outside edge of a galaxy, and that we are doing so from a previously unconsidered position and attempting to use maps, which are themselves now almost half a billion years out of date. Have you heard of the three-body problem?"

"I have, and although I ignored some of the briefings, I imagine we are facing something far more complicated than just three-bodies?" Hacker asked.

"It might be the closest example of the phrase 'infinitely more so,' being more than just chaotic exaggeration that I have ever considered." BOB answered.

"Do we need to discuss how we were just hijacked by that amulet?" Jason said to Kate.

"We do... But first, I need to eat. Who's hungry?"

"Sod off..." Impact said.... Only continuing to speak after he had been enthusiastically sick again. "But I could go for a sandwich, actually."

Mission Date: Day 1                Emergence.

                         *      *      *

## Mission Date: Day 23

## An unbalanced force.

A little over three weeks later.

Three weeks spent working hard with the two starships' extensive sensor arrays to better understand their current situation. Where, when, and even why...

Almost all they had were questions. Far too few answers. She was exhausted.

Not physically, that was no longer a thing. Mentally, emotionally. It had taken a toll.

Katherine had the largest dedicated office within the Pequod. Not purely an indulgence, although it had always been that, too. It had originally been designed so that heads of various scientific departments could meet. A Provision, created so that a less dreadful mission, one of exploration and pure scientific endeavour, could have been better managed.

But those had been the dreams of another life.

She had the other doctor, the one spirited away from Hermentia. A man who had uncovered so much before he had originally died. That man had a second chance at this. He would be able to see the fruit of his works. He was coming to see them all later today. That was at least something.

Something which might not be connected to this other work.

She could use a distraction, herself. So could the other scientists.

Here, on the Pequod, her office was her sanctuary. Squirrelled away as it was, in the starship's heart. There were no external windows. But from the far end, she could overlook the hangar. She even had a small door which would allow her to enter the hangar via a simple open stairway down to the deck below. A complicated door, one capable of holding back the vacuum of space when the

Mission Date: Day 23     An unbalanced force.

hangar was depressurised. One capable of sealing them off from any other potential hazards. Chemical, biological, even radiological. The entire wall, even her door, it could be transparent or opaque. Right now, it was opaque.

There was her desk, to the other end, and in the centre of the room was a large table. One with the holographic projection systems, which would allow for almost any data-set to be presented.

She was here to meet with her small team. Apparently, Jansen and BOB, they had something important to show her.

She entered the room through the other door, the one leading from the science-deck. The three scientists were already there, waiting for her.

Summers looked expectant. Jansen, anxious. BOB, hell... he would only ever share emotion deliberately. Harder to read. But Jansen was anxious. That might not bode well.

Looking around the room, she allowed herself briefly to consider what once might have been. But only briefly. She moved across the room toward her desk. The hologram of the nearby galaxy was hovering over the conference table behind her. Although, much of it lacked any actual definition. Where assumptions were still being made, the scientists had resisted the urge to paint a picture of things they were yet to understand.

The round conference table was in the middle of the room. It looked like wood; she accepted that it was, really. Even if it had never been a tree. One of the few things in the entire ship that wasn't carbyne.

She sat facing the room. It was still uncertain that it was the Milky Way. But even she sometimes tired of the scientific process. It was bloody obvious that it was the Milky Way.

BOB moved. Animating himself for the first time in days. The floating tic-tac shape of his hull, folding outward. His limbs and head, appearing from his sleek body, leaving the familiar, instantly recognisable slots where they once had been, were clearly visible. His legs extending to reach the floor, taking his weight. Moments later, he began striding up and down alongside the hologram, and peering at it with his pixilated face. His slender arms clasped behind his back in a deliberately human fashion. Katherine knew that he did

Mission Date: Day 23     An unbalanced force.

not need to physically look at the thing, that this was entirely for their benefit. Also, for his own. She hated that she was so tired that she was more fascinated by how he was attempting to mirror a human's walk with three legs than she was by...

"You have something for us?" She asked. With her elbows resting on her desk's oiled surface. Her hands supporting her chin. Staring at the small team across the room. Nodding toward Summers to indicate she was including her colleague, who was clearly also in the dark.

"We do." BOB responded.

"This isn't just about the proposed jump-points which are needed for us to better build our maps?"

"It is that, but it is not only that. There is something interesting we need to look at along our way."

"If we are staying here?" Summers queried.

"We are staying here. You have made your feelings known, Dr Summers. You have made your points, well, and you were not wrong. But we are staying here." Katherine replied. Regretting that her tone had been so dismissive. "We can achieve our original goal in this time, as simply as we could if we had only travelled back a few hundred thousand years."

This had been kinder.

"Once we have found the Progenitor planet?" Summers added. Raising her right eyebrow into a questioning arch. An ability that Katherine had been jealous of, ever since the first time she had met the woman when she had been one of her students. Decades ago, now.

"Okay, that would be a lot easier, a little closer to our time..." Katherine conceded. "But there are risks to time-travel. Forward or backward... and until we know why it was that our last time-jump behaved as it did. We risk the mission by risking ourselves."

"We all know it was the amulet,"

# Mission Date: Day 23  An unbalanced force.

"We all assume that it was the amulet." Katherine could not entirely keep the frustration from her voice as she corrected her colleague. "But what Jason and his team did in defeating the Progenitor fleet at Epsilon... It has earned them a level of trust. Certainly, more than enough to buy them a little wriggle-room."

"The number of jumps outside the galaxy?" Jansen interrupted. Clearly attempting to bring the meeting back on track. "I would say another six. We believe that we will eventually need to be here..." he indicated a spot almost on the other side of the image and deep within the galaxy itself. "But not with enough confidence to risk going straight there, just yet. We will know more, as we continue to move in a corkscrew fashion around this section." He was now indicating a line along the outermost edge of the galaxy, leading immediately away from the location image of the Pequod. "Six more, but not super far each time."

"Measure twice, cut once. BOB, what do your calculations tell us?" Katherine asked.

"Katherine, I agree with Dr Jansen. We cannot say for certain, and we may see more as we continue to progress further. But as far as our current knowledge sits, this plan still offers the best chance of success." BOB replied. "Also, we have modified things a little to allow for the other thing."

"So, you suggested there was something else?"

"BOB and I were working through these jump-points, reviewing the wide-spectrum data-set we have already captured. We spotted an anomaly." Jansen moved over to the table. Using a pencil to indicate a small section of it. A significant distance from where they were now, but the proposed path of the mission would eventually take them close to it, and then pass it. Katherine studied it. Carefully. Idly wondering why the man had a pencil.

"Okay, so why is this object highlighted?" Katherine asked. As she did so, her bio-technology filled in the gaps for her. She knew that she would have simply stopped. Frozen in place before the others as she processed everything. As she attempted to. After she was done, after many long seconds, she reached for her water glass and attempted to sip from it with a shaking hand. Spilling far more than she managed to drink. Her bio-augmentations warning her of

Mission Date: Day 23         An unbalanced force.

adrenaline spikes. Working to subdue those. Moments later, reminding her to breathe. "Oh," was all she said. She looked over at Summers. It had been news for her, too. She saw tears running down the woman's face. Shock, not sorrow. Katherine knew the woman well enough to tell that.

"What do we know?" Katherine asked. Finally able to speak.

"We cannot be sure, not yet, not of everything. But what we do know is that it is a supermassive star, and one which is close to the end of its hydrogen-cycle. It also appears to be travelling extraordinarily fast." Jansen started. "We are basing this on estimations built on far too many assumptions. But we expect that it should reach the galaxy's edge, and perhaps even its end-times…" the scientist paused. "Katherine, our best estimations put both those events happening within a year of today. Worryingly, they seem destined to happen very close to each other."

"Okay, we will need to improve on those estimates. The age of this image?"

"We are over thirty-thousand light years away. We are looking at it as it was thirty-thousand years ago. We can predict its path, but obviously only to a level. We have baked in more jump-points so that we can draw closer to it, carefully. Every step closer, we know more. As we learn, our math tightens, and the risks shrink. If we take small enough steps, we remove the risk of appearing out of FTL, and back in real-space in the midst of a nova-event."

"Reduce, not remove," Katherine corrected.

"Fair point, well made." Jansen accepted. "It seems to be an unlikely coincidence, though. That we are here, so close to the event that we could potentially witness it."

"They happen, though. We even have a word for them."

"Pardon?" Jansen asked.

"Coincidences… Okay, so we approach carefully, and we will know better where it is going. Do we know where it came from?"

"It is possible that it was ejected by another galaxy. Also, that it may have formed alone, out in the void." Jansen shrugged. "We know that there are

# Mission Date: Day 23        An unbalanced force.

gaseous nebulae, many of them, out there in the darkness. It is theoretically possible for something like this to be born outside of a galaxy. Its size is limiting. It should live only perhaps ten million years... There are no galaxies close enough, even at its current velocity. We don't know enough yet, to do much beyond speculate about its origin," Jansen added. "But we know its approximate mass, and its approximate velocity... Katherine, we are looking at a supermassive star, one with over eighty times the mass of our own sun. It is a proper brute, and it is one that is travelling at forty-six percent of the speed of light."

"It is impossible..." Katherine replied. Her brow furrowing. "Sorry, it is improbable."

"It is everything, and it is singularly the most fascinating scientific event any of us could likely imagine. Everything else aside, and just the opportunity alone to be able to study this. To witness an event of this magnitude. The importance of this, to humanity, to our search for knowledge." Jansen's voice was tinged with wonder.

"Were the galaxy ever to need a better example of the effects of an unbalanced force as it... Jesus Christ? Okay, team. We need to collate what we know already, and we need to take it to the rest of the crew. Summers, are you in?"

"Katherine, there is nothing in this universe that could keep me away from this," the woman replied. She had moved to the plotting image and had zoomed into the star itself. Data scrolled to its side, as the ball of burning plasma sat large in the centre of the room. Its image was tinged with red. Its velocity, and the fact it was moving away from them at an oblique angle, stretching the wavelength of its emitted light. Red-shifting the image. "If this star continues on this path, it will enter this spiral arm around here..." She had zoomed out a little, and had followed the indicated path. "There are solar-systems in this section, any number of which, whose gravitational effect may draw this thing into them..." The doctor turned to face the others in the room. "We do not know exactly when we are. But we know the approximate time. We are assuming that Earth is in this direction. The wolves, all of them, can point toward her moon." She had zoomed out even further, indicating a spot almost a hundred-thousand light-years away, in another spiral-arm of the

Mission Date: Day 23                 An unbalanced force.

galaxy. "The theoretical event, of the collision of two stars of significant mass, with this much potential energy. Its effect will ripple out for…"

She left it hanging. For a long minute.

"If that magic-eight-ball dragged us back here for a reason, it would be unwise to not consider the possibility that this is related, somehow." Summers.

"You have made the same connection I did. The Ordovician-Silurian extinction event on Earth… it ties in." Jansen.

"Jesus Christ…. This event…" Katherine whispered. Her mouth had run dry again. She reached for her water again. Taking another sip. This time, her hand was steadier, and she spilt none.

"If we are right, it re-writes much of the galaxy." Jansen said.

\*     \*     \*

Mission Date: Day 23     Capability Brown.

## Capability Brown.

Later that afternoon, Dr Thomas 'Capability' Brown made his way into the Pequod's science deck. After birthing, it was the largest section within the ship that was dedicated for a singular purpose. Deck four. A deck, like deck five, which was truncated by the large hangar, which dominated the starship's rear quarter. The singularity was above him. Decks one-through-three needed to move around the enormous sphere that somehow contained a captured a primordial black hole with a mass close to that of Jupiter.

Because that was apparently possible.

A dead-man, walking. A man who was all too aware that everything he experienced, moving forward, was a gift. A man who had originally died on Hermentia before time had been rewritten by the crews of these starships. A brutal line in the sand that was hard to ignore. Which haunted him. But for a scientist, what lay before him filled him with such extraordinary wonder that he could push the ghosts away. Smiling away to himself as he finally reached the hatch, aware that there was an airlock between him and where he needed to be. He waited for the doors to detect him, to flash green, and to open for him. Making his way inside.

Katherine would be there. Her, he knew. Even if just a little bit. An impressive woman, one who he had got to know over the last few weeks. So would Kate, although apparently much later in the day. He had known that woman for years. For her, it had been centuries. The others, the opportunity to speak to scientists who had learned their craft on another world, filled him with such glorious anticipation.

It took just a moment to pass through the airlock. Waiting for only a couple of seconds with the two doors shut. Then the door before him flashed green and whisked to the side on barely audible actuators. The doors were covered with the same eggshell-white tactile surface of the rest of the ship. He had not been able to detect how either door had flashed green. Like the diffused light which illuminated the starships, there was nothing to show where any of the light came from.

Mission Date: Day 23        Capability Brown.

One day, he promised himself, he would remember to ask how that worked.

Once through, he processed that there were labs to either side of the corridor which continued to run through the centre of the ship. Eight in total, with four on either side. He knew that all disciplines were represented. Biological, chemical, Astronomy and geology. Archaeology, too. History. His own particular bag. A starship, initially designed for scientific endeavour. A wonderful thing. To the end, he could see Katherine's office.

Initially, in the first weeks, it had been too easy for him to consider the two starships to be almost full. The claustrophobia of his new reality, going somewhat to magnify that feeling. Although, unjustly. On the rare occasions when he had joined those gathered in the social areas, he had understood a little better the true size of the Pequod. The galley, the improvised gym on the hangar deck. The hangar deck itself...

... The large room under the fabulous dome, which Jason was attempting to transform it into a jazz-club. Even Capability accepted that space was going to be fabulous.

A man who he had known well, just years ago. A man who was now, like Kate, centuries older. He knew why. But that did not stop the feeling being odd.

He believed that the starship had been enlarged following her initial construction. That perhaps additional decks had been added. To allow for potentially longer missions. But he was not sure of the details there.

Today, he was going to see the preserved data from the library in Hermentia. Ancient text, which had been held by these people for centuries. Never forgotten. Apparently, it had changed the world.

This, even amongst everything else, was almost entirely overwhelming.

Katherine appeared in the corridor ahead. Leaving her office and moving to greet him. A warm smile spread across the youthful face of a woman who was somewhere in her nineties.

"This, none of this is my field, Dr Brown. It was still considered sensitive. It was still blocked from casual access. Even in my time. But from what you have

Mission Date: Day 23          Capability Brown.

told me... and I have peeked a little already. It is going to blow your mind... It did mine."

*   *   *

## Mission Date: Day 60.

### The old man and the sea.

Weeks later.

In the medical room of the Pequod, within a transparent tube filled with a green liquid, hung the shape of a man. Suspended by a complex harness, his head lolling to the side. No one else was there. No one else needed to be, so automated were the treatment and life-support systems.

It was a young man. Perhaps in his forties, somewhere. Fit and strong. Pale, and with puckered skin which, even through the viscous fluid, appeared oddly new.

A screen to the side flashed, a subdued alert which did not reach out further. Which understood that it didn't need to. The head moved. Just a little at first, then the man's eyes opened. Filling with sudden, unmistakable shock.

\*     \*     \*

Mission Date: Day 60.                The old man and the sea.

Julien woke up, his body jolting, and he felt himself immediately panic. There was a mask over his face, and he was… in a fluid. Suspended vertically within some sort of harness. Drowning, for a second he forgot to even try to breathe, and when he did, it was a desperate hacking attempt.

It took seconds, then he remembered. He had woken up like this before… He also felt the tubes which were… inserted. Then the panic grew. Then the drugs came again.

Which was nice. He decided, as he felt himself falling asleep once more, that he didn't mind the drugs.

Perhaps he would dream again. He liked dreams.

Perhaps he might dream about baseball.

Although, that would be odd… that was a sport loved by Americans. By Hemmingway. Perhaps cricket, then.

Then he slept.

\*     \*     \*

Mission Date: Day 60.      The old man and the sea.

Elsewhere on the ship, another old man considered the enormity of the open-space they were currently moving through. Lost in the void between galaxies. A position which would have seemed impossible at any other point in his life. Which should have still been impossible today.

Almost.

Sometimes, when he would be caught up by the romance of the endeavour, he considered space almost as an ocean, although, an infinite ocean...

Alistair had crossed Earth's oceans during his first life. Doing so at a time where not all the lands on the other side had yet been mapped. Heading into the great unknown, whilst there were still worlds out there left to conquer. Jason shared those memories, almost as if they had always been his own.

Today, and what they faced; it was more complicated. Arguably more terrifying.

Equally wonderful.

His constant companion. His greatest friend. He could feel the old man there, with him... always there. Often, now only sharing his presence as a warmth, a feeling... as a love that they had shared for centuries. Reassurance, for when Jason would face difficult things.

As he would today. As he would until this terrible mission was finally done.

"Are we still sure this is the best course of action?" Katherine asked the room. Shaking Jason out of his reverie. The woman was looking round to see if there was still a consensus. People didn't speak. A few nodded. Most were simply watching her.

"If we agree on this. We have two missions now... One old, and one new, which may only prove to be a fascinating distraction. We also need to consider that the amulet, and its purpose in bringing us to this exact point in history. So, two missions, but three concerns. Any of which, even all of which, may be connected. It is hard to look at the dreadful purpose, our original purpose, and not allow ourselves to be too easily swayed to instead head off

Mission Date: Day 60.  The old man and the sea.

in another direction... to follow that amulet hoping it leads to something which is less bloody awful." Katherine said.

"We should pay it heed?" Jennifer asked.

"Good question, and I suggest a qualified 'yes' for now." Katherine responded. "We trust it until it puts us at risk, or the overall mission."

"Why?" the ex-president pushed a little further.

"We went to Earth, to that Greek island, to track down the amulet based on a brief conversation outside of a café in Bordeaux, centuries earlier. An extraordinary act, and one based entirely on trust. But a trust in a man who has earned that from us. Time and time again." She nodded toward Jason. Who just looked uncomfortable. "... I worry that it has purpose, also that we do not understand that purpose. Kate, you knew the stone. From before. Do we know more today than we did even yesterday?"

Kate looked around nervously. Uncharacteristically so. Pulling the amulet from around her neck and laying it on the conference room's table before her. Uncertain eyes followed it. Nervous eyes. "You know my nature. The wolf came from my father, and I was not the first such creature that any of you encountered. Apart from you, Jason. My mother, from her, came the magic. It allowed me to reach-out, beyond myself. It allowed me influence over others. Something which I pushed back against... although, not always." She idly lifted the amulet on its chain. Holding it before her and staring into it. Her curly red hair falling past her shoulders. Shadowing, but also framing her pale, freckled face. From which her piercing green-eyes beamed forward. "The lady who owned this... She used it to allow her to know things she should not have known. She was powerful, more so than my own mother..."

"More than you?" Colm asked.

Kate merely shook her head. "Not without this, but with this? I don't know, maybe? But it is changed. It carries something else with it."

"What?" Jennifer asked.

"Purpose," Kate shrugged. "Which is equal parts fascinating, and terrifying. But I don't detect any malice. All I know is that we are currently doing as the

Mission Date: Day 60.      The old man and the sea.

stone wants us to. I feel anxiety from it, every time we question what we are doing here. But I have never sensed doubt from it. The science team, whilst we are mapping what is out there, whilst we are still hunting for the Progenitor's home world. We are not going against its wishes, not yet... But we are not only mapping that; we are also charting our errant star. In that, I can sense interest. When I think of the star, I sense urgency."

"But you don't think it is related to the star?" Katherine asked.

"No, not directly. But the event itself may be driving a timetable..." Kate shrugged.

"To be fair, this entire section of the Milky Way is under... well, quite a lot of time-pressure." Jason said. "How are the dreams?"

"Fewer now... I would not like to test the theory. But if we were we to stray too far from what this thing seems to want, I would not be hugely surprised if they returned in earnest."

"You are still convinced that this is important?" Katherine asked.

"As far as I can be sure. I am as convinced about this, as I have ever been about anything." Kate replied.

"...okay... Witchy stuff aside, anyone else?" Katherine asked. Seeing Jason staring at her. A flicker of animosity passing across his face. A logical man, one she had trusted now for years. But one whose weakness would always be his desire to protect Kate. From anything, including from any slight. He was also preparing to speak. Intrigued, she waited to see what he had to say.

"We do not forget the Progenitors. Because they will keep coming until Earth is gone. Unless we kill them first. I know that I am digging up old ground, but it is perhaps the most important ground any of us will ever cross. Because we cannot stop them when they are already amongst the stars. But we can now, here..." Jason said. Hearing the murmurs of agreement which came from most there. "We came back much further than we expected, much further than we had planned. Even if they are not there just yet. Not yet spat out, by whatever bastardisation of evolution created them... we can still kill their planet. We do

# Mission Date: Day 60.  The old man and the sea.

so, because we must do the bad thing. Because doing that bad-thing falls to us," Jason finished.

His voice had been fierce, perhaps more so than he had planned. But it had also been certain. Alistair had been there in the background. Sharing his sentiment.

"We cling to our resolve. We must not forget our original mission, and we execute that mission with the fury of an otherwise dead race. We did not start this. But we will finish it."

Now he was done.

The leadership team was gathered in the Pequod's conference room. Buried in the starship's core, on deck three of the five. There were no outside windows here. Just a functional square room about twenty feet along each side. An oblong table in the middle, with modern chairs built to replicate the Eames office chair, around its edge. Every surface was covered with the same padded material as the rest of the ship. The hard carbyne hidden by a far more tactile, far more pleasant, eggshell-white covering.

Jason was there, as was Kate. Katherine was chairing the meeting and had taken the seat at the top of the table. Colm was sitting to her left, with Jennifer opposite him. Daniel had cried off, insisting that he didn't want to be part of such things, not yet. But Natalie had joined them. The young woman was listening far more than she was talking. Horribly outside of her comfort zone. But representing the mission team rescued from Hermentia.

"Jason, grandfather, please do not doubt our resolve or our support." Jennifer replied. Her voice was stern, marred by disappointment at his grandstanding. "BOB, the next steps?"

"We continue to make these relatively short-FTL-jumps, and we continue to travel at an obtuse angle to the galaxy's edge. We skirt the galaxy, and we continue to build better maps as we do so. The better we understand the star's fate, too." BOB responded. "Also, the more different things we do, the more likely we are to be told we are doing right, or wrong, by Kate's magic eight-ball. There are multiple strings here. This approach, it pulls on each of them."

Mission Date: Day 60.                    The old man and the sea.

"Fair enough," Kate said.

BOB was standing at the table himself, resting on his deployed legs. One arm was extended out, and he was inexplicably spinning a pencil between the three fingers of his mechanical hand. A thoughtful face projected across the pixels on the dome of his head. Articulated on the mechanics of his neck, and tilted forward, it turned to look at everyone else seated there. Jason reflected that his friend was using more redundant expressions in his speech. Probably deliberately... Probably again to appear more like the more fallible meat-puppets he liked to complain that he was surrounded by. It was not just what he said; it was also how he carried himself. The mannerisms that the artificial life-form portrayed had made him appear more human to those present. For most of them, even seeing the elongated cylinder of BOB's body, floating along the starship's corridors, with his legs, arms and even head, recessed again to form a seamless shape, felt right now too.

The flying tic-tac.

BOB was one of them. He had been ever since the benefactors had saved the survivors of the ambush at the comet. He had stepped in now, to placate the emotional humans. Jason idly wondered where the pencil had even come from. He also tried to remember back to the last time BOB had used the phrase 'meat-puppets'...

"Have we detected any further signals which appear to be manufactured?" Jason asked. "Anything that might suggest that there is life out here, anywhere?"

"We haven't, not on either of the last two times we exited FTL. Those three, the signals we heard during the rest period after the first jump, they were brief and very faint. We are still only eighty percent sure that they were even artificial at all. However, we are still a long way from the galaxy. We would not expect to hear much of anything this far into the void." Katherine replied. "Even if it were a galaxy teaming with life."

"The star, do not think that I am not as fascinated as anyone else here. But parking that, how long now until we head back in?" Colm asked.

# Mission Date: Day 60.                    The old man and the sea.

"at least three more jumps. With a few days for us to collect data at each waypoint." BOB responded.

"But you still think that we cannot find the home-planet of the Progenitors, not until we..." Colm probed.

"Not until we then take further readings from a different angle. From positions within the Milky Way itself. We will know where those positions are, perhaps as soon as the next waypoint. But more likely, the one after. Also, there is the other thing, the star. As I said before, we will also learn far more about that, as we draw closer to it."

"Thank you," Colm replied.

"Jason, Natalie, how is the team from Earth doing?" Katherine asked. Finally, breaking the silence that had fallen across the room.

"Well, I think we are doing extraordinarily well, bearing in mind what everyone has been through." Natalie responded.

"It is not a straightforward thing to easily process, to be told that you should have died. That another version of you died," Jason said softly. "I would like to say that you get used to it... However, for me, that is still a lie. You do eventually become more accepting of it."

"Eventually, I hope that I do. That we all do." She replied. "Treatment wise, and Julien is still in the bacta-tank. He will be for a few more days. He was far more beat-up than any of us realised back there. Watching the years drop away from him... it's unsettling for all of us. Alien, impossible... but part of a new reality, and one that we all need more time to understand. The others... Jennifer, your daughter's friendship, it means the world to the young girl. To Alice. The soldiers. Flaherty, Herrick, Impact and Crater... They are an odd breed, but they are taking it all in their stride... Hacker and Cleo, the gunner. I know neither of them very well. But Hacker just seems to just roll with it all. The man is fascinated by the entire process. I am not sure if that is healthy or not. Cleo, she was so badly injured, and her modifications are further along than the rest of the team. As much by necessity, to save her, as by desire. She was a Royal-Navy officer. One who was entrusted by that navy with the weapon systems onboard their most powerful gunship. She should be solid.

Mission Date: Day 60.            The old man and the sea.

She is enjoying her training. Doc Brown, Capability, he is fascinated by any opportunity to explore the unknown. He would have signed up anyway, gladly, if any of this had been even vaguely optional. It is still very early days for all of them. Daniel is watching over them all. That man has a great deal of compassion squirrelled away."

"He keeps it well hidden, but he is not as much of an arse as you might initially think." Jason replied. Getting a dirty look from Kate for his trouble. "Doc Brown, he wasn't interested in coming to this meeting."

"I didn't ask him. We're in the middle of an argument." Natalie shrugged. Clearly not wanting to expand. Jason didn't push.

"Bacta-tank?" Colm asked.

"Star Wars. It's a thing from an old movie." Kate explained. "The treatment tanks, they're not a million miles from those in the movie. In appearance, anyway."

"The treatments for the wolves? Including the non-purestrains?" Colm asked. Looking at his wife, smiling grimly.

"We are getting there. Or... perhaps it would be more accurate to say that we are getting somewhere. We initially tried to push past the healing factor. To use force alone, to resist a wolf's ability to reject foreign material, or... more involved changes. We are now looking at a process that can alter those modifications, both genetic and bio-tech, to leverage parts of the material secured from the mining of Earth's moon. To see if Theia's magic can change things. This will hopefully one day allow for the internalised technology for the Purestrain, and to remove..."

"My mortality?" Jennifer interrupted. A little surprised that the alien sentience, that BOB, was becoming far more comfortable discussing magic.

"Again, early-days, but watch this space." BOB replied.

"Interesting," Jennifer replied.

Mission Date: Day 60.    The old man and the sea.

*   *   *

Mission Date: Day 61.      Battle ready.

# Mission Date: Day 61.

## Battle ready.

The next day.

Lance Corporal Coltheart, Cleo, swung the nimble fighter through a tight arc. Knowing that the g-forces, those that she could feel pushing against her, were simulated, seemed to be an almost entirely abstract fact. It felt so real to her. The stars moved around her as her ship turned, but as she accelerated hard on her new vector, she knew that the feeling of speed was also only artificial. It was also almost entirely imperceptible, visually. There was no blurring of star-lines around her cockpit. Nothing was moving at all. Even if she were. Checking her vector and speed, she whistled. Her reality, in the last few months, had been turned upon its head.

It was a moment of peace. Or it was until the buffeting of weapon fire against her shields became more pronounced. Until the chaotic energies painted the shield's shape around her cockpit, and she forced the small craft through another tight turn to face her attackers.

Thousands of miles above the planet, where her team were fighting a desperate battle of their own. She had had allowed herself to be drawn away. Chased away.

She remembered the briefing. She would often be the fastest thing in the sky. But she must never presume that she always would be. Thirty-three years old, just months ago she had been a gunner on an Apache helicopter in the Royal Navy, and now here she was piloting an advanced starfighter, which could travel through space as easily as it could a planet's atmosphere.

Flying above the atmosphere of an alien planet, in an alien solar system light-years from Earth. A life far less ordinary. Piloting the beautiful star-fighter, a craft shaped like a streamlined teardrop, with stubby atmospheric wings to aid its flight closer to a planet's surface. Three wings, two at an angle

Mission Date: Day 61.                Battle ready.

protruding from the fuselage's tapered rear, and another immediately behind her cockpit. The fighter was elegant. Stunning. Its shape only marred its missile pods and gimbaled guns.

It had been an experience which had been a hell of a lot more enjoyable before her sky had been filled with aliens determined to kill her.

She smiled grimly. A strand of her blond hair dangled in her eye-line, blurring in the corner of her eye... blowing it clear, from behind her helmet's visor. She could not see her own face, but as her eyes focused, and laughter lines deepened around her brown eyes, creasing against her lightly freckled face, she became a picture of focussed determination.

The Progenitor drones, far smaller than those face by the Thunder-Child, during the battle of Freja, but still deadly, had drawn close, and were attempting to reach out with focussed energy beams. EM only, for now. Splashing against her shields, but not uselessly. They were abrading the shields faster than her onboard power-storage could replenish them. They were also draining those same storage modules.

They were doing so worryingly quickly.

Drawing a bead on the first of her attackers, she opened up. Flashing past the expanding debris of the destroyed drone only moments later. The one missile she had deployed taking care of its wingman perhaps a second later.

"Maverick, where the hell are you?" came the desperate call from the planet far below, and she opened up the taps.

"Incoming, coming in fast and I will be there in T-Minus three minutes." Cleo fought to make sense of the data scrolling across her screen. Knowing that once her bio-tech augmentations had completed, that she would be better able to make sense of the colossal amount of data she was being fed with. But there hadn't been enough time to wait for that.

Three minutes... her display told her two, but she was not convinced that it was considering the fact that she planned to slow down from the...

The alien planet ahead grew exponentially larger, horrifyingly fast. Far faster than she had thought possible, and she braked as hard as she could. The small

Mission Date: Day 61.               Battle ready.

fighter coming down from the what had appeared to be seven-hundred-thousand knots, to a little over twenty-thousand... doing so before she slammed into the much thicker atmosphere. The ship shuddering in protest, as the shields, which had elongated themselves to a distant point, to dissipate as much of the resistive gasses as possible, worked their magic. She regained control of the fighter before its auto-pilot was forced to do so for her.

As her heartbeat slowed, as she forced herself to calm down, she reflected that she had just experienced the sensation of speed which had been lacking just minutes earlier. Things were happening so much faster than she had ever experienced in her previous life.

It was a dead planet. Even though it had an atmosphere thick enough to play havoc with her fighter, there was nothing here that could provide for life. Co2, but to toxic levels, and with no plant-life to create oxygen... A dust-bowl, a dead rock existing in the goldilocks zone of the small solar system to the galaxy's edge. Mountains, which she assumed might never have been seen before by a considered mind, flew past far below her. The cockpit of the sleek ship allowing her to see down to the side, if not everything directly below. Her helmet was sealed, the visor down, so she triggered pass-through mode. Allowing her to look around the craft and see only the controls before her and the ghost of her own body-shape. Dissociation, it had made her unsteady, even nauseous, on the first flights. It hadn't mattered then.

This was combat. It mattered now.

Still travelling in the high-hypersonic range, she arrowed towards her team.

"One minute out." She updated. Pushing the ship even faster. Seeing the atmospheric shielding beginning to protest at the abuse.

The alert came, even as she was reacting to the movement herself. Three more of the Progenitor drones, surging toward her from behind a mountain range almost... It was to her front-starboard-quarter and at her current speed, closure distances were fleeting in their relevance, and entirely subjective to a moment already passed. She banked hard, and to starboard. Pushing her fighter toward the new enemy. They were fast, and had she given them her retreating back, it would have sealed her fate. Six interceptor missiles left, two each, but she gave each only one. Firing desperate volleys of weapon fire

Mission Date: Day 61.                    Battle ready.

towards them as her shields blazed as they returned with their own. The directional focus of her weapons was not yet as comprehensive as those in her old Apache helicopter. But they did, at least, now move. They were also now slaved to a targeting sensor that followed her eyeline. A change she had requested herself.

Two died. One exploding into fire. The other, collapsing toward the valley floor below it. Sweeping through the chaos and smoke left behind by the fallen, Cleo sent her craft arrowing skywards once again, as she banked hard to avoid painting herself across the mountains that had hidden her attackers. Conscious that she was bleeding speed, fast. More weapon-fire, and for the first time she saw her shields fail, and alerts populating her display as her ship reported damage. Light damage. Her controls felt fine, for now. Thankfully, the shields had dissipated most of the energies deployed before their failure. She spun the craft, relying on the atmospheric shields to stop her from losing control in the desperate manoeuvre, and blazed at the pursuing ship with her cannons. Killing that one, too.

For the time being, her sky was empty, and she righted her craft, and set a course for the ground-team, in their shuttle, and cursing the lost time.

"Status? I was distracted there for a minute. On my way, thirty-seconds out." She called over the comms as soon as her voice had steadied enough to trust it. Watching the ground tearing past beneath her. Valleys which might once have known water, and which were now little more than red-dust and rock. All there was as far as the distant horizon. A desolate planet, bereft of anything of much significance at all.

"Herrick is damaged and hurt. Moving to assist. Maverick, we have no response to this thing. Get here fast." Neil shouted over the comms.

"Incoming." Cleo replied. Only seconds later. Her display painting the monstrous walker which was threatening to kill her friends. "Lock, danger close. Firing... Nuke away."

Because, apparently, nukes were still a thing.

Mission Date: Day 61.                Battle ready.

\*   \*   \*

The team from Epsilon had never encountered a Progenitor walker before. The first team had, though. Although, only once. It had been during the first century of their desperate fight, the first time around it all. Forced to destroy one from orbit before it had reached the last remaining base on the planetoid they had thought hidden. One of many that the remnant fleet had scattered across a much older Milky Way.

From orbit, it had not been a threat. Destroyed by weapon fire from the first Pequod, only a year before that starship had been lost, herself. They had recognised the war machine from the recordings that had been preserved, and shared with them, by that first team.

On the ground, and facing it with only Tanks, the behemoth had proved a far harder kill. Standing on four-legs, each the diameter of a road-tunnel, and with an enormous body which was little more than the expected octahedron. Standing an almost impossible two-hundred metres above the ground, it was a terrifying sight. The remnant fleet had never determined if they were even crewed. It was also shielded by energy plates which proved invulnerable to all but the fastest kinetic weaponry.

…. and nukes.

Cleo had seen shared information from the Tanks, watching as Neil had dragged Herricks crippled machine back over a hill. She had seen both machines reporting shields at full. Automatic handshakes between her attack and their defences, coordinating their response to her tactical nuke. Her weapon system had automatically timed a burst from her particle accelerator and, moments later, her railgun, all to hit the thing after the nuke had…

The explosion was spectacular, and she knew that she had saved the crippled and downed Thunder-Child from the attack. But she also knew that the drones which crowded her sky behind her were about to kill her. She had known that inevitability before she had even started her run… The first impacts were softened by her inertial dampeners, but the subsequent ones

Mission Date: Day 61.  Battle ready.

sent her into a brutal tumble. Her shields were exhausted in seconds... her ship was dead a heartbeat later.

\*   \*   \*

Mission Date: Day 61.              Battle ready.

"That was too bloody real." Cleo squeaked as she pulled back the canopy on the fighter, which was resting safely in the Pequod's hangar.

"Whilst you saved us, I am still not calling you Maverik." Herrick said. Clambering free from the open hull of his Tank.

"We, none of us here, are any longer in a military who had thought to still ban that callsign. You are just sad that I thought of it first." Cleo replied, winking.

"You still died, again." Jason said.

"Captain, yes..." Cleo started. "But not quite as quickly this time."

"You were moments away from attempting re-entry at fractional relativistic speeds." Jason said. Exaggerating slightly. "You survived the skirmish out in space. Very well. But after that point, you were too focused on getting to the team. On saving them. Commendable, but you cannot save anyone after you're dead. I want you running simulations as often as you can. Not just on the fighters, but the shuttles and even the Thunder-Child herself. Her stick is empty most of the time we're docked with the Pequod. You can run simulations from that seat. You might enjoy flying her. She's possibly the most powerful ship any of us will ever know. Until we meet the ship that finally kills her. Cleo, Maverik, you're one of the most instinctive pilots I have seen. I want you able to fly everything we have. As soon as your augments are completed, you will find everything ratcheting up another level... Or so I am told." Jason said. Patting her on her shoulder a little awkwardly. "Just work through the missions until you know it backwards, and get Dani to fly on your wing. You will learn a great deal from her."

"Captain, thank you." Cleo turned, walking away so that no one could see the delight on her face.

"Herrick, I noticed that you managed to get blown up again." She heard Jason call across the room to the American.

"Hey, I just lost a leg..." the man protested.

"... and most of your left arm, and also your..." Neil replied. His voice faded as the young Lance Corporal headed deeper into the starship.

Mission Date: Day 61.  Battle ready.

\* \* \*

## Mission Date: Day 73

## Awake.

Almost two weeks later.

"Hey old man," the familiar voice greeted him as he woke.

"Natalie, Christ... I feel..." Julien forced the words out.

"Terrible?" The young woman asked, holding his right hand in both of hers. The warmth feeling wonderful.

"No, I feel amazing. Terrified, but amazing." Julien opened his eyes. Seeing the same face he had got to know over the weeks they had fought together on... who had visited him ever since he had been removed from the treatment tank, and apparently many times whilst he had been in there. "For the first time in as long as I can remember, I do not hurt. I do not have a part of me that aches, that is swollen... Also, we're not dead, either of us. I assumed we would be, you know?"

"So did I... right until those last moments, I assumed we would die that day," Natalie replied. "... that day, and almost every other day after the first day." Her face was still haunted. Julien wondered if those were only old demons, or if some were new.

Julien looked around him at the medical bay. Crater was resting on another bed across the room. undergoing his own treatment. Far less intrusive treatment. The man was wearing headphones of some sort and was staring at a ludicrously skinny screen he was holding in his right hand. The other held a mug of coffee. The room was a brilliant white. It was lit, but he had not yet been able to discern any source for the diffused light. There were the physical resistance machines, ghastly devices designed to restrict every mechanical part of their human victims, and to allow for every possible range of motion to be evaluated, then refined. These were in the far corner, beside the door. Beds lined the walls, with small monitors and panels on stands placed to the

Mission Date: Day 73  Awake.

foot of each. There were eight of them in the room. Only two of which had anyone in them. Just him and Crater.

"It is time for you to leave this room. It has been for a little while now," Natalie said. Her best reassuring smile painted across his face. "I have been here myself, you know. For treatments of my own. But you have always been asleep. I didn't want to wake you."

"Are they turning you into a cyborg, too?" Julien asked.

"We all need to be modified. There are precautions because of things, radiations and pathogens, that we might all be exposed to. There are improvements, too. A great many, and I have questioned my own acceptance to go through such... invasive changes... but there are apparently benefits. I was terrified, so very scared... I imagine, that for you things were..." she trailed off.

"I was a little more pressing for me. Apparently, I would not have lasted much longer. But I am also scared. I have spent much of my life facing things that terrify me. All of which... is almost entirely Daniel's fault... and his carelessness with his bloody diary. This is the first time I have ever been too scared to face..." He paused. "... and look at me. I look like I did when I was barely forty. Only if it was a different me. One who ate better, drank a hell of a lot less, and one who went to the gym a hell of a lot more consistently... does that make me, still me?"

"Who else were you planning to be, old man?" Natalie replied. "Hey, we all now get to live forever. Or at least until we all absolutely get killed by some vicious alien, or horrible accident in the void. Far harder to kill, but with perhaps a lot more things trying to kill us. Get to your feet. As much as it is terrifying, we are out here amongst the stars, and that is wonderful."

She led, and he followed. He was wearing his light grey trousers and a vest top. Shoes that appeared to be little more than deck-shoes, and which were very similar to ones he had practically lived in on the Greek island. Natalie was wearing almost the same thing. As he walked along, subconsciously he wondered where they were going and into his eyeline appeared a directional display. Into his mind came the answer. His quarters first, because apparently he had his own room on the ship. Then to the bridge. The bio-tech augments.

Mission Date: Day 73              Awake.

He had always pushed them away before. This time, he allowed for them to help him.

He was, he reminded himself, famously a very adaptable old sod.

*     *     *

## Perhaps we are not alone.

"So, it is the Milky Way?" Herrick asked Jason.

"We are now ninety-six percent sure. If we take just the information we have, and we then compare what we see on our maps to the objects out there alone and it is merely probable. But if we add to that the likelihood of another galaxy being close enough to where we found ourselves... to be this close in composition... it rises to almost an absolute certainty. Unless there is something we really do not know about moving through time." Jason replied.

"Aren't there many things we do not know?"

"Okay, that is fair. But also," Jason raised his right hand and, miming a pistol, sighted it out into the beautiful image which dominated their view. "Right there... is Earth's moon. A tiny little splinter of light in the night's sky that all the wolves can see... We are sure we are in the right part of the universe."

"I know. Man, I just like to hear it." Herrick squeezed Jason's shoulder. Both men staring forward.

"One day, I am going to ask you about the years that followed what happened on Hermentia. The fracture." Herrick said. But only some minutes later.

"This is not the first time you have skirted this. It was punchy there for a while. For quite a few years... Interesting times, but we had a way to fight the threat. To eventually contain it. What you all did there. Your sacrifice... it made a difference." Jason said. "It is possible that it also united a world which had become fractious itself. You cannot prove a negative... but I remember being very concerned back then that the world might be on the brink of wars which..."

"So, why did you call me here?" Herrick asked. Bringing the conversation back on track.

"Because we have picked up a signal, and we want to investigate the signal." Jason replied. "We will need to be very careful... we will only do this if your team is comfortably up-to-speed in their defensive roles on these starships.

Mission Date: Day 73          Perhaps we are not alone.

Or, at least as far as you can be. We were lacking in numbers. Militaristically. You are all about to become more important than you might consider yourselves ready to be. I need to take my team with me. I need people back here, military trained people, in case. Are you ready for such things?"

"In case of what?"

"If we ever knew that for sure, we would have never needed Marines."

"Not a Marine, dude. As for being ready, I always have been… for most things. If not always everything." Herrick said. "For this, though. I think so. Although, you can only imagine how bizarre my life now is to me. Because, apparently, I am now a spaceman, man."

"Yes, indeed, you are," Jason replied.

"King would have loved this…" Herrick added. Again, staring out into space.

"Too many who have died along the way would have loved to be here. So damned many. But I am sorry for your loss, and that we could not simply have arrived sooner. Not soon enough for your friend."

"He was your friend too, Jason."

"In the centuries since, and for years before, I have buried so many friends that I have genuinely lost count. But I have carried none of their deaths lightly. None." Jason replied. Turning now to face the American. "We had to wait until the last manned-vehicle left the area before we could hijack the feeds. There was a line, a moment, which we could not cross. By then, King was already dead. We saved who we could."

"Mark-one eyeballs, never bettered and too often, far too inconvenient." Herrick replied. "Only, of course, now they have been." He added, as his ocular-feed fed him more information about the galaxy laid out before him like a… he hated a little that the singularly more beautiful sight he had ever seen looked a little like a frisbee.

"Now, tell me what you think you have found out there."

Mission Date: Day 73          Perhaps we are not alone.

\*     \*     \*

Mission Date: Day 73    Sendler: The handshake protocol.

## Sendler: The handshake protocol.

There was a signal. A message radiating out into space, one which had contained an entirely wondrous thing. An otherwise completely unexpected component built into the signal; if objectively, it was also almost an impossible thing.

A data-packet. Almost undetectable, it was so degraded, having travelled an almost impossible distance. One which BOB had carefully inspected. Within it was a progressive map of the language of the beings who had created it. It took even BOB's incredible processing powers hours to understand it. To even make enough sense of it, to realise that it was data itself. Beyond what was obvious structure, nothing was standard. Nothing could be. There were no standards. Nothing had been constructed in a way that either humanity, or their benefactors, had understood.

But within the packet, recognisable things were found. Making themselves known, as he had dug deeper. Universal constants, drawing his eye, and from which a translation matrix was revealed.

The first of those constants had been the simplest of all. The hydrogen atom. Unmistakable, unique and the building block of everything. It had been expressed as a pattern. From that, then grew the rest of the periodic table. Then Prime-Numbers.

Slowly, carefully, unravelling the first building blocks of the language of those who had created the signal.

Naming stars, planets. Objects which made the galaxy. Defining sentient life-forms.

Focussing again on the elements, but this time specific ones. Carbon, oxygen, water. The cornerstones of life. Carbon-based life. Like humanity. Like the people who they now considered only as their benefactors, BOB's people, had once been.

Mission Date: Day 73          Sendler: The handshake protocol.

Constants, all made recognisable to any being, eventually. Certainly, any which were technologically advanced enough to accomplish space-travel. Life, able to recognise life.

A language appearing from amongst that. A way to structure your own language to fit within the same protocol.

Life, able now to communicate with life.

As BOB had delved into the data-set, he had seen such wonder in a protocol created by a sentient mind. One who had wanted to make themselves understood. A Rosetta Stone, a cohesive mapping grid. An established handshake, he had translated as being named 'The Sendler Protocol.'

Attached to the packet was only a single line.

"Help us."

\*     \*     \*

Mission Date: Day 73         Sendler: The handshake protocol.

"So, you're going to do this thing?" Julien asked, looking across at Jason as they strode together through the lower-deck of the Thunder-Child. Kate was on Jason's other side. Apparently, she would be flying the ship during the mission.

"We are. But we are going to be very careful. Hell, we don't even know yet if we will find it… if the signal is already dead… it will probably be lost."

"Because we're looking at a decades old signal, and as we draw closer, we are effectively moving through time, to now," Julien confirmed. Noticing that Jason and Kate were holding hands as they walked together, albeit discreetly. But it was not the first time…

"Do you two kids ever look back to those first weeks when you met? The chaos, the adventure?" Julien asked.

"Yes," Jason replied. Julien noticed that they had both looked at each other with a smile before Jason had said anything. "Neither of us had a simple time getting here, to this point… But we are always happier when we know the other is close. Neither of us can forget any moment that we have spent together, nor can we forget the pain of being apart."

"Yours is a complicated story. But I think also a wonderful one… You both keep berths on this ship, not the Pequod. Jason, your team, too."

"It is the fighting ship. Its job is to protect the others, if it is needed. We are warriors first. Julien, you're also here?" Jason turned the statement into a question.

"Yes, it looks like this ship is where most of the fun will happen." Julien replied. Laughing. "Now, show me the new galley, if is about time you had somewhere a little more comfortable to kick back on this boat."

"Follow me, one deck up and… I think you will like it, old friend. But don't get too excited," Jason replied.

\*     \*     \*

## Mission Date: Day 75.

## Mission.

Two days later.

"So, this can be many things… but it is hard to not think it could also be a trap…" Daniel addressed the room. "… a honey-trap."

He looked around. Processing that the president's husband was looking on thoughtfully. Also, that Jason's three marines were still deferring to the man. Subtle cues that he could easily see. A retired man, but one who had once held the highest rank amongst their specialist team of war fighters. A man whose wife had held the highest authority. Complications? Maybe not now, not today, but perhaps later.

"… and you know enough to spot a honey-trap, Dad?" Kate asked.

"By the third time, yes…" He winked toward his daughter, who looked back at him with a disturbed look on her face. "No one knows that we are here, not yet. We take this step; we risk ourselves being discovered."

"It is not safe at all, dad…" Kate replied. "But little that we do here can ever be truly without risk." She ignored his sideways glance. He would know this. "We just have to ensure that we understand the risks that we are taking as best we can. That we mitigate those risks, as far as we can. We are not looking to offer help. Not as any primary goal. It is what it means for the mission, that there is a protocol which is constructed for one technologically advanced race to communicate with another… They were expecting to speak with someone who they did not know."

"Meaning, that life out here, today, it is something that might be far more commonplace than it is half a billion years from now," Daniel replied. "Technologically advanced races."

Mission Date: Day 75.                Mission.

"The signal is old. We picked it up at over fifty light-years away. So, the theory is…" Colm started.

"That the people who sent the message fifty years ago, if they really needed help, are likely already gone or dead." Daniel finished.

"It is an opportunity to learn something of the galaxy before we set foot within her. I think it is too good an opportunity to miss," Katherine said. "But we are not looking for a vote here. Jason, you have operational command of this mission. It is your decision."

"We go. We separate, and the Pequod sits half a light-week away from the site. The Thunder-Child gets as close as possible, and we see what's what." Jason confirmed. "It is unlikely that they are even still transmitting. The signal we have is as old as hell. Chances are, as we get closer, the signal is gone, that it stopped transmitting years ago, and we won't find whoever sent it, anyway."

\*   \*   \*

Mission Date: Day 75.　　　　　Mission.

There were protocols in now in place. The dangers of separating, of moving away from each other, of losing each other, were many.

Waiting a few days to receive a signal and patience alone should mean that they could not lose each other in the vastness of space. So, and certainly whilst out in the dead space between galaxies, the Pequod and the Thunder-Child would never separate by more than a few light-days. Right now, and whilst starships could travel faster than light, data could not.

They had an agreed meeting point, a solar-system on the edge of the distant galaxy. To be used only if everything else failed. But that was days away in FTL, and they had no way of knowing if any dangers awaited them there. It would be better not to lose each other at all.

The Pequod had taken them all to within spitting distance (in galactic terms) of the origin of the signal, and the Thunder-Child had headed out alone. Not entering FTL, but rather staying at three-quarters of the speed of light, and hammering into the darkness on a journey that would take days.

As they had drawn closer to the source, the signal only increased in strength. Whoever had come asking for help, their signal was still being sent.

It was what they had hoped for. But few of those onboard the Thunder-Child were still quite as sure of that as they drew closer.

\*　　　\*　　　\*

Mission Date: Day 75.  Mission.

"Mission, we are drawing close enough now to begin throttling back. I am planning to approach to within a thousand clicks, and come to a full stop. We sit, we look, and we evaluate." Jason said. Speaking to the rest of the crew from the cockpit on the nose of the Thunder-Child. "BOB, what is the status?"

"Jason, the cloak is fully operational, and we are fully passive. Monitoring the source, and we are only seeing the original signal on repeat. No change. The translation matrix, the Sendler protocol, that is coming through every seventeen minutes. Nothing has changed." BOB reported. "We can see the outline of the object which is radiating the signal. It appears to be a starship. It appears to be derelict. There are no signs of any other radiated energies. We cannot, as yet, determine her size. But she appears to be very large."

"Coooooool..." Jason replied. His statement trailing off for a moment as he considered the enormity of what might be about to happen. "ETA, five minutes until we come to a full-stop relative to the target. Everyone be ready, every weapon armed. But no-one is to act without my orders. Dani, Neil, are you ready in the Tanks?"

"Ready boss." Dani replied.

Jason knew that he needed to get the rest of the expanded team ramped up. Colm was at the helm in the Pequod. But he had brought the rest of his recon team with him. Leaving the Pequod with little in the way of true starship combat experience.

TT was in one of the Thunder-Child's turrets, and in the other was Cleo. The Lance Corporal, the Apache Gunner, who had been plucked from Hermentia moments before the entire island had been turned to nuclear ash. A woman who seemed to process things surprisingly well. But untested out here.

To be fair, they were all a little outside of their comfort-zones.

The Thunder-Child throttled back, and he brought up the images of the alien vessel. Filling the cockpit with the holographic rendering of the thing he had come to see.

It still appeared dead. But it was not completely dead. Something there was still transmitting the mayday. BOB had detected EM-band radiation, which

Mission Date: Day 75.    Mission.

suggested systems were still active. Which didn't help them understand what those systems were.

[Well, that is a hell of a thing.] Jason said. Reaching out internally to his oldest friend.

[Pretty much everything we will face on this journey will be a hell of a thing, my friend. Remember to step with caution. To look for danger behind every corner. These things we find out here, they are born from civilisations so very different to our own. There will be danger where we might not expect to find it.] Alistair replied.

[Agreed,] Jason replied.

"Kate, be ready to take the stick." Jason called over the intercom. Reaching behind him and grasping the handle there to pull himself through the already opening hatch.

Because he was going along too.

\*    \*    \*

Mission Date: Day 75.                           Mission.

Kate had flown them closer in, with Jason readying himself for the mission alongside Dani and Neil in their Tanks. The heavily armoured fighting machines dwarfing him in his own armour. Beyond their checks, none spoke of the upcoming mission after the Thunder-Child had come to a full stop.

"Ready?" Jason asked. Staring through the open hole in the floor below his feet. Only barely registering the two Marines, confirming that they were ready. Before him lay the blasted, and pitted, hull of the Alien starship. Surrounded by the void. "Then, let's go."

He stepped into open space and pushed himself away from the safety of the Thunder-Child. Leaving the depressurised drop room and using his armour's zero-g manoeuvring function to approach within metres of the derelict hull. The sensors, already deployed and now before him, were connected to his own internal systems and projected onto his visor were the assurances that it should be safe to proceed.

Probably.

Despite that, it still took a determined effort to force himself to reach out and touch it for himself. The technology in his gauntlets allowing him to secure himself to the surface. He rotated his body and brought his feet down. Until he was finally standing. Failing to even begin to ignore the equal parts terrifying, and hauntingly beautiful, image of the Milky Way hanging over his left shoulder. Turning to face it. Spellbound by what he saw. The isolation, the knowledge that they were all so far away from anything… the void. They should not be out here.

Nothing should be out here.

Certainly not the derelict starship.

Because the ship he was now standing upon was scaring the hell out of him.

"Well, I am not dead. Does anyone wish to join me?" He called over the comms.

"No, it is clearly a terrible idea, but if I wanted to be the master of my own destiny, I would not have signed up and become a Marine. So, we're coming,

Mission Date: Day 75.                    Mission.

boss," Dani replied, and he saw his proximity sensors reporting on the two Tanks moving towards him.

He was eager to get going.

The derelict starship was half a kilometre long, if only a fraction of that deep. A block of a composite of carbon and titanium. Enormously strong, if not as strong as the material of the Thunder-Child's hull. It was vastly easier to manufacture than carbyne.

The ship itself was a flattened obelisk, an oblong, and its structure, whilst otherwise almost featureless, was marred by dozens of weapon platforms. The engines lay to what they assumed was the stern. There was also what appeared to be a bridge. Standing proud of the hull by almost fifty metres, another obelisk, but with windows to the very top. The hull itself was torn and ruined across swathes of it, from what appeared to be multiple strikes of what they were currently assuming had to be brutal weapon fire. Showing clear signs of battle, which they assumed might have been what originally disabled it.

But they were still over ten-thousand light years away from the edge of the galaxy. The damage, it appeared to have destroyed what they were currently assuming, were the ship's engines. What had brought it out here, and what had followed it out here and destroyed it?

The bridge itself, it was also where the signal was coming from. Two domes, on the very top of the… he struggled to consider it a roof. But it was a roof. It was also where they were heading, and Jason felt it was impossible to tear his attention away from it. He watched his readout, in the corner of his eye, as the two Tanks landed. He felt the soft impact as it reverberated the short distance across the hull to where he was stood.

"Let's go, follow me." Jason ordered. Striding forward, with his mag-boots holding him when they needed to hold him, releasing him when he needed them to release him, enabling his easy progress. Doing so without relying on magnetism at all.

"Jason, team. There are solid indications that the ship has been in this state for decades. Possibly centuries." BOB said. Speaking over their comms. "We

Mission Date: Day 75.                    Mission.

are still not seeing any other activity. Also, its power source is almost depleted. It appears to be some form of atomic-fusion devices. There is radiation, but nothing which your armour's shields will struggle to repel... another thing, though..."

"Go on," Jason prodded.

"We need to learn more. But if their FTL engines use the technology, they appear to use... There is no way that they could travel this far, with the reactors they appear to have."

"So, what brought them out here?" Jason asked.

"That is something you can hopefully find." BOB replied.

"So, nothing here is going to try to kill us?" Neil joked. Tempting fate.

\*     \*     \*

Mission Date: Day 75.        Mission.

Stepping from the ship's hull and onto the bottom of the bridge was briefly disorientating, as his perspective changed. Feeling the Tanks following as their heavy footsteps reverberated through the hull behind him, Jason strode onward, toward their destination. Toward the opening in the hull, through which they had decided to make entry. As he drew closer, reaching the gaping hole which had been blasted through the thick material, he looked in. His armour and his preternatural eyes showing him the empty room before him. He deployed a drone, commanding it to fly inside. Waiting for it to check that it would be safe for him to follow.

"Are we doing the right thing?" Dani asked.

"Rarely," Jason replied. Pulling himself through the opening.

The hull was thick, but only about two feet thick. When considering the horrendous power of ship-to-ship weapons, the danger of collisions, it seemed carelessly thin. The edges were sharp, warnings pinging him across his helmet display, letting him know. But his suit was strong. Nothing here should be able to compromise it. It was dark, but his eyes and his armour's technology could handle that issue.

He had entered a small room. Empty, square and less than twenty feet across each side. There was a door before him, one which was inexplicably shaped like an octagon. It had two handles, one to the left, the other to the top centre. He manipulated both, and was pleasantly surprised that it opened for him.

"Drones," he ordered. This was unfamiliar territory. Let the tech continue to blaze the path ahead. "Dani, Neil... it's time. It's too damned small in here. Set the Tanks into sentry mode and get your arses' in here.

Moments later, both Marines surged into the room to join him. Moving elegantly through the room, now only in their armour, to follow him deeper into the ship.

The corridor was also hexagonal. About ten feet across each dimension. It took a moment for any there to process, but the corridor ran vertically up the length of the bridge section. Perhaps the race who had built the ship had not discovered how to create artificial-gravity, but that did not explain a design

Mission Date: Day 75.            Mission.

which would not work if the ship were accelerating or decelerating. A little confused, he made his way slowly onwards. Moments later, he was suddenly caught out by a high-pitched scream from behind him. The directional source of what was effectively a radio signal, carefully replicated with wonderful fidelity by his helmet's speakers. His sensors reporting a sudden pressure change, the vacuum lessened but only momentarily. Trace gasses passing sensors which immediately recorded their composition.

"Neil, what is it?" Dani responded first. Jason had spun and deployed his weapon. Sighting towards the two Marines, ready to support them. Seeing immediately what had shocked the man.

Frozen in a rictus of death, it was the shocking nature of the monstrous damned thing which made his own heart jump in terror.

Three heads. Blocks of black, fur covered… like the torso, which was round, like an oversized beach ball. Eight legs, devil legs… Like a mutated spider.

"Did you open a hatch and have that thing… what were you thinking?" Dani asked. Her own weapon trained on it.

"Clearly, I was not thinking at all…" Neil replied.

"I think we found one of the crew. Also, some of the ship might still be pressurised." Dani mused. "There wasn't much oxygen in the gas that escaped the room, but there were toxic levels of carbon dioxide. Perhaps it was asphyxiated?"

"Perhaps… if we knew what the thing breathed… Proceed with caution… Neil, was that door powered?" Jason asked.

"Boss, it was. I pressed my hand against the lighter section below it, and it just opened." Neil replied.

"Okay, that is not good." Jason's concern went up a notch. "Let's get to the bridge and see if BOB's toolset can access some of their data."

"Copy, boss." Dani replied.

They made their way toward the bridge, the shape of the corridor making far more sense now that they had seen the species that had likely built it. The

Mission Date: Day 75.          Mission.

team moved carefully. The doors which lead into the bridge itself did not open, and Jason and Dani needed to combine their strength to force it.

BOB's little device, deployed from Jason's equipment belt, was very similar to the spider device he had used on the gantry of the shipyard orbiting the Iron-Moon back in the Epsilon system, what now felt like a lifetime ago. Its multiple legs, after their experience with the dead creature, drew an uncomfortable comparison. But the device did its thing, and guided them across the alien bridge, and to an access panel in the room's ceiling. Once there, the device let Jason know exactly where to place it. Its legs extending, pushing into the material, the metallic-carbon composite, and shortly after, the machine reported that it had started to collect data. Doing so a little too quickly for Jason to entirely trust that the ship was as dead as he hoped it was.

Jason gazed across the wreckage of the room. Taking in alien stations, displays. All damaged by an ancient fire. There were no bodies here, and the stations would not have made sense had he not first seen the creature's corpse. Everything was just off. Nothing looked correct, not to his human eyes. Designed for spider-like creatures with multiple... heads? He had assumed they were heads. It was unsettling. The race of their Benefactors, BOB's people. He had only ever seen images. Absolutely alien. But bipedal, with two arms and a head with sensory organs. Alien, but familiar. Then he had met the insectoid Progenitor race, vile creatures whose appearance resonated with every fear response baked into his soul. Even if he considered them by appearance alone, and not by their genocidal mission.

Now this, and with no subjective mechanism to understand the character of the creatures. With no way, not yet, to know if they were kind or cruel. With no way of knowing if attempting to judge a truly alien species with a human value-set.

It was hard to not find it all hugely unsettling.

Looking around, seeing a room that was exposed to space. But only through holes too small for the creature's body to have made it through.

So where were the dead?

Mission Date: Day 75.                    Mission.

Anxiously, he waited.

\*     \*     \*

"Kate, we are making our way out of the hull again. We are not going to learn more about this here." Jason reported, as he pushed himself across the bridge. Dani and Neil following close behind. Everyone was eager to leave. He had BOB's device attached again to the equipment belt at his waist. They had been within the ship for a little over an hour. To the entire team, it was more than long enough.

"Confirm, Jason. It will be good to have you out of that bloody thing. I don't like it."

It took only moments to reach the torn hole in the ship's side, the one by which they had originally entered. Once outside, and attached again to the hull, Jason waiting patiently for the two Marines to re-board their TANKs. Moments after that process was completed, they had pushed off, and made their way back to the Thunder-Child across the kilometre of open space which separated the two vessels. Drifting slowly, barely using any thrust, not wanting to pick up too much speed. Speed which they would have needed to shed before they reached their destination, anyway. They completed the short distance at only a little over walking pace.

But the journey was terrifying, almost overwhelmingly so, and with his mind threatening to betray him as his panic response surged and waned. Coasting away from a dead starship lost in the void between galaxies. The Milky Way painted across space behind the waiting Thunder-Child. Isolation, the realisation that they were so far away from anything else but… just his ship and a ghost ship and its monstrous dead. Alistair was silent, but he could sense the same turmoil from his permanent passenger, from his oldest friend.

Reaching the ship, entering the drop room, and seeing the doors seal below their feet. Waiting for the room to go through its decontamination protocols for the next hour. With Kate already piloting the starship back to rendezvous with the Pequod. The uneasy disquiet would not leave him, and he settled into his own funk. Silent, processing.

Mission Date: Day 75.  Mission.

Whatever happened next. He was anxious to get the team back into the distant galaxy with all haste.

*   *   *

Mission Date: Day 75.　　　　　Revolver.

## Revolver.

Later that day.

Daniel looked down at the weapon in his right hand, the familiar shape taken from the weapon he had carried ever since he had inherited it from his father. The heavy revolver was... It had been pretty much redundant since he and Alistair had returned from the second world war, and Alistair had proven more than capable of making silver bullets for almost any calibre.

But he had loved the ancient percussion revolver. He had never stopped carrying it.

Things had changed again... his world had been turned on its head, and too many things had changed now to leave his old revolver as anything more than a curiosity. But BOB had indulged him and had found fascination in the challenge. A creature whose very core programming had been built around pacifism had found such surprising fascination in the weapons of humanity.

Looking at the new thing, he rejoiced that its balance was still exquisite, that it pointed naturally toward its target simply as he raised his arm to lift it. It was not the same as the old, but it was immediately so intimately familiar he felt his heart swell.

"The power-pack itself, that sits within the grip of the gun. I have built two. One for your bare hands, and the other to fit better with the gauntlets of your armour. That one, it can even draw power from your armour if you need more. The chambers, at first it seemed like we were hunting for an arbitrary reason to make those still relevant. Which, to be completely honest, we were. But in the end, it proved to be a solid answer to an intrinsic problem with plasma-based firearms. Certainly, hand-held weapons. You need to move the plasma into an area where it can be contained by the electromagnetic fields, prepared and energised before firing. Effectively, there are steps required to make it ready. These chambers, they were perfect for that. Those chambers then need to be purged, cooled, and prepared to be loaded anew. So, we load from the bottom chamber for you, and it is ready by the time it rotates to the top." BOB explained. The pixilated grin across his face, entirely genuine. "You

Mission Date: Day 75.     Revolver.

need to prepare the weapon. Press the small button just below the rear of the chamber, on the right. Your trigger finger can reach it easily, even before it is drawn. That takes five seconds, and it can only be left in that state for an hour before it will go through a cleansing state to be ready to be used again. Draw the weapon, and pull back the hammer, and it's off to the races."

"Thank you, BOB." Daniel grinned, looking at the jet-black pistol in his hand. The weight felt so very right. Everything felt right.

"I can put better targeting solutions in play. But what you call a 'guide-rod', the lever you used to re-seat the old lead ball... obviously, that wasn't needed. However, I kept the form, and introduced a new function. One which is a little more relevant." BOB was indicating the rod which sat beneath the barrel. Thinner than the barrel, and shorter, it really did visually resemble the guide-rod on his old pistol. Only now with what looked like a glass lens on the very end. "This now connects to your armour's targeting sensors, or even just projects a laser red-dot exactly where it will hit. That's down to you. I kept the single-action function with the hammer moving the cylinder, and preparing it to fire. It is, as you requested, how it will need to be operated. There is a motor, which will move a prepared cylinder forward once the weapon is activated. But apart from that, it will be down to you. This, it offers an additional level of fidelity, of control. But in reality, it is nothing but theatre."

"Nice," Daniel ignored the gentle criticism, self-aware enough to know that it was entirely valid, and spun the weapon backwards on his trigger finger, as he lowered his shooting hand toward his right hip. The barrel stopping as it struck the edge of the holster, and he lowered it inside.

"When you have made yourself happy with this. I am working on something else," BOB said.

"Go on?" Daniel asked. Intrigued.

"There was a weapon in a movie, a fast-firing gun with revolving barrels. I am planning something for the Tanks."

"Was that a movie called 'The Predator'?" Daniel asked.

"It was," BOB replied.

Mission Date: Day 75.                Revolver.

"Nice,"

"You know that you are not actually a cowboy, don't you?" Jason asked. Watching the pair of them, from where he had waited just outside the Thunder-Child's armoury.

"You know that you actually are a weirdo who did too much soldiering in the 1990s and are still fascinated by a weapon which was pretty much obsolete before it was ever issued?" Daniel quipped back. Indicating one of Jason's precious, P90 based railguns, which were mounted on the rack across the small room.

"Oh, yes. Abso-fucking-lutely," Jason replied. Inside, he had such delight for his old friend. It was critical that he not show that delight... "Marine, not a soldier..."

"Because soldiers are all well and good. But if you want soldiering done right, ask a Marine." Daniel called after him. "So, how do we test this thing?"

"Not in here," BOB replied.

\*     \*     \*

## Mission Date 79.

### Living in the now.

Four days later, with the Thunder-Child and the Pequod successfully reunited.

That evening, the Pequod's bar.

Dani was watching them both, Jason and Julien, grinning away as she did so. Enjoying a rather wonderful chicken and mushroom pie. Julien was sitting beside her, opposite Jason. He was not smiling, his own food appeared forgotten. His drink, not so much. The man was staring at the whisky glass resting on the table between his two hands. His shoulders hunched.

"This... it had its hooks in me for years. Most of my adult life. Perhaps all of it. I lied to everyone, myself, as often as anyone. Now it doesn't. I am the same man, but I am not all the same man... I have been remade, anew."

"You have." Jason replied. Carefully.

"Damnit man. I do not begrudge these changes within me. I just worry perhaps if I am even the same man, without my little quirks."

Dani was idly wondering if what sounded like decades of being a functioning alcoholic could be called a quirk, when the man went off on a different tack.

"So," Julien looked across the table now, directly at Jason. Meeting his eyes, his brow furrowed. "Time travel is possible. General Relativity explains that... Forwards, and what you say, made a level of sense. With the caveat that I am buying into some stuff that is demonstrably stupid, I will accept that mass itself bends space-time, and that curvature is, in part, what we call gravity..." Julien said. He raised his hands, waving down Jason, who was clearly about to interrupt. "It is close enough for cricket, my friend... for the sake of this conversation. But the piece about travelling backwards being impossible because of the 'Causality Lock'," his hands indicated 'air-quotes,' "... because the multi-verse theory around that would have the time-traveller appear in a

Mission Date 79.          Living in the now.

copy of the actual universe. Not the universe proper. That the alternative universe would be built around that time-traveller as they emerged from something you call a 'relativity bubble'. Only not here, someplace else, someplace new, and with nothing approaching the information, or the energy, which would be required to build that universe... and then everyone involved immediately dies. Am I right so far?"

"Dies, perhaps. It is more accurate to say they cease to exist." Jason shrugged.

"It is the same thing." Julien admonished.

"It sounds the same, but it really isn't..."

"We can agree that it is bad, though?"

Jason simply nodded.

"A theory which was actually first proven by the nephew of the man who was shot-dead before my eyes in my old police-station?" Julien continued.

"Yes, him... Although, not proven. That could not really happen until the first FTL drives came onto the scene... but he qualified a theory which was later proven after his death." Jason replied. "Neither matter nor information can be sent back in time... information it's an odd concept, too, perhaps... Okay, so writing on a book is data. But it is also matter. Energy, it is only ever energy, really... but if you modulate energy, you can carry data within it. Like radio-waves... Energy, information, matter, nothing could be sent back."

"Okay, so... this is fine, immutable, right up to when another version of our Kate, your robot friend, BOB and Katherine, the doctor from your time... Another version of that group discovered that moon-rock, taken from Earth's Moon, which is in part made up from an ancient planetoid..."

"Called Theia," Jason said. Seeing his friend struggling to remember the name.

"Theia yes... A planetoid which survived the big-bang. The theory of the cyclic universe. Theia... it was outside of the previous collapse?" Julien asked. "... and now, if you travel in time with a piece of that moon rock, and wolves... it is possible... because magic?

# Mission Date 79.    Living in the now.

"No, or rather perhaps...Let me see where to start... So, this is where too many people go wrong. I did, for years, myself. You imagine the big-bang, as if you were watching it from the outside. To see the singularity, and for that singularity to explode and expand into the place where you were already watching from?" Jason started.

"Yes, kind-of... you're going to tell me that is wrong?" Julien asked.

"Yes... The universe is always the universe. It is not infinitely large, well it is... but it is a little more useful to consider that it was always, everything. There is not an outside to look in at it from. It just used to be far smaller, but everything was always inside that singularity... your vantage, if you could exist back then... which you really could not. Only energy can exist within the singularity.... But your vantage point would have been inside, too. It would have expanded around you... energy at first, then, as it cooled, the first particles, then atoms... The great expansion. Before that, it would only have been energy..." Jason said. "To be fair, if you look at matter closely enough, deep enough, it is just energy... and every part of you came from that singularity. So, in a way, you were already there."

"Not strings?" Julien smirked.

This time, it was Jason's turn to raise his hands. "That, my friend, is an entirely different conversation... we are too drunk to head off into those weeds."

"... okay, so if Theia came from before, where was she?" Julien asked.

"We honestly have no damned idea." Jason replied. Shrugging.

"Perhaps she survived in one of these alternative universes you claim can't exist for long. Because, from what you said, they exist someplace else. If the universe is everything, then there is nowhere else... apart from those created by your causality-locks. So, is it not possible that perhaps that information portion you speak of... that which tells that brand-new universe what it should become... If that information told the new universe to be smaller, would it not be possible to create one large enough to carry Theia? Perhaps it could be called a pocket universe?"

Jason just stared at the man; his brow furrowed.

Mission Date 79.                    Living in the now.

[Fuck me,] He said. Inwardly.

[did he just solve it?] Alistair replied. Genuine interest radiating from the old man's soul.

[no, he didn't... that is not how the scientific method works... As you bloody well know. But he has suggested a thing, which might be an interesting thing... which is interesting.]

[Go, Julien... the ancient grumpy policeman does something your scientists have failed to...] Alistair started. Jason tuned him out. Which was a little rude.

"So, you were a really old dude?" Dani asked, making use of the break in conversation, and leaning across the table to help herself to another bottle of wine. Filling her glass worryingly full. Wanting to save the conversation. Looking at the middle-aged man sitting beside her in the booth. Strong, handsome in a rumpled sort of way. Very rumpled. With a hairline that seemed to fascinate him. Like most of the men from Earth that she had met, the first being Jason, he seemed to prefer a beard. She watched as he ran his hand through his hair again, her enhanced eyes spotting a flash of delight over his face as he did so. He hadn't been bald before, but had it been thinning?

"Did you not see me when I came onboard?" Julien asked. The young Marine just shrugged her shoulders. "I felt guilt at first, that I was cheating... that I was getting another run at things, and one that I have not earned. But Daniel is here, and there is no way I can survive many more adventures with that lunatic. So, it is all very temporary..."

"You don't seem to mind that?" Dani asked.

"Well, mostly it's horrible, and too often it's terrifying. But..." Julien started. Leaning forward, a somewhat maniacal smile across his face, and his eyes, full of both certainty and mischief. "Sometimes, though, I feel the magic of the moment. The magic that is in every given moment, but too often, hides from us all. The electric charge, the miracle of life, of existence, almost sparking at my fingertips." Julien said. Raising his hands in front of his own eyes. Waggling them. "Those moments, when everything feels so very real... Delight, ever so tenuous, where your entire body tingles, and is born from nothing more than

Mission Date 79.  Living in the now.

the ability to see existence... and the understanding of the miracle of it all. That blows its way through normality with such sharp detail... which laughs at the humdrum. I have memories of brief moments of time where I remember feeling so very present. So locked into the moment... An immediacy... a vitality of just being... Everything is turned up to eleven, and there is such a wonderful clarity... Sometimes those fleeting moments stay with me. There is one where, as a child, I felt such power... I remember a bridge, or perhaps it was the end of a street. It is the feeling you see, rather than the thing... But since I met that bloody man, I have far more of those moments. Terror too, a great deal of that... but those other moments, they are the more important." Julien paused. Taking a drink, before raising a toast. "To simply being alive."

Dani raised her own glass to meet his, also meeting his eyes. Sharing the toast.

"But to your original question. I am still an old dude. I just look young... That man," he indicated Jason. "He is younger than me, but then something funky happened one day and he bonded with a soul of an immortal werewolf... A werewolf who was centuries old. But he was still younger than me when I last saw him before the summer. Just months ago... Now, and that summer won't happen for half a billion years, and he is somehow now four-hundred years older than he was a few months ago... and out there, that big, beautiful, mass of stars that is painted across the sky there." He indicated the domed ceiling above them with a drunken hand. "That is the Milky Way.... Weeks ago, and I was about to die on a Greek island, attacked by zombie vampires and now... I am on the outside looking in on a galaxy where the planet... my planet... it is lost out there... it has become that sort of life, ever since that first day. An interesting life, perhaps that is more important. It is one that I sometimes thank God for, but other times, I curse him. But I curse the humdrum, more. I fear normality more. Cherish the adventure, young lady." Julien finished. For a moment, he looked like he was struggling to decide between whisky and wine, before sticking with whisky and filling his glass with a relatively steady hand.

"You mentioned God. Do you believe in a god?" Dani asked. Genuinely interested.

Mission Date 79.                    Living in the now.

"That is hard to say... if you had asked me decades ago, before I found a diary in an old loft in London... I would have said no. But then I found out that many legends were indeed true. Too many. So, our friend here, what he is... then, perhaps." Julien said. Leaning back. Staring thoughtfully into his glass. "Then there was the ancient vampire, and she thought herself an angel... The other, he called himself a god. Perhaps the truth is a little more complicated..."

"Do you believe?" Dani pushed.

"I believe that what we think we know, today... is far less weird than the truth of it will one-day prove to be. I believe that we will see such wonderful things here... on this little adventure. So yes, perhaps even God." Julien replied.

"You think that the fact I am a wolf speaks of other things that exist beyond humanity's understanding... of higher powers... that it speaks of God?" Jason asked.

"That's not what I said. However, it tends to render several of the stronger arguments to the contrary, a little redundant, mate." Julien replied. Winking at Jason.

Jason didn't reply immediately, instead he reached forward onto the table between them with an unsteady hand. Grabbing an object there. Holding it aloft for his audience to see.

"There is miracle enough, right here... Yet so few see it. This is a group of molecules that I believe is a pencil, and I am a group of different molecules which are looking at this pencil with a considered mind. It is only that mind that considers this a pencil. The carbon in the pencil's core allows it to write. The carbon in this starship's hull allows for so much more... but I am life, and I am a life form whose building blocks are also carbon. What is a wolf? It is nothing close to as extraordinary a thing as any group of molecules that can think. What is thought? What is life? That is the magic... Perhaps life is everything. Perhaps it is all the magic, and yet it is taken almost entirely for granted... The most impossible thing." Jason trailed off. His point was there, held in his focus. Hard sometimes to voice. He rarely knew if it was harder, or easier, whilst drunk. "Gwilym, he died before we even left Epsilon. Dying, as he saved us all... Do you remember when that man used to speak about the moment we live in?" Jason asked. Directing the question to Dani, who nodded

Mission Date 79.   Living in the now.

her head slowly. "To this pencil, time has no meaning. It simply is. Meaning, it can only ever defined by a conscious mind. Time, beyond the entropy of the universe, is only given relevance because we perceive it... If no one was paying attention, what would time even be? But it is more than that. To us, we understand that we live in the now, in the moment, and we remember the past, and we expect the future to come. But we live in the now. A line between past and present which is undefinable, unmeasurable. The future simply becomes the past. It does not stop and pause. One simply becomes the other and we exist only in the line between the two. We live in the moment. But that moment, if you consider it fully, you realise that it does not exist. That it cannot. Gwilym, he would say that the sharpest blade, were it able to cut time itself... that it could never be sharp enough to find the moment which is all that exists. Think of a second, the second that follows is the future, the one that has passed, it is the past... but you could say the same of a thousandth of a second, a hundredth of a thousandth of a second... That next fraction, it is the future, and then immediately it is the past. No matter how small a section of time you consider... it is only ever the future, or the past. The now, the moment, any moment, it is something that does not exist. But it is also somehow all that exists... the only other time that exists lives either in expectation or memory... for that, we require the considered mind. So, perhaps we forget about thoughts of Gods, and instead focus on the miracle that we even exist at all..." Jason leant back, studying his old friend. Lighting and then taking a draw from a fresh cigar and waiting for Julien to respond.

The man took a healthy pull from his whisky glass, meeting Jason's eyes for a long time.

"Twat," Julien eventually said. Wondering why the hell there even was a pencil onboard a starship. Dani giggled.

\*   \*   \*

## Mission Date: Day 81.

### Exercise.

Just two days later.

The resistance machines in the Pequod's medical centre were amongst the best options for exercise on either ship. Natalie knew that Jason's Marines were working to set up a gym in an unused room on the lower-deck. Close to the hangar. That many preferred the free-weights already set up in a corner of the hangar-deck.

But for her, for now, this was her best option.

The movement felt more natural now, the explosive sprinting action where her arms were also forced to move through an extensive ark. A movement which had no other reasonable application, not beyond testing her improved musculature.

... and she wasn't tired.

She thought, just a flicker of a request, and was immediately presented with all the information she needed. Portrayed just out of her line-of-site, but swinging into focus as she looked towards it.

She had been working out like this now for over an hour, pushing hard through the equivalence of a hard marathon, one which was up a brutally steep hill. Whilst also... Maintaining a pace which would have put her ahead of the fastest competitors...

... and she wasn't tired.

The last fire-fight surged into her mind. Her fighting with Crater and Impact, whilst Cleo lay beside her, dying. A woman whose name she had barely known back then. Assaulted from each side by zombies and more evolved

Mission Date: Day 81.     Exercise.

vampire variants. The knowledge that she had at that exact moment, of her inevitable death, was never far away. Even now.

When everything was so far away.

"You spoke with Jason recently?" Flaherty asked. The Royal Marine was in the machine next to hers. Undergoing as punishing a workout.

"I did. He suggested that I look for the wonder of it all..." Natalie replied.

"Did that help?"

"It is wonderful, you know. If you stop and think about where we are..." Natalie said. Smiling across. "It does not make it seem any more possible... I know enough of what makes humans, human... to recognise that I am weighing myself down with survivors' guilt..."

"Clearwater, we have another chance at this thing. At another adventure. But we must both be careful of our ghosts." Flaherty said.

"... I don't think I will ever be rid of them." She replied.

"Then take strength from that alone. Collins is dead, but I think he would have loved this. I speak with him most days." Flaherty replied. "My family, too. But that's different. They weren't there..."

"I know, I miss my family... Hell, even my car... it was finally sorted and apparently Jason, he took it after I died... Now I will never see it again."

"Took it?" Flaherty asked. Horrified.

"Okay, it's a little more accurate to say that he met with my parents to share his condolences, and when they told him that they had no idea what to do with the thing, he saved it and loved it... Apparently, almost as much as I did." Natalie admitted. Ruefully.

"What was it?" Flaherty asked. Genuine interest in his voice.

"Have you ever heard of the Subaru Brat?" Natalie asked.

Mission Date: Day 81.                Exercise.

... he hadn't, and for the next half hour, two young warriors joked and chatted as they pushed their enhanced bodies harder and harder.

"This I can get used to. I have never felt so powerful." Natalie replied. To a question she had already almost forgotten.

"Race you..." Flaherty said. A big grin painted over his face as he exploded into an even faster pace.

Natalie laughed as she matched him, and then pushed faster herself.

The laugh was genuine. Mostly.

\*   \*   \*

## Hacker.

"We fly through FTL docked to avoid losing each other if something unexpected happened. If either ship were disabled, to find each other in the void would be hopeless... Also, we cannot communicate with each other." Jason answered Hacker's question.

"Also, the kitchen in the Pequod is far better." Daniel added.

"That makes sense. Thank you..." Hacker downed his glass. Refiling it immediately afterwards. "So, whilst I appreciate the opportunity to not be dead." The alcohol was slowing his words, although only ever so slightly. "I should point out that it was this man saving me, the first save." He indicated Daniel, "Or would it be better to say that you spared me?" Hacker laughed... hiccupped, looked mildly concerned, and then seemed to gather himself a moment later.

He was clean shaven again. He had sported a beard for a few weeks into the mission. But seemed to have abandoned it. Stocky, a shade under six-foot, and with the weight of his fifty years subsiding as the treatments, those he was currently undergoing, continued to work their magic. Brown hair, brown eyes and a careful gaze that indicated a strength of character that was there, too.

"Spared," Daniel replied. His voice was like rolling thunder. "But if it makes you feel better, I am glad now that I didn't kill you."

"Good enough," Hacker saluted the man. "I just hope I can bring more to the table than simply being a reliable drinking buddy."

"I hope so, too." Jason replied. Keeping his face deadpan. Messing with the solicitor.

"I am not entirely sure how I should take that. But I am sure that was your intent, old man." Hacker replied. His voice was suddenly far more sober, his eyes measuring him. There was iron there, too. Jason reminded himself that everyone brought something to the table.

Mission Date: Day 81.                    Hacker.

"We expect to be a long time here, on this mission of ours. We don't know if it is even possible, or if we will survive either the attempt, or even its success. Or our potential failure. We also don't know where we might go after." Hacker asked.

"Correct," Jason replied.

"Then I will not press you about answers you do not have." Hacker said. "I would ask about our current distraction. How do you know if it is dangerous? If it is perhaps a little too dangerous? Or if it even has any value at all, anyway?"

"We don't. Typically, we wait to find out until we get there," Jason replied.

"Okay," Hacker replied. His tone indicating otherwise. "I know that our original mission, the reason for even coming here at all, that it is important. Vital for the survival of humanity. That it is likely very important for the survival of many other sentient species out there. I am concerned that our eye seems to be straying from the ball."

"Okay," Jason replied. Still studying the man.

"Is that all I am getting? That is a little unfair."

"True," Jason replied. Leaning in. "We are all concerned, too. We are working the problem."

"That is all I am getting. It will have to do, for now." Hacker replied. Changing tack and gesturing around himself. "This ship is an amazing technology. Many amazing technologies. But not to just me. You have come from centuries in my future, and I think that much of this starship is magic to you, too?"

"Much was. Although, much of it was theory made real. The science of it, most of it, was understood already. Not all. But a great deal..." Jason replied.

"That makes sense. So, from what I can tell... from what I have seen, what the benefactors brought to the table was their ability to manufacture complicated things, easily. Much like our own industrial revolution. It is the ability to make a thing, rather than necessarily the thing itself... it is that which is the trick?" Hacker asked.

Mission Date: Day 81.     Hacker.

"Often, and yes, there is a great deal of truth to that. Carbyne was theoretically understood for centuries, for decades even before your own time. It is devilishly hard to make, though. Without the ability for the benefactors to stitch together molecules on the atomic level, it would have remained that way. Without their technology, it was unlikely to ever become more than an interesting curiosity." Jason replied.

"Aren't all curiosities, by definition, interesting?" Daniel asked. Smiling to himself.

"... and now, we make almost everything from that wonder-material..." Hacker said. "Your power source. Initially, I took for granted that power should not be an issue. There were aircraft carriers whose keels were laid before I was born, whose nuclear engines only ever needed re-fuelling once in their lifetimes. I have learned that things here are different. That thrust in a vacuum is not a straightforward thing. That to travel in a vacuum it is not enough to simply have power, you need fuel. Or, at least, a propellant. Or you need to mess with gravity itself. Doing so, as we do, with engines that are miracles, even to humanity hundreds of years into my future... That our power-supplies are of such incredible... We are powered by primordial black holes... That energy shields, might be little more than science-fiction, to most. We need to do our best to hide our more exotic technology," Hacker said. Struggling to voice unfamiliar concepts, but also resolute. "We are planning to head into a galaxy, which we now expect to be teaming with advanced civilisations. It might be sensible to not look too tempting a target to such beings who might look upon us with jealous eyes."

Hacker still hadn't finished. Pausing only briefly to consider what he was going to say next.

"Then there is the other thing. We are at a time which is potentially hundreds of millions of years before the Progenitors even become a threat... I do not buy into this magic-roundabout crap, not all of it... and perhaps nowhere near enough for a man who was rescued from an island overrun by zombie-vampires, by werewolves and who was then spirited away on starships which were also time-machines... built by the remnants of a lost race... Even beyond all that noise, a rational man would not, should not, be so careless as to trust the intent of a piece of jewellery. But I am not always a rational man. From

Mission Date: Day 81.                    Hacker.

what I know of her, I trust Kate. That is not the same as trusting that she cannot be manipulated..." Hacker paused. "I don't think that we are on our original mission, not any longer. I think that you know that, too. I am not saying that we do not do this other thing. I just want us to step forward carefully, with our eyes wide open. We know what is coming... Hell, we have been close enough to that thing now, for more than long enough, to have a pretty good idea what is about to happen to this part of the galaxy. Something else, something with its own intent, its own goals, it is steering this ship. But it can only do so as far as we let it. Remember not to be so fixated by one bogeyman that you miss another. One which is potentially pretending to be a friend. There is always something worse out there."

"What did you say that you did?" Jason asked. Leaning forward.

"A lawyer. But mostly, I worked as an intermediary. I arrange for the sale of businesses, and also the purchases, and mergers. I negotiate for a living. I have learned to never go into a deal expecting to win, and for the other to accept losing. To instead, look always for a win-win... and to achieve that, both-parties need to compromise at least something. Even those whose interests I served. I know that it is vital to understand the value of what you have, but also the value that thing has for the other party. They are not always the same, or even often the same. I have learned to be fair, and I have learned to be careful." Hacker replied.

"... and you worry that we might not be quite careful enough?" Jason asked. Genuinely intrigued.

"You are soldiers..." Hacker said. Jason smiled, Daniel did not. "... and do not protest too hard, Daniel. Your brain is wired in almost the same way as his is. If half of the stories I have heard were true, then neither of you could have even made it this far if you had always been careful enough. Sometimes, the universe needs warriors, and in those moments, I could imagine few better. Sometimes, though, and the world needs a more careful hand."

"Your hand, Hacker?" Jason asked.

"It is not like I do not have skin in the game. I would resist casually writing myself off. Not fully. Not yet. But I did not mean me. Katherine, she is solid enough. But she is a scientist first. Jennifer, she was once the president of

Mission Date: Day 81.                Hacker.

your colony. Although she is delegating overall control of the mission to a soldier and a scientist. She seems to have solid instincts. The time will come when you need to listen to her, and perhaps later to pull her back in... watch for those times carefully."

"She resigned her office before we left Epsilon. She considered herself a distraction. Video evidence had leaked, showing their daughter fighting back against the police, who were trying to assassinate her family. It did not go hugely well for the police. Nor was it easy watching. Clare is extraordinarily powerful, and she was highly motivated that night. Jennifer fled the colony with her family, with this mission, because there was no place for her there anymore. I have tremendous respect for her. But she holds no authority here." Jason replied.

"Okay, that explains things. But make sure that you do not forget to pay attention. People follow soldiers in times of war. They will hitch themselves to a different star in quieter times... Months already onboard these ships, and I get the picture that we will spend far longer getting places... than we ever spend doing whatever it is that we need to do in those places. Do you make as much sense when things are safe?" Hacker asked. Turning to look at Daniel, who had been watching quietly up-to-now. "I believe I once told you that I know where the line is... Not necessarily that I never crossed it... But I have learned that the trick is to never lose sight of where the line is."

"You did," Daniel replied. His voice, deep, and barely now more than a distant rumble.

"You are a more interesting man than I had first thought." Jason said. "Also, I am a Marine, not a soldier. Soldiers are fine. But if you need soldiering done right, you need a Marine... If I promise to take everything you have said onboard, can we get back to drinking?"

"We can," Hacker smiled. Reaching over to fill first Daniel's glass, then Jason's. Then his own.

"You're planning to take a more active role?" Jason asked.

"I am," Hacker answered. "Sometimes, I just cannot help myself.

**Mission Date: Day 81.**          Hacker.

\*    \*    \*

Mission Date: Day 83.     Prepare.

# Mission Date: Day 83.

## Prepare.

Just another two days later.

"You know that we were happily retired, right until everything went to shit on that island?" Crater grumbled, as he moved across the floor in his new armour. Green, not black like Jason's Marines. Apparently, a colour called 'olive drab green'. Or OD green.

On his shoulder-pauldron was a golden picture of an eagle, resting on an anchor and holding a trident and a flintlock pistol in its talons. The badge of the special-warfare group. Of the US Navy SEAL's. Beneath it was a zero.

He flexed in the armour, moving through a series of motions clearly designed to test his flexibility. Delight, such a wide smile, immediately painting itself across his face.

"So, exactly what level of protection does this stuff offer?" He asked.

"I watched Jason's eat .556 at close range without even picking up a scratch." Flaherty said. He was resting at the side of the room. Still just wearing the light ship's-gear that they all wore now, every day. A vest over a pair of loose trousers and what appeared to be deck shoes.

"It will also keep you alive. It has a pressure rating of comfortably over 30 atmospheres in fluid and can keep you alive in a vacuum." Jason added. Walking up to the American to check the fit of the armour. "Internal oxygen-reprocessing can recycle the liquid-oxygen built into two pods along your spine. It can separate the oxygen from the $CO_2$ of your breath. That can give you enough air for hours. Longer, if you're not working too hard. With the right modules, we can move that timeline out to days. Those modules, and others, they are mounted to the back of the armour. It can also survive temperature ranges, from horrifyingly cold to incredibly hot. As Flaherty said, mine could shrug off bullets, easily. But energy weapons, railguns with

Mission Date: Day 83.                    Prepare.

enough power behind them, and intense plasma weapons, any of those can chew through most things, eventually. I have told you about the fight with the Progenitors. The state that my armour was in after that... That was the Mark-One. You are wearing a later iteration now. It will last longer, protect better, but you are not invulnerable. You have internal-power. Power which is automatically recharged when you come on board. Either as you wear it, or when you store it. That can power flight through a zero-g environment, and for quite a while. It offers limited flight in standard-gravity. There are shields, like those of either starship, or the Tanks, the fighters, or the shuttlecraft, but that sucks power hard if it is asked to work hard."

"How much better is it than the armour you have had us training in?" Crater asked.

"Exponentially. Although much of that are the environmental functions. The powered systems. The old armour was not terrible. It was effective enough if you were hit in the right spot. Far less so if you weren't. Today's step, this step, we needed to wait for your bio-tech to bed in. For you to finish your genetic... improvements... before we could tailor this armour to you," Jason replied.

"You mean, you needed for your magic machines to remove his gut and his enormous ass?" Impact shouted across the room.

"Hey man, not cool... we were retired." Crater replied. Genuine hurt in his voice.

Jason seemed satisfied with the fit, and stepped back.

"Now, if you are ready. Command the suit to seal up, and the helmet should deploy.

"Helmet, seal." Crater ordered. Looking only a little nervous as the helmet lifted from where it was stored on his right-shoulder, moving on invisible actuators to position itself onto the back of his head. The faceplate rotating away, to move to cover his face. A moment later, and it sealed. The visor, opaque at first, cleared to reveal a smiling face behind it.

Mission Date: Day 83.                    Prepare.

"Okay, this works..." Crater said. His voice, now with a slight electronic-tinge as it was relayed through the invisible speakers in his armour.

"Right, your bio-tech will now work seamlessly with the suit. You will eventually be able to call on many of its capabilities, simply by thought. However, each of those functions will remain disabled until you have got used to it... baby-steps. Then, and you will have an advantage here that the wolves, including me, will never have... The technology, the way you can interface directly with technology... Including your armour and the weaponry, even including the Tanks... That, I am afraid, is still a few weeks away for any of you... until then, you will control those machines the old-fashioned way." Jason said. "The Tanks have also been updated. Although, not significantly. The Mark-4, the same shells, but now with an internal-environmental grav-field. To be used to reduce the effect of fighting in high-g environments. As Neil faced fighting in the Progenitor mothership. The Tanks are now called Ogre 1-8. We may one-day find a planet we cannot go to, not without one of those and that functionality. We cannot equip a function like that, not in your armour."

"Okay, thank you," Crater replied. Thoughtfully.

"So, you're Seal-Team-0? Flaherty asked, moving to look at the new emblem on the man's shoulder pauldron. "I don't recognise it."

"There isn't one. Like we keep saying, we were effectively retired. Although, we were already in the scrap on Hermentia days before our president called us back into service, officially... Who we were, before we retired? We walked away from that. This, zero... We are, in a way, now the first SEALs." Impact added from the sidelines, resting on a stool beside the wall of the Hangar.

"You will fight for this, for us, on this mission?" Flaherty asked.

"Apparently, we are all doing our level best not to get involved in anything here. There is part of me, as there is no doubt in everyone, that is fascinated to see alien civilisations, to explore this galaxy. We are not pacifists, but we want to be. If we are needed, we will do what is necessary." Impact added.

"Give peace a chance," Flaherty grinned.

Mission Date: Day 83.     Prepare.

"Every time." Impact nodded.

"But, just on the off-chance, things get messy. Can you show me the equipment pods and the weapons, and how they work with this suit?" Crater asked.

"I certainly can," Jason replied. Moving across the room carrying the small, and now standard-issue, railgun. Making it safe, ensuring that it was powered, but not loaded, as he did so. Handing it to Crater when he reached the man. "You might like this."

\*     \*     \*

Mission Date: Day 83.　　　　　Awake.

## Awake.

Kate awoke. The dream staying with her. As these dreams tended to do.

She was again on her feet, only this time she was fully dressed. Although, her vest-top was on backwards. That, she could tell immediately. It felt so awkward against her body.

Her heart rate came down. It had been racing in her chest. But this time, there had been no terror. There had been... She had felt still an urgency. But they were heading in the right direction. Leaving to re-enter the Milky Way. Just a couple of days.

She only needed to ensure that they went to where they might also be needed.

The dream, though. She had been running across grass. Wild grass, on a planet which felt like Earth. Only, it had been a far too warm Earth. One that smelt, ancient. There had been a moon in the sky. Immediately familiar, but it had not been her moon.

... an imposter. But she had felt assurance that this was okay. That it was important, too.

What had she been running toward? The sun had been there, rising just above the horizon... dazzling her, and throwing wild shadows across the landscape. She believed that there had been a building ahead, certainly an artificial structure of some sort. But it had been indistinct, and she had been entirely unable to focus on it.

She hadn't been scared though... running beside her had been her father. His shape had been nebulous, not something she believed she had actually seen. She had known absolutely that it was him. She could never be scared, never be truly scared, not with him there.

Mission Date: Day 83.        Awake.

They had both been chasing the shape in the sky. The dragon, flying high above them. Circling them, encouraging them on. Showing them where to go. Where they needed to be.

Then the star had changed. Its colour morphing, it became a brighter blue and then... Then she had felt an unease pushing through her.

That star had been wrong, too. It was not Earth; it was not Earth's sun. It was an imposter.

Everything had felt like it was an imposter.

The amulet wanted them to move on. It was growing more and more frustrated about how long they were standing still.

Checking the ship's time, she was not surprised that it was again the early hour of the morning. She straightened her top, kicked on her deck-shoes, and went to meet her father in the bar.

They were so used to this now that she didn't consider needing to check with him first.

Reflecting, as she stepped through the opening door of her quarters, that routine and traditions could build around the oddest things.

\*    \*    \*

## Mission Date: Day 84.

### Piano man.

The next day, and Jason rejoiced as his hands glided across the familiar keys on the piano. The music filling the large room. So focussed on the keys, the piece, that he barely noticed Julien sit beside him on the long bench seat. Joining in, picking up on the lower notes.

"Fly me to the moon… Let me play amongst the stars…"

They sang together. The song, a horrible cliché, was also one which fit perfectly. One which they had played last, together, centuries earlier for Jason, and a handful of years for Julien.

Jason looked over, the grizzled face looking back at him was decades younger. Younger even than the first time they had met. The smile, though, the smile was the same. God, he had missed that man.

They were parked, taking their last measure of the galaxy from the outside, looking in before they headed in.

Looking up into the room itself. Ignoring the stars painted across the transparent dome of the room's roof. Jason looked at the small groups which had formed. Katherine, TT and Dani chatting with Cleo. About what, he didn't feel the need to eavesdrop to find out. Flaherty, Impact and Crater were showing Neil how to play poker. Also, BOB. Jason hadn't noticed his friend sitting by the group of humans at the small both. The groups seemed to have formed a little too much around gender, but Jason pushed his concerns away, knowing that it was little more than chance.

There was laughter. Herrick and Daniel were sharing a bottle of excellent wine, standing by the bar, lost in conversation.

He knew that his granddaughter, that Jennifer and her family, were taking the two young children into the zero-g room beneath the Pequod's bridge. That

Mission Date: Day 84.        Piano man.

the children loved to play there. That was lovely. Even if the starships were not the ideal place for them to grow up, they would at least find family here.

He had.

The errant star. The lost super-giant. They had watched it now for long enough, from a position more than close enough, to know for sure where it was heading. Disaster, such terrible disaster. The scientists were working to hide their fascination, as the dreadful reality had shown itself to be inevitable. Such unimaginable horror of a truly galactic scale.

They had come close, deliberately very close, just to be sure. Now they were sure, and he could not wait to be far away from this part of space.

Jason missed a key, his left-hand faltering. But he picked himself up and forced himself back into the moment.

Impact had bought his guitar. It was resting beside the man now in its case. An acoustic, Jason had been surprised that it was the one he had selected. A guitar that Alistair had won during a card-game not too dissimilar to the one Impact was currently teaching the colonist Marines. He wondered if the retired SEAL would get a kick out of it, if Jason ever shared who it had once belonged to. Perhaps the man would play again today. Perhaps he would lose his nerve.

Tomorrow was going to be important. Tomorrow, and they would begin their journey to finally once again enter the Milky Way.

Unless something went wrong first.

*     *     *

Mission Date: Day 84.                    Cook off.

## Cook off.

It felt right. This, more than anything he had ever felt in his life, it felt right.

Kate's head was warm against his chest, her long red-hair a tangled mess there. Just having her close was enough. More than enough.

He looked around his room. The stateroom, the VIP quarter on the Thunder-Child. It had been his since the president and her family had moved over to the Pequod. Larger than the others, with an office/sitting room between him and the rest of the ship. The second bedroom was often Kate's. They were not strictly a couple, but they shared a love which had crossed centuries. It was complicated, but wonderfully so. The bedroom was larger than those of the rest of the crew onboard. A small desk, even a dressing area. All very neat, the padded surfaces were the same pleasing eggshell white colour as the rest of the ship. Each surface was a myriad of clever storage and useful displays. His armour was mounted there. Hidden behind the wide doors of its dedicated unit. Stepping to it, and the unit would present itself, repaired, cleaned, from whatever had happened during its last outing, and extending out upon its mount, so that it could be quickly worn… he was considering additional requirements, refinements. His mind wandering to things which were not strictly important when…

"Emergency. Cook-off… Cascade failure to starboard MOAM. Pequod released, and I'm triggering TSR remotely. Pequod clear. Thunder-Child is still ejecting one and two, starboard…. Failure, failure, unknown cause… compensating… Christ, trying something…. just release, damn you. Thunder-Child, brace… brace." Cleo's voice came through. Thundering over the cabin's speakers as, moments later, Jason and Kate were suddenly thrown from their bed. Crashing into the far wall, as the artificial gravity simply disappeared, and the ship seemed to punch itself backwards, bloody hard. Shuddering, catastrophic vibrations continued to hammer through the ship as they both struggled to untangle themselves. "MOAMs are clear. Running under TSR. Shields to full power. BRACE-BRACE-BRACE."

Mission Date: Day 84.   Cook off.

"Jason, what the?" was all he heard when he felt like God itself had picked up the ship and brutally thrown it across the universe.

\*   \*   \*

"Nice for you two to join us…" Julien said, his voice unsteady. Addressing Jason and Kate as they entered the Thunder-Child's control room.

"Is everyone onboard present and correct?" Jason asked.

"Neil has a broken arm. He is in the infirmary. Natalie received a head wound that would have killed her if you hadn't modified her. Impact is a trained medic, and he is familiar with the equipment there. Everyone else, just bumps and bruises."

"The Pequod?" Jason asked.

"She managed to get further away. Her shield's absorbed it with barely a bump." Cleo answered his question as she swung out from the tunnel leading to the cockpit. "BOB was onboard the Pequod, so he didn't notice what was about to happen. The alerts came through, and I followed procedure."

"She saved us, is what she did." Julien responded. "That godless damned antimatter is terrifying and just tried to kill us all."

"Fair enough. Okay, damage report?"

"Early doors, but as far as I can tell, we lost power-relays to the shield's in the surge. Although, we have maintained redundancy still. TSR burned itself out, but that is what it was designed to do. A small stress concern to the starboard rear-quarter… nothing else, but niggles. We should be moving again in a couple of days. Apparently, the door to your bedroom lost its motor, Jason. That explains why you were late… Kate?"

"Clearly, I was helping him get out from the other side," Kate lied, convincing no-one.

Mission Date: Day 84.　　　　　Cook off.

"Cleo, you called it a cook off?" Jason asked.

"Captain, that might be an ancient term, but we used it for our own explosive ordnance in the fleet. The containment reported as failing on one of the two on that side of the ship. It could not say which. I ejected both. Or I tried to. The standard operation failed. I had to reverse the ship to get the malfunctioning MOAMs out of their bays. The ship was attempting to prevent their launch... it was stuck in a logic-loop. I got us clear of the Pequod, the weapons clear of us, then us clear of the weapons."

"You saved us. Thank you. Sincerely, thank you. None of those things should have been possible... The precautions... They were supposed to be far more robust than that. We will find out what caused the weapons to fail, and we ensure that it cannot happen again. However, hands up, who doesn't think it is a good idea to carry anti-matter warheads within any of our internal bays?" Jason asked the room. Not entirely surprised by the response.

"Okay, open a channel to the Pequod. Let's get going, people," Jason said.

Because it might also be nice to have weapons which could respond to the threat of capital warships, and which were not quite such massive overkill.

　　　　　　　　　　*　　　*　　　*

## Mission Date: Day 85.

### Heading back.

Just two days of frantic work, later... a battered crew prepared for the next stage.

"Engage," Katherine ordered. The command bringing a wry smile to Jason's face.

Jason stood before the enormous dome of the Pequod's bridge. Gazing at the edge of the galaxy as he felt the starship beginning to accelerate towards FTL. This would be the first time he had watched from here. The first time he had not taken the stick in the Thunder-Child's cockpit. Neil had that responsibility today. Looking to his right, he saw BOB right there with him, standing with him. His torso supported by his three powerful legs, and his slender arms crossed across what could be considered his chest. The articulated head turned on the gimbaled neck, and the pixilated face drew a smile, and winked at him.

"Uneventful so far, Jason. Although I must caution you that I might be getting a little bored with the inaction." BOB said.

Jason heard Dani snort with laughter at this from behind him.

"Are you back in the game now, Jason?" BOB asked. "It makes sense that you and Kate are better placed to help the new team acclimatise than anyone. But you have been missed here."

"BOB, I have full trust in you all... and as for a lack of excitement, we will see what we can do... I thought that the Thunder-Child's antimatter weapons, attempting to turn us into little more than a memory, might be enough excitement for a while." Jason replied. Looking around the room. Seeing little in the way of shared laughter at his joke.

Mission Date: Day 85.         Heading back.

"Too soon?" He asked. Greeted by further silence. "Tough room... This next location. It works for the mapping project and also keeps Kate's amulet happy? Also, it's been a few days now. Have you been able to get anything more from the data we brought back from the alien ship?"

"Yes, it is, and also yes..." BOB responded. "Mapping wise, we need to hit two additional points, ones which we have already defined, and we need to capture extensive readings from those points. Both of which will need to be deep within the Milky Way. It is not exactly triangulating, although to consider it that is not a bad shortcut to understand the logic of the thing. It will allow us to draw more accurate maps. It will give us enough to find the Progenitor system... Also, from the list of the possibilities put forward, Kate became quite excited about this one."

"Lightyears away from the event, too?" Jason asked.

"Far more than enough to be safe for years if we stayed there... It is a shame, though. To have been able to witness such a thing, first hand..." BOB said. Wistfully.

"Like a flee, attempting to watch a nuclear explosion sitting on the bomb... it would be a hard thing to witness, and to survive..." Jason replied. "Do we understand more about the true velocity of the orphaned star?" He asked.

"We do. Also, we were able to ascertain that it would not have lasted long, anyway. Even if it were not set to collide with the other star... Its main sequence is almost done. Its death, a supernova of rare power... It is a supergiant of an unusual size. I would recommend coming to the science deck... it is fascinating." Katherine replied.

"Dreadful?" Jason asked.

"Dreadful, yes. But also, fascinating. Also, we have something else, potentially also worrying."

"Something else to worry about?" Jason asked. incredulous. "Other than that?"

"Subjectively, possibly. Harder to compensate for. That Data-dump, from the derelict starship, it was corrupted to hell, but we believe now that we have

Mission Date: Day 85.　　　　　Heading back.

untangled all we will be able to... and we need to brief the team... Jason, there appears to be a war currently being fought in this part of the galaxy. One that has been going on for generations, and one which might complicate things. What is still very odd, though... BOB theorised this at the time. He was correct to do so. That derelict, from the information we gleaned about her FTL engines, her fuel reserves. There is no way that she should have been able to get as far out as she had."

"Is it possible it was towed out, or was on a trajectory which allowed it to continue to drift?" Jason asked.

"Both those things are possible." Katherine replied.

"... and where we are going. Kate signed off?" Jason said. Circling back.

"Yes," Katherine replied. Carefully. "Had she not told you?"

"No," Jason replied.

"We went through the destination points for the mapping exercise, and Kate was very insistent that we picked this one." Katherine indicated a spot on the projected holographic star map. "It should be safe. We picked it as potentially a point that should be safe. But now a stone in a magical amulet finds that spot interesting. We really want nothing there to be interesting. Why do you still trust it?"

"I don't, not fully... but it has been that sort of life." Jason shrugged. "It has also been an outstanding life... it has often been that, too. But I have put far too many sizable decisions on naked trust based on very tenuous things, far too few of which could be considered even vaguely objectively sensible..." He finished. Katherine didn't push further.

Pushing everything away, and ignoring any of the chatter on the bridge as the crew continued to prepare. Instead, watching as the first signs of the transition to FTL begun to show against the otherwise invisible shields before the Pequod's bridge. Sparking at first. Energies coalescing, flaring, and then immediately dissipating as the waves of energy begun their protest at the starships breaching of relativistic physics. Cheating nature itself to corrupt space around them. Then the overwhelming burst of radiation from across the electromagnetic spectrum flared brighter, the transparent-carbyne of the

Mission Date: Day 85.    Heading back.

bride's dome darkening to protect the crew. Moments later and the bright-white light separated to form compressed waves of the colours of the...

"This is Pequod actual. We are riding the rainbow." Dani reported from the helm behind him.

"Outstanding," Jason murmured.

This time, he meant it.

\*    \*    \*

Mission Date: Day 85.                    Heading back.

"What do you see when you look out there?" Crater asked.

"I see something hauntingly beautiful, but also terrifying." Impact replied.

They were both standing inside the small office, which was otherwise unused. One of many on-board the Pequod. There was no proper furniture. Apart from two bean-bags, the retired SEALs had spent days attempting to have the Pequod manufacture for them. They were still not entirely right. But the beer was.

"You know, we have yeast, even fermentable sugar... but no hops. We could have worked to make our own beer!" Crater said.

"Instead, we are cast adrift in a cruel universe with only this..." Impact replied. Inspecting the bottle of ale he was holding.

"I like it. I feel that if we ever return to Earth, that we should visit 'Newcastle' and see where their brown ale is made." Crater replied.

"But this is all we will ever have until we do..." Impact replied. Laughing. "You're struggling with this old friend?"

"I am no longer the master of my destiny... we retired, you and I, because we were tired of the killing. Because we were tired of watching our friends dying. But also, because it was long past the time that we needed to follow our own star... and now we are here... thrown into utter insanity. I am not entirely convinced I am not in a padded room somewhere, with a straight-jacket on and some awesome drugs."

"I would be right there with you too, buddy. What freaks me out is that... well, that would be a far better explanation than... well, than this crazy world we find ourselves in. I used to get claustrophobia on submarines... not because they were cramped hell-holes that stunk of feet and farts... but because we were surrounded by an ocean that wanted to kill us. Because all that existed was a metal tube... and here we are, and we are in a universe where there might not be a planet out there that we can stand on, and even take a single breath without dying. These two starships, as comfortable as they are, as incredible as the technology is... This is everything, this is everywhere...." Impact replied. "On Hermentia, we did what we had to do. We were prepared

Mission Date: Day 85.  Heading back.

to die doing it... So this is... all very unexpected. But it is an extension to a life we had both believed we were giving for the greater good." Impact started.

"Unexpected... ha." Crater laughed. Taking a swig of the cold ale. "If either of us had expected such things..." He stopped.

For a long time, neither man spoke.

"I am no longer human." Crater said.

"I never have been." Impact replied. Carefully watching his friend.

"I am stronger than I should be. Faster, too. And not just physically, my mind works faster. My head is clearer... I am younger, and I need not age again.... Ever. But am I still me? Am I even me, anymore?" Crater finally asked.

"Do you feel you are?" Impact asked.

"When I ask myself the question, the answer is yes. But who is answering that question?" Crater replied. His eyes haunted. "Nothing hurts either. My leg, where it was broken in Kandahar, back in oh-nine. My shoulder. How many times have I dislocated that damned shoulder? Nothing aches."

"You have always defined yourself by your collection of knackered body parts. To quote that British marine." Impact replied. "On the plus side, you are thinner again.

"I am struggling, Impact...Peter..." Crater was staring again out of the window. Watching the rolling colours that sparked and shone through the protective carbyne. Watching the rainbow.

"You and me both, my friend."

\*  \*  \*

## Mission Date: Day 92.

## Catch.

In FTL Transition, seven days into the journey.

Jason looked at the people before him in the Pequod's hangar bay. The survivors from Hermentia.

Today would hopefully be a break from the brutal combat training he had been putting them through for weeks now. Today, and hopefully, they could also have some fun.

"So, I am going to take it easy on you today. This is something entirely new. This is Earth Standard, plus fifty percent." Jason said to the room. "BOB, if you please?"

"Jason, done." BOB replied. Hovering in place, close to the ceiling, and directly above, the two fighter-craft, which were positioned near the ramp.

Immediately afterwards, Jason felt his body suddenly become half again as heavy as it had been. Hearing exclamations of surprise from his audience. Groaning from several. He had been expecting it. They hadn't.

"With the exception of the wolves, all of you here have been through enough of your modifications for your bodies to better cope with the strain of the additional gravity. Your armour will assist even further. However, today we are going to look a little deeper at what that gravity means. I want all of you to disable your bio-tech. No cheating."

"Cheating, I was struggling to climb into my jeep those last few years… trust me Jason, I feel like a million damned dollars. Everything I do moving forward is cheating." Julien replied. A grin painted across his face.

Mission Date: Day 92.              Catch.

"All of that work, to make him a younger man. Did you not consider making him prettier?" Flaherty jibed. The marine was bouncing from toe-to-toe, testing the change.

"Hey, why mess with perfection?" Julien replied. Laughing.

Jason held the ball in his right hand. Scanning the room. Not the wolves. Their nature was more cunning, they might guess. Hacker, the solicitor, Jason noticed the man looking at the ball, and saw a grin on the man's face. Not a soldier, but a man whose lateral thinking would make...

Natalie watched on. Jason thought it likely that she had guessed the truth of it, too. He knew he would catch Flaherty out, probably. But he found himself reluctant to embarrass the young man. A fellow royal marine. The SEAL, or Herrick. One had a better sense of humour. So, the SEAL it was then. Crater. He was big enough, and ugly enough, to hopefully not take this personally.

"Crater, catch..." Jason threw the ball through the air in a gentle lob. A practiced throw, which would look mostly natural on its way up. Predictably, the man missed the ball, his hands closing around empty air moments after the ball had fallen past them.

"Well, that is fucking horrible." Crater said. "That genuinely hurt my brain." The man moved across the floor. Picked up the ball and lobbed it back to Jason.

"Things will fall faster than your brain has evolved to expect. Things will move differently, and the chances are that we will never set foot again on a planet with the same gravity that we know instinctively how to work with... Now, everyone, I want you to jump up... into the air."

They all did, several of them muttered in surprise as they fell, faster. As they landed, harder.

"On the way up, and it feels like you're simply carrying a heavy pack. It is how you slow, and how you fall back down. Your mass is still the same, but it is not correct to consider that only your weight has changed. Gravity is a force of acceleration. It is why that old footage of the first astronauts on the moon looked a little funky. Get used to it here, not out there where you might be

Mission Date: Day 92.              Catch.

fighting for your life. Your instincts will want to lie to you. The feeling will be nauseating for some of you..." Jason said.

"Apart from Earth," Natalie said.

"What?" Jason asked.

"When you said we might never again set foot on a planet with a gravity like Earth's, you meant apart from Earth. We are going home one day, aren't we, Jason?"

Jason tossed the ball to her, the woman catching it in her left hand, never once taking her eyes from his. He was pleased to see her here, joining in with the training.

"Natalie, I bloody hope so," Jason replied. Honestly. "Okay team, let's play catch."

He missed the ball that Natalie threw back to him.

[I hope so too, Jason... you did the right thing, by not lying to her.] Alistair said.

[No more lies...] Jason replied.

[There are always more lies, my friend, no matter how good our intent might be today.]

\*     \*     \*

Mission Date: Day 92.　　　　　　Elite-Recon.

## Elite-Recon.

"Our team grew," TT observed.

Neil was initially a little surprised that she had spoken. None of their group had. Even Colm, who was relishing spending time again with the troops after years spent hobnobbing in political circles, had been unusually quiet. He raised an eyebrow at the comment.

"Deliberately open-ended statement there, TT?" He said. A few long seconds later.

"Deliberately so, yes." The young Marine replied.

They had gathered in the small mess on the Thunder-Child. It was their space, one that had been precious to them all since the starship had first launched. Not a clandestine meeting. But deliberately a private one.

"Do they concern you?" Neil asked.

"Everything concerns me. It is what makes me a good Marine," TT answered.

"Do I concern you?" Neil asked. His tone and face painted with mock outrage.

"Like I said, everything concerns me..." she replied.

"Fair enough... The boss. He is very excited about Flaherty. To have one of his precious Royal Marines onboard made his day." Neil said. "Daniel, Christ, that man is scarier than his daughter, and a hell of a lot less easy on the eyes."

"I would not go so far as to say that..." TT replied. Winking. "But our team has grown, and we have unknowns in the crew. I like them. As their modifications progress, they will become stronger, better. Several were already very accomplished warriors, already. But they are not Elite-Recon, they are not us."

"We need the numbers. To crew both ships and to put together teams for ground missions... we needed more numbers." Colm said. "I hold my old rank as little more than an honorary title. I have clarified that I want to be one of

Mission Date: Day 92.          Elite-Recon.

you now. But I have a level of wisdom here, perhaps... We get them up to speed, and we trust Jason. The captain has the measure of what is happening. We know him well enough to see that."

"... for now, perhaps... but if the cracks come back?" TT asked.

"We all know him. We love him as a brother and a leader... he has our backs, we always have his," Neil said. Finally relaxing back in the booth, wishing the conversation could be a little lighter. "Cleo, she saved us when the anti-matter tried to kill us. She is a hell of a pilot. We watched those two SEALs work through their training exercises. They fought together for years... They're exceptional warriors."

"We trust them?" TT asked.

"We trust them, right up to where we don't..." Neil winked.

"We had better pay attention, then..." TT replied.

"We would not be very good Marines if we didn't." Dani finally spoke. Grinning away.

\*     \*     \*

## Mission Date: Day 103.

### Finding balance.

Still in FTL. Eleven days later.

The ship had fallen into an easy rhythm. The scientists were lost in their work. Building their maps. Studying the information gleaned from the derelict starship. Fascinating themselves with every detail of a race they knew almost nothing about.

Still unable to explain how that starship had come so far from the Milky Way. With neither the engines, nor the power, to achieve a fraction of its last journey.

Apparently, the expedition would have its own Sendler Handshake shortly. One, with a carefully curated introductory package about a species which wanted to hide its truth. A fiction, but one which should enable them to communicate with anyone they met.

Originally, before they had left Epsilon, both starships not yet ready to fly on their own, and still carried within the Ark's hangar bay, he had briefly considered preventing the science team from coming along at all.

This mission, it had a military focus, but scientific inquiry, it would likely keep them alive longer than the ability to scrap.

The Hermentia survivors' training was progressing well... inquisitive minds, keen to learn and faced with such wonder that few had maintained a jaded eye for long.

This was the sticky bit, though. Close-quarters combat. Much of which, it had not changed a great deal in centuries. But it had changed. He had a lot of strong egos, and he had a lot of disparate mind-sets amongst the war fighters.

Mission Date: Day 103.                Finding balance.

But he had TT and Dani, and they were proving exceptionally useful in training.

He walked around the corner to find Dani proving herself very useful. Entering the hangar, to find the marine squaring off against Daniel. Remembering back to when the elite Marine had tested herself against Kate.

This was something which should prove interesting.

Jason walked up to Kate, standing beside her and...

"So, what is this lesson?" He whispered.

"This is actually Dani making a point which might save their lives. I am a little surprised Dad is going along with it." She replied, her voice as low as it could go. Idly, Jason wondered who amongst the modified team had heard their quick conversation. He suspected that they all could.

No matter. That was not important. This was.

*     *     *

Mission Date: Day 103.　　　　　Finding balance.

"Team, you have seen a great deal over the last few weeks. Also, all of you have now been issued with your new armour. Today, I am going to show you some of the advantages you have... Suit, rapid-seal," Dani said. A heartbeat later, and her helmet slammed closed over her head, hiding her cropped blond hair and her youthful face, which was marred only by the scar she refused to have fixed. A moment later, and the visor became transparent. Revealing her crooked smile.

"Daniel, if you please." She asked. Her voice relayed now through the invisible speakers in her armour. Jet black, with only the emblem of the Elite-Recon, Colonial Marines, visible. Sleek, deadly.

What happened next was terrifying.

Daniel was wearing his standard outfit. Jeans, a vest and cowboy boots, that he had bribed Impact to retrieve from Jason's apartment. The man took those off, putting them carefully aside. He also removed his holster and laid his sidearm down. He grinned at Dani, and...

Jason had not watched Daniel move like this in centuries. The memories shared by Alistair, of finding SS guards fleeing... such awful things... even now, centuries later, and his own fury had barely dulled. Many Nazis had died very unpleasant deaths that day. This was not that fury. It was controlled, deadly.

He exploded across the floor as Dani drew and fired her pistol. Jason hoped that the rounds were less than lethal. Although, where Daniel was concerned, such determinations existed only in the grey. She got off two shots. Daniel rolling across the floor, under the weapons field of fire, and surged upward to grab her arm. Twisting it and forcing the weapon from her hand. Moving her into an arm-lock with her body now twisted away from him, and facing the floor.

"This old-git, he is faster than I was... he has disarmed me, and he is strong enough to hold me in this position. But his options are also limited," Dani said. Daniel, clearly waiting for her to share this, continued to hold her in position. "But he could not injure my arm by forcing it past its point of articulation. Daniel, please try."

Mission Date: Day 103.			Finding balance.

Daniel's expression intensified as he increased the pressure he was exerting on Dani's arm.

"Effectively, the armour is tailored exactly for each of you. It can follow any motion you are capable of. But critically, it is also incapable of being forced past the point where your own bones can't go, anyway. This hurt. I am disabled, but there is no permanent damage. He is stronger, significantly more so than I am. Even with my enhancements. But your armour can also add its own power. Watch my arm."

Slowly, barely, Dani's arm bent again at the elbow. Breaking the lock.

"Jesus Chris, the suit is telling me how much power it is using. This is insane... that you're actually this powerful?" Dani was clearly startled. "So, I can free myself, but it is slow, and he isn't. Daniel respond, if you please."

Daniel flowed away from the armlock, spinning on his heal, and sweeping the woman's right leg out from under her, dropping her to the floor. Rolling her onto her back and crashing down on top of her. Pulling back her helmet and holding it a foot above the floor with both hands. He again stopped. Waiting.

"Right now, and I would struggle to keep up. The speed of the attack, his response to my defensive moves. I would struggle to process it all fast enough to save myself. He could never crush the armour, not by driving my head into the floor. But all of you understand about accelerative and decelerative concussive injuries, and he could turn my skull and my brain into porridge in moments... So, I need to respond. What options do I have?"

"Electrocute him!" Kate shouted. Before mouthing an apology as her father looked across at her with genuine hurt in his eyes.

"There is that. The suit can generate electrical charges across its surface and enough to disable even Daniel. I will not show that. Even to make his daughter happy. But the options should appear on your screen. You should all now be able to select and deploy defensive measures with just a thought and a glance. Or, if you are confused or injured, they can be instigated by voice commands. There are also the shields, which, like with the electrical discharge, the energy field around the armour would disable, or at least, dislodge him. Or... there is,"

Mission Date: Day 103.        Finding balance.

Daniel was still on Dani's back. Crouching on top of her and holding the armoured figure to the ground. In the blink of an eye, the suit surged toward the ceiling and spun around, dropping Daniel thirty feet to the floor. He landed easily on his feet, genuinely laughing.

Jason, watching on, promised himself to ask later if Dani had let him in on that last thing.

"Because you can fly... not for long. It is a mechanism to get you into, or out of trouble, quickly. If you are losing a fight, don't react to a fist with a fist, react with whatever you have."

The figure righted itself. Dani rotating to float there, standing upright near the hangar's roof, and then lowered herself gently to the floor to stand beside Daniel.

"The Pequod, the Thunder-Child, they excel for two reasons. For many reasons, but I am focussing on just two. Their power-sources will outlive all of us, no matter what we ask of them. But more than that, it is the ability to tap into those power sources. There are batteries on this ship, in this armour, which would stagger you. Which were exceptional even in my time. The trick is to get the power into those batteries. You all saw the damage both ships had following the antimatter incident. Damage that was not limited just to that caused by the energy of the detonation. But also, as both ships tapped into their power at unsustainable rates. TSR, the acceleration that offers is greater than could ever be achieved from batteries alone; that was a sacrificial function burning out as it drove power directly into the Chasers, from the singularities themselves.

Once you are off the ship, your power reserves are finite and cannot be replenished until you return. Watch them. Learn what takes the most power and use those functions sparingly."

"Can we practise these things?" Crater asked. Herrick looking almost as excited. "Because I want to fly."

"That is how we are all spending our afternoon. Suit up people. This is going to be fun..." Dani replied. "Doc, Daniel, Impact... I need to work with you all. Jason and Kate have tailored suits able to work without the bio-tech

Mission Date: Day 103.         Finding balance.

enhancements. Right now, and your armour is configured in the same way. We need to find the best way to work for you all."

Jason smiled, watching his LT looking after his people, too. It was pleasing.

\*   \*   \*

Mission Date: Day 120.  Lessons learned.

# Mission Date: Day 120.

## Lessons learned.

Over two weeks later. Still in FTL. Still heading deeper into the Milky Way.

The science deck also had a small lecture theatre. Barely capable of seating the ship's full complement. Up to this point, it had only been used as a cinema room. Jason showing his old movies to a fascinated group. Some watching films from their future, others from such distant past that they had never known of their existence.

This had not been that sort of movie.

"... that was a lot." Hacker was the first to speak. "Briefings aside, and I know that you have spoken to us at great length about the Progenitor threat. To be told about that threat is one thing. That was a lot..."

"We have fewer antimatter weapons today than you did back then, and it was barely enough. Was making ourselves weaker?" Natalie said. Losing her own question as her mind fought to process what they had just watched. "The Thunder-Child, she is so powerful, and she barely survived that encounter."

"We thought long and hard about how to show you this. If we should allow you all to watch the footage, that which we were able to preserve, alone in your quarters. Or to do so in a briefing. It seemed better for you to be able to ask questions." Katherine said. Addressing the room before her. "This mission has fallen somewhat out of focus over the recent months. Since we arrived at this point in time. For us, those who fought the creatures at Epsilon, those of us who witnessed their awesome power, and their singular focus. We will never forget. We will still do this thing, not because we want to. But because there is a threat that is this powerful and which is relentless. Which will keep coming until they are stopped. Which cannot be stopped then, so we came back in time to do so... and we have been... diverted. But we cannot forget what else we must do."

Mission Date: Day 120.   Lessons learned.

"We just watched the Earth die. The first time around and the Earth died... Even if that footage was faked, it was faked by someone who watched it happen. By another Kate." Herrick said.

"As Hacker said, it is a lot. It took all of us a while to process it." Katherine said.

"Gwilym was a good Marine, one who might have saved everything... it's a shame we will never get to meet him..." Crater mumbled. "I say we discuss this for only half an hour, then take the rest of the conversation to the bar. That we raise a toast to that young man."

"I second," Impact slapped his oldest friend on the shoulder.

\*   \*   \*

Mission Date: Day 120.                Friends.

## Friends.

Alice ran along the deck, weaving between the scary English man and the old policeman. Now a young policeman... which was weird. Hearing the two men laughing as they watched her disappear around the corner. Behind her, and Clare was hot on her heals... Alice knew that her friend would catch her easily. That the mythical creature she should have been terrified of, but now loved like a sister, was so much quicker...

But that would have ruined the game for both of them. The end of the corridor was only twenty feet ahead, and the ship, knowing their game very well by now, had opened the hatch before she reached the entrance. Giggling, she threw herself forward... and flew.

Alice preferred it when they were not running faster than light itself. The rainbow was beautiful, but even the surging colours which rippled past the vast, transparent dome could not compare to the sight of the galaxy laid bare.

She loved the stars. Her mum had loved the stars...

Alice twisted expertly, as she floated through the large space, bringing her legs forwards to cushion her against the glass. She knew it wasn't glass... Perhaps when she was an adult she would relent and think of it otherwise, correctly, but not yet. For now, it was enough.

Clare landed beside her. Her friend's long raven hair and darker skin, reflecting the beauty of the corrupted universe outside of the starship. A huge smile painted over her face, too. For long minutes both girls stared ahead, holding hands and lost in the view. Soon they would play here. Bouncing from the walls, flying through the space without gravity.

Flaherty had promised to meet them here with the ball and the bat. The man had said he needed their help to develop zero-g baseball for the Americans.

Alice knew that he missed his own family, too. That was okay. They all did.

Mission Date: Day 120.                Friends.

This, what they had found here, it was beginning to feel like her family once had...

Before, they had been taken.

\*   \*   \*

Mission Date: Day 120.    Evening.

## Evening.

The steel-acoustic guitar was not the only one which they had spirited away from the London apartment. But it had been the one that Impact had chosen for himself. Its tone was simply exquisite, and as he moved the fingers of his left hand across the frets. Crater was singing, crooning enthusiastically. Suspicious Minds, by the King.

Jason was waiting patiently with his violin, the impossibly old instrument which had been the same instrument, as one of the matched pair he had looked at in the music room in his old home.

Impossibly, the same instrument. They hadn't needed to steal it; Jason already had it. Time travel, it made odd things possible.

Natalie moved tentatively forward; she was holding the trumpet shyly beside her. Clearly wanting to join in.

The original crew watched on as Neil sat down on the drum set. The colonial Marine, spinning the drumsticks expertly in his hands, and then immediately picking up the beat. Nodding for Natalie to step forward. To join in, too.

TT, Cleo and Dani were watching on, laughing. Drinking the exquisite wine.

Impact knew that he was not actually drinking an almost eighty-year-old Macallan. He was drinking a perfect replication of that whisky.

They had another hour, then it was going to be a night dedicated to the Electric Light Orchestra. Because, apparently, quite a lot of work had been put into it.

Wonderful.

His heart still felt the pain of missing his world, his family. But he was living now a stolen life, and his mission was to make his world safer.

He had a new family now.

Mission Date: Day 120.  Evening.

\*   \*   \*

## Mission Date: Day 134.

## Clear.

A fortnight later. Still in transit.

Flaherty moved forward carefully, with Herrick just a few paces behind him. His weapon to his shoulder, and tracking the superimposed images of his targets as he stepped carefully through the virtual-building. He was being careful to not touch the walls, not too much. His armour was carefully manipulating his movement, restricting it where needed, to best represent the structure which was being painted within his bio-tech. But it was still possible to tell it was not real.

The uncanny valley. Almost there, but where it wasn't, that was where the pantomime went away.

But for a virtual training simulation, it was insane. Not to the extent of the experience that the Tanks could offer. Or the various vehicles, ground and flying. But far better than it had any right to be.

It had been disorientating at first, with the limited space, the necessity for movement to be sustained, and that the building they moved through was larger than the space it was painted in. The mission had paused several times, and he and Herrick had needed to turn and 'reset'.

The enemy troops, faceless AI creatures based loosely on those found in the derelict starship, were terrifying. They moved onwards, testing their 'sensor' mapping. How it would help, where it would be limited and where they still needed to maintain old-school field-craft. Covering each other as they rounded corners, clearing rooms.

The spider-creatures. The race had a name, one that he thought had been found in the data-set. If he had ever heard it, he had forgotten. He resisted asking his bio-tech to find the answer for him.

Mission Date: Day 134.                Clear.

Using them in this way, portraying them as the villains. It was useful to have opponents other than the Progenitor foot-soldiers. Useful, not only because these were far smaller. He just hoped that the race did not turn out to be pacifists if they ever met them.

Grinning, he surged around the last corner, already firing. The simulated recoil, again not quite there, was convincing enough. Until such a time as he could fire the weapon for real. This was the best they could do.

After he finished the last virtual enemy, he reconsidered his last thought. Pacifists... it was an odd thing to wish them not to be.

"Clear," He called.

Which would have been excellent, had it been the last training run planned that day. It really wasn't. Doc Brown was showing them all how to make the perfect Pasta-Bolognese this evening. Flaherty was looking forward to that.

"One more time. This time, Impact, Crater, I want you both to come in through the second entrance and make your way to coordinate the final assault as a combined force. Herrick, watch how they move together. Work together. I am going to want your take on where we can improve. After that, Neil, Colm, TT, you're all getting involved, too. We are going to go through this one until we have everything down pat," Jason said. "Herrick, that night in Afghanistan, when we were attacked in the mountain camp. That was the first time I watched a coordinated team working together that seamlessly. With every member of your team equipped with rehearsed roles and responses to almost every scenario. We are getting there. We have technology which will make our responses fluid, and predictable only to ourselves, never to our enemies. We need to keep running scenarios until we are... We need to become a cohesive, responsive force. We need to become..."

"Marines?" Herrick asked. Raising an eyebrow.

"How did you possibly guess? Jason replied. Winking at the man. "If you want soldiering, done right..."

Mission Date: Day 134.    Clear.

"... and those two?" Herrick said. Interrupting Jason's favourite saying, as he nodded towards Kate and Daniel, who were sitting watching what was happening.

"We will always be the wildcards..." Kate said. Smiling innocently.

"What they are, actually, is difficult. A pain in my arse. But we will get them involved." Jason promised. His professed certainty fooling no-one.

\*    \*    \*

# Mission Date: Day 151.

## Sword.

A little over another fortnight later. Still in transition.

Kate held the weapon in perfect balance. The Katana resting upon her extended index finger, only about five inches from the guard. The blade pointing upward. Hacker watching both the weapon, and the woman holding it, with rapt attention.

"Carbyne is harder, and far stronger, than any other substance we know to exist. If built perfectly, if every single ordered atomic bond is formed to make a singular molecular structure... it is a simply incredible material." Kate said. Meeting his gaze. She flicked the weapon into the air. The movement seeming to come from her finger alone, and she caught it deftly, in a two-handed grip, as it came back down. Her economy of movement, the precision, all was spellbinding.

"We can make it perfectly here, with the benefactors' machines. But is has little weight... a sword, no matter how sharp, it needs weight to be... to be its most effective... To the core of this blade is a tungsten alloy... in its centre is a tungsten-rod. Carbyne becoming alloy, then alloy becoming tungsten. One, becoming the other through perfectly ordered atoms. For you, we would make a blade slightly lighter. For my father, a heavier one."

"So, you will make one for me?" Hacker asked.

"If you are sure, you are ready to learn first how to use one. We will make you a sword." Kate replied. Re-sheathing her own weapon into its scabbard, which she was wearing across her back.

She would not know this, but the way she could find the scabbard behind her, do so with such unerring accuracy, as if it were the easiest thing to do in the

Mission Date: Day 151.                Sword.

world... it was perhaps the most inhuman the immortal creature had ever looked to Hacker.

He watched her as she moved gracefully across the room to the rack on the far wall. Taking a training blade, throwing it across the hangar deck toward him.

It was a shame that he missed it.

\*     \*     \*

## Mission Date: Day 180.

### Survey.

Thirty days later. Emergence.

It was a long time in FTL. Months spent riding the rainbow, before the two combined starships slipped back into real-space. The crew, both old and new, finding their places in the new order of things. Getting used to each-other. The survivors from Hermentia, the human ones, getting used to the changes they were being put through.

Then finally, the ships re-entered the universe, proper. Their velocities dropping back under the speed of light, and then further, until they reached a point where matter would behave more, as matter should. Still tearing through space, but now space was again visible to them.

"Pull up a local map and start populating it. We should be alone out here. But let's find out..." Katherine ordered. Knowing that the team would know exactly what to do, that they would reach out passively first. The procedure was standard. It had been since the first flight.

They were safe, too. Or rather, they damned well should be. This was the first stop inside the Milky-Way for the mapping efforts. But they had not needed to aim for a star-system. Instead, they had pointed at an arbitrary point between the stars. General location was important. Specifics, exact position, had been less so.

Safe. Relatively safe. There were LIDAR, focussed lasers firing only directly ahead. Ensuring that it would be unlikely that they smash into anything unexpectedly. Not fully passive... but risks needed always to be measured against risks.

Mission Date: Day 180.                    Survey.

"Katherine, there are no errant signals that appear to be artificial. Not in any of the expected bands. We are expanding the filters to ensure we miss nothing." Jansen replied.

"Dani, bring us to as close to a stop as possible when Jansen clears it." Katherine ordered.

"Clear," Jansen replied. Only a couple of minutes later.

"Bringing us down to relativistic stationary." Dani responded. "We will be stationary, relative to local space, in twenty minutes."

"Thunder-Child?" Katherine grinned.

"Ready-to-go, and seeing nothing ourselves, either." Jason reported from the helm of the docked starship. "But we are ready to get stuck in, if we're needed."

"Okay, we sit like this for half-an-hour. Everyone stays at their station until then. Then we go active, carefully. Then we map this galaxy." Katherine ordered. "All we need is a little peace, to be left to do our thing... This should go without a hitch."

"Boss, you know about not tempting fate, don't you?" Dani queried from the helm.

"Sorry, what? I was already miles away," Katherine replied. Staring off into space.

\*      \*      \*

Mission Date: Day 180.                    Survey.

Jason closed the connection to the Pequod's bridge and reached behind him to grasp the bar there. Pulling himself through the short tunnel where he landed with a thud in the standard gravity of the control room behind the Thunder-Child's cockpit. Kate and Daniel were already waiting for him.

"The amulet?" he asked. "Is this where it wants us to be?"

"It is happy that we are here. Just as it was happy when we decided to come here, to travel to this very spot. I can sense that it wants us to wait," Kate said. Staring at the green-stone.

"For what?"

"It is not sharing. There are no words between us. There are still only feelings, and sometimes the chaotic dreams. But mostly just feelings. It is getting insistent, impatient. I can sense frustration from it. If I wasn't sure before, not completely, I am now. It has a purpose entirely beyond our own mission, and one which it does not want to share with us. I still trust it, instinctively, and I do not think that it is manipulating me to gain my trust. It is asking for help. It is prepared to insist. I worry that it seems to enjoy that our decisions are what it expects them to be," Kate added. "That they are what it wants them to be."

"What is your biggest concern?" Jason asked.

"What it wants us to do. It believes that it is very important... That does not mean it should be important to us," Kate replied. Shrugging.

"It speaks poorly of any considerations we might have about predetermination." Daniel said. His arms crossed over his chest. Concern written over his face. "It speaks poorly about who, or what, is actually controlling this mission now."

'We knew this already. Before we set off to come here. We agreed then." Kate said.

"Coming here, that met our requirements, too. Waiting indefinitely, it does not. We will need everyone's buy in if this goes on too long."

"Agreed." The other two said in unison

Mission Date: Day 180.  Survey.

\*       \*       \*

Mission Date: Day 212.                Alone.

# Mission Date: Day 212.

## Alone.

Thirty-two days later.

Katherine was satisfied that they were alone. They had been alone since they had arrived. Here, which was as close to nowhere as anywhere could be...

Every day since that first day, it had haunted her that this position meant something. That they were waiting now for something... because her work was done. They really should be going.

Magic bloody eight-balls. Herrick had finally explained the etymology of that phrase. Describing a child's toy which professed to speak psychically to the child playing with it. A larger copy of the eight-ball from a game called pool. Shake it, and a message would appear against a transparent section on its surface. Offering wisdom. Advice.

Smiling to herself, she wondered how that man was getting on recreating a pool table. Doing so from memory, and with the help of BOB and his magic machines... Apparently, the cushions were not yet right. A project which had grown around a throwaway phrase. As such things, might.

Weeks ago, and they had needed only two low-power pulses to confirm that there was nothing nearby which might be a threat to them. Signals which would have nothing even approaching the power to reach even the closest system. A system which was five light-years away, anyway. Immediately after that, and the Pequod's hugely powerful astro-navigational sensors had gone to work. Mapping every star, every stellar body visible within the Milky Way, from their new perspective. Watching the skies. None of the cartographical equipment needing to radiate any energy to do so.

Mission Date: Day 212.          Alone.

That alone had taken weeks. Even with the power of the Pequod's sensors, it was a task of biblical proportions. But that was done now, and she was eager to move on.

They really should be going.

They still needed to build on their charts, to compare positioning data separated by thousands of light-years in the constantly changing galaxy. Data collected from wildly differing points in space, and with the distances in question being so colossal, therefor also being points in time separated by millennia.

This they could do as easily in transit. Whilst riding the rainbow.

But they were waiting.

During that time, most of the ship had fallen into its now familiar rhythm. Training of the military assets, scientific study, and the ongoing treatment for the Hermentia survivors. Most of which was practically completed by now. But there were also lectures on fields of interest for the crew, offered by specialists in those areas. Jason's fascination with music, and his offering tuition to the team was a wonderful distraction for many. But there was also far too much hard-drinking for her like.

There was little for the crew to do on either vessel, for maintenance or upkeep. Little service-bots, tiny, wheeled devices, would scoot past the bemused crew. Moving on to take on some task or other. Larger machines, those capable of construction, of structural remodelling or repair, were needed less often. The most significant challenge had been the changing out of the antimatter weapons from the Thunder-Child's internal bays.

Those weapons were now limited only to the external missile pods of either starship. The precautions, the checks and balances to respond to any issue, with any of the weapons, they had been refined, further.

But it was still a long-damned time to spend out here on their own. For all of them. In the older universe, the isolation had still been difficult for some to process. But back then, there had been two planets populated by humanity,

Mission Date: Day 212.          Alone.

with either capable of providing them somewhere. Here, so far back in history, and neither could offer the same. Nothing known back here could.

They were truly orphaned here. Cut off, with only the two starships offering them a home. Sitting still like this. It wasn't good for anyone.

She knew she was more fortunate than most. She had her labs, the star maps. Complicated work. This took most of her focus. Enough of her focus. These distracted her. Capability Brown, his project. The ancient texts from Hermentia. The preserved library. What limited free time she had, she spent with him.

Healthy distractions.

But everyone was distracted by the other thing. Because the amulet wanted them to stay exactly where they were, right now. That was unsettling everyone.

\*     \*     \*

Mission Date: Day 212. Perhaps there is proof in the pudding.

## Perhaps there is proof in the pudding.

Natalie watched with interest as Impact strode into the club. The powerful wolf moving lithely across the floor. Deliberately peacocking. His hair, the tight afro, and thick black beard framing a rather wonderful bone structure. She thought the wolf to be somewhere in his fifties, but the energy, the vibrancy, which radiated away from him was...

Hypnotic.

But not ageless. Not this one.

He was stocky, heavily muscled. But not so much that his grace and agility would be compromised. His thick arms hanging from broad shoulders. Wearing only a singlet over light trousers, he was the epitome of power.

Flaherty, the royal marine, was sitting with her. Younger, taller and with the modifications he had been through, now fully part of him, he had always been an impressive figure. Now, and he was even more so. But the wolves, they had an aura.

Today, this was going to be interesting. The club was crowded. Looking around, she wondered who was even on duty on either ship.

Kate walked in. Wearing pretty much the same thing as Impact. To be fair, she was wearing the same as everyone. Moving to stand beside Jason.

Within their crew, Jason was practically a giant. Broader, stronger in appearance to everyone else, and beside him Kate looked... Dainty?

Impact received a round of applause as he strode into the middle of the dance-floor. Crater, ever loyal, leading the celebration. Whooping for his colleague. His oldest and dearest friend. Impact took a bow. Then addressed the room.

"Today, and we are here to answer the speculation that has become a distraction amongst the crew here. Who is stronger?" Impact bellowed.

Mission Date: Day 212.   Perhaps there is proof in the pudding.

Flexing his enormous arms for show. The clapping intensified. "This will also help you all understand the differences between wolf and the purestrain."

Natalie watched the small woman moving to stand beside him. Graceful, also with an elegance that betrayed a strength which was immediately obvious to those watching. Built like an Olympic sprinter, an explosive athlete, but far smaller in stature than Impact. She bowed before those gathered. Her hair falling around her face, and when she rose again, a wide smile was painted across her face.

Her father, Daniel, he led the round of applause and Flaherty joined in. Jason stepped back, proud, and joined in himself. Hacker was out there, standing with Julien, and both men had unhealthily large glassed of whisky. Both men used their free-hands to clap against their chests'.

Natalie still remembered seeing the woman for the first time. Onboard the shuttle as it had pulled desperately away from Hermentia. Moving from the cockpit to help the injured Cleo as she had lain, dying. With her head resting in Natalie's lap. Her red hair, her green eyes, and freckles. Just as beautiful today as she had been then. The Royal Navy Apache gunner had been saved. But that was not what Natalie thought of when she remembered that moment.

Natalie only then realised then that she was clapping for her, too.

The two opponents moved to the booth. The one which had been deliberately kept free for the match. Sitting opposite from each-other, and grasped each other's right hand's. Preparing for an arm-wrestle. Kate's hand looking miniscule in the much larger hand.

Impacts smile threatened to split his face in two, right up to the point where his enormous shoulder bunched, and he tried to push Kate's hands toward the table.

It didn't move. Perhaps it did, just a little, but it did not seem to do so by very much.

Natalie smiled to herself when she saw Kate wink at Impact, and then poke her tongue out at him.

Mission Date: Day 212.     Perhaps there is proof in the pudding.

This was absolutely going to be very interesting.

    *       *       *

## Mission Date: Day 231.

### Rudely interrupted.

After 19 more days of peace, things suddenly became far more exciting.

"Is it still tempting fate, if we waited weeks for this to happen?" Dani shouted from the Pequod's helm.

"Separation in ten. All teams tell me now if you are not ready. Hold on fighters. We are seeing only capital ships out there," Katherine repeated.

"... and in four, and two, one... release!" Jason said over the comms. Feeling the Thunder-Child's controls weighting up as his starship prepared for battle. "Tanks. All teams remain ready in case boarding actions are needed."

Jason was pleased to see the confirmations coming back through. This would be, could be, a baptism of fire for the new team. Herrick, Flaherty, Crater... Fighting with Neil. The four Tanks in the drop-room of the Thunder-Child.

Colm and Cleo were waiting onboard the fighters... both buttoned up in the Pequod's hangars.

As bad as it felt, powering hard into combat this unprepared, with this little knowledge about what they were about to face, it felt good to have a starship almost fully crewed. Fully able to respond with its full capabilities.

"Kate, can you confirm one more time? We are to help the ship that is being attacked?"

"Confirm, as far as I can interpret what is little more than a feeling... I am sure." Kate came back from one of the Thunder-Child's turrets. He saw that it was the starboard module. Impact was in the other. "I will let you know if the nightmares come back tonight. But apparently, the crew, the captain, they can help us find the beings we must speak to."

Mission Date: Day 231.          Rudely interrupted.

"What are we seeing out there by way of detection technology?" Jason stumbled through the sentence. Hoping that there would even be a tonight.

"We are seeing crude radar only, although we cannot understand the capabilities of their passive detection."

"Crude radar? What do we have?" Came Hacker's voice. The man was apparently on the bridge of the Pequod. ", sorry... please don't answer. I know you're all busy."

Jason could practically feel the man wincing across the radio.

"Better radar. For active detection, all we can really do is send out energy, electromagnetic, and wait for something to bounce back... interestingly, passive detection can often see more... quicker, too. When objects in combat can be light-minutes out, not needing to take the round trip can be a significant advantage. The last to know, they are the first to die. We can detect gravimetric mass, its effect on spacetime. We can detect anything they accidentally push out there. These are all part of our passive suite."

Jason tuned out Dani's technical response to the man, although he did smile when he heard Marine at the Pequod's helm mention "... and now, we also have Kate's magic eight-ball."

"Pequod, hold back. Remain cloaked. I want to move in front of the attacking ships and see if we can't disable their offensive weaponry without destroying either of them. I want to do so without looking horribly more advanced than any of the ships we're seeing there." Jason called.

"Agreed, godspeed." Katherine replied.

"BOB, can you quickly confirm we can outmatch these ships, ideally horribly so?"

"Jason, we are. Probably."

Jason throttled up. Feeding on the power further and moving away from the Pequod. Dropping his own cloak, only when he was sure he was far enough away from Katherine's ship to not give away her position. Leveraging the thrust-engines to complement the acceleration of the Chasers. The solid-fuel

Mission Date: Day 231.          Rudely interrupted.

engines burning bright through the sky. Looking a little more correct to inquisitive eyes. Drawing the attention of those out there.

The battle had emerged into real-space only a few thousand miles from where they had been hanging in space, themselves. Carrying huge velocities as the corrupted space-time collapsed behind them. Jason hadn't thought it possible for ships to track each other through FTL, and certainly not to emerge so close to each other. He told himself to remember bringing this up with BOB later... Also, their FTL tech looked unusually familiar...

"BOB, that looks like they're using technology more similar to ours, rather than WHITs drives?" Jason queried. "Natalie, can you attempt to communicate with the lead-ship? And then share our protocol with the attackers, but don't establish communication, not yet."

"Sending our own Sendler handshakes now, captain." Natalie replied.

"You are correct. It looks like all the ships leverage a rudimentary version of our own Chasers. But only to fracture space-time and create a warp-bubble. They are using Ion-Drives to push themselves through space. Although, I have no idea how they are dealing with the power-requirements."

Jason was drawing closer. The lead ship had attempted to accelerate away from those pursuing it. Failing to gain any ground at all. If it was because of the damage it had already taken, or its comparably laughable engines, Jason did not know.

"Jason, we have the captain of the damaged ship online. Be careful, the translation matrix is warning of high probability of error." Natalie said. Jason processed this. Realised the magnitude of what he was about to do, and reached out to the first biological sentient life form with which humanity had ever attempted to communicate.

"Captain, I am in command of the fast-moving warship just off your starboard quarter. Are you in need of help?"

"Captain, I am Redroot-Tessera'd of the Boylston Armada. We are a civilian ship carrying only farmers and food-stock. We have done nothing to warrant this attack. Please help us." Came the electronic reply. The level of such

Mission Date: Day 231.  Rudely interrupted.

obviously synthetic noise indicated that the translation had been quite punchy."

[Jason, I am sure that 'Boylston' is a street in Boston.] Alistair interjected.

[Old friend, it is all we have for us to work with.] Jason replied. Grinning inwardly.

"Captain, I will see what I can do. Keep flying. We will work the problem." Jason said, closing the call and routing all comms back to just the two human starships. "Okay, Natalie, force communication with the attackers and let me know when they're listening." Jason ordered. Swinging the Thunder-Child ahead of the two attacking warships, positioning himself between them and their prey, deliberately spinning his ship to face them both.

"Now, Jason." Natalie confirmed.

"This is Captain Jason Young of the warbird Thunder-Child. We are ordering you to cease hostilities against this ship and to stand down."

[Warbird?] Alistair asked.

[I like it... we never defined a class.] Jason replied.

"Die and burn alien...." The rest was garbage, unable to be translated into anything of use. Jason assumed he was being sworn at. Possibly imaginatively. Certainly, damned enthusiastically.

Immediately, he felt the ship buffeting as huge amounts of chaotic energies were pumped into her shields. Jason returned the favour. Opening up with his forward weapons on the closest of the distant ships' hull. A combination of his preternatural eyes, and the Thunder-Child's forward cameras, and he could see the massively accelerated steel-tungsten rounds smashing into the hull, accompanied by the chaotic energies from his particle accelerators. The hull tore, tremendous damage smashed into the material, which seemed metres thick. He knew immediately that it would take too long to chew through. The railguns and particle accelerators only pitting the ferociously strong material. The weapons, their emplacements, they were an entirely different matter.

Mission Date: Day 231.  Rudely interrupted.

"Impact, Kate. Target only their weapons, but keep firing until they can no longer return fire. BOB?"

"Copy, we are on it, Jason." Kate replied. All he got from Impact was a grunt.

"They are firing projected energy weapons only, Captain. At least so far. Our shields can take it, but not indefinitely. Without ramping up the transfer buffers to close to maximum, and risk damaging those, we are going to see shields failing in less than five minutes." BOB replied.

From the corner of his eye, he saw the two turrets flowing around the halo on the Thunder-Child, which now ran for the full circumference of the ship, and meeting only yards apart from each other on the ship's dorsal surface. Fire erupting from both, even before they even came to a rest. Jason targeted the weapons on the closest ship with his own cannon, orientating the Thunder-Child to do so.

As he fired, he took in the attacking ships properly for perhaps the first time.

Both were significantly larger than their prey. The closest one was over a kilometre long, perhaps a tenth of that wide, and a sharp wedge shape. The shape making sense, as the vessel appeared to have no energy shielding. The angle of the hull, and the clearly thick armour of its nose section, would deflect objects it ran into at speed. Deep scarring across its surface making that assumption even more likely. As he had already guessed, their armour seemed to be simply no more advanced than ludicrously thick hulls. Dumb, but effective.

However, the weapon systems on each ship had extended out from behind armour plates which had folded clear. With many standing proud of the hull itself. Some were projector style, EM based weapons. Others looked like missile ports. Possibly. Although, those had not fired yet. None withstood the withering fire from the Thunder-Child's far more advanced weaponry for long.

It was only a few brief minutes before they had crippled much of the offensive weaponry of both ships. Both ships continued to avoid any attempt to communicate further and, instead, accelerated away on an obtuse vector. Burning hard. Not only ion engines. But solid-fuel boosters, too. Lighting up

Mission Date: Day 231.     Rudely interrupted.

the sky behind each like a candle. Jason assumed they would jump to FTL once they had built enough velocity.

"BOB, what is your take?" Jason asked. Watching the starships powering away.

"They were ludicrously outmatched. However, had it not been for our shielding, we would have potentially been destroyed first."

"To be fair, had that been the case, I would have been flying around, dodging it all with quite a lot of enthusiasm." Jason replied. "Also, there are the MOAMs. Now, we also have the TOAM weapons in the inboard weapon bays. We would simply have remained cloaked and turned them into a rapidly expanding dust cloud..." Jason trailed off.

"It is nice to have an intermediate step. Something between the small missiles, and our cannons, and the anti-matter warheads. We needed something which is not such massive overkill." Kate said.

"It is also quite nice to not have anything locked tightly inside the Thunder-Child's hull which wants to kill us so enthusiastically." Impact added.

"Also true... Now, let's see if that ship needs an assist." Jason replied. "Let's see what we can learn from Captain Redroot-Tessera'd..." He was proud not to butcher the name too badly.

*   *   *

Mission Date: Day 297. Frontier planet: Corkier-Shay.

## Mission Date: Day 297.

### Frontier planet: Corkier-Shay.

Months later. An even more cohesive team found themselves somewhere very new. Months of travel. Months of pushing the starships faster than ever before. Months of work to finally meet with...

Hopefully, someone with answers.

His armour was sealed. Fully closed-up, and working with only its internalised air-supply. A hugely efficient system, one leveraging multiple reservoirs of oxygen, which were compressed into liquid. This alone provided enough air for perhaps three-hours. It could also reprocess the exhaled $CO_2$ in his breath, splitting the oxygen away from the carbon once again, and feeding that back to him. The functions expanding further into the sleek backpack, which was attached to the rear of his suit. Extending significantly, although not indefinitely, the time the wearer could spend in inhospitable environments.

It was currently promising Jason that it could also take oxygen from the surrounding atmosphere and ensure that any pathogens or poisons were cleaned long before they reached him. This, currently, it was still a step a little too far. He trusted BOB, but he was loath to take the step where he risked such things. It would have to be a last-ditch option.

He was walking on an alien planet...He was surrounded by aliens from many planets. That was already a lot. So, perhaps another time.

Corkier-Shay, a brutal place, and a world so close to the edge of the galaxy that half the night's sky was almost empty. Seen from orbit, and it was painted only by the light from distant galaxies, and the few errant stars closer to the edge of the Milky Way than it. The Andromeda galaxy, for they knew now it was that, displayed so wonderfully in the darkness. The planet itself, its own star, was pretty standard. The handful of small moons which orbited around the planet disturbingly quickly, were less so. Certainly to human eyes.

Mission Date: Day 297.　　　　　　Frontier planet: Corkier-Shay.

Smaller, and far closer in than Earth's own, they were also not uniformly round. Little more than lost asteroids, captured by the planet's gravity. Passing him, easily visible even against the cloudless morning sky. Flicking overhead in their startingly quick orbits. An unfamiliar sky. An alien sky.

They had backtracked again. Travelling thousands of light-years away from where they had last appeared from FTL. From where they had met a ship's captain whose gratitude had led them here. Heading back towards the galaxy's edge.

Heading back closer to such unimaginable... disaster.

It was eerie. Knowing what lay in store for this planet, for this region of space... Rationalising that something that was already inevitable, was only a few years away from reaching here. Unstoppable, and beyond devastating. Difficult to process. Not relevant, not to the mission, not to this mission, today... Hard to ignore, so hard to... They were here to destroy a world to do that awful, unpalatable thing. Sidetracked, and now walking upon another world whose fate was also sealed. A Marine once again, and no longer wanting to think about being a scientist, or of pictures so large, he often awoke drenched in sweat from some barely remembered nightmare. So, right now, he was focussing on his three-foot world.

They were here to meet with their contact. A mercenary, a smuggler who existed in the grey. But a being who could introduce them to the higher echelons from the resistance.

Because that was apparently also a thing, too.

Because the amulet had focussed on the wedge ships, the aggressors who had pursued Captain Redroot-Tessera'd and his single remaining ship from the Boylston Armada, and had told Kate that it was not them... Nor was it even the Boylston Armada... But that they must seek those who fought against the aggressors.

The resistance.

Mission Date: Day 297.					Frontier planet: Corkier-Shay.

Captain Redroot-Tessera'd had pointed them here. He had supplied a signed message for those they had come here to find. The captain, he could not introduce them to the rebels. Today, they should meet someone who could.

For a price.

So, they had come here. To a planet which was bereft of much in the way of life. Little more than sand and rock. Unforgiving, and almost unrelentingly harsh. Only the hardy could come here and prosper. The dangerous, too. He should not forget that.

He was, at least, somewhat able to enjoy the gravity, which was only five-eighths of Earth-Standard. Even though his armour was powered anyway, he still felt he had an extra spring in his step.

Daniel was with him. By his side, the terrifying bastard wearing armour in the same blood-red as his daughter's. Not a Marine, not a part of Elite-Recon from the colonial Marine force. He had rejected any suggestion of wearing their colours. Out of respect. But it was a wolf's armour. Within its shell, above the heart of the wearer, there was the additional pocket. Gold, not carbyne, which would open at just a word... against his chest, exposing the moon-rock held there. Releasing its power, its glory, and its song.

The man was also wearing his new pistol in a low-slung holster on his right hip. The charged-plasma weapon built for him by BOB. Jason smiled to himself. His friend had always wanted to be a cowboy.

This was the first time Daniel had stepped into an alien world. Only the second time Jason had. The first having been Epsilon, and that had been considerably over a century earlier. His old friend seemed to be taking it in his stride. Or hiding his distress, well. Jason kept a wary eye on the man.

His own. His first time. He had arrived in a burning spacecraft, plummeting into a swamp and upsetting a family of... well, there had been dragons. There, back then, and everything had been a frantic reaction to a rapidly devolving string of chaotic events. He had also been on fire for a disturbingly sizeable chunk of it. This, today, it had to be different. It had to be a measured, considered action. Control, both of themselves, of the situation. Chaos, it would not be their friend here.

Mission Date: Day 297.    Frontier planet: Corkier-Shay.

Neil was following them both. The Tank's footsteps thudding as each foot moved the gigantic machine forward. The heavily armed, and armoured, war machine. Jason felt a measure of confidence that he was also armed, himself. Confidence that took a significant knock when he remembered that so was almost everyone else.

Everyone? Was that even the right word? Perhaps 'everything' was better? Were the aliens things? The grammatical evolution of the English language, of any language born from humanity, none had prepared him for this.

His brain had threatened to crash into a tattered ruin as they first made their way from the dirt landing-strip that the authorities had called a 'spaceport', and found the road into town. It was alien, so utterly alien. Feeling far more so than the Progenitor mothership had felt. Or even Epsilon. He glanced quickly back towards the shuttle. Unthreatening, just a tube on four landing struts which resembled the legs of a mechanical insect. The load-out was light, with just the two harnesses at the back, behind the truncated fuselage. Those to carry the Tanks. Herrick was there, waiting in the second Tank. He was a little threatening. Cleo, she had flown it in. This, the shuttle, it was his lifeline to a world he better understood.

But one that might have drawn a little too much attention. Her unusual reaction-less drives raising the equivalent of an eyebrow amongst the small crowd that had gathered around her after she had landed. A crowd which had slowly dispersed when the two Tanks had detached themselves and made themselves known.

He reflected quickly on Hacker's warning. Weeks ago, now. About standing out with technology which might prove enticing to the wrong eyes. Promising himself that he would revisit it.

The planet was a dust-bowl. One which was apparently filled with the waifs and strays of a cruel galaxy. But it was habitable, and maintained a stable orbit of the yellow-dwarf star, which had only just risen above the distant horizon. The atmosphere was not a hell of a long way from Earth's, or Epsilon's. But there were trace inert gasses which would render the human team unwell in only a few hours. Which would kill them in days.

Mission Date: Day 297.　　　　　　Frontier planet: Corkier-Shay.

Which was why they were all buttoned up tight.

That and the terrifying thought of funky alien pathogens.

Daniel had pulled slightly ahead now. He had scarcely noticed his friend doing so, so preoccupied he had been. The road was little more than a wide flat surface carved into the dust and the rock. They were making their way towards the small town about two kilometres away. Little more than a trading hub, it rose through the dust and heat distortion, barely. Still over two miles away, and made from the same rock and dirt that surrounded it, it was hard to see. Indistinct, even to him. Wheeled vehicles trundled past them. None were moving quickly. Most were rustic, as if life here had once prospered, but had run into significant decline, and now continued to survive as they eked the last tough years out of ancient technology. Machines, which were close to their useful end. A failing civilisation, a planet scratching its last before its own now inevitable loss.

Once, they would have had scientists. They must have had, for them, to be able to create ships capable of interstellar travel. But did they lack the inquisitive nature of humanity? Had they pushed into the stars for other reasons beyond simply wanting to know what was out there?

Was that why no-one was aware of what was coming?

Captain Redroot-Tessera'd had told them only a little of the planet's history. Whatever the town had been, or even the planet, it was little more than a trading post now. With the scourge of the local systems, meeting here to exchange goods and services on neutral ground. Jason had been a little unsettled that the translation had been so very precise.

Waifs and strays. Once only meaning abandoned or neglected children. Broken in English, centuries earlier, to cast a far wider net than its original intent. But what did the translation actually mean?

The captain had also told them to be careful. Because it was not safe.

It was not safe, but there was a general understanding that no one should start trouble. But that anyone was fair game to everyone else if they did. A

Mission Date: Day 297.        Frontier planet: Corkier-Shay.

broken, tenuous way to provide a level of peace in a very hostile corner of the galaxy.

The Aliens that they passed, all bar the natives were wearing some level of environmental protection. Some wore only masks, covering whatever part of their anatomy that Jason assumed, were where they breathed through. Most, they wore far more complete protection. Like Jason and Daniel.

Some were bipedal, a group of four looked startingly almost human. Even if they only did so for a moment. Wearing red-robes, sweeping as far as the floor, and with silver spheres over their heads. The spheres were opaque, so Jason assumed that below that...

They would probably be just as alien as everything else.

The locals, though...

He knew it was coming, but he was forced to stand aside as a four-legged creature, one with a head mounted at the rear of its long torso, surged past him close enough to have hit him had he not moved out of its way. The creature had two clawed arms protruding from the other end from its head. Like a backward horse. Only one with arms, and one with the head of a fly.

It looked back at him and hissed in fury. Moments later, seven more surged past.

It was not even the freakiest thing he had seen, although he thought it might be the most outwardly unfriendly. The Sendler protocol package for the planet had explained how to act, how to react and not cause offence to the local species. Whilst it had not strictly said that he shouldn't knock the aggressive prick the fuck out, he assumed that would be taken as rude.

Other aliens move around him. Scuttling creatures, half the size of a man. Insects with over a dozen legs and with almost as many arms. Bird-like creatures the size of Emu, but with articulated arms, and not vestigial wings.

Many others were bipedal, and after the shock of everything that was so very different wore off, he processed that many, perhaps most, seemed to follow a similar design. Symmetrical, to a level. Two arms, two legs. Few faces were visible, not beneath their environmental protections. Those that were, they

Mission Date: Day 297.   Frontier planet: Corkier-Shay.

seldom followed anything approaching a consistent design. Eyes though, and only after a little while, Jason noticed that evolution seemed to either dictate two, or many. Insectoid eyes, or simply stereo, which would offer depth-perception. Mouths, these seemed to be commonly built into faces. But he had no idea if the creatures he saw would eat through the same hole they breathed through.

Similar problems, similar drivers. Evolution seemed often to march a path toward similar solutions.

So, whist it might prove true that many of the aliens were humanoid in their general structure, they were not the ones towards which his attention was drawn. This was not what his highly stressed brain was trying to tell him.

"So, life requires the opposing thumb." Daniel grunted. "Certainly, for life to become dominant and to build... tools. It is an odd reality to consider that we are the aliens here. It would be less alien if they looked a little less..."

"Agreed." Neil replied. "We should also be happy that no-one has tried to kill us yet."

"We should..." Jason responded. "Kate, do we have any sign of the contact yet?"

"We have just heard from them. They are flying in now. I suggest you make it to the town square quickly if you plan to get there first." Kate replied over the comms.

"Okay, keep your head on a swivel, everyone. Hope for the best, and prepare for the worst." Jason ordered.

[We find something today, or we abandon this side-quest.] Alistair added.

[I understand your reluctance, my friend. But if it is important to Kate, it is important to me,] Jason replied.

[You would follow that woman into hell.]

[I would. I have,] Jason answered.

Mission Date: Day 297.          Frontier planet: Corkier-Shay.

[Be careful who you drag along for the ride, Jason.] Alistair finished.

Jason didn't reply. He grunted and kept moving.

    \*       \*       \*

Mission Date: Day 297.     Frontier planet: Corkier-Shay.

They were meeting in the town's square. A prearranged spot suggested by their intermediary. Traders lined the square's edge, selling their wares. All three men bided their time, watching the melting pot of potentially dozens of different civilisations interacting with each other. Each was fascinated by the fabulous diversity of alien artefacts on sale. Some were unrecognisable to the human team, but many were instantly recognisable. The juxtaposition of both realities, hammering their current situation home to each of them.

They were very far from home.

Daniel was scanning the distant wall. Turning his body deliberately to do so. Telegraphing his intent. Doing so deliberately.

"You happy with this arrangement?" He asked.

"No, not at all." Jason replied.

"This armour, with the shields, we can take a few hits?"

"Probably. But these things very much depend on what they use to shoot you with," Jason replied. Holding his armoured right hand up to the sun. Spreading his fingers and turning it to see his palm, then the back. Making a fist, before stretching the hand to its maximum span, again. For a moment, he was quiet. Lost in some internal dialogue. "Be wary of your hands, though. The fingers, the armour, it is thinner there. It needs to be, if you want any useful dexterity."

"Cool, thanks." Daniel drawled. Continuing to scan his surroundings. It took Jason longer than he might have expected to realise that had been the extent of the conversation he was going to get today.

They waited for over an hour for their contact to arrive. When it finally did so, the creature entered the square and deliberately strode toward them with an escort. Doing so whilst five more aliens, who looked a hell of a lot like it, had surreptitiously positioned themselves near the exits.

His deployed micro-drones were scanning, finding more from the same species and highlighting those as potential danger. Internally, he blanched a little at the level of racial profiling he was now relying on. Blanching further, as his technology linked the species, and also now their technology/clothing.

Mission Date: Day 297.		Frontier planet: Corkier-Shay.

Twenty-three were in the surrounding area, which seemed to be part of the same group.

It was not impossible that this precaution was designed to enable for their contact to flee via any exit, and to receive help from members of his team as he did so. However, it did also look a little too much like they were preparing to seal the place off.

The Sendler Protocol request came across as the large, three-legged, four-armed creature drew closer. It had an elongated face, not too dissimilar to a kangaroo. One which was visible through the clear shell which covered it. Three eyes, a first for Jason today. The middle one was hidden behind a block of some sort of tech.

The first pair of arms were thick and powerful, hanging from broad shoulders beneath the creature's head. The other set was positioned below those, slender by comparison, and with claws that looked far more dextrous, useful than those on the larger limbs. These were clasped over its... Jason allowed himself to consider that part, the creature's belly. It was wearing armour. Heavy plates of something or other. Not great coverage, but not entirely horrible either. Beneath the armour was a shapeless tunic of what could easily have been sack-cloth. Coarse, simple, and a light blue.

"Jason, thank you for meeting me here." The translation came through clearly.

"Cordax, I am pleased that we can finally meet in person." Jason replied. Still stunned that his own reply was translated in real-time. That he was speaking with an alien, on an alien world. Hopeful that alien could not tell that he was terrified.

"You promised us technology. The potential for trading technology for information. Information I have and that you need. Our scans are showing unique attributes in your protective clothing... this might be something we will insist you share with us," Cordax replied.

Jason forced himself to not react to a perceived threat. Reminding himself that they were conversing as two separate beings, from entirely disparate

Mission Date: Day 297.　　　　　Frontier planet: Corkier-Shay.

races. That the translation alone might bring inflections and insult, where none were intended.

He noticed that Daniel had tensed at what had been said. The man's right hand moving imperceptibly closer to his side-arm.

[Trust the man. He will not make a move, not unless you take the lead. But trust yourself. That sounded a little funky to me, too.] Alistair advised.

Cordax moved closer to him, one clawed hand reaching out to touch the chest of his armour. Careful to keep far enough away from the weapon he wore there. This Jason appreciated.

The casual way by which the alien was prepared to invade his personal space, less so.

"This is the strongest thing. But it is impossible to make this much, and this well. Its value should not be underestimated. You should be careful... I am tempted to take it from you myself." Cordax replied. Before leaning back, and screaming...

It took a beat for Jason to realise the creature was laughing. For the Sendler translation to confirm that. A beat which nearly cost the alien its life.

"Team, I am not sure we were ready for this." Jason sent the comms to the local team. Copying in Herrick and Cleo at the shuttle, and Kate in the Thunder-Child. Careful not to let the sentiment be spoken out loud by his armour. "Shields up. Be ready for anything."

"Let me test it..." came the sinister threat. The unexpectedly rapid escalation, catching him completely off-guard.

Jason felt the impact striking the back of his helmet. A terrific blow, which sent him staggering forwards two full steps. Processing that Daniel had immediately drawn his own weapon and was firing it across the square. He barely processed that Neil had immediately moved to put his Tank between him, and whatever had taken the shot. The shoulder-mounted railgun firing a quick burst.

Mission Date: Day 297.                    Frontier planet: Corkier-Shay.

Jason was struggling to process the reports from his armour. That the shield had stopped the projectile, even before it had reached the carbyne shell. His decision to raise shields, just moments earlier, had possibly saved his life. But he had kept moving, too. His staggering steps forwards, caused by the shot... he kept going to reach a backpedalling Cordax. Drawing his sword as he did so.

The carbyne was light, but the blade was horrifyingly sharp and at its core was a tungsten rod. That gave the weapon enough weight... Jason had smashed it into Cordax's middle leg, almost before he realised he meant to. The blade crushing into armour which was proven wholly unable to do much more than slow it, not with Jason's strength behind the blow. He had swung the weapon from high-right, continuing with its natural arc as it left the sheath on his back, finishing to his low-left. The armour, Cordax's armour, it had resisted, but barely. Cracking in such a way that reminded Jason of ceramic plates. Better at dissipating heat, better at energy weapons.

Horrible against his blade.

His head was still muddy. The blade was stuck fast against something. Perhaps whatever passed for the aliens skeleton, or the armour. Rearing back, he Spartan-kicked Cordax in his treacherous chest, and he watched as the mewling creature fell to the floor. Noticing blood, which seemed a greenish-yellow coating his now-free blade. Stickier... was it even blood?

His sword, though... at least that was free.

"What did you do???" Cordax screamed.

It was the other screaming that jolted Jason from his almost daze. The panicking crowd, which was fleeing the town square, finally bringing his concussed brain back into gear. Sheathing the sword again, Jason released his railgun from his chest mount, and sighted towards what remained of Cordax's team. Dialling up the weapons power, and firing the tiny projectiles at the downed alien's escorts as they struggled to ready their own weapons. Flakes of shattered ceramic flying into the air as the railgun chewed through. The blood, the viscous green-yellow substance, erupted from the wounds in the armour as if it were under horrendous pressure. The aliens staggered backwards. One lay still. But the others twitched upon the floor, wailing.

Mission Date: Day 297.          Frontier planet: Corkier-Shay.

Shrieking. The sounds, the sights, all completely... He was not in Kansas, he hadn't been for centuries, and everything was so damned alien.

Everything had also escalated damned quickly.

He was fast, though. Blazingly fast. With the wolf, with everything that made him the creature from myth, from a planet hundreds of millions of years away from even considering that myth, he was faster, stronger.

Today.

"Cleo, we need a pickup. Kate, air-support we are seeing fast moving craft coming our way." Jason was studying the reports from the circling drones he had deployed when he had first got there.

"We see them, too. Already on our way," Cleo shouted. "Scrambling, two minutes out."

"Jason, I am pushing through orbital insertion. We are ten-minutes out. Wait for me, don't die."

"Wilko," Jason replied. "Neil, Daniel, on me." He started sprinting towards the edge of the open space, towards the wall. Some level of concealment. Perhaps even marginal cover.

The Thunder-Child had been mimicking the need to maintain orbital speed. Hammering around the planet. She had been out of position, but not horribly so.

Jason sprinted past the bodies of two fallen attackers. Both of whom had been killed by Kate's father. Daniel's handgun, it was beyond devastating. Where his own railgun could punch holes through the enemy. The plasma weapon was blowing larger, molten holes through the same targets... The nature of their armour had not made this success immediately certain. Jason was relieved that Daniel was not hobbled by carrying the wrong weapon.

"Aircraft, here in thirty seconds. I am tracking, I am ready to respond... Jesus Christ." Neil shouted, as the first rockets tore into the space. Missing the three of them, but wiping out an entire structure where dozens of beings had sheltered themselves. Killing many. Wounding many more. Further weapon

Mission Date: Day 297.    Frontier planet: Corkier-Shay.

strikes, some sort of energy-based thing, Jason had no idea what, tore into the surrounding area.

Carnage.

"Just kill those things." Jason ordered.

"Enabling brutal murder-mode, right now, boss." Neil responded.

The Tank could not fly for long, or with much in the way of grace. Designed more to allow for it to be dropped from orbit into battle. But it could manage flight well enough for what it needed here. Jason assumed that Neil required the additional height to get a line on the attacking aircraft. Four of the missiles on the left shoulder mount fired immediately. Jason tracked them for as long as he could until his attention was needed elsewhere.

Cordax's people carried unusual weapons. Mounted on their torso and apparently guided by their gaze. Two were skittering towards him across the square. Daniel's attention was on another group and Jason took these two. Weapon fire still splashing off his depleting shield, he took a bead on both and put three shots through the helmets of each.

"Jason, this is Kate. We have two capital warships entering lower orbit. The Pequod is remaining cloaked and moving clear. We are coming for you. But things might need to happen quickly." Came the familiar voice over the comms.

"Regulators, mount up!" came the other voice as the shuttle hove into view. Herrick dangling from the rear cradle. It swung through a tight arc, and came to land immediately beside Jason, Daniel, and Neil.

They didn't need to be told twice.

Moments later, with its own shields now peppered by weapon fire, the shuttle craft erupted back into the sky and accelerated hard. Fleeing the scene.

Jason fought his way towards the cockpit, moving to sit beside Cleo on the cradle which extended from the rear-bulkhead to receive him. The controls coming immediately to hand.

Mission Date: Day 297.  Frontier planet: Corkier-Shay.

"You want control?" Cleo offered, giving him a quick sideways glance. Her face was invisible beneath her armour.

"No, you are better with these things than I. Tell me what you need from me," Jason replied.

"Thank you. We have fast-movers coming from behind. Faster than us, and I cannot stay ahead of them for long. I believe that we are on the best course to meet the Thunder-Child's approach. Confirm that, then watch our six." The young Royal Navy Lance Corporal ordered. Fully focused on piloting the shuttlecraft as fighter-craft attempted to kill them all.

The shuttle rocked violently. He heard Daniel swearing enthusiastically from behind as he watched the shields falling significantly. He could see the aircraft, almost ten clicks behind them. But he could not see enough to tell if they were space-worthy. He had to assume they were. Two more strikes. Then he watched as fast-missiles were fired against them. Gaining quickly. Frantically, he worked through the defence protocols, attempting to confuse the weapons from the unarmed shuttle. Then, with relief, he watched as first one, then the other, were destroyed. Momentarily confused how.

"Jason, we can turn and face behind us in our cradles. Although, not easily. We have decent coverage for our railguns but cannot use the missiles this close to the shuttle." Herrick called over the comms from his Tank.

"Nice work." Jason replied. "Kate, how far out?"

"Here," Then the sky above them darkened briefly, as the Thunder-Child flashed past.

"Kate, thank god." Jason breathed.

\*  \*  \*

Mission Date: Day 297.   Frontier planet: Corkier-Shay.

The shuttle was going to be a problem later. The Thunder-Child could not carry it. Kate pushed that thought from her mind and focussed instead on the two fighter-craft which were attempting to kill her friends. Watching the display projected before her, she selected two of the small missiles and fired. The destruction of the small aircraft, moments later, was almost an anti-climax.

"Impact, Crater. We have a half dozen more fast movers coming down from orbit. They're different. They look far more powerful. Be ready. I am moving to intercept." She swung the Thunder-Child through a tight-loop, the shields automatically morphing to control airflow to help her. Staring ahead, she saw the powerful display highlighting the threats, prioritising them. "Natalie, try to establish contact. We don't want this to be simply a misunderstanding.

"Will do," Came Natalie's disembodied voice, over the comms from the control room behind her.

"Kate, we are both ready. Both turrets are operational, and we are using the full halo track." Impact shouted back, glee in his voice at the potential for combat.

"Don't get too excited. We appear to be more powerful than these threats. But that might change. There are also the capital ships coming around in their orbit of the planet. We want to get out and clear before we are forced to engage with those." Kate called back. Pushing the Thunder-Child to entirely unadvisable speeds for a planet's atmosphere. Waiting for the fighters to fall into range, she was momentarily horrified to see a swarm of missiles fired towards them.

"Countermeasures active, targeting and responding to threat." She called over the comms, immediately enabling the smaller, close-defence turrets to operate automatically. The Thunder-Child buffeted as she flew through the expanding debris of the destroyed missiles. Moments later, her own weapons reported a lock, and she replied with several of her own. Lining up the forward guns and moving the starship's nose across the attacking fighters, she released a charged mess of railgun slugs and highly energised particles in a stream towards the enemy which seemed hellbent on killing them. She hit only two with her own guns. One more was destroyed by a missile. Soon

Mission Date: Day 297.  Frontier planet: Corkier-Shay.

afterwards, the combined weapon-fire from the turrets manned by Impact and Crater joined the fight.

The last one died close enough for its fractured hull to be falling past them as they surged through the space recently vacated by their destroyed enemy.

"Team, anyone, have we received any contact from the attacking forces? Natalie, have you got through?" Kate asked.

"They are refusing the handshake. I cannot establish contact with the warships. But they do not seem to be moving to intercept." Natalie's voice came over the comms again. "We have other vessels moving toward the shuttle, though. It seems that others might want to have a go."

"Shit, it's the bloody way, here... Apparently, we're fair game. Okay, warn them off. Let them know that any aggressive actions taken against us, or the shuttle, will result in their destruction. Tell them politely, but firmly, that we will suffer absolutely no fucking about and that if they want to play stupid games, they will win stupid prizes." Kate grunted.

"Colloquialisms are not the friend of a translation matrix. But I will share the sentiment. If we cannot avoid conflict?" Natalie responded.

"Then we kill whoever puts the mission, or our friends, under threat. That's okay. I love a fight." Kate replied. "Jason, Cleo, get that shuttle over here. We might need to transfer you all into the Thunder-Child at speed. We can't save the shuttle, not without bringing the Pequod out of hiding. Prepare her for auto-destruct. We might have no other choice."

\* \* \*

Mission Date: Day 297.  Frontier planet: Corkier-Shay.

In the end, nothing caught them. There was nothing out there which could simply fly directly away from a gravitational mass the size of a planet. Those that had headed toward them gave up. Either realising that they did not have the legs to catch either ship. Or, in response to the less than subtle threats made by the Thunder-Child.

So, they ran, and when they thought it was safe to do so without being noticed, they hid beneath their cloak. They managed to do so without needing to kill anything else. Which was always nice.

The shuttle was lost. In the end, Crater was forced to vaporise it with his particle accelerator.

An annoying waste of resources.

"What do we see?" Jason asked, finally free from the extended decontamination wait in the drop room. They had time to kill. It had made sense to take additional care, to spend longer, ensuring that there was even less chance that they could drag something microscopic onboard which might inadvertently kill them all.

Because that would be bad.

To consider himself invulnerable. Or for any of them to believe they might be. It was as a luxury, based upon untested assumptions, and within which there was baked far too much risk... Wolf, or humans who had been enhanced by their benefactors' technology, they should be okay. But the gap between should, and would, was where everyone might die. The unknowns were terrifying. All of them had waited for the radiation, the chemicals, to do their thing.

So finally, he strode into the Thunder-Child's control room. There, above the holographic mission table, hung the images of two starships. Both were made from a series of spheres, each connected by a thick tubular section. One ship had five spheres, the other seven. Almost like broken jewellery. The forward sections showed clear portals, which Jason assumed to be before a bridge. To the rear, and unmistakable engines protruded. Weapons dotted each sphere. But there were many more upon the longer of the two. The ships were oddly beautiful.

Mission Date: Day 297.　　　　　Frontier planet: Corkier-Shay.

"They have picked up Cordax, and carried him away in one of their shuttle-craft... we watched that happen on the drone you left behind. Good thinking there. He is now being brought onboard the smaller of these two ships currently in orbit. The current assumption is that the larger one is the escort. She is clearly more heavily armed. None of the other ships out here are responding to their attack on us. So either Cordax has many friends here, or he is considered too dangerous." Kate shrugged. "From what we can tell, the smaller ship is the faster of the two. Although, everything is relative, of course." She was standing beside the hologram. The ships, and their position relative to the planet below, were mapped out. "We are following their orbit. The cloak is hiding us."

"Kate, thank you... also, nice flying back there... Okay, so he is alive, that is good. We still need to know what he knows. We were happy to pay. Now, I will be happy to beat it out of the duplicitous sod," Jason replied. "BOB, we can assume that they will break orbit soon, and that they will start making their way toward achieving FTL-jump-speed. If they are planning to make a swift exit, we can assume that they will head towards the star, not away. That they would plan on picking up speed from the gravity assist. Is it possible to disable Cordax's ship at a point where the escort is committed? Disable, but not destroy."

"It should be possible, yes."

"We just have to hope that they send the escort ahead..." Natalie added. "But it was the first to arrive here, and it makes a level of sense strategically."

"... and if it doesn't. We kill it. I would rather not, but I do not think I will lose a great deal of sleep if our hands are forced... Good, we have a general approach, and we have some planning to do."

\*　　　　\*　　　　\*

Mission Date: Day 297.          Frontier planet: Corkier-Shay.

It was straightforward for the Thunder-Child to match the performance, and course, of the two starships, even cloaked. Both leveraged ION drives, and although they also had far more powerful reaction engines, neither seemed keen to waste reactive fuel. Their acceleration, even with the gravitational assistance from the star, was lamentably slow. The Pequod kept her distance, some several thousand kilometres away from risking detection. It took almost two days for the ships to make their final run.

Even if the interdiction was hopefully going to be relatively straight-forward, this had been a tedious wait.

Finally, approaching speeds which would allow them to leverage their FTL, Jason felt his heart-rate increase as they swept around the yellow-dwarf star, hot on the heels of their target. Jason was very aware that this was the closest they had yet come to a star. There was no danger, and he monitored the shields as they performed exactly as they should. But they were close, barely a million kilometres from the outside edge of the corona. His cockpit was dimmed, to where the only detail left was the almost infinite sea of burning plasma. Staggering in its beauty.

Then, as they had hoped, Jason watched as the first ship, the larger and more dangerous escort, accelerated to reach FTL. The second ship, the one carrying Cordax, starting its own charge just half an hour later. It didn't matter that the escort was surging away. That was the plan. Jason waited patiently until BOB green-lit the engagement and immediately fired the single anti-fighter missile with the very precise fire-mission.

Tracking it in his monitors, he saw it hit home and the starship's acceleration tail off. Impacting barely seconds after the escort had disappeared in a raging storm of impossible energies. Leaning over to open the comms, he opened a channel to the crippled ship.

"Cordax. This is Jason on the Warbird Thunder-Child. We have disabled your ion-drives. We have left your thrust engines operational. We have done so deliberately. We would rather leave you with a way to stop yourselves from eventually falling into the star, but if you engage those engines before we have what we want, we will disable those, too."

Mission Date: Day 297.    Frontier planet: Corkier-Shay.

He waited patiently.

"What do you want?" a disembodied voice said. Jason did not think it was Cordax. Even through a translator, it sounded different.

"We just want the same information we had originally asked for," Jason said.

"Our payment?" The voice came back moments later. "To share what we know about those you are looking for, it does not come without significant risk to us."

"There will be no payment, beyond me sparing your lives. You tried to kill my team. I am surprised that I am even considering letting you live... but I am considering it. Right now, there is only one current threat to your continued existence. I would warn that you should not test my patience."

"Please pause before you act. I will need to speak to Cordax." The voice replied. For ten long minutes, the line was dead.

"Please forgive us. Cordax is hot-headed, but our relationship with the rebellion is very profitable and we are angered that he put it at such risk. With this contact, the one we share, I hope that you do not feel the need to report that we acted in bad faith. We will offer you him, too. With the information. If you insist on such a trade."

Jason stared at the ship before him. There had been no inflection in the alien's voice. Such things were lost in translation. Was the alien trying to protect the rest of their crew? Or was he making a play for command? Jason tried to find within himself anything which cared either way. Entirely failing to do so. He hadn't even dialled in a second missile-strike against the crippled ship's other engines. He had no desire to kill so many simply because he was pissed. It had been a bluff.

Probably.

If they told him what he wanted to know. They would live.

He corrected himself. If they told them what the amulet wanted them to know. They would live.

Mission Date: Day 297.    Frontier planet: Corkier-Shay.

Probably.

This distraction, it was proving more complicated than he had first thought.

[Let's see what they say. Let us see where it leads us next.] Alistair said.

\*   \*   \*

Mission date: Day 335.   Rebellion.

## Mission date: Day 335.

### Rebellion.

A few weeks later, and a couple of dozen light-years further up the spiral arm.

They were friendlier here… Or, at least, they appeared to be, and she hoped that they would continue to prove to be.

Dani swung the hover-bike to a stop just inside the compound's wall. Parking beside the four, which were already there. Flaherty pulling up just behind her. The Marine's armour, almost identical to her own, was painted a dark green with a camouflage pattern Flaherty had called MultiCam. With greens, greys and much of it, surprisingly, a grey which was almost white. Hugely effective for a passive solution. On his left shoulder's pauldron was a badge, a numeric four and two, separated by an image of the dagger Jason had always carried. The same dagger that their team, the Elite-Recon of the Colonial Marines, had always carried. A weapon which she was currently carrying on her hip. Just behind her sidearm. A Weapon that Flaherty was insisting on calling a blaster.

The knife was an interesting callback. That much she already knew. She suspected that 'blaster' was, too.

The Royal Marine had been fascinated by the hover-bikes, insisting on calling them speeder-bikes instead. Apparently, they looked similar to a two-wheeled sports bike from his own time. Only, with the faring extending around the vehicle's front, where the wheel would have been, continuing underneath, and extending almost to the rear. Carbyne, not plastic, but otherwise, apparently, the similarities were surprising. The terrain was terrible. Between the landing site and here, and the speeders had been the best solution to cross the open ground.

Swinging her leg over her seat and striding away from the vehicle. She monitored it as it sunk to the ground. Burning fuel simply to look cool whilst parked. That was not why they were here.

Mission date: Day 335.   Rebellion.

They walked across the dark-blue grass analogy. Moving past the scrub, which could have been a plant taken straight from the Epsilon woodlands, Dani walked towards the fortified buildings ahead. Cleo was over the horizon in one shuttle. Two fully armed Tanks waiting in the drop-harnesses behind her cockpit. Neil and Herrick. They would offer support if it were needed. Jansen, a scientist who had proven himself a surprisingly capable pilot, he was in the other. That one had the cargo/personnel attachment mounted behind its cockpit. Blending seamlessly where it joined with the cockpit. Troops waiting within. Impact and Crater.

They had been pulled into a conflict, simply because they had stopped to draw measurements for their maps, and had stumbled upon a colonist's ship being hunted. An event, which Kate's magic eight-ball had somehow predicted. Following that, they had been misled, ambushed and betrayed. That had led them here. Simply because an amulet had... had what? Magic now, too.

A distraction.

She was here, on this mission, to kill the monsters that had come for her home. Monsters who had killed her friend. This was not her mission.

They were getting involved. They should not be. She saw the rebel soldiers nearby. As it seemed to be the case surprisingly often, the rebels here were bipedal, two arms... one head. Humanoid. Cruder, bulkier environment suits with patchwork armour. But even their movements were oddly familiar. Almost human, unless you looked a little closer. They were watching the new arrivals carefully. But none had raised their weapons. She hoped that her instinctive reaction to trust their new allies was not from those similarities alone.

Flaherty was walking behind her. His primary weapon, far larger than hers, was slung over his shoulder. One that would be more capable of defeating heavier armour than her own. Less wieldy though, and his hand was not far from the plasma-pistol at his waist. A weapon very similar to the one carried by Daniel. Kate's father. He was five steps back, a little to her left. It would look like an innocent stroll, a casual decision, but his position would offer him a better field of fire, should things go wrong.

Mission date: Day 335.        Rebellion.

Things were already going wrong. They should not be here at all. A diversion, pulled from pillar to post, and further and further away from what Dani considered being far more important things. The irony, that this was driven by the woman who had sent them on their original mission, was not lost on her, either.

A woman. One who Dani had rescued during a desperate assault on a very different rebellion's stronghold, and whose subsequent actions had first shattered, and then rewritten, a timeline that would have seen Dani already killed.

Things were complicated. Things were getting more so. Complicated…. and what the hell was that?

"Dude, is that a fucking compass?" Dani asked, glancing quickly again at the Flaherty's wrist.

"Yes, it's my issued… I now realise that it will not help here."

"It could, more than you think, most habitable planets will have a magnetic field protecting them… that will mean a pole, and that will mean that your compass will at least point in a consistent direction… Speak to Jason or Kate about the rare-Earth theory. One from your back in your time, actually. Fascinating stuff," Dani replied. "But your armour will give you far better location data than that thing… moons, though. Sometimes they're magnetic, and it's possible that one close enough might confuse that thing."

"So, this thing might save us, if technology fails us?" Flaherty asked.

"Dude, if technology fails us, we will both die choking to death on an atmosphere which is beyond toxic." She laughed.

"Valid point." Flaherty replied. Laughing himself.

"How are you coping with the higher gravity? We are at about one hundred and eighteen percent of Earth here?" She asked.

"Fine. The armour is compensating for most of the difference. But to be fair, whatever else the changes that I have gone through might mean… I am stronger than I ever thought I might be."

Mission date: Day 335.                    Rebellion.

"Just be careful and think back to your training. Things drop faster. That is hard for your brain to adjust to." Dani advised.

"Fair point." Flaherty responded.

Both Marines, the Colonial and the Royal, were talking without taking their focus at all from their surroundings. Warriors who were separated by centuries, but not by everything.

She saw movement from the buildings ahead. Watching as Jason left the larger structure, making his way across the ground toward them. Raising his right hand in greeting. Hopefully, he had managed to disentangle them all from this cluster-fuck.

"How's it going, boss?" Dani asked. Marvelling at how instinctive it was to direct conversations across the armour's radio. This was private between the three of them.

"Surprisingly well. Hacker and Jennifer are attempting to negotiate passage to the last waypoint. It's deep within their territory." Jason responded.

"... and we could simply have dropped into the space between stars, and taken our readings from there. In and out..."

"Kate's amulet... it wanted this. It took a lot to stop Kate from being here, too. Assurances from Jennifer that her questions would also be asked."

"... one day and it might betray us," Dani warned.

"... one day, and it just might." Jason replied. "Hopefully not today. It wanted us here, though. It wanted not just for a negotiation team. But for ground-forces to be close enough to respond. For the Thunder-Child to be waiting in orbit... That doesn't suggest that it is expecting this to go smoothly."

Dani subconsciously adjusted her side-arm, her blaster. The pistol she had carried ever since her one-woman assault on the Iron-Moon. Its load-out, on the mechanised belt around the armour at her waist, was brutal. Nothing she carried today was less-than-lethal. The railgun. She held it across her chest at low ready.

Mission date: Day 335.        Rebellion.

Everything was ready. She was ready. Just for what, she did not know.

\*        \*        \*

Hacker was resting beside the President. His earlier enthusiasm to become more useful, waning. It wasn't heated, the overall discussion was still civil, and he trusted the tribal leader, who was doing most of the talking. Babalich-ThrunderArch, Hacker, enjoyed rolling the name around his mouth. Wonderful. The president, Jennifer, she was paying attention to that guy. Hacker wasn't. He was fascinated by the alien sitting closer to the back.

They were negotiating with creatures who wanted something they had. They wanted to understand their energy sources. They wanted to understand how they manufactured what they had. Carbyne, the hardest substance, understood to exist... making it was the trick. That trick could define a species, it could win a war.

Wars won. They could shape a galaxy.

They were kneeling opposite each other. With a low table between them. Hacker was very glad of his recent 'improvements', which had meant that his knees hadn't exploded after a few minutes. The armour he was wearing was also locked in place. Helping him further. On the table was the gift they had bought with them. A sword, wearing the symbol that belonged to Alistair, who was bonded to... more crazy shit. It was made from carbyne. Impossibly strong, impossibly sharp. But with a tungsten core to give it weight. Carbyne, to their hosts, this was some of the magic that had pulled this meeting into existence. A sword, one not unlike his own. A Katana.

Jennifer's armour was pearl-white. His own, it was a light pastel-blue. Her visor was transparent. His own, it was not. The blue was his daughter's favourite colour.

She wasn't born yet. Neither was his son. They would have lived and died hundreds of years before the Progenitors arrived and exterminated humanity. He was here to protect his species. But first, he would protect his own family. It sounded like the same thing, and he genuinely believed that most

Mission date: Day 335.     Rebellion.

oftentimes it would be. He was keeping an eye out for the other times. Carefully... This side quest, it was a dangerous distraction.

So, he was paying attention to the other guy.

"BOB, the guy I am focussing on. He is hidden more than the others. I cannot see his face." Hacker asked over a closed link.

"Steven. So is your own..." BOB responded.

"True, but I am not up to anything nefarious. All I am doing is worrying that he might be. I can ask my armour, my bio-tech, to hack into any communications that are coming out of his suit. But I do not understand the risk of being detected, or even how to mitigate those risks, even if I am unsuccessful." Hacker replied.

"Why do you mistrust this one?" BOB asked.

"Body language, he moves and responds to what is being said... It is close, but the beat is slightly off. Also, his suit. It is better armoured than the others, but not as completely as it would be if that was what was wanted to be achieved... Almost as if someone wanted the protection, but also did not want to stand out. He was also interested more in carbyne manufacturing than he was in power. The rebels, fuel is an issue... a constant issue. Those who control the area, those they are fighting against, for them, it is less so. For them, fuel is not a problem. But mostly, it is my gut," Hacker said.

"I have grown. Since I met my first humans, I have grown to trust the guts of some... In this, if I am careful enough, then it should not be a risk to trust yours today. Let me manage the hack from here. I am going to need to hijack your systems to do much of the work, and borrow your armour's, too. You will see a request come through. Please give me authorisation." BOB asked.

"Done, thank you." Hacker said, mentally responding to the request that moved across his minds-eye. Marvelling at how he was taking such crazy stuff in his stride.

Then he felt BOB pushing into his own mind, accessing the technology that was now so much a part of him. This was harder to take in his stride. His armour locked him further in place at his frantic request. Not just his knees

Mission date: Day 335.          Rebellion.

anymore. He needed to remain still. Whatever it was in the alien opposite him, that which had caused his initial concern, he did not wish to escalate things by his movement telegraphing anything at all about what he was now doing.

He was aware that Jennifer was still talking to the rebel leader. A conversation which was stalling as the desperate alien pushed harder for the technology that he so desperately needed. Even through the chaotic information that was surging through him, he could tell that she was stalling. Wondering why she was even there.

The rebels, they knew enough to know that they were objectively the good guys. They knew enough to know that not everything was so cut and dried. Certainly, to risk making such powerful technologies available.

It also wasn't their fight.

The onslaught lessened slightly. But only for BOB to communicate.

"You were correct. This man appears to be a mole. He is speaking to other traitors in their midst, and they are currently considering if we are a prize worth throwing away the years spent imbedding him here.

"Man?" Hacker was shocked that this was his first question. "I have referred to him as a 'he' but that was only so that my feeble brain could look at an alien and still make sense of things, but you call him a man?"

"Biologically, their approach to reproduction is more similar to the way you humans go about it than not." BOB responded.

"Have you made the others aware of this?" Hacker asked.

"Reproduction?" BOB asked. Hacker knew the artificial intelligence well enough to recognise the inflection of surprise in the response.

"No, damnit, I meant the betrayal?"

"The greater team, yes. They are getting into position. Jennifer, no. We don't want her reaction to spook a reaction before we are ready." BOB responded.

Mission date: Day 335.        Rebellion.

"He has other agents here... there might be something else, a little more worrying, out there too."

"Okay, she is going to be pissed." Hacker replied. Genuinely surprised that he was intrigued to see what happened next. That he was a little excited.

"She is. I will give you as much warning as possible, but be ready." BOB replied. "Daniel, though... His face is visible. I have not warned him, either..."

"Then, I want to go on record right now that I do not agree with that decision." Hacker replied. Considering the terrifying warrior, who was sitting on Jennifer's other side.

\*        \*        \*

Mission date: Day 335.      Rebellion.

"Right, team, we have eyes in the sky already. But I want drones out here, too. Flaherty, one of yours and I am going to send one of mine up. Confirm?" Jason said over the comms.

"Confirm, ready. On your order, Captain." Flaherty responded.

"In five, four, three…. One and launch," Jason said. Noticing that Dani had deliberately ambled away from them and stumbled on a loose piece of brush. A distraction, one taking the attention of the rebels nearby. The subtle drones, each no larger than a matchbook, released from his, and Flaherty's, armour. Moments later, his situational awareness feed baked in additional data from the two devices. He knew that Dani and Flaherty would have experienced the same.

"What do we have, boss?" Dani asked. Her new position was solid. It would allow her to respond to… almost anything.

"We have concerns. There is a mole in the meeting, a man who is talking to his controllers. They are currently weighing up taking action against the meeting." Jason replied. "We don't know where the others are, not yet, nor how many, but they are close enough to communicate in real time. The shuttle-teams have been made aware, and they are ready. The Thunder-Child, she is in position and ready to respond."

"For now?" Flaherty asked.

"For now, we wait." Jason replied. "But be prepared for things to get a little more exciting around here. Our job is to survive first. It is then to protect the rebel leaders, if it is possible."

"Awesome," Flaherty said. Honestly. "You said man… does that mean?"

*    *    *

Mission date: Day 335.		Open space.

## Open space.

"Incoming disturbance, we are seeing signs of FTL... They're here." Colm called. Shouting over the comms from where he was currently sitting in the port turret at the Thunder-Child's waist.

Kate stared down at the same information, which was populating the feeds across the displays before her.

"Responding, bringing the ship up to combat speeds, and moving to intercept. What is the Rebel Fleet doing?" Kate replied. Feeding on the power. "BOB, shields to maximum, and watch our backs. We are going to use the solid-fuel engines to create the impression we are not too damned odd. But sparingly, and more for show... TT, Colm, hold fire until I order otherwise."

She moved the starship through a tight turn, accelerating hard towards the radioactive disturbance, which had first alerted them to more ships being in their sky. She watched in horror, as a half dozen warships surged out of the maelstrom of corrupted space that had once been their warp-bubbles. They were already firing.

Wedge-shaped, and although these were all smaller, they were also familiar, and she knew just how hard they were to kill.

"Did we ever get the name of these aliens?" She asked.

"Checking... Okay, we have a rough-translation to 'Orga-Loathe'clichemere'. Although, that is subject to change as our translation matrix improves." BOB responded.

"Okay, force communication, and tell me when they can hear us," Kate ordered.

"Will do, bear with me. Okay, we're through." BOB replied, moments later.

Kate paused, studied the display, and the flashing icon, which would open the channel. Pressing it moments later.

Mission date: Day 335.                Open space.

"This is the warbird Thunder-Child. I am ordering your retreat. Any aggression shown will be responded to immediately with violence."

"Thunder-Child, this is not your fight..." The heavily modulated voice came back only moments later.

The Rebel ships had been in orbit of the planet. Without the ability of the Thunder-Child to hang motionless above a planet, their options were more limited. Many had achieved a geostationary orbit, by necessity, sitting far further out. Bunched together, tens of thousands of miles above the planet's atmosphere. Directly above the meeting, so very far below. Sitting ducks. Others, they were hammering around the planet, far closer, and although they passed directly above the meeting, on the surface, they were spaced out. They could still only provide a limited amount of cover during the brief time any were in range.

Missiles, probably energy weapons, too, fired from the advancing warships toward the closest rebel ships. The Rebel Fleet, attempting to change position, to respond... they were too slow, too late. Too many died there in the opening seconds of the attackers arriving. Warships, torn to shreds by an incredible salvo of nuclear ordnance. They had been firing almost as soon as they had arrived, and Kate watched on in horror. Unable to do anything to change what was happening.

But she could enact on her threat. Kate moved to intercept the new fleet. Knowing that their shields, their ability to manoeuvre outside of standard physics, these secrets were likely to be about to be laid bare. Even with the heat-trail of her solid fuel engines. A simple analysis of the energies radiated, and the Thunder-Child's performance, and the pantomime would be revealed.

That could not be helped.

She reflected, that to be this precise, to know exactly where the rebel ships were. The attackers would have needed to be elsewhere within the system. Light-minutes out, not light-hours.

"BOB, is there any way to backtrack where they came from? Can we detect if there might be others?" She asked.

Mission date: Day 335.    Open space.

"Not yet, but I will continue to try," BOB responded.

"I am targeting the lead two ships first. Nukes only for now. We will use only TOAMs, until a time comes when we need to hit harder." Kate selected the weapons held within the Thunder-Child's internal bays. Preparing them to fire. There were six attacking ships. She had only four conventional warheads.

The pods, attached to the Thunder-Child's hull, they contained anti-matter warheads. Not something that they wanted to reveal to their potential allies, or enemies, not yet. Nor were they weapons anyone wished to detonate this close to a habitable planet.

"Oh, what a web we weave, when first we practice to deceive." She murmured, as she selected the first two warships and let fly.

The TOAMs, or the 'Toddlers of All Missiles', were still leveraging chaser drives and cloaking tech to reach their targets. The first warship stood no chance, and the weapon reached it before its crew even realised that they were under attack. It borrowed deep and erupted in fury from the ship's core. The second, a few thousand kilometres from its friend, it may have had more of a warning. But it did them no good.

The ships died, and a flare of anger ran up against Kate's soul as she attempted to ratify the lives she had taken, with the childish naming of the missiles used to kill them.

"Bringing us around for another pass, I want to see if we can drive them off. How long until the remaining four reach the planet?" She asked.

"They're in range now. I assume that they will not fire for risk of killing their own, or risking their prize..." BOB responded. "Aerial bombardment of the settlement will unlikely achieve their goal, here."

Kate felt the first buffeting as the Thunder-Child's shields warded off return fire from the remaining warships.

"Until the point where they consider their attempt to win this, failed. Then they might decide to instead ensure that the Rebels cannot have the prize, either. Warn everyone on the ground. They're about to encounter whatever

Mission date: Day 335.  Open space.

phase two of this attack turns out to be," Kate ordered, raking cannon fire across the distant hull of an enemy ship.

Two TOAMs left. Should she kill two more and leave herself exposed? Decisions, decisions.

"BOB, can you coordinate with the rebels that are still flying? It would be nice to not be doing this alone," she asked. Feeling a little mean when she considered how many had just died.

\*     \*     \*

Mission date: Day 335.   Phase two.

## Phase two.

Daniel was stunned by how quickly everything descended into chaos. Chastising himself that he had allowed his attention to wander, for himself to get bored. The creature, just to the left of the rebel leader, surged to its feet as suddenly his armour marked it as a threat. It was pulling some sort of weapon, fumbling it from within the cape thing it had worn over its armour. Everyone was reacting, and the information dump which hit him was a little distracting, even if it had clearly been curated to be as less so as possible. Frantically, he looked for danger around him. Before him.

He watched as the being finally managed to draw its weapon, the capabilities of which he had no way of quantifying. He surged to his own feet, drawing his own pistol. It was charged. Readied. He had been cycling it through the hours of the interminable meeting. Doing so subtly, and only feeling marginally twitchy for those long minutes whilst it was effectively useless. His draw was blindingly fast, the holster retracting immediately after he had taken the weapon's grip in his right hand. The base of his thumb had already drawn back the hammer as he had closed his hand around it. The bolt of energised-plasma struck the alien dead-centre in its chest. Blowing a hole clear through the armour and its body, then burning a hole through the concrete wall behind it.

He had not seen the weapons damage from this close before. He was staggered by the ease it blew through what he assumed was solid armour-tech. The alien blood, a dark red with an unusual green-tinge, surprised him.

The others were reacting. Jennifer was on her feet, herself. Her hands forwards, attempting to calm things. Daniel ruined her moment by shooting another assailant in the face. The shot burning a terrible hole through the alien's head.

Seconds later, and Daniel realised that three of the four guards had revealed themselves to be traitors. He had only done so, as he had shot the third in the face. Traitors, or perhaps just startled guards, looking to protect their primary.

Mission date: Day 335.                    Phase two.

Whatever else the alien race was capable of, their reaction times seemed lamentably slow. But he was having a very hard time telling friend from foe, and was a little disconcerted when his armour's display highlighted more enemy for him. Even if it made his job a little easier.

There was a ruckus behind him, and he saw the lawyer struggling on the floor with another alien. Looking for all the world like he was attempting to use some sort of wrestling move. Commendable, but it was one that was failing horribly as the limb Hacker had trapped, proved itself capable of moving comfortably past the lock the man had been trying to find. He helped the man out. Putting a third shot through that one, too.

"Jason, what in the name of...?" he shouted.

"Incoming heavy armour. Get Jennifer out of there." Jason's voice called over. "Now."

Hacker had picked up the sword. Unarmed, he had slung it over his shoulder and now held the blade before him in two hands. The president had grabbed the panicking leader by his arm, and was attempting to pull him after her. Daniel looked at the last guard, the creature turning its armoured head to look at the fallen, then to look back at Daniel. Only then raising its long, ungainly weapon. Daniel shot him, too.

"Everyone, stop. You, Babalich, you have enemies in your midst. They are coming for you and us. We have our team mobilising right now. But we have to leave this structure. We have armour incoming." Daniel had not addressed the rebel leader by name before, and he stumbled over that name now. His mouth stumbling over the unfamiliar sounds. "Jennifer, stay behind me. We will need to fight our way out to Jason. Hacker, do your best with that sword, but let me know if something happens behind us."

Turning, trusting the others to follow his lead, he strode from the room.

"Jennifer, Hacker, apparently BOB was hacking the bad-guys as they planned this. He cannot guarantee that he will know all of them. But those he has identified will be marked in your displays." He shouted over a closed-loop between their team.

Mission date: Day 335.        Phase two.

"I know, dude. I called it." Hacker exclaimed.

Daniel briefly reflected on that comment. Looking around as he did so, and seeing the wireframe graphics populating the rest of the building. Identifying two approaching enemies in red. Just around the corner ahead of him.

The structure was some sort of crude concrete shell. Mostly a rounded structure, which they believed rebels formed over an inflatable bladder-system. Quick, dirty and effective. As they moved to clear the building, they were picking up an entourage. A group of aliens who were crowding after them. Panicked, but reacting to what was happening in a fairly typical way. Military leaders, aides, perhaps even cooks — they could be literally anyone. But all of which had just had their world turned upside down. Hacker was indicating that they stayed far enough away to make him happy. Doing a half decent job of it.

As the two marked bad-guys approached the corner ahead, Daniel raised his pistol. This was almost like cheating.

They died as they emerged, neither making a bad effort of clearing the corner. It just hadn't been good enough.

"Hacker, if you take my railgun, how confident are you that you won't shoot me, or the president, in our arses?"

"Fifty-fifty," Hacker replied.

"Good-enough," Daniel replied. Turning to present the weapon, which was slung across the oxygen-breathy-thing, which was on the back of his armour. Feeling it detach as the man grabbed it. Hearing the man fumbling the sword back into its sheath.

"Let's go."

\*    \*    \*

Mission date: Day 335. Phase two.

Mission date: Day 335.          Phase two.

Jason saw Daniel emerging, his great-granddaughter dragging their contact behind her. Appearing from within the pitted ruin of the building behind her, as one corner sagged further. The attacking armoured vehicles were hitting it, but not with their main guns. They were not trying to... destroy it.

"Get to cover. We have support only seconds out." Jason hollered, his own weapon on his shoulder. Stitching weapon fire across the attacking soldiers who were sprinting across the purple grass, the rugged ground, toward the rebel encampment. The railgun devastating the attacking aliens. But doing little more than digging holes in, not through, the armour of the tracked vehicles which were getting worryingly close. They were larger than the old Challenger tanks, but followed basically the same design-principle of old-Earth tanks. Tracks, running around the edge of their angular hulls, and a turret, an eerily familiar turret, which was mounted on the top. Only, with two barrels, each only five feet long. Jason knew that their world might easily complicate with the naming convention of their own Tanks. Their walking armour. Which, although capitalised, were very different machines.

He also questioned their own technology. Which had failed to detect an enemy who seemed to have done little more than bury themselves in the soil.

"Cleo, how far out are you? We need heavier weaponry to take out their death-machines." Jason hollered over his comms.

"Climbing for altitude, Neil and Herrick wanted to approach the problem from a more interesting angle... Perhaps a weapon pack for the shuttle itself might be a good idea at some point?" She asked. "I am faking it with the new engines... but it seems odd that we don't arm these things."

Jason tracked the shuttle, watching through his situation-awareness-display as it climbed high under its new solid-fuel engines, and then two Tanks dropping free. Staring back at the attacking enemy armour, he appreciated that the Tanks would have an excellent vantage point.

"We have ten machines approaching, prioritising." Neil reported. Jason saw the reported release of all four missiles from each Tank. Then their railguns opening up, moments later.

Mission date: Day 335.          Phase two.

Several projectiles hit him, one actually making it through his shield to punch against his armour. It held. It dented worryingly, but it held. It did wonders to bring his attention back to his own situation.

"Danger close. Everyone down," he shouted. As their Tanks missiles found their targets. Noticing that Flaherty was doing his best to draw fire from their allies. Running and gunning with his larger-railgun and engaging with the enemy fighters. The man should be far enough away, so should... possibly.

Jason dived to the ground.

Then the missiles hit the armoured vehicles, which had been in the process of breaching the camp's wall.

They hit blazingly fast, a line of fire surging down almost vertically. Punching into the tracked vehicles' upper hulls. Nothing happened, but a split second later, fire burst from every seam.

"That was a bit of an anticlimax. But we have two left... Make that one." Daniel said, as the vertical heavy-calibre, railgun slugs smashed through the top of the first of the last two. The fire blazing through the sky, as the ordnance, moving fast enough to burn the atmosphere, hit home. Chunks of armour flying clear as the weapons dug deep. A torrent of horrific death. No less dramatic than the missiles. Just different.

Whichever Tank pilot tackled the first. The other killed the second in much the same way.

"Okay, we have another cluster, about two hundred yards out." Jason shouted. He was moving forward and was happy to see Dani and Flaherty both flanking him with no need to be asked. Neil and Herrick landed beside him a moment later, and he felt indestructible.

"Kate, how are things going on up there? We have pretty much everything handled at our end," He asked, over the wider-comms.

\*       \*       \*

Mission date: Day 335. Phase two.

Mission date: Day 335.                Not quite as smoothly.

## Not quite as smoothly.

"Not quite as smoothly. These ships are powerful, and very well armoured. Unless we chose to start firing off anti-matter warheads, we might be forced into a retreat... The rebels don't seem to have anything that can hurt them, and those that survived the initial attack are taking forever to get into position, anyway. It is too easy to forget how inconvenient gravitational masses were in space-flight. The Pequod is cloaked, running silent, but she is listening, ready to rock and roll. We can destroy these ships in moments. But we show our hand if we do... we will also irradiate much of the planet. Our shields are down to fifty-five percent. I am attempting to take out their weapons, but if I hit fifty, and I am taking out two of the four with the last of my nukes..."

Kate threw the Thunder-Child through another tight turn, able to stay ahead of the physical ordnance fired toward her, but not from the EM energy weapons. Her shields were holding, but would not do so forever. Fifty-three percent. The close-defence pods were roaring their own fury, defeating any missiles which got close enough to be a threat. She felt entirely free, flying the starship. Even if things were a little desperate now, it was a wonderful machine to pilot. This was the second time flying her into combat. Also, it was only the second time without Jason sitting beside her, with the cockpit configured for both seats. There was, she reflected, far more room without the enormous bastard there.

"You don't want to keep doing that..." Kate whispered. Addressing the ship which she was currently shooting past, and which was proving the largest threat... Fifty-two percent. "Please, don't make me kill so many more of you."

"Boss, we're doing what we can, but we will need to concentrate fire on a single vessel to win until... pause." Colm started. "Okay, so BOB is working on a thing."

"BOB?"

"The anti-fighter missiles. I have a new configuration that should allow us to target only the weapon modules on the warships, much as we did with the

Mission date: Day 335.   Not quite as smoothly.

cannons the first time we met these brutes. Much as we are still trying to do now. It is ready to go... just a moment." BOB went silent. Kate continued to fight the good fight. "Now," BOB said. Possibly a minute later.

"Good timing," Kate said. Smiling as her threat board suddenly opened up with a bunch of new options. Her shields dropping to fifty percent at almost that exact moment. Targeting the two with the most functional armament remaining, she fired off the last two anti-ship nukes at them. That done, she moved her selection function over to the smaller missiles, selected every emplacement on the last two warships, and unleashed hell on them.

Those which she had not just killed.

The subtle 'thuds' of the smaller missiles releasing was a reassuring sound. The tracking data from each lighting up on her virtual-image moments later. The tiny devices had been designed to be as invisible as possible, and they were difficult even for the Thunder-Child to monitor. Although, they lacked the cloaking tech of the TOAM and MOAM weapons.

Those weapons, the nukes, they struck home. Fast, invisible. Deadly. Enormous explosions tearing the ships from deep within their hulls.

Then the smaller weapons reached their targets, and she watched, hypnotised, as they hit home. Explosions rippling across the surface of the two starships, realising that the enemy had not even noticed their approach until they had hit.

"Thunder-Child to ground. Things are going a little smoother now." She reported. "Threat neutralised."

\*    \*    \*

Mission date: Day 335.    In the dirt.

## In the dirt.

Flaherty approached the last building within the fortified wall of the rebel camp. The one where the last holdouts were currently making a stand. He deployed a drone; it flew in and seconds later, his vision showed a wireframe of the internal structure and visualisation of the fighters there. Two of them. Three legs, the four arms. Cordax's people. Probably mercenaries like that duplicitous fuck had turned out to be.

"Those inside throw your weapons clear and make your way out with your arms held high." Flaherty shouted. His amplified, and translated, voice speaking what was essentially garbage to him at a deafening volume. He hoped that the translation made sense.

If it did, the explosive which was thrown through the crude pre-fabricated doorway, seconds later, might mean that the bad-guys had a sense of humour. Glad to spend precious power for his armour to attempt flight, Flaherty threw himself far and low. The explosion came moments later, peppering his shield, but not compromising it.

Rolling over, raising himself to his left knee, he brought his railgun to his shoulder. It was larger, and perhaps more cumbersome, than Jason's. It was also more powerful. Feeling only a tinge of guilt, he drew a bead on the images of the two mercenaries, which were still superimposed into his eyeline by his bio-tech, turned his weapon up to eleven, and murdered the buggers through the building's wall.

"Clear," he shouted. Moments later.

\*     \*     \*

Mission date: Day 335.					In the dirt.

"So, how are the delegates?" Jason asked. Looking around at the smoking mess of the rebel camp.

"They're still in a level of shock. But they are glad of the assist." Jessica replied. "Jason, I am sorry. I put us all in danger."

"You didn't. I know I pushed for this. That I am more focused on following that damned stone to wherever it is trying to take us... I know that I am more than I should be," Jason replied.

"Whilst that is true, I do not understand why?" Jessica asked.

"I trust Kate." He replied.

"With your life?" Jessica asked. Turning away from the carnage, to face him. Her own face revealed behind her helmet's clear visor.

"With everything, always." Jason replied. Meeting her gaze. "The new deal is that we trade what we did to keep them alive for the information we need. I do not know about you, but this is not our fight, and we might already have done too much. We might already have changed something."

"Even if they are all doomed, anyway?" Jessica asked.

For a moment, they both gazed down and to the left. Their visors displays', painting the distant star... frozen, with the only relative movement being the spinning of the planet they were stood on. No matter how fast the rogue star was travelling, it was too far away for its own speed to be visually noticeable.

"I will get the information," Jessica said. Not moving for another minute, before turning towards where the rebel leader was waiting. "Hacker, with me. I might need you." She called.

Jason watched as the man in blue armour made his way to join with his granddaughter. Unable to take his eyes away from the looming disaster for too long.

Watching something, the predictive mapping of the image, ignoring the relativistic distance, and showing where it was thought the object was, today... right now.

Mission date: Day 335.　　　　In the dirt.

A stella-orphan, a supermassive-star, which was in the last stages of its own life, and also an ancient collision course with the Milky Way. It would hit. It was now almost certain that it was going to hit the other star, the smaller star. What happened next, though... that was still uncertain. A nova event, an impossibly powerful super-nova... But what was left would be a singularity. A black-hole. One which would have been slowed by the collision. But it would not be stopped.

Was that why they were here? Was that why they were chasing ghosts? It had to be connected. Two missions, only one was taking his focus. He felt that was right.

He trusted Kate, always. He always had. He always would.

So, standing amidst the wreckage of a brutal fire-fight, on another planet barely capable of supporting plant-life, He was again staring at the image of a dying super-massive star, one travelling at a not insignificant fraction of the speed of light, and which only was months away from its journey's end.

A collision with a yellow dwarf star, one not too dissimilar to Earth's, and one which was about to end all life in this corner of the Milky-Way.

\*　　　\*　　　\*

Mission date: Day 335.　　　　In the dirt.

Hours later, once they had been satisfied that the shocked rebel leaders had shared what they needed, Jason had finished the preparations for the teams to finally leave.

Everything was loaded back into the shuttles. Everyone else was, too. The Tank drivers would be eager now to return to the Pequod and to get themselves free from the machines. The other shuttle, the one with that cradle, was waiting patiently a couple of hundred yards to his left with the Tanks firmly attached. He was the last to step onto the other shuttle's ramp. The one configured to carry people and equipment. Their hover-bikes.

They were waiting for him.

For a moment he was distracted, looking down at his armoured feet. Seeing how the treads on his boots had left indistinct footprints, as they had discarded soil there. Alien soil, resting on the hard-carbyne of the shuttles entrance. A juxtaposition which would be far too easy to ignore if it had not caught his eye. His attention. He bent over and picked up some of the dirt with his armoured hand. Letting the soil fall between his fingers as he stared at it. Turning, he indulged himself on a sudden whim and stared out of the hatchway, and out across the alien planet. Taking in the impossibly coloured grass, finally questioning how chlorophyl could be... but it wasn't Earth, it wasn't Epsilon. It was a completely unique planet, and he had walked across its surface as if were merely an incidental thing. He stared away from the carnage of the battle, and toward the distant hills. Processing the foliage that covered much of the land between him and those. Alien plants doing their alien thing on this alien world. Looking skyward, and even with his over-laid charts, it was not his sky. The moons, two of which were in sight now that the sun was gone. A star, an unfamiliar star that was not his sun. Moons that were not his moons. One was spherical, although its surface shone an impossible blue. Scarred, like Earth's, hammered through millennia by ancient impacts beyond count. The other, it was little more than an asteroid caught in the planet's gravity. Irregular, ugly.

He looked elsewhere. Higher though, far higher than both, and searching the sky there for the familiar splinter of light in the night's sky. The wolf locking onto it. Marking it for him. Calling for him. Earth's moon.

Mission date: Day 335.            In the dirt.

His moon.

Earth, which was today populated by creatures ancient even compared to the dinosaurs. His own planet would be unrecognisable to him were he to travel there in his impossible starship. Inhospitable to him, too. Likely more so even than the alien planet upon which he was now standing.

For a moment, for a long moment, the incredulity he felt about his current position was overwhelming. Not unpleasantly. But in such a way that the magnitude of everything became so starkly real. His heartbeat in his chest sped up. Thudding, almost the only sound he could hear. His life, his energy... He was the alien here.

It was all a little overwhelming.

"Right people, let's close up and get off this rock." He ordered. Stepping into the shuttle's airlock and closing the hatch behind him.

*        *        *

## Misson Date: Day 336.

### The next step.

The next day.

"So, this next stop, it's not too far?" Jason asked. A rhetorical question, and one he already knew the answer to. He was seated on the stool before the Steinway, and was facing the room. Turned away from the piano on the stage in the Pequod's jazz-club. The rainbow scrolling above his head. This time, everyone was there. Kate was on his left, Katherine to his right. He was sitting, to better avoid towering over everyone.

"It is not too far. We will be there in around four days." Katherine replied.

"Okay, so this mission is a snatch and grab. I am afraid that we need to collect an… an alien, and that we need to rely on that alien, showing us where to go next." Jason said.

"Isn't everything out here an alien?" Daniel asked. Ever helpfully.

"Yes, okay, and thank you. This is a very specific alien, obviously. One who might well be the last link in the chain. I am planning to take only a small team. Subtle, careful. We will need a shuttle, one which does not look too out of place, and a way to better hide ourselves… The modifications we put in place, to meet the rebellion, should be enough. This will be camouflage and sneaky-sneaky. Also, if possible, I want to dock the shuttle to the Thunder-Child. Ideally, we do not abandon another one during our exit…"

"Jason, it should be achievable. The docking function on the Thunder-Child's ventral surface, we just need to add the same component to the shuttle's cargo-pod. We can do that in time if we start now," BOB responded.

"That means no second shuttle, with Tank support." Neil said.

"It does, but if we make a noise, the mission fails anyway." Jason added.

Misson Date: Day 336.        The next step.

"Great, and I appreciate that, but the last two missions were simple conversations. Both times, things kicked off. We're expecting violence this time… I don't want to leave you out there, alone." Neil said. His point was entirely valid. His concern was obvious.

"True… but if things always went to plan, no one would ever have needed Marines…" Jason said. Grinning at his friend.

"I can fly you in," Cleo offered.

"No, I want you on the stick in the Thunder-Child. You have the right instincts, and I want Dani flying the Pequod. If we die, she completes the mission." Jason replied. The young officer smiled. Perhaps for the trust shown, perhaps just for the idea of flying the starship. Hopefully both. "Our exit, if we need it… there will be no margin for messing about. The old-girl picks us up, and we can be clear, far faster.

"What do we know about the planet?" Herrick asked.

"A fair amount. The planet is… It is called Darla. Rather, the name translates to 'Darla'. I believe that it is something to do with 'beloved'. For the Sendler Protocol to work, it must make some arbitrary decisions for us," Katherine replied. "It is also more industrialised than any we have yet encountered. Far more heavily populated, too. Billions live here. Obviously, there is far more evidence of what we would consider being an evolved and established societal structure, although it does still sound a little unruly."

"Thank you. This is the home world of the Orga-Loathe'clichemere. The race behind the Teghra-Dorne empire. Those of the wedge-shaped warships we have encountered twice now. Against which we have also fought twice. This is very much the belly of the beast. The target is a rebel-operative. A member of a race which we are not yet familiar with. A Tarka-Jebshate. It is called 'Karma-Yermic-Tata'. It works with the local government there." Jason continued. "It is also an operative who may already be exposed. The aliens who had infiltrated the rebels would have had access to the target's name. They may not have dug deep enough. He may be safe. Or they might be already watching him."

"He?" Flaherty asked. Smiling.

Misson Date: Day 336.          The next step.

"Damn it, for the sake of this conversation, let's say probably?" Jason asked. "We have a data packet, honestly I have not researched their mating or reproductive functions."

"Is this truly the last stop, before we reach wherever the hell it is that we are meant to get to?" Herrick asked.

"We hope so..." Kate replied. "Because things are about to get exciting around here."

"Exciting?" Herrick asked.

"No, it is going to be horrible... entirely horrible... Our timeline could rapidly compress at almost any moment. We know something that no one here seems to yet know... Certainly no one who has been forthcoming about it. Our first stop, the dust bowl Corkier-Shay, it has less than a decade left before it is irradiated. Granted, it is a shithole and populated mostly by arseholes. But it is hard to wish that on anyone. It will take almost half a century for the effects to reach out this far... But all we need is for one astronomer out here to look in the right direction, and see something dreadful about to happen... then things are going to get exciting, quickly." Jason replied.

"Will they be safe this far out?" Hacker asked.

"From the initial gamma-ray burst, almost no chance. Perhaps, but only if they are fortunate enough for their own star to be between them, and it... but the chances of that happening are miniscule... the radiation that will follow for years... it will kill the planet." Jansen added. "Then, when we consider the neutrinos... they hit a few weeks after the first burst. No, the planet cannot survive."

"Can we save them?" Hacker asked. Leaning forward from where he was sitting in the booth. "... and should we, even if we could?"

Natalie was sitting opposite him, a deck of cards laid out before her. The chess set was pushed to the back of the booth. They had been playing something. She raised an eyebrow and turned to look at Katherine.

"We can save some. Or, rather, we can help them save themselves. Their current FTL tech is a relatively clumsy version of our own. Mirroring those of

Misson Date: Day 336.    The next step.

the Thunder-Child's, the Pequod's. The power requirements for such devices are incredible. We have far more efficient engines, and our power supplies are phenomenal. Our power concerns are taken care of… We cannot share that tech though. Just to find their first primordial…" Katherine said. Pausing and nodding to BOB.

"It took my people centuries to learn how to harvest primordial black-holes… to capture them. We did it out of necessity. We had a rogue-singularity, with the mass half of that of our own planet, wandering through our solar-system. It was never originally meant to be a power-source, that was just a by-product of the technology we used to hold it. A fortunate happenstance, if you like. There was a cluster just half a light year away from us. What we have here…. What we have available for ourselves, I am afraid that it is not repeatable for them." BOB said. His face turning to look toward each of the human crew, his familiar smile painted upon it.

"However, humanity first travelled to the stars using a very different technology." Katherine continued. "Less flexible, perhaps, than our Chasers. But capable of similar velocities once in FTL. The short-incident wormhole technology, WHITS Drives, they require far less power. Levels that the races here can easily generate. We could share that with them, and some could flee." Katherine replied.

"My people, they faced a similar threat. Although one which was, in galactic terms, far more localised. It was to be equally devastating to our home world. They built a fleet of Ark ships to flee the planet… The people here, they have decades to prepare and to build their own fleet." BOB spoke up. Floating into the air, and still only extending his domed head module from his tic-tac body. Painting his familiar face on the dome's surface. His expression was now neutral.

"We don't have to think about that today." Jason said. "But can we build a package containing what they would need to know, and package it within a Sendler Protocol Packet?"

"We can do that." Katherine replied.

"It is something that needs to be put to a vote. Before that happens, we will need to fully consider the risks. Not to us, but to humanity as a hole. If we

Misson Date: Day 336.     The next step.

allow them to travel further, they will travel further. None of us has seen a planet here that is half as attractive as Earth, or from what I understand about Epsilon, her either. We scatter dozens of races out there, looking for a new home and... This will need to be an educated, but subjective decision, based upon objective facts." Daniel rumbled. Surprising everyone.

"So, you're saying we should not do it?" Hacker asked.

"I am saying that I wouldn't. But then I am a dick... I am saying that we should vote on it, but that we should do so carefully."

"Okay," Hacker replied. Thoughtfully.

"So, back to the mission. There are challenges. Preparations to make and unpredictable timelines?" Herrick asked. Jason just nodded.

"Just to find a creature who will apparently recognise Kate's amulet?"

Jason just nodded again.

"Have you picked a team yet?" Herrick asked.

"Why, I am glad you asked." Jason replied. Smiling.

\*     \*     \*

Misson Date: Day 336.                    The next step.

Together, they sat, staring again at the amulet. The three adult Purestrains. Family. This time, Katherine was with them. So was BOB. They were in Katherine's office. Five conspirators, six including Alistair, discussing things.

Uncomfortable things. Secrets.

No more secrets. Jason pushed away the memory. The traitorous thoughts.

"It wants us to do this. It wants us to find this spy, and it wants us to ask where he saw something like it... I still get little more than feelings, ethereal memories... Barely there, and I know that they are not mine. Messages, but it's like a voice screaming into the void to be heard, but knowing that it will barely be heard. This is not our mission.... But it is important. Of that I am convinced." Kate said. Running her fingers through the curls of her red-hair.

"It is not the Progenitors..." Jason said.... "This, it was never that. We have always believed that this is a distraction."

"Yet we allowed ourselves to be distracted." Katherine responded.

"Whilst there was a manageable risk, it seemed worth the risk... but we have run into situations, arguably every time, where we faced far more violence than we expected. Violence, which we proved we could handle. But we have risked potential disaster... It seems like we must risk ourselves once more."

"At least once more." Daniel said. "This is not the last of it. We then need to go to where this spy tells us we should."

"I pushed back. I have since the meeting with the rebels... I pushed back against the amulet's wishes, wanting to test it. It has shared a little more. We are looking for something. It is no-longer the Progenitors... Christ, I think we all know that it was never that. But the answer was also that whilst that was true... it is also all connected." Kate said.

"... Connected?" Katherine asked.

"What did it tell you?" Jason asked. Leaning forward.

"That we are not here for the Progenitors, not yet... I think we are here for the thing that they were built to fight."

Misson Date: Day 336.            The next step.

"Oh, for fuck's sake." Jason sighed. It was his turn to run his fingers through his long-blond hair. He stared at the ceiling and seemed to lose himself there.

"The Progenitors, they were built?" Daniel asked. His daughter merely shrugged with an apologetic look painted across her face.

"Built by whom?" Katherine asked.

"Honestly, I have no idea... It is little more than feelings... Apparently, we are heading towards that answer," Kate replied. "But if that is true, there might be something else out there. There might be something out there that really is fucked up. But we need to move fast now. The timeline... we must hurry."

She looked lost. Jason had seen her like this only once before. Kneeling amid the carnage at the police-station in Hammersmith, back in London at the tail-end of the twentieth century... a dead friend, only a few feet away from her. Terrified, furious... sometimes desperate. He had seen these things far more often than he would ever have wanted to.

But not lost.

"Let us hope that this contact, this Karma-Yermic-Tata, that he has answers." Jason said.

\*     \*     \*

## Mission date: Day 341.

### Teghra-Dorne: Planet fall.

Just a few days later.

"So, this is all very different," Jason said. Voicing pretty much what they were all thinking. Staring down at a city which would rival New Austin, back on Epsilon. Unlike Epsilon, this was one amongst many cities on the overpopulated planet. However, it was that planet's capital. Captea D'Laghas. Although, the translation made little sense to any of them.

Overflying the city by thousands of feet, he moved through the designated flight-path that had brought them in from orbit. He hadn't faced any level of traffic control since they had first left Epsilon on their original mission to the comet, years ago. A lifetime ago. Certainly, none that he had obeyed, he thought ruefully, as he remembered their return to that planet onboard the brand-new Thunder-Child.

So many bloody years ago now... was that where it had started? He thought that was likely far further back... When he had met a beautiful woman at a west London university in the tail end of the twentieth century.

Looking across at Kate, and processing that quite a lot had happened since then. He winced a little. Even after all these years, most of it seemed entirely improbable.

He leant forward, checking quickly through the request from traffic-control to take control of the shuttle on the console before him. He hesitated. But they had been careful here. They should be safe. They also really didn't have any choice. The request bleeped again. Conveying that he was taking too long, and he accepted the request. Leaning back, and trusting the system. Whatever else happened within this empire, good or bad, it was unlikely that this was doing anything but working to avoid incidents.

Mission date: Day 341.        Teghra-Dorne: Planet fall.

He may as well enjoy the ride.

There were other planets almost as populated, but these were apparently further up the spiral arm. Although not many, and only a few of those might consider their own importance to be as significant as Darla's. None who could do so with absolute honesty.

"That star dying, it kills all of this?" Herrick asked. His voice was tinged with sadness. The man leaning in from the pod behind them.

"Yes, that is inevitable now," Jason replied. "Overflight, how are things up there?"

The congested mess of broad-spread em-radiation, the vast majority of which was absolutely comms data, had led them to trust that it was unlikely that they would be detected speaking with one another. Still, they would only speak ship-to-ship sparingly.

"Jason, The Thunder-Child is cloaked and exactly where you need us to be... godspeed." Cleo responded. "Be aware that some of the empire's warships are looking worryingly capable. I am sending through updates and estimated capabilities now."

"Thanks, stay safe." Jason replied. Flicking through the data-packet sent through from the Thunder-Child, Jason winced.

"The space-port is up ahead. The authorities have checked our registration again. It seems to hold up well and I do not believe that they are concerned we are not who we are pretending to be. The rebels did not screw us, after all." Kate said from the copilot's seat. "I have loaded our course down to the surface and our landing spot. In the event that we lose traffic-control's... well, their control. Interestingly, we are saving quite a few credits by the shuttle being capable of VTOL. Apparently, not all craft here are."

"Okay, good. I have it. She is handling well with the standard thrusters. We are using the grav-field to reduce our weight. But all propulsion is solid-fuel. This should not be something they notice..." Jason added. Idly wondering what the actual value of the credits was. Those gifted to them by the rebels,

Mission date: Day 341.  Teghra-Dorne: Planet fall.

and now loaded to their Sendler Protocol. "It feels odd to fly this way. Wasteful, too. Burning physical fuel. Even if it was all I knew for centuries."

[A gentleman can often soften quickly, if he allows himself to be surrounded too much by the trappings of his improving position in life.] Alistair added. Ever helpfully.

[Ha, we both look back with fond eyes at our far more comfortable, less exciting lives.] Jason replied.

"Hey, if this goes to our standard success rate so far, we can expect to be leaving again, in far more of a hurry," Herrick added, also helpfully. Bringing Jason back to the present.

"Hopefully it will not come to that," Jason replied.

They were following an altogether too familiar warship down to the ground. The wedge shape, now unmistakably that of the Teghra-Dorne Empire. Smaller than those which currently orbited the planet. Smaller, also than any they had yet fought. But still close to a thousand feet long. Not as wide as the Pequod. But the length was only a few feet different.

"BOB, you ready for this? This is your first mission away from the ships for..." Jason started.

"Jason, I was born ready..." BOB said. "Literally. I was created to be immediately effective from the moment I was first activated."

"Were you?"

"Christ no, it was an entirely overwhelming experience. To be suddenly one, but sharing so much with so many more. My identity, I felt its importance to me... Then, with the hive mind, I felt its immediate dilution."

Jason looked over, needing to look backwards from his seat to see his friend where he was currently resting before the rear-bulkhead of the cockpit. "My friend, one day we need to talk about this properly. Are you okay today, though?"

"I am, Jason. I would also enjoy that."

Mission date: Day 341.          Teghra-Dorne: Planet fall.

"Excellent," Jason replied, turning back to his console, and watching the shuttle navigate down the highlighted path. Still not fully trusting that the systems were fully calibrated to the old-style engines. Not knowing how the empire's control would handle any errors, his hands did not stray too far from the controls.

"All of this talk of rebellions and empires, it seems a little too familiar...?" Daniel muttered.

"I know, but if a species moves clear of their own planet and rules others... what do we call them? If species out there are not happy, and if they resist...? do you see the problem?" Jason replied.

"Okay, fair enough." Daniel said. Seeming happy enough with the answer.

"Shuttle, play Carter, USM. Sheriff Fatman." Jason ordered. Smiling, as the powerful rhythmic synthesiser kicked into the intro.

"Who the hell is 'Carter USM?'" Herrick asked.

"This, my American friend, it was perhaps a little before your time." Jason attempted to run the maths, but was too distracted to complete them. "I have no idea if they even made it stateside... But this is also an education. They are Carter, they are the unstoppable sex machine.... and I give you Sheriff Fatman."

"The Prince of Wales award for pushing Valium and amphetamines?" Daniel asked.

"Drugs? Christ..."

"It was the late eighties... also, the Sheriff was not a good guy... he was, after all, the undisputed king of the slums." Jason said. His smile turning into a grin as the rhythmic music powered through the cockpit."

"Nice," Kate added.

They landed half an hour later. Not finishing the album, and not yet fully winning Herrick over to the band, not yet. Once on the ground, it was only Jason, the registered captain, who was permitted to disembark at first. Standing at the lowered exit door on the shuttle's stern. Meeting a small, two

Mission date: Day 341.          Teghra-Dorne: Planet fall.

wheeled, customs robot there. It was not true-artificial intelligence, but it was apparently designed to mirror sentience. It struggled more with Jason. Even with the Sendler-Protocol shared, it was not familiar enough with Jason's race, with humanity, for the interaction to avoid being a little clumsy.

This suited Jason. Everything he was sharing, even the breadth of the shared language files, was carefully curated. Nothing could be learned about humanity today. Even if the machine was alarmed by this, it did not share that it was. After a few boring procedural steps, he was pleased when the machine authorised their arrival. Beeped at him, and turned to trundle away on its small wheels.

"Ready team, let's roll out." He was still watching the disappearing robot when he heard the rear-ramp descend, and felt the rumbling as the wheeled vehicle rolled out. The rear-pod, it could carry people, or cargo. Here, it had carried both. The team, and their latest vehicle.

"Ready to go?" Herrick asked.

"Yes." Jason replied. Still distracted, he moved over to sit beside Herrick in the open cockpit. He could see his armour reporting on the warm sunshine, on the cool breeze. Looking into the cloudless sky and at a sun which looked so much like Earth's, he longed to one day move again through a world unencumbered by armour. To feel these things once more against his own skin.

Their ground-vehicle had been dragged together quickly. Modified from the lower chassis of one of Katherine's original exploratory vehicles. An agricultural mess of a thing. But there had been no time to build anything fancier. It had four wheels, a front bench seat, and further benches running along the sides at the back. It reminded him of an ancient amphibious military vehicle from before even his time in the Royal Marines. Although that one had six wheels, and theirs would sink like a stone since they had... effectively, since they had ruined it. It was grey. As innocuous, as boring a colour, as they could imagine.

Innocuous was the key. The shuttle itself was almost unrecognisable. With lift engines on its rigid landing struts, with two larger thrust-engines to its rear. As they drove away, he looked back at the machine. The camouflage was

Mission date: Day 341.　　　　　Teghra-Dorne: Planet fall.

even more extensive than it had been for the meeting with the rebels. Everything was covered with high-carbon titanium. The Heath-Robinson docking attachment bolted onto its starboard flank, only helping to disguise any elegance in its original design.

... and it was not only their vehicles. Their armour. They had needed to retain atmospheric protection, even if the air was almost breathable this time. Covered, where visible, now in blocks of rudimentary technology they had copied to resemble items they had seen during their brief, and eventful, trip to Corkier-Shay. With long fabric robes covering as much of the rest as possible. Whilst hopefully looking as natural as possible. The carbyne of the armour was painted a pleasant pastel blue. Spectrographic analysis should not cause them too much issue... unless someone paid too much attention to their visors. BOB looked the most ridiculous. Hidden beneath a barrel of titanium, and only able to move on small tracks.

"BOB looks like a dustbin." Daniel laughed.

"Jason, Daniel is lucky that I am a pacifist." BOB responded.

Their vehicle moved off the track to the side of the airfield and towards the exit. Or rather, an exit. Their designated exit. This was the first time they saw any function created to enforce authority. A tower, to the top of which was some level of energy-weapon. Emitters, like funnelled radar dishes, which were about ten-feet long and mounted on a dome which could clearly traverse in all directions. Jason had seen images of the indigenous race before. Humanoid-ish, with three legs but oddly only one arm-appendage. Mounted on a shoulder joint which pointed only directly forward. Eight feet tall, and slender. With a head that was perhaps twice as large as a human's would be. One eye, a first, but multi-faceted like an insect's and apparently capable of depth perception. The one hand looked more like a claw than it did a hand. As much a weapon, as it was the limb which first allowed the creatures to develop tools, to evolve. To dominate on their own planet.

There was no breathing gear. Nothing in the way of environmental protection. It was their planet.

Clothes would have been nice, though.

Mission date: Day 341.    Teghra-Dorne: Planet fall.

So would symmetry. Jason realised that he might be a fan of symmetry. But was self-aware enough to know that this was just a little xenophobic.

Christ alone knew why he had first thought to define the things as humanoid-ish.

Everything was electronic. The Sendler protocol, the handshake, also sharing the relevant ID data for the team. All forged, but apparently the forgeries were acceptable. They appeared at the gate and were quickly processed through.

If any of the security personnel were taken aback that the humans were not a species that they had seen before. If they could even tell past their armour, then they didn't show it.

Jason relaxed back in his seat as Herrick piloted their clumsy vehicle along the road separating the spaceport from the city in the distance. From this far out, it could almost have been a city back on Earth. Tall buildings in its centre, and lower ones spreading out from that centre. It was half an hour before they started making their way through what he would have once thought of as suburbia. Buildings, obviously dwellings, lining both sides of the street. Oddly, they were taller than they were wide, and Jason idly considered how that worked. If they wasted space with stairs, or if the species was happier climbing. Otherwise, there were doors. Scaled for the Indigenous people, obviously, but so damned familiar. Windows, too.

So very alien to look at. But the same questions, they often would create the same answers. He hadn't noticed before, not until now. But even back on Corkier-Shay, the first planet, there had been pavements running along the side of the road. Was there even any other way to do it?

Grinning to himself, he continued to stare around him.

The buildings had become taller, although they were, for the most part, still residential. They had passed what clearly had been shops, and something which had appeared to be a school... unusual, but also so oddly very familiar. Either the buildings themselves had become more human-like, or Jason was desensitised to it all, and was concentrating more on the similarities than the

Mission date: Day 341.          Teghra-Dorne: Planet fall.

differences. Although, the native species' insistence on not wearing clothes was wearing on him.

"Jason, we are drawing close to the target's residence." BOB said. Perhaps ten minutes later. "As discussed, we are planning to stop the vehicle at least a hundred yards out, and your team can lose yourselves in the crowd in the arena, whilst I do my bit."

They had not reached the more industrial centre of the city. They had not needed to. Their target lived out in suburbia.

"The hack?" Jason asked. Knowing that he was vastly simplifying what BOB was attempting to achieve. "How does it look?"

"The air is full of data-transitioning from point-to-point. With directed signals between dedicated transmitter-receivers. The encryption level is entirely alien, as is the data. But it is not unfamiliar anymore. I can sniff signals without risk of detection. Breaking the encryption itself, it might take minutes, it might take weeks."

"Weeks?" Jason exclaimed.

"Probably hours," BOB replied. "Hopefully less. With the keys shared by the rebels, it should be minutes... They're less careful here, even than your own twenty-first century. Or perhaps they are less paranoid. Hopefully, both."

"Good stuff. Now, let's go watch the fights." Daniel said. Excitement in his voice. He had already climbed out of the vehicle that Herrick had just parked. The man reversing it between two others, both were far nicer vehicles, in a way which so closely mirrored parking a car in London, that Jason was genuinely shocked.

Because, whilst BOB worked his magic, waiting in the car, camouflaged as whatever piece of utility equipment a passerby might consider him to be, the rest of the team would attempt to blend in at the open-air arena.

An arena which was only a block away from their target's residence.

Because the agent knew something... hopefully. An agent now, he had not always been that. An anthropologist, who had been a scientist for decades.

Mission date: Day 341.　　　　Teghra-Dorne: Planet fall.

One who had apparently travelled more of the known worlds than any other member of the rebellion. Or were they being used to extract a valuable asset?

Jason, and the rest of the wolves out there, they were beginning to really miss their ability to catch someone in a lie.

From the outside, looking in, and the arena looked like any sports arena taken from any city on Earth. Modern, with its structure made from metal frames, and not stone. A steel-carbon composite. Purposeful, circular, and enormous. Two hundred feet high, and a circumference which apparently held a running track almost a kilometre long.

Because sometimes, it was not just about fighting.

Today, though. It was.

The seating areas were structured not about race, not entirely. Instead, they were entirely driven by physiological requirements. They needed to work for whatever creature needed to sit upon them. Creatures who were often of a very different shape. Jason was initially a little taken aback to find himself amongst creatures similar to his own species in appearance and size. That most, those not covered by pelts of fur, were clothed, was nice. Walking alongside familiar bipeds, ones identical to those which they had seen back on Corkier-Shay. Silver spheres for protective helmets, clothes that looked almost like religious robes. He had seen them first on a planet which was also as good as dead. Far closer to the epicentre than Darla, Corkier-Shay would be dead within five years.

The thought left him immediately fighting his fight-or-flight response, which was screaming to him that it was impossible that none here knew that. That some must know that this planet, and everyone on it who did not flee, were also doomed.

Because he was as nervous as hell. As he had ever been. So, he forced himself to instead focus on what was happening in the moment. His three-foot-world. The mission, his team.

Mission date: Day 341.          Teghra-Dorne: Planet fall.

Something which would have been far easier to achieve, if immediately surrounding his three-foot-world, had not been a myriad of alien races he knew nothing of.

They followed the crowd. Also, following the map outlined in a shared interface positioned beyond the Sendler Protocol Buffer. Its firewall. Safe, hugely efficient. The scientist in him was fascinated by such a successful technological achievement.

Their seats were distinctly average. That had not been a priority. Jason didn't care, none of the wolves would. Their eyesight was more than capable of seeing what was happening.

Which was pure carnage.

"So, this is a little more Roman than I had expected." Kate said. Leaning forward, staring at the spectacle unfolding before them.

[This is barbaric,] Alistair said. Horrified. Jason was speechless. Herrick, too. Daniel just seemed to be watching, his face and body position, dispassionate.

\*     \*     \*

Mission date: Day 341.          Teghra-Dorne: Planet fall.

The fighting was barbaric. Alistair had been correct in that. Creatures, most with articulated limbs, ending in what might be analogous to a human hand. They also used weapons.

They were sentient to a level it was impossible to fully quantify whilst they fought for their lives. They were larger than most of the audience, and clearly selected for their brutal strength and ferocity. The spectators wailing, screaming, making whatever noise signified their pleasure and excitement at the gruesome spectacle. Some were giants, and as Jason and the team took their seats, forcing their slightly too large frames into chairs, which were just a little off. Their knees, especially Jason's, were forced just a little too high. They were also forced to lean forward, just a little too far. Their environment packs, mounted to the back of their armour, forcing them all a little further forward than was ideal. Glancing around, Jason saw that many of the other spectators had units which could be removed and rested on the floor before them. Theirs, the human team's solution. It was a one-size-fit-all. Hugely capable, but not hugely comfortable. Chances were, that it was far better technology than most of those brought by the other species. But it would have been nice if they had been able to detach the damned things.

"It's not your height, it's your enormous arse." Daniel leant over and whispered discreetly. The armour's comms kit, capable of making judgement calls about what he was planning to achieve, and replicating that. The link, he assumed, would be restricted to just Daniel and him.

Then Jason heard Kate snort with laughter. Apparently, the armour had been able to more correctly judge what Daniel had planned.

Whatever joviality had spread amongst their group, it was soon crushed by the gradual understanding of the brutal fighting playing out before them for their entertainment.

The creature, clearly a crowd favourite, was surrounded now. Over fifteen feet in height, it stood on bulbous, pink-skinned legs which were wildly disproportionately short for its body. There were, at least, only two. Its upper body had four arms. Radiating out from its central trunk and its head, with four eyes equally spaced around a smaller cylinder of wrinkly pink skin. There was no hair or fur anywhere on it, and except for what had to be providing whatever it was that it needed to breathe, a brutish suitcase sized piece of

Mission date: Day 341.        Teghra-Dorne: Planet fall.

battered metal which was surgically grafted onto its trunk, it was naked. Its pink skin crossed with countless scars from countless battles.

It was larger than the dozen aliens which were attacking it. The closest was a clear five feet, and probably half a metric tonne, smaller. But they were working together to kill it.

An enormous creature, this one covered in bright red hair, but otherwise almost humanoid, leapt through the air to attempt to drive an axe into the central creature. It didn't get there. One arm shot out and caught it by its lower torso, snatching it from its desperate attack and then swinging it into the ground. Once, twice, and by the third strike, the body was flopping against its broken skeleton. Or whatever the clearly dead creature had once used to maintain its body's structure. Two more attacked together. Smaller, rounder with scurrying legs of a number Jason didn't have time to count. Both died whilst he was still processing the red monster's brutal demise.

The arena was behind a huge fence. None of the spectators had a view which would not have needed to first look through the gargantuan structure. The arena was simply sand, stained with bodily fluids from creatures from dozens of worlds. As the giant continued to fight, as it moved forward, towards a weapon rack which extended from the floor and seized two spears almost ten feet long, each, even more attackers, were released into the fray. Now armed with weapons which looked tiny in its massive hands, it surged forwards. Killing, fighting, taking wounds itself. It was only when a spear, a tiny weapon by comparison, was thrown and sunk into one of its eyes' that it finally made a sound. A roaring, screeching sound which was translated for the stunned audience.

"Help me!"

Jason felt his heart tearing.

The crowd roared, jeered, called out for blood in a dozen languages. Then, finally, the creature killed the last.

For a moment, there was silence, and Jason dared hope that it was all over. Then there was a stamping sound as the audience beat against the stadium in a terrible rhythm. Their calls starting soon after. 'encore' 'final' 'family'... all of

Mission date: Day 341.   Teghra-Dorne: Planet fall.

which lacked context until Jason saw another structure rising from the beneath the sand. Cleverly hidden mechanisms rising through a hidden doorway. Then, when all was done, there stood a large pole in the ground and tied to it a far smaller version of the surviving creature. Struggling against its chains. It cried, faintly. Within his armour, and without his armour's enhanced audio, Jason would have missed it.

"Parent, help."

It was clearly a child, clearly that of the surviving gladiator, and Jason felt himself surging to his feet as a dozen more aliens, all armed, were released into the arena. A powerful hand grasped his shoulder. Forcing him back down. He didn't test it, immediately aware that his reaction was not thought through. That the alien behind him was protecting him, not the horrific events unfolding before him. He turned and nodded to the being behind him. Knowing already that it was one of the humanoid figures, the ones wearing the silver spheres over their heads.

Jason commanded his suit to reach out across the Sendler Protocol. A little taken aback that the protocol did not seem to recognise them.

Then a message, plain text, appeared before him in his own helmet's display.

'Be careful, human, do not allow yourself to become noticed here. Not too soon, not for the wrong reason. You cannot fight every battle, you cannot right every wrong.'

A sentiment he was intimately familiar, and one which had been a mantra for much of his impossible life. It had also appeared the wrong side of the protocol's firewall. Both things were terrifying.

"Do we need to talk?" Jason asked. Confused, but not feeling under threat.

"Not yet. We will find you when it is time. Besides, I believe that you have other places to be right now." It answered.

Jason was wondering what to say to that cryptic bullshit when he saw the alert on his display. It was from BOB. Things were about to get damned exciting.

Mission date: Day 341.  Teghra-Dorne: Planet fall.

Jason stood, raised two hands towards the alien behind him, and mimed two pistols firing.

"Catch you later, alligator." Jason said. He would never know why he did that.

\*     \*     \*

Mission date: Day 341.   Running and gunning.

## Running and gunning.

"So, what's happened?" Jason called over the comms as the small team fought their way off the stands and down the stairs leading towards the arena's exit. Forcing from his mind what was happening behind him. Forcing their way through the throng of excited onlookers. Not freaks, just unfamiliar… not monster's, either. Apart from those fascinated by the spectacle in the arena. They were monsters. He glanced quickly behind him. Daniel, Herrick and Kate were hot on his heels.

"The local authorities are aware of the rebel agent. They have been for a while now. Things became a little more exciting when news of the failed ambush at the rebels' planet reached them. Apparently, there was fast-courier, a specialist FTL-capable vessel. It got here an hour ago. It wasn't much slower than us." BOB updated the team.

"Okay, what's there now and what is coming?" Jason asked.

"We have local police only. But there are more troops on their way." BOB replied.

Jason increased his speed into a slow jog. Not quite fast enough to panic the aliens he was moving past. But quick enough to draw attention to their small group. Just hopefully, it would not be the wrong sort of attention.

"Straight to the car, arm up and we move directly to the house. We get our friend, and we get the hell out of Dodge. Daniel, Herrick, you two take the back. Kate, you're with me. BOB, can you paint the authorities on our HUDs?" Jason asked.

"I can," BOB responded, and Jason saw the icons populating before him. They were still five hundred metres out, so the figures were indistinct. Within neighbouring buildings. Another warning, this one telling them of the larger team's approach. This time there were two ground-vehicles, and two airborne. By the time they had arrived at their own vehicle, BOB was already

Mission date: Day 341.            Running and gunning.

waiting at the back, and he quickly opened the hidden compartment at its rear. Their weapon load-out revealed.

Daniel and Herrick grabbed their weapons. Daniel holstering his enormous pistol under his robes, and even he relented and grabbed a railgun. They both disappeared along the side-street, making their way to the target's property from the rear. Jason knew that they would be spotted at any moment. That they may already have been. Momentarily indecisive, he saw that Kate was already armed and had jumped into the driver's seat. Jason jumped into the passenger's. Noticing that she, like he, had grabbed her sword. Looking up, he saw the highlighted images of the police painted within two buildings opposite the one they would need to reach. They all seemed to be preparing themselves. Presumably for the vehicles, which were currently less than five minutes out.

He had to assume that some, or likely all, of those vehicles were full of troops.

"BOB, I imagine that they are monitored. But we have to risk it. Send the message the rebels gave us, and we then have to hope that our new friend trusts us." Jason said.

"Done, and it was detected immediately. Chatter from the authorities has just raised the alarm. I am afraid that the cat is out of the bag."

"Shit, let's move people." Jason said. "Drones skyward. One each, and let them work out their own disposal patterns between themselves." He felt the pop from his shoulder as he released his own contribution. Sending the tiny device on its way. Reflecting, and not for the first time, that his wonder was not only about the complicated things which the technology could do. It was also how the tech could be asked to do those complicated things, simply.

Things were about to get exciting.

*    *    *

Mission date: Day 341.        Running and gunning.

The armoured figures that surged from the watchers' house were hurrying on their three legs. Jason's mind lazily drawing comparisons to Cordax and his team. How differently those aliens had moved on their own three legs'. Cordax, his people. They had used the centre leg for power, and it had looked like the two to the side were mostly for steering. These aliens, their legs rippled side to side with each stride. The single arm was still distracting. At least these were clothed. Although, this was mostly armour.

The heavily armed team were heading directly toward the building, where their contact was currently hiding. Moments away, and far closer than they were. Kate drove the heavy vehicle directly at them. Jason braced himself, only realising what was happening as she smashed into three of them. The car slewed around, its front shrugging off the impact. But the motor driving the wheels to the left fizzed alarmingly.

Looking ahead, he saw one of the figures pushing itself upright, clumsily doing so with its one arm, before its central leg folded straight forward and pivoted impossibly. It was horrifyingly alien to watch. It turned its armoured face toward Jason, shouting in a fury his armour entirely failed to translate. He raised his railgun and fired. The alien's armour shrugging off the shots with a worrying ease.

Jason had his weapon to four, he moved it up to eight and only the second shot made it through. Killing the thing. He switched it to eleven.

Kate had already exited, and the world seemed to slow as Jason swung himself free of the vehicle himself. Leaping over the side of their ruined car, landing hard, and moving fast across the road to flank the threat. Two were down already, one smashed under their vehicle, and the one he had just shot. Five others surrounded the car, and Jason watched as a pivoted weapon swung free of the backs of each of the clearly startled troopers. A noise from his right caught his attention, and cursing, he rolled fast across the ground as weapon fire hunted for him, crashed past him. Rising to his feet again, he took a quick aim at the creature who had almost successfully ambushed him. A short burst from his railgun into its torso, and he watched it fall. Wondering why it had only become visible to his armour at the last moment.

"Full power to beat their armour," Jason called over the comms, as he spun on his heel to bring his weapon to bear on a second target. Putting two

Mission date: Day 341.                     Running and gunning.

through its face. The shot, which struck him in his back a heartbeat later, it slammed him forward with terrific force. Picking him up and tossing him through the air like a child's toy. His armour screaming its warning as the shields barely absorbed the blast. He was attempting to turn himself, to land well, but didn't have time before he crashed into the floor. Skidding for several feet effectively on his face. Alerts flashing across his display before him.

"Plasma, sodding plasma!" Jason shouted. "Luckily, they're not focussing the weapons. The impact is dispersed enough. Our shields can catch most of it... but it hits hard."

[... that still bloody hurt.] Alistair quipped.

[Just our pride... this armour, these shields are enough to make a difference. The wolf, we still seem to react faster, move faster...] Jason replied. Watching from the corner of his eye as Kate rolled across the ground blindingly fast, about twenty feet away, keeping ahead of the confused creatures as she fired into their midst with her own weapon. [For example,] Jason had regained enough of his composure and killed another himself.

"This was fortunate timing," Jason shouted as he dived for cover behind a sturdy-looking wall which ran around their target's home.

"Fortunate timing would be us arriving yesterday, and missing all this excitement entirely." Daniel called back from the other side of the house. There was firing from there, too.

But no matter how powerful their foes had been, surprise had been on the side of the human team. Enough to have made a difference, and moments later it was done. It appeared done.

Jason raced to the house. Very conscious of the approaching vehicles. Very aware of his rapidly shrinking timeline. Barely aware that BOB had ejected himself from his disguise and was moving quickly across the ground on his three articulated legs. Crashing into the building's wall and drawing himself as flat as possible. Jason didn't know if it was still a deliberate affectation, or if the delighted pixelated face was now just reflecting his friend's actual mood.

Mission date: Day 341.                Running and gunning.

"Jason, you're on fire." BOB said. Jason checked his robes and found them to be enthusiastically burning away. He tore them free and threw them across the small front yard.

"BOB, get the Pequod heading away from the planet as fast as possible." He ordered. Leaving BOB to sort out the details with the larger ship's crew. "Cleo, we are going to need a pickup. Come in cloaked, but do not hang about. We are going to need an exit."

[That bush, it looks like a rose-bush... that is so odd.] Alistair said. Jason, attempting to ignore his permanent passenger, failed, looked over and couldn't help but to agree.

Kate was knocking frantically on the door. It cracked opened slightly, and she clearly grew bored and kicked it in. Surging in immediately afterwards.

Jason followed her.

"Herrick, Daniel, cover the front, and watch out for the other forces." Jason ordered the men, who had already fought their way to the back of the house. "They're not far out. It is going to get messy."

"On it," Herrick replied for both of them.

\*   \*   \*

Mission date: Day 341.         Running and gunning.


Herrick allowed for his bio-tech to move forward almost fully. His body, just over a year ago it had struggled to keep up. Deep enough into his fifties to be really feeling it, and he had been fighting to keep himself fit enough, strong enough, to still be relevant. He had looked for jobs which would require less from him. He had been looking forward to retirement.

Of course, that had been about the time he had followed his boss over to an island just off Greece... A gig which should have proven to be relaxing, as specialists in such things had faced the problem of dragging an enormous cargo ship off a beach.

Now, with his body enhanced, changed. Pushed through millennia of evolution, humanity would never have needed to achieve. He was stronger, faster, than he had any right to be. His armour was adding to everything. The technology allowing him to be immediately aware of... very worrying things which would likely soon try to kill him. He had just engaged with alien police in a brutal fight that had left three dead at his own hands.

Herrick had sprinted from the rear of the house, and was back at the car, pulling out the heavier weapons, and readying himself to potentially fight off ground and air-attack vehicles. On an alien planet, far across an ancient version of his own galaxy.

Because, once upon a time, the problem of the beached ship had seemed like it might actually be the most unusual thing he would ever see.

He laughed to himself, ruefully, as he prepared the shoulder-mounted missile-launcher. Inserting its magazine. Four missiles. Readying himself to face whatever the universe threw at him next.

Ground vehicles, they would not come into line-of-sight, not for a little over a minute yet. The airborne forces were further out, but moving faster, and were only seconds away. Daniel was pulling free a heavy railgun. Herrick trusted that the terrifying bastard would know what to do.

Sprinting fast toward the closest house, he leapt high and caught himself with his armour's zero-g and flight functions. Battling against the additional weight of the launcher, but the complicated systems ran the maths and landed him

Mission date: Day 341.                    Running and gunning.

precisely where he wanted to be. Even if the whole thing had seemed horribly ungainly.

The roof was flat. He was genuinely delighted to see the same water-damage and puddling which had killed his own garage roof a half dozen times since he had bought the place from his father. The pleasure he found in that moment, that aliens might also make the same dumb-ass mistakes, helped to ground him.

He had initialised the launcher as he had collected it, and he forced himself to control his breathing as he raised the weapon skyward. Looking out, across the rooftops of a city on an alien world, seeing just buildings, homes, streets populated by vehicles which were equal parts terrifyingly unfamiliar, as they were instantly recognisable. The two attack-vehicles were surging toward him. About two kilometres out. Both were sitting underneath two rotor-pods, which extended away from their hulls on articulated arms. There were mounting solutions for what looked to be missiles, alongside the tubular block of white... something. He drew a bead on the first and fired.

Because things had already gone loud and there was no time to fuck about. He watched in dismay as the missile was destroyed before it reached his target, and immediately fired two more.

The attacking flying machine was either too close, or struggled more because he had fired two, but it only stopped one. The other hit it directly in its fuselage, and it exploded into burning chunks in mid-air, barely five-hundred yards from him.

The second was on him before he could swing the weapon over to fire against it. Overflying the building only moments after he had thrown himself clear. Firing some sort of chaotic weaponry at the very spot where he had just been standing.

He had dropped the launcher as he frantically dumped power into his flight module. Powering himself as quickly as possible skyward. The explosion caught him and tossed him through the air like a rag-doll. But safely, with his shielding and the carbyne absorbing the shrapnel and energy. He righted himself before he landed, crashing into the ground. Cushioning his momentum on knees, which would have shattered in his last life.

Mission date: Day 341.  Running and gunning.

Disorientated, but barely as his bio-tech forced him to focus, he pulled his railgun free, selected the flying assault-vehicle as a target, and tracked it through the air.

It swung round, ignoring his weapon's fire, and faced him...

Herrick accepted that this was where he died, when the aircraft burst into flames and fell crashing to the ground before him.

The Thunder-Child hammering into the cloud of smoke, to hover before him.

"I believe someone called in for an exit?" Cleo called over the comms.

\*  \*  \*

Mission date: Day 341.                Running and gunning.

"We're friends, Babalich-ThrunderArch sent us to find you." Jason said. His arms held high, and his weapon slung. Attempting to placate the angry...

It was a seven-foot-tall teddy-bear. One who was staring at him with dark red eyes, and baring teeth which looked a lot less friendly than the rest of him. Brown fur with patterns of fawn. Long legs, thankfully only two, and two powerful arms. The jaw was damned terrifying, too, Jason thought as he attempted to process everything horribly quickly.

Looking to the rebel spy's side, Jason spotted the smaller version moving to its parent to cling to its right leg.

"The handshake checks out. But I do not recognise you." It bellowed. The human-team were all immediately supplied with real-time translation. It was wearing some sort of block around its neck on a looped metallic chain, a small ear-piece in its right-ear. Jason assumed it was its Sendler-Device.

"There was a double agent. The Teghra-Dorne empire has known of you for weeks. They were watching you from across the street. They're dead. There are more coming. We are here to get you out," Jason replied.

They hadn't been. Originally, the plan would have been to warn the bugger he was at risk, and to be paid back with the information they needed.

The explosions from outside that followed, they helped Jason sell his story. The enormous noise of the Thunder-Child's ferocious arrival sealed it.

"Okay, my son, he is coming with me." The alien shouted above the racket.

"Agreed, but we also need information that apparently only you have. Bring that, too, and follow me." Jason replied.

Daniel had come in from the front door, his railgun slung, and his preferred plasma-pistol in his right hand. Clearly taken aback by the talking teddy-bear.

"Jason, we are fucking off?" He rumbled.

"Right now. We go right now," Jason ordered. Nodding toward the figure before him. "We will keep you alive. We will keep your son alive. Grab some food, grab what you need to breathe, and follow me now."

Mission date: Day 341.          Running and gunning.

The fluffy bear did not need to be told twice... whatever was in the bag it grabbed and slung over its shoulder; Jason assumed it would be everything the two would need.

*   *   *

# Mission date: Day 341.  Running and gunning.

"Jason, we have bogies moving fast towards us. Moving clear to draw their fire." Cleo shouted.

She was already surging skyward, drawing the missiles, fired against her, away from the besieged suburban street. Still, some hit. Blowing a building opposite Jason into a fiery crater. Others landed streets away. Deafening, but their damage hidden from their perspective on the ground. Seconds later, and a swarm of fast-moving aircraft exploded past. Jason watched as half of the aircraft pulled a tight-enough turn to convince him that they were bypassing a chunk of Newtonian physics themselves.

Which wasn't good.

Jason moved fast between the still burning wreckage of the recently downed attack-helicopter-thing and the bodies of the soldiers already killed earlier. Herrick was crouching behind a sturdy-looking piece of wreckage, and was firing toward the approaching tracked war-vehicle with the much-larger railgun that Flaherty preferred. It was chewing into the heavy armour, but it was not chewing through.

"Jason, we need to get out of here... Cleo left a special-package." Herrick said. Nodding behind him.

"Yes, bless her, she did." Jason smiled.

The speeder-bikes, four of them, were hovering a few inches of the ground just to their side.

"What's your name?" Jason shouted. Asking a question, the answer to which he already knew.

"Karma-Yermic-Tata," the bear responded.

"Good, nice to meet you... I am Jason... This machine, it should carry you and your son. Right hand is throttle, twist the grip. The right-trigger is braking. Left twist-grip changes altitude and whilst turning the bars will turn the thing, I suggest leaning with it. Body weight and position do far more than the bars ever will. I hope you're a fast learner." Jason shouted back. Really hoping the translation had not screwed up this one. "Kate, on with me and pillion. Everyone, we are leaving now." Jason leapt onto the vehicle, feeling it sag

Mission date: Day 341.	Running and gunning.

slightly as it compensated for his weight. He felt Kate's weight adding to it, and the reassuring pressure of her leaning against his back. Looking around and Daniel was already on his, firing toward the approaching troops with his pistol. Jason could not see his face, but he knew his oldest friend would be having a whale of a time.

Because the man was not right in the head.

"Herrick, we are leaving." Jason shouted. Watching as the man moved swiftly backwards, staying in cover from the approaching horde, and climbed upon his own vehicle. "BOB, get on there with Herrick. Watch our backs and help us with a route out of here." Jason was pleased to see BOB surging across to Herrick, and attaching himself to the bike's rear. He did so by tearing holes in its fuselage, and Jason could only assume that BOB would know what bits not to break.

"Kate," Jason directed this only to her, "Sync, with our new friend's bike, if you need to, help him not die."

"On it, Jason." Kate replied.

Jason looked over to Karma-Yermic-Tata, the creature nodding back to him from the speeder-bike, doing so in an oddly human fashion. His child was sitting on his lap, grabbing its parent's pelt firmly and looking suitably terrified.

"Right team, off we fuck..." Jason shouted, and opened up the taps.

\*    \*    \*

Mission date: Day 341.　　　　　Running and gunning.

The speeder bikes were little more than Dani's own special project. They were not designed for war. They were designed for messing about and tearing ludicrously fast across a planet's surface. But they had been designed by a Marine, so there was absolutely that, too. Dani had used one to escape the rebels' stronghold on the Iron-Moon, following her rescue of Kate. The machine had been critical then. These would be now.

They were fast.

Bloody fast.

He had a route calculated. BOB had done as he had been asked, and now there were highlighted maps portrayed in his eye-line. The world was tearing past him, and with the rest of the team showing themselves capable of keeping up, he increased his speed still faster. Feeling the air-pressure telegraphed carefully to him by his armour, feeling Kate holding on a little tighter.

"Tell me if anyone has a problem, if there is anything I need to know. Otherwise, focus on not dying." Jason ordered. Very conscious that he could not verbally communicate with their new allies. He forgave himself for not sharing some level of comms. There had been a lot going on.

BOB had picked longer, straighter streets. Deliberately picking a route which would allow their vehicles' performance to maximise its benefit to them. The streets which tore past to either side of him were wide. Filled with alien vehicles, it was child's play for them to fly over. They stayed as low as possible. The power required to keep the vehicles close to the ground was significantly less than it would be just a dozen feet higher. Power which could be pointed forward, rather than down.

So, it was a mixture of absolutely terrifying and fabulously exciting.

There was an intersection ahead, one which BOB was very keen for them to take. Jason banked his speeder, pushing its undercarriage, its lift module there, toward the outside of the turn. Feeling his weight compressing him into the seat, as they chewed through an easy six-g of force. The others followed. Karma-Yermic-Tata, able to replicate the same manoeuvre flawlessly. A fast learner, and clearly prodigiously strong. Jason risked a glance back, and saw

Mission date: Day 341.          Running and gunning.

the fluffy-bear with its fur flattened against its powerful skull, and a massive toothy smile painted across its face.

That was good. Or it was unhinged. Possibly a bit of both.

"Okay, BOB. Where are we going?"

"Space-Port, we are breaking for the shuttle. At these speeds, providing we don't need to change our route, we are five-minutes out." BOB answered.

"Can we make it through the security there?" Jason asked.

"We don't need to." BOB replied. "I am bringing the shuttle to us."

"Was there anything in the car which might betray us, which might share technology we would not want known?" Jason asked.

BOB did not answer immediately. Seconds later, he did.

"Not anymore."

Jason's feed letting him know about what BOB had just done to their abandoned vehicle.

Seconds later, and things went to shit. Just a little bit further.

Weapon fire exploded into the street before him. Smashing into the vehicles there, which Jason knew to be full of civilians. The Teghra-Dorne military did not seem to have an issue with collateral damage. His HUD alerted him to the attacking aircraft. One more of the rotor-vehicles that Herrick had killed earlier. That he had only seen the wreckage of himself.

"Kate, is there anything you can do?" He shouted to his passenger.

"I will try," she replied.

Jason felt her shifting on her seat, and immediately firing her weapon. It was firing slowly. Likely meaning she had it set to full-power.

Mission date: Day 341.	Running and gunning.

"Jason, it's not enough. I am afraid I am going to have to do this the other way." Jason felt his seat lighten, the speeder-bike climbing as the weight it was carrying, suddenly lessened.

Then she was gone.

"Daniel, Herrick, get Tata to the shuttle and if you can, come back for us. But do not risk the mission. Tata and his son, they're the mission." He ordered, swinging his own vehicle into a tight, braking arc, as he brought it to a stop. Diving skyward himself.

The armour's-flight was incredible, and although this was the first time he had used it in anger, he was stunned by how effortless it felt. The vehicle hammered toward him as he used everything he had to power through the same hole Kate had already made in its windshield. This time, he did not draw his railgun. This time, he pulled his sword free from its sheath.

The pilots were dead. Kate had clearly killed one as she had crashed into the cockpit. Possibly just crushing it where it sat as she had smashed into it. The other, its head, was at an angle that no creature should easily be able to survive. She had already forced her way into the rear of the craft, and as Jason burst through, he saw her driving her own blade into one of the heavily armoured soldier-creatures. Finding a gap in the plates. It was a terrible melee, close-quarters fighting of the most brutal form. The robes covering her armour billowing as she flowed through the cabin. There were two others already dead on the floor. As she moved forward, Jason saw one of the surviving creatures holding some sort of firearm up in its one arm, levelled against the back of Kate's head, and firing it. Jason heard himself screaming in fury as he closed the gap, smashing down on the alien's only arm with his own sword, severing it. Driving his elbow into its head, he smashed his foot into the same spot as it staggered backwards. Kate was down. He had no time to check on her. There were an easy half-dozen of the creatures still fighting. Roaring with fury, Jason let the wolf have its head, and went to furious work.

Mission date: Day 341. Running and gunning.

\*   \*   \*

Mission date: Day 341.　　　　Running and gunning.

Kate was not dead. His armour was constantly speaking with his own, and he knew this immediately. But she was massively concussed. Jason had pulled her unconscious body away from the carnage he had left behind him in the cabin. The back of her helmet was scorched, layers of the carbyne had been ablated away. But it had not broken through. His own armour was sticky with the viscous yellow-orange substance he now knew to be the blood of the aliens he had just killed.

He had her over his shoulder as a dead weight and was just about to climb free of the aircraft when it smashed into the ground. Realising, only at that exact moment, what the strident alarms his armour had been sharing with him had meant.

It was not a soft landing, and it took precious minutes for him to pull himself out of the wreckage. Emerging with a still-groggy Kate, back into sunlight.

Staggering to the side of the eerily quiet street, Jason summoned the speeder-bike as he frantically searched for news of the rest of the team. Including the Thunder-Child.

The shuttle hove into view as the bike arrived, as he received an update from Cleo. She was not having a great deal of fun, but she was keeping a lot of attention from them. So, there was at least that.

Kate helped him to bring the bike onboard, joining Herrick and Karma-Yermic-Tata, and his son, who were both already buttoned up in their seats. The adult alien barely fitting into the generous space.

"Who is flying?" Jason asked.

"Daniel," Herrick answered.

"So, we are absolutely going to die..." Jason replied as he felt the machine surge skyward. "Hey, are you okay breathing this stuff?" He added. This last was directed at Karma-Yermic-Tata, who hadn't worn any level of breathing apparatus since they had met.

Mission date: Day 341.     Running and gunning.

"My species, we are happy to breathe almost anywhere. Just as long as there is oxygen." The alien replied. Holding up its thumb and little finger to either side of its clenched fist, and waggling its enormous paw.

[Jason, be careful. It is a big cuddly teddy-bear who apparently seems to be a surfer. It is important to remember that we do not know this creature, that it is not a cuddly teddy-bear who was ever a surfer.] Alistair advised.

[True, but you have to admit that was pretty cool,] Jason replied.

[Okay, yes. I can admit that was cool.] Alistair replied.

Jason leant back in his seat as Daniel continued to fire the shuttle directly upward. Not bothering with the pantomime of the solid-fuel engines and instead pushing the gravity-drive to full tick. Pleased that his oldest friend had not killed them all on take-off, Jason reflected that they might survive this one.

Possibly.

\*     \*     \*

Mission date: Day 341.  Fight and flight.

## Fight and flight.

Cleo pulled the Thunder-Child through a tight-turn, attempting to shake the atmospheric craft from her tail. Failing to do so. They were damned fast. The starship shuddered, as fire raked across her rear-shields. More than a little worried that their attempt to draw as much of the planet's atmospheric fighters, away from the ground-team, had been perhaps a little too successful, and might easily kill them.

"Ship, chart the shield's strength, and warn before anything becomes critical. Update on the close-defence. Are you confident we can keep their missiles off us?"

"Maverik, I am confident that I can continue to defeat their missiles. Shields are holding for now. But the power is degrading faster than we can replenish. The advice is to evade the attackers' fire more effectively." The computer's synthetic voice was familiar, even if the crew were more used to speaking with the AI through BOB. It was not sentient, but it was advanced and now understood its human crew, their capabilities, and many of their nuances, far better.

"Okay, wonderful. Everyone is a sodding critic. Impact, Crater, how are you two getting on?" She called out. Shouting to the two gunners, fighting to maintain control as the ship shuddered as her energy shields struggled to resist more enemy fire.

"We are not making enough of a difference. There are too damned many of them and you keep moving the bloody ship. For every one of them we kill, another two seem to take its place." Impact hollered back. "The turret's systems, even our own augments, they can't see the bloody things. We have needed to disable most. We're doing this by eye…"

As if to illustrate his point, both of his points, Cleo was forced to dive hard for the ground as a destructive wave of fire almost overwhelmed the starship. Continuing to arrow the Thunder-Child downwards for over ten-thousand

Mission date: Day 341.	Fight and flight.

feet, to stay ahead of a second group of aircraft which came at her from the sun.

"Ship, why the hell did we not detect them?" She asked. Desperately scanning the mountainous terrain below. Only levelling off as she approached the level of the summits. An incredible landscape of towering mountains, incredibly closely packed. She had an idea, and she mulled it over as she awaited her answer. The current state of the landscape, far below, would make it impossible for a little while longer.

It was not her worst idea... Patience; she needed that. Because if the enemy could only come at them without missiles, it was time to make them work harder, still.

It was not a great idea. I just wasn't her worst.

"They have a level of stealth. Excellent passive technology, we spotted that immediately. But they are using something active which I do not yet understand." The ship replied. "It is very effective,"

"Update, Cleo. Are you able to listen?" Natalie asked over the comms.

"I am, hit me." Cleo replied.

"These are assumptions. But based on good intel."

"Natalie, it's cool. There are no absolutes." Cleo fired back.

"So, they can manoeuvre like us. If not to quite the same level, and with nothing like our level of fidelity. They do not care as much about gravitational inconveniences as almost everything else we have seen out here. But they still do, to a level. They will struggle to cushion their crew as effectively as us. They also can't do what they're doing for long. We have detected evidence of fusion power in the aircraft, which will melt-down in less than half an hour, unless they dial it back. Although, obviously, that is more than long-enough to kill us,"

"Natalie, thank you. Are you working on a thing?"

Mission date: Day 341.     Fight and flight.

"Cleo, we are working on a thing." Natalie replied. "We have a small margin where our capabilities are stronger. We will need to move the fight into those margins."

"Good. Can you hurry, please? Ship. Were you able to map the ground-clutter ahead of us whilst we were at altitude?"

"Maverick, we have solid predictive maps of over ninety percent of what's down there. I advise against doing this." The computer replied. Second guessing her intention.

"But you saw what I saw?"

"I did, but I strongly advise..."

Cleo watched the terrifying scenery moving below her. Took three deep breaths. Making the call only as she actually did it and taking the devil of a chance. Diving hard into the towering mountain range which dominated the planet's surface between her and the distant ocean. Moments later, and now at less than two hundred feet, she was forced to manoeuvre violently to navigate the canyon she was flying through. Her speed plummeted, but she watched her monitors and saw the aircraft gathering in her wake. The sides of the mountains, which were hammering past to their port and starboard, towered above them now by kilometres. Snow, and dead-rock to either side... and mere feet below her belly, forests marching alongside a fast-moving river. Terrifying mountains which would kill them in a heartbeat if her attention wavered. But mountains, which might just keep them alive. Because she had seen a way through.

"Ship, watch out for attacks from above. It's harder now, but not impossible. Expect more missiles. Gunners, watch the canyon and the skies. This should funnel those dumb enough to follow. Natalie, Colm, any closer?"

"Okay, there might be a way where we can put them all exactly where we want them. Watch this space. I have to be sure we can detect them properly. What they're capable of, it should be impossible... not unless they're far closer to us in technology than we realised. But we think that we have seen a pattern. Keep us alive. I am working on this," Natalie replied from the control room behind the cockpit.

Mission date: Day 341.              Fight and flight.

"Colm?" Cleo asked the older Marine.

"It is a better plan than anything I have come up with. I am assisting." Colm replied.

The close-defence solution roared, and Cleo watched on in horror as the Thunder-Child was buffeted by enormous explosions which had detonated worryingly close to her hull. Fighting to keep the starship from smashing into the valley's floor as the concussive forces pushed her downward.

They had shields... At least the enemy did not have shields.

"Ship, we are three-minutes from running out of ground-cover, then we will be out over the ocean. Can we get more speed than we had last time we were running in clear skies?" Cleo asked.

"Not enough to out-run our pursuers. Not in an atmosphere." The ship replied.

"Is the ground-team out of the atmosphere in their shuttle, yet? Or do we need to keep running interference?" She asked.

"They are airborne, but they are also in trouble." The ship replied.

Shit.

"Natalie, we need your plan." Cleo demanded. Her voice strained.

"Got it, on your display now, and we have a new button." Natalie replied.

"What does it do?" Cleo replied. Frantically working the stick, forced to use the rudder pedals to turn the Thunder-Child as the scenery flashed past, horrifying close, and horrifyingly fast. The starship responding flawlessly. The damned thing was magnificent.

"When they brake hard, we can see them. There is an intense flair we can lock onto if they burn hot enough, for long enough. We just need to brake harder." Natalie replied. "The button says you're happy. It will stop us just as fast as it can do so. But only when the ship is happy that none of our friends behind us

Mission date: Day 341.  Fight and flight.

will immediately smash into us... then we paint them with the missiles, then... we kill them."

"They will fly right by..." Cleo said. A smile on her face, which only dimmed slightly as the shields were peppered again with fast moving ordnance. "Right, I am going to be a little erratic, and hopefully I can gather them behind us. Impact, Crater, get ready to paint everything you can. Authorise all firing solutions. We are the hunters now, and we eat what we kill."

She knew that the last bit made almost no sense.

\*   \*   \*

Mission date: Day 341.  Fight and flight.

The Thunder-Child erupted from the towering mountain range which had led to the ocean. Each had been larger than most of their contemporaries would have been on Earth, far larger. A difference which might have been down to the slightly lower gravity, or perhaps simply a very different tectonic history. Magnificent, objectively stunning. All totally irrelevant from the moment that they were clear. The starship firing itself forwards using its thrust engines. But complemented fully by its Chasers, and cheating relativistic physics with great enthusiasm.

Normally enough. Typically, far more than enough.

Today it wasn't.

The dappled sunlight which reflected the clear sky upon the fresh-water ocean sparkled in the fierce midday light. Painted upon that ocean were the tiny, silhouetted images of the Thunder-Child, and those of the smaller pursuing atmospheric fighter-craft. Almost two dozen advanced machines, whose sleeker fuselage and unusually powerful engines, gave them the match on the far larger fleeing starship. Each reflected image was distorted by the undulating surface.

But the Thunder-Child could still climb a little harder, turn just a little faster, and she erupted into the sky. Only to be immediately followed by the horde of fighters.

None of the craft had been close enough to the water to disturb the ocean's surface with the wake of their passing, and soon, even their reflections were lost. Long seconds later, and the hypersonic boom of each, combined to fill the air with a furious sound. Disturbing the tranquil world and sending panicking sea-bird analogues surging into the sky themselves.

The Thunder-Child reached the apogee of her climb, a little over thirty-thousand feet, rolling onto her back and immediately fled hard for the planet's south-pole. Her pursuers were now seconds further behind, gathering into a formation which allowed each to fire upon their quarry. Few had any missiles left, and those that did had learned that those weapons would not reach their enemy. But they had cannon. Those, they could tell that

Mission date: Day 341.    Fight and flight.

those weapons were eroding the energy-field technology that protected their target.

A few died, targeted and hit by the turrets which flowed around the circumference of the enormous craft on some insane track. But the pilots trusted their technology, that it would continue to hide them. They would mourn their fallen, but they understood that those had been lost to chance.

Because their enemy could not understand how easily their technology could be tricked.

It was only a matter of time.

Then the starship stopped. One instant it was travelling in the high-hypersonic range. The next, and it wasn't. They did not use humanity's measurements. But had they, and the Teghra-Dorne aircraft, would have seen the vehicle drop from a shade under six-thousand knots, to a standstill. Doing so, inside of two-nautical miles. They all reacted almost immediately, themselves. Braking hard with technology that had only recently been developed. Each pilot put through almost enough g-force to render them unconscious, but shielded from orders of magnitude more. Still, every one of them blew past the stationary starship still at supersonic speeds, their engines flaring before them to kill their own terrific velocity. Radiating energy at enormous temperatures. None realising their catastrophic error before it was too late.

Because it was then that the starship reached out with its own furious anger.

Inside her hull, missiles which had been refined, shrunk, refined again. Perfected over the brief handful of years that the Thunder-Child had existed. Each was now only a little over two feet long. Feeding into their launch-tubes from automated magazines which held dozens in each. Four missile tubes, each firing two of the deadly weapons at each of the targets they could finally see. Doing so instantly, they had pulled ahead far enough to do so. The two tear-dropped-shaped gunner-seats, opening fire with their weapon systems only moments later. The armoured figures within, working their cannons with deadly intent.

Mission date: Day 341.          Fight and flight.

The sky blazed with terrible fire. With the explosions of almost two-dozen aircraft, dying. Smoke following much of the wreckage as it plummeted toward the ocean, far below.

"Confirmed kill. Every pursuing fighter has been downed. We have only a half dozen bogies in our sky now, and they are too far out to reach us before we get to the shuttle." Natalie quickly updated the team from the control room.

"Confirm. Ship, are we close to understanding a little better how to see these fighters?" Cleo asked.

"A little. That helped. Bear with me, it could be a little while." The ship replied.

"That might not be soon enough. Where is the shuttle now?" Cleo asked.

"She is exiting the upper-bands of the atmosphere and is climbing out of range of the fighters which were pursuing her. It does not appear that they are designed to fly outside of an atmosphere." The ship replied.

"Thank you." Cleo replied. Climbing skyward. "Team, we are cloaking, and I am moving over to Chasers only. The time for pretence is over. We get our friends, and we get the hell out of Dodge."

*   *   *

Mission date: Day 341.  Capture

## Capture

They had not got far. The shuttle's cluttered hull had corrupted her cloaking tech, and their attempt to sneak out past the fleet had failed.

Catastrophically.

"We cannot move... we are being restrained by some sort of energy field." BOB reported. Jason moving fast through to the cockpit to help Daniel, processed this, and the terrifying visage now filling the sky before him, as he sat down.

"It's some sort of tractor-beam." Daniel shouted over, fighting a clearly futile fight with the shuddering shuttle. Its controls, its engines. Nothing, it seemed, was doing what they were supposed to do. Nothing Daniel was trying was helping.

"Tractor-beams are not a thing." Jason corrected. Looking across to BOB.

"Jason, it is an energetic dampening force which is collapsing our gravity-field from the Chaser-module. That is useless, and we don't have near enough power from our thrust engines to compensate. It is also pulling us toward that damned capital ship," BOB replied. stealing Jason's favourite swear-word.

"See, a tractor-beam." Daniel repeated.

"What's occurring?" Herrick asked. Appearing in the cockpit's hatch as Jason threw himself into the spare chair.

"A tractor-beam," Daniel replied. "Although, apparently, they're not a thing."

"So why can we not fly away?" Herrick asked.

"A tractor beam... Okay, it is a damned tractor-beam." Jason replied as he frantically tried, and failed, to understand the readings the shuttle was pushing at them. "Pequod, if you can still hear us, they are far more powerful than we thought. Get out of here..."

Mission date: Day 341.  Capture

The Pequod would not reply. She would not risk discovery, and Jason knew that his team there would get that crew to safety. That they would continue their original mission if they could not make the rendezvous themselves. So, there was that... at least.

"This is the Thunder-Child. Do you want us to bugger off, too?" Cleo's voice came through.

"Christ, no. Come and rescue us," Jason hollered back. Before taking a moment to centre himself. "Scrub that, Cleo, get the Thunder-Child to safety. Rendezvous with the Pequod and complete the mission. There is nothing you can do for us now."

"That is a crappy order, Jason."

"But it was an order," Jason replied.

He didn't get an answer. He hoped she would not do something stupid. But thought she still might.

Staring ahead, the shuttle's passengers, those able to stare through the cockpit's canopy, watched in horror as they were drawn towards a vast opening hatch on the belly of an enormous warship. A plate of armoured hull, itself easily two-hundred meters square, and which swept aside as they drew closer. Forty-feet thick of carbon-metal alloy.

The warship itself was the now familiar wedge-shape, but was hanging in space, stationary above the planet's surface. Doing so, with no outwardly visible sign of propulsion. One of the advanced warships that Cleo had warned of earlier, as they had approached the planet's capital. It was enormous, kilometres long.

The hatch had revealed an enormous hangar beyond it. Fighter craft hanging from racks against the far wall, looking for all the world like the mechanism of a terrifying vending machine. Larger craft were parked across the floor. Some were built for war, still others which were far more utilitarian. Crucially, there was an open area to the far right of the gigantic room near the towering bulkhead. Empty of anything at all, but encircled by armoured troops. With walker-type armoured vehicles amongst them.

Mission date: Day 341.          Capture

Not a million miles away in design from their own Tanks. But these had three legs, and only one mechanised arm. Like with their own Tanks, it was immediately obvious that the Orga-Loathe'clichemere people, the Teghra-Dorne empire, based some of their fighting machines after their own physiology.

They passed through a hazy-event border which was somehow projected across the opening in the warship's hull. As they passed through it, Jason saw alerts flashing across a display just out of his line of sight. Warning of an energy field of some type. Immediately they were on the other side, Jason saw a report of a pressurised atmosphere...

"Orac told you that atmospheric shielding was difficult to achieve. Not impossible." BOB said. Clearly guessing where Jason's mind was going.

"Team, we might be screwed." Jason whispered. "But they want to take us alive. Otherwise, we would be dead already. Arm yourselves. We will not find an easy-day waiting for us here. Nor is it likely that we will survive this one. However, we can fight harder than they might ever imagine. We can be magnificent bastards in our last moments." He looked over at Kate, meeting her eyes. She could so easily read him. He knew that.

"We will be magnificent." Kate said. Reaching over and grasping his armoured hand in her own.

"So, sneaking back in time and not getting involved once we arrived. How is that plan holding up? Daniel asked. His helmet re-sealing around his head. Having to hold his too long beard to stop it from fouling against the mechanism.

"Not hugely brilliantly at this moment." Jason admitted. The helmet; he hadn't processed the man had opened the bloody thing. The decontamination threats... hell, they had two aliens in the cabin behind the cockpit. They also had far larger problems.

"Where is the Thunder-Child?" Daniel asked.

"Hopefully, they are already far away and still running hard." Jason replied, grimly. Finally shutting down the shuttle's engines and allowing the

Mission date: Day 341.　　　　Capture

shuddering machine to finally settle. "You wouldn't want them steeling our fun, would you?"

"Honestly, I would not mind." Daniel grinned at him through his clear visor and winked.

[Once more into the breach, dear friends.] Alistair said. Jason felt trepidation there. But also excitement at the prospect of a proper fight.

Waiting now for the inevitable, the team watched as the shuttle continued deeper inside. Moving slowly toward its fate.

Then, after long minutes, a text-only message appeared before each of them. [We had an idea. There was, perhaps, one thing we could still do to change. Delay your exit from the shuttle and wait for a timer.]

Unnecessarily cryptic. Either the Thunder-Child thought their comms might be intercepted, or their idea was so messed-up, they had not wanted to share it.

"Fuck me," Herrick swore. "I will get our passengers ready."

\*　　　\*　　　\*

Mission date: Day 341.                    Capture

"Unknown vessel. You are under arrest by order of the Teghra-Dorne empire and you are currently held upon our flagship 'Strenuous'. You have taken violent action against our safety officers on our planet, you have killed many within our air-force, and you are carrying with you two spies who are guilty of high-treason. We order your surrender." The voice said. Echoing through the shuttle's hull. Transmitting itself through their own speakers as their comms system security failed them.

Jason was just considering this, when a countdown from two-minutes appeared on the display inside his armour.

"You all are seeing this?" Jason asked. Looking round, he saw nodding heads.

"Jason, team. The hatch into space, it is opening again behind us. The soldiers waiting for us out there… they appear surprised. I am seeing confused activity around us. This might be our window." BOB said.

"The shuttle is still disabled. The only way is… Christ!" Daniel said. The last exclamation coming as weapon fire tore into the shuttle.

"Stop your current actions, or you will be destroyed." Came the order from outside.

Jason rushed across to the comms.

"This is the shuttle 'Cuddly Peace'. We are taking no actions against you, or your ship, whatsoever. Please stop firing at us," Jason said. Kate looked over at him, mouthing, 'cuddly peace?' Jason shrugged.

The weapon fire against their hull did not stop. If anything, it intensified. Jason knew that by now their titanium skin would have been blown through. Their camouflage ruined. The miracle-material which actually made up her structure below, would now be visible. That even that would be showing substantial damage already. If this gave the commanders of the warship pause, or their scientists, they did not relay that to those who were currently firing at them. Then they all felt the shuttle hit the ground. Harder than any of them expected, and Jason needed to grab a nearby rail to stop himself from falling.

Mission date: Day 341.        Capture

"Fuck me Jason, we need to exit," Herrick shouted over the din.

"We wait for the timer. We trust the team." Jason replied. Shrugging. "Does our new friend want a weapon?"

"He took my big gun," Herrick said. Hefting his smaller railgun. "We need to protect his son..." The old Delta operator could not ignore the plight of the child.

The timer ticked down, the last minute so impossibly slowly as the small shuttle continued to rock under the onslaught. Then it reached zero, then a new message appeared.

[Go, now. We have your backs. Operation Harry Potter's Cloak...] The message came through.

Which sounded like it might be promising.

\*        \*        \*

Mission date: Day 341.          Capture

The sheer extent of open space over Jason's left shoulder was terrifying. Even buttoned up in his armour. The shuttle's ramp had dropped clear, and he had erupted onto the deck of the warship's hangar. There were a dozen armed troopers before him. Wearing what appeared to be even sturdier armour than those they had fought planet-side. His own weapon was turned all the way up to eleven, and even then, not every shot punched through.

But their own armour had charged in the shuttle. Everyone with armour was on full shields, and as those first away from the shuttle were immediately bathed in a deluge of plasma-weapon fire, this proved to be a good thing.

Jason watched in horror, as he saw his shields first struggling, and then faltering... but he had sensed something. Daniel had to, so had Kate. Through the noise, the chaos, as they had erupted onto the decking outside of their refuge. They had detected the unmistakable presence of moon-rock hugely close.

"Follow me, it's the Thunder-Child," He ordered. His voice was full of glee as his eyes, fighting to see through the horrendous energy of the burning matter which continued to strike at him, spotted the unmistakable distortion of his starship's cloak just feet away.

Then, below the shimmering illusion.... Below the mirage, crafted with energy even his own keen scientific mind had struggled to understand, dropping below that, were the unmistakable shapes of two Tanks.

"Captain, we will cover. Please get to the drop-room," Natalie called.

Then the cloak dropped away, and a wall of energy shielding erupted before the suddenly revealed Thunder-Child. The starship entirely magnificent in its glorious power. The two weapon turrets were on her dorsal surface, and they tore into the hanger with savage fury. He thought he saw several of the fighter craft attempting to launch, but they were ripped to pieces, still in their cradles.

Both Tanks carried only the powerful railguns. One on each shoulder. Dual wielding the weapons for the first time, opening up against the handful of soldiers who had found themselves within the shield's influence. Those, they did not struggle with the alien troopers' armour as he had. Running across the

Mission date: Day 341.    Capture

floor, watching as Daniel and Herrick accompanied their new friend and his son, Jason sprinted for the ship. BOB moving faster than any of them. They made it to the drop room, clambering up the ladder there. The two Tanks attached themselves to their harnesses' again, and were dragged back into the drop-room moments later.

"Jason, all onboard. Sorry we could not share the plan. The risk was that they could intercept and break our encryption," Cleo shouted. "We are going to break for space. This thing can still kill us. Can I have your permission to use a TOAM? To leave a present?"

"Christ, okay... go for it. It's not like we're making friends here, anyway." Jason said. "Hold, where will the wreckage land if we destroy this damned thing?"

"We are over the ocean. Providing we kill her engines with the blast, she should fall directly downward." BOB responded.

"Okay, well, screw them, and their fucking fish." Jason replied. Greenlighting Cleo's plan.

"Didn't we technically attack them?" Kate asked. Speaking for the first time in a little while. "We're not necessarily the aggrieved party here."

"I never really did enjoy context. Certainly, when it is used against me," Jason replied. He pulled himself over to the emergency restraints situated against the otherwise empty wall beside the drop room's interior hatch. Opposite where the Tanks hung in their cradles. Helping Karma-Yermic-Tata and his son to restrain themselves as best they could. The rest of the team doing the same. Kate bracing herself beside him. Holding his hand. "What was the Harry Potter reference? Was that a code?" He whispered over.

"Jason, yes, it was a code. Even dad got that one... Harry Potter, his cloak of invisibility?... Jason, have you never watched the movies... did you never read the books?" She looked at him with surprise. Squeezing his hand tighter.

That felt good.

"Your missions suck." Daniel growled.

Mission date: Day 341.          Capture

"Bullshit, old man. You had a whale of a time." Jason replied. Winking at his friend.

"Yeah, well, I am not right in the head." Daniel replied. Winking back. "For God's sake, strap yourselves down!" he bellowed.

[Topol, Zarkov…. Flash Gordon, nice.] Alistair said. Jason smiling back.

"Cleo, get us out of here!" Jason ordered… a completely redundant order as the Thunder-Child was already swinging free from the shattered hangar-bay.

\*     \*     \*

Mission date: Day 341.   Capture

In the end, the Thunder-Child was briefly slowed by the warship's tractor-beam. A brutal tug-of-war. Jason would never find out if it were her engines or the exploding tactical nuke, which freed them.

Cleo had not fired it as a missile. Rather, she had merely ejected it onto the hangar deck. Leaving it behind. The warship was immense, singularly the most powerful ship they had encountered so far. Since the Progenitor fleet in the far-future. But nothing flying could survive a nuke going off within its hull.

Once free of the warship, they cloaked as it died and ran hard for the outer system. Docking with the Pequod, who had been waiting for them out there.

Fleeing into FTL only moments later.

\*   \*   \*

Mission Date: Day 342. Transit.

## Mission Date: Day 342.

### Transit.

The days that followed were difficult.

The Thunder-Child had been evacuated by those who had not been planet-side. They were now onboard the Pequod. The fighting ship was now a quarantine zone. They had two new guests. Alien guests.

Unknowns, with bodies potentially teaming with micro-organisms, any of which could prove horrifyingly dangerous to the human-team.

Karma-Yermic-Tata, and his son Karma-Tata-Ye, were taking it in their stride. Still shaken that they have been plucked from almost certain death.

But they were safe. Even if such determinations were always subjective, they were relatively safe. The docked starships were riding the rainbow and hammering away from Darla, the Teghra-Dorne Empire's home-world. On a very specific course.

Herrick, Jason, Kate and Daniel were restricted into the forward section of the Thunder-Child. Jason and Kate were still in their own cabins, the two within what had once been the guest suite. Daniel, he had somehow managed to retain separate quarters onboard both ships, and was entirely happy in his. It was only Herrick, whose cabin had been on the wrong side of the bulkhead. He was borrowing Neil's. To the other side, Tata and his son were sectioned off into a dedicated space, chosen because it also included the medical-bay. Creating a space where their two guests could stay. Where they could be run through a barrage of tests until the human crew could be sure of everyone's safety.

BOB was with the two Tarka-Jebshate. Working the science.

This was not a new concept. The eventual, almost inevitable, necessity of taking this step had been prepared for. Hell, even the original colony ships to

Mission Date: Day 342.                    Transit.

Epsilon had been along this path centuries earlier. Although most of those plans had fallen to the way-side, after the explosions, the death and the survivor's fiery descent to the planet onboard whatever was left which was still capable of the attempt.

It was possible, even probable, that it may already be safe to walk upon an alien planet if the atmosphere was not toxic, with no need of environmental suits or their armour. So confident were they of their medical advances, the evolutionary steps they had been pushed through, and the tailored micro-bots, which coursed through the bloodstreams of the modified humans. If not yet the wolves.

The wolves, their claim, it was still that they could survive almost anything. This was a harder thing to prove. Nebulous, even if, in an uncertain universe, it was understood perhaps as well as it ever could be. For magic, this existed in the gaps between scientific knowledge and gods.

But wood-chippers, they might one day come as little more than a tiny bacterium.

The crew, they were clean, themselves. Cleared of anything which they might inadvertently carry with them. Something that had been implemented, even before the Sendler Protocol had shared that requirement with them. They had already known that they would need to avoid any chance of inadvertently wiping out an entire planet.

Obviously.

Or, with interstellar transit, a common thing… half a bloody galaxy.

Their guests would have followed the same protocol. They were theoretically clean, too. But the human crew were still not fully comfortable, completely trusting such things.

Trust, but verify. 'Probable', it was not a word without wriggle-room.

BOB had also been able to easily identify, and then formulate, meals to match the dietary requirements of the agent and his son. They were living on water and a grey-paste, which was very similar to that which the original crew,

Mission Date: Day 342.                    Transit.

rescued and taken onboard the Ark a lifetime ago now, had once learned to enjoy themselves.

They were, as Tata had promised, entirely happy with the atmospheric make-up of the starships.

Adaptable buggers.

Jason had asked BOB about this. The rest of the team had been equally fascinated. Asking how long their new friends could live like this. Bob had shrugged.

"Indefinitely."

Which was a hell of a thing.

It was days before the first doors opened. Not between the Pequod and the Thunder-Child, not at first. Just the doors separating the isolating ground team and their guests.

\*       \*       \*

## Mission Date: Day 346.

### Conversation.

In the end, it was four days before Jason could finally sit before with new passengers.

It was perhaps still pushing things a little. But they had needed to talk, and the risk would never drop all the way to zero. Jason was delighted to finally be sitting before Tata and his son. Able to study their new friends, not encumbered by either his armour or a comms-link. The enormous bear had a pleasant smell. Like lilies and woodland. He smelt of nature.

"We are already well on our way, Jason. Have you told the crew where, yet?" Tata asked.

"Not yet," Jason replied. "Not all of them,"

Tata raised an eyebrow. Jason noticing for the first time that the alien had any eyebrows.

"I like that you were careful, with possible contamination... That we waited this long to sit together. To break bread... I like that phrase. Your being as careful as you were, it suggests that you are new to this all, which is interesting... either you are not used to meeting other races, or you haven't had this technology for long. Also, I don't recognise you, your species. Which, although unlikely, is not impossible. However, I do not think that you are from around here. Then there is the other thing. Whilst you are terrified of tiny little critters that might kill you, you fought with a ferocity and bravery the like I have not seen in centuries... bravery when facing combat... a propensity for it, which is rare." Tata said. Barely pausing between bites. "This is superb." He added. Waving toward the grey-paste. "

Jason laughed. His Sendler unit plugged into his right ear was doing a wonderful job of keeping up. Only a little jealous of his teammates' internalised bio-technology, which made the whole thing practically seamless.

Mission Date: Day 346.          Conversation.

But Tata and his son, neither of them, had any internalised technology, either. Both relying on devices not entirely dissimilar to his own. In function, if not in form.

"It was all we had for months ourselves. Different, tailored for our needs, instead… We will know more about what you can eat from our more standard food shortly. Although…" Jason replied. Ignoring Tata's other probing comments.

"Although, we all evolve alongside the nutrients which were available upon our own worlds. A horrifyingly large amount of food out there is entirely toxic to other races. My race, my son and I, we are different. We are the galaxy's favoured survivors. Born to push into the great-unknown… we are tougher than most." For a moment, the enormous teddy-bear stared wistfully toward the bulkhead over Jason's right shoulder. Lost in thought. The moment oddly human. "But even we need to be careful. To us, to have a food so specifically tailored to meet our bodies' needs… it is wonderful. Besides, did you not warn me to bring food of my own?" Tata replied.

"That I did, my friend," Jason replied. Delighted when Tata leant back in his seat and unleashed a demented belly laugh. One that Jason was getting far more used to. Although, this was the first time he had seen it outside of the holographic video-link. This close, it was also terrifying.

They were in the small mess on the Thunder-Child. Not uncomfortable, despite it being far more utilitarian than the Pequod's more wonderful expansive spaces. Just a series of booths along one wall, and the food-prep area on the other. Little more than a row of cabinets built into the wall. Each cubby-hole presenting whatever the crew member had wanted to eat. Not quite Star-Trek level replicators. If you wanted something other than the paste, you needed to request it at least an hour earlier…

Or an MRE. Flaherty had dragged a holdall full of them from the compound on Hermentia. Now, there was a solid stock. MRE 'Meals Ready to EAT', it had taken him back to his service days back on Earth. He was still thinking jealously of the Pequod's full kitchen when he realised his own attention had drifted away.

Mission Date: Day 346.     Conversation.

"Why a rebellion? Why fight the empire at all?" Jason asked.

"It is difficult, where resources and territory are contested. Where there is value to one species, there is inevitably to another. They grew faster, first, and they laid claim to vast swathes of the local systems before many other races had even left their own planet's surface. Testing waters.... I like that phrase of yours, human. We must all be careful dipping our toes into unfamiliar waters," Tata replied. "Other races tested those waters, perhaps some did it too aggressively. Perhaps the response was disproportionately strong... You saw their arena... They are a cruel race. But they are not only a cruel race... Just the other side of things."

"I understand. We have wars on our own planet. Based on borders, resources and beliefs... Beliefs have often been the most dangerous. But borders form around a connected people, and so do ideologies. It is easy to conflate one cause for the other..." Jason started.

"My friend, this is a story repeated by almost every sentient race yet found..." Tata interrupted. "These ideologies?"

"... I wonder if you have gods... I guess you do. The Sendler Protocol found the word and translated it. Many, almost all, of our ideologies were based around gods. Gods, created by more primitive humans, looking with wonder at the world that surrounded them all, and searching for answers. The first humans, those who built the first societies, and finding that those societies needed rules, would imagine those rules being greater than themselves. Laws are easier to follow if the laws come from God, not man... Fear of others, fear of the barbarian at their gate... beliefs, formed centuries ago by people who really should have feared barbarians at their gates. Barbaric times need barbaric people... It is difficult if those beliefs are never questioned later. That a people who once rightly feared their neighbour might include that fear within their ideology as a righteous anger and hold on to that anger long past the point where it served them, and to where all it does is tear the world apart. Because those who feared their neighbours... too often their neighbours also feared them. Often for just as good a reason." Jason said. Losing himself a little. "Science came, and gods were forced into the gaps between the true understanding of what governs the physical world, and

Mission Date: Day 346.   Conversation.

what was still not yet known. The gods lived only in the gaps. Those gaps shrank. But they never went away entirely."

"Stories, as old as time. That talisman you wear, Jason." Tata indicated Jason's gold locket around his neck. "That others amongst you wear... I think that has power. I also think that there is a little magic in you, too. Isn't there Jason? Not all of you, but some. I am a creature of science, but I have travelled many worlds, and I have seen many things. Not everything out here sits comfortably within science's embrace. Even my people, we have our gods, just as you do... Only," Tata paused, leant forward, and winked. "Mine are real." He leant back and roared with laughter. Before suddenly stopping. The mirth evaporating from his broad face. "Only, they are..." His voice was deadly serious. Before immediately lightening again. "So, your team... your people. You are not from around here, are you?" Tata asked this again. His huge round face, suddenly far more serious. Jason looked at the creature. His enormous mouth, large teeth and powerful jaw. His skull was huge. His mood changes were an emotional rollercoaster to behold.

But he also looked a lot like a teddy-bear. Which helped.

"We are not." Jason replied, carefully.

"... and your ships. They have capabilities beyond their size. Beyond the capability of a race so unused to existing amongst others. You defeated the empire's flagship. That should not have been a straightforward thing to do. Nor would it ever be something advisable to do. They are powerful enemies to make," Tata said. "It makes me think that perhaps you are not planning on hanging around."

"We can always run faster. We have only bumped heads here, where there have been things we needed to do. There are only a few of those things left. To be fair, we defeated them with a nuclear warhead. We did cheat quite a bit," Jason replied.

"Why did you come for me?" Tata asked. "Why are you so keen to go where you really should not go?"

"These are where things get a little less, certain... We received intelligence that someone amongst your rebellion would recognise the amulet. We were

Mission Date: Day 346.          Conversation.

led to believe, by the leader of your rebel-group, by Babalich-ThrunderArch, that this was likely you. We are supposed to go to where you pointed us next." Jason replied. It was not the whole truth. But it was also not strictly a lie, either.

"No one is supposed to go there, my friend. Certainly not now."

"... and absolutely not later." Jason added.

"No, absolutely not later... I have travelled far and wide... and I recognised that pretty necklace your friend wears. As I told you, I have only seen its like, once. Although, only from orbit, and using powerful cameras."

"... and despite everything, you are happy to come with us?" Jason asked.

"Happy, it is possibly a word which was not translated very well. My life, it is not what I have wanted it to be. It hasn't been so for years. Personally, I am not looking to fight anymore. The fight has left me... After that last mission finished, I was hoping to drift away into a peaceful retirement." Tata's face lit up when the Sendler Protocol so quickly found the translation. "Retire... such a wonderful thought. But I can embrace perhaps one last adventure... and I still have questions I would still like to ask of this place you are looking to visit. Even if those questions might kill me, I am still keen to ask them. Also, I need to keep you alive. These starships of yours they may be the only answer for my family's survival. On Darla, where you found me, I was on one last mission, and I only took on that mission because we were promised a way out. I took it to save my son," Tata said.

"Because you know what is coming..." Jason said. This time, very carefully.

"Few do. Even if it is only days away now. Although, perhaps more of your annoyingly short days than they would be of mine." The bear grinned. "The knowledge of the event, any knowledge, it is carefully compartmentalised. It needed to be. It is vital to avoid panic across all the known worlds. There is nothing that can be done to save everyone. There is little to be gained by terrifying everyone. We have FTL, but nothing that can travel far enough... Perhaps, if it had been seen sooner..." Tata paused, leaning forward. "Of course, rumour is the bad thing that hides in shadows. It is said that it has been known about for centuries. That those races who first saw it, they have

Mission Date: Day 346.          Conversation.

already enacted plans which will save their elite... contemptible creatures to so easily sacrifice so many of their own. But then, when I find out for myself... When I came to understand that I could not save my people... I decide to save just my family, instead. When there are no good options, do we not all become a little contemptible?" Tata finished. Looking across at his son. Seated only a few feet away, eating his own dinner. His eyes glistening. Again, oddly human.

"It is not impossible. But contempt, it is, by definition, subjective." Jason replied.

"Pah, you are too timid to judge me, Jason. But do not worry. I take care of that myself. I just take care of my son first," Tata said. Reaching across, picking up, and then downing the water in his glass. Holding it up before Jason. "There are worlds out there, where even having water to drink is a luxury... Here, you live with magical machines, which I suspect make such concerns... no longer concerns." He was inspecting the empty glass himself, before looking back across the table. "So, Jason. You needed something from me. The rebellion, their promise of a seat on their transport... That, I think, was probably smoke and mirrors anyway..."

"You didn't trust them... Yet, you took the mission?" Jason asked.

"I took the mission. A remote chance is better than none. So, Jason... can you do better than none?"

"I can do better than none. We have the legs on this starship to stay ahead of the event. We can offer you both passage here, and to anywhere you want to go. Within reason. The other ship, the Pequod, we have sections, relatively sizable unused sections, which we can even tailor the environment to more closely match your species. Your own requirements. The ships themselves, neither of them, are vast. Although the Pequod is far larger than the Thunder-Child... but we are a small team. We have space for you. We can make space for you."

"What if we have no-where else to go? What if we wanted to stay?" Tata asked.

"That is an interesting question... We would not abandon you." Jason replied.

Mission Date: Day 346.         Conversation.

"Unless we misbehaved?"

"Our responses to that would only ever be proportionate." Jason replied.

"So, we can reach an understanding. Providing we don't all die during what you plan to do next?"

"Providing, we don't all die." Jason replied.

"Because you seem intent on testing just how far your luck will hold."

"Don't we just?" Jason grinned.

"Okay, Jason… Then I believe we have the beginnings of a deal." Tata smiled back.

\*     \*     \*

Mission Date: Day 348. We must hurry.

## Mission Date: Day 348.

## We must hurry.

Two days later. The entire crew finally re-united.

"So, what, or who, the hell are we looking for when we get there?" Katherine asked. Unmistakable frustration in her voice. "I thought we might perhaps get a few more answers."

"I do not know. The amulet, it is not speaking anymore. Not after Tata told us about the planet." Kate replied. Placing the amulet on the table before her. The tiny thing vibrating busily against its surface. It actually moved a few inches before Kate snatched it up again. "It is just doing that now."

The room was silent. Staring at it in her hand.

Tata and his son were watching on dispassionately. Jason knew that they were unlikely to speak during the meeting. But they were part of the mission now. They should be here.

"We were pulled back here, to the moments before this part of the galaxy is effectively sterilised... At the epicentre of perhaps the most violent event to strike this galaxy, possibly since its creation. For what reason? What is it that your magic eight-ball does not want to tell us?" Katherine asked pretty much the same question again. Her voice was a little more heated. Jason hoped that the veiled reference to time-travel, lacked enough context to be ignored by their new guests.

"Honestly, I do not know... It has almost become a weird mantra, for Jason and me, to say that it has been that sort of life... We say it... because it has been, and so many times we have acted so completely on-faith... and sometimes, just because how the fate-fuckery of it all struggles for any other explanation. We say it because it is amusing... but it is also, so very often, fucking exhausting." Kate answered. Her words, perhaps a little jumbled. They were heartfelt. The strain in her voice, her face, was clear to everyone there.

Mission Date: Day 348.     We must hurry.

"I dragged you on our first mission. Now I feel like I am dragging you all of at a tangent, and I can't tell any of you why…"

"This diversion, at least it is a little less dreadful than our original purpose," Flaherty spoke up. The quiet young man rarely doing so in the larger meetings. "I, for one, am happy to put off that other thing, even if it is only for a little while."

There were murmurings of agreement which rippled through the room.

"I say we do it… Everything we have done since we got here. From those first moments where we all stared out of the window to see our galaxy whole… From the outside, looking in. Through every piece of barbaric violence. Every tragic moment when all of us have stared at the charts which show the star which will soon end, everything. Which will destroy civilisations beyond count. We do it, because a magic-eight ball tells us to. We do not stop now, just because we do not know the end-point… Besides, what can go wrong?" Jennifer said. Laughing to herself as she finished. She was leaning back against the side of a booth's table, her beautiful brown skin reflecting the pulsing rainbow moving past the window above her. A very large whisky was held in her left hand. A cigar held in her right. Colm was sitting in the booth. Clare was there tucking into a pizza with Alice. Both girls were paying scant attention. Not even Clare, to her drunk mother.

"It is a fair point. A fair question, too. I have been chasing shadows, and the monsters which hide amongst those shadows, for too many years now." Julien said. He looked at the transparent dome above their heads. Watching the colours surging past. Feeling everyone's eyes following his. "Chasing rainbows, those too. Doing so, only ever to see what lies at their end. Often to be disappointed to find more horrific things there, than ever hid in shadow… An incurable curiosity which has been a bane of my life. We have come so far, perhaps a little too far, but I have learned to trust Jason, Kate…" He paused. "I say we do it. At the very least, it will be interesting."

"It is not about trusting them, though, is it?" Crater asked. "It is about what they are trusting."

"Then we trust their judgement," Julien shrugged.

Mission Date: Day 348.    We must hurry.

"What are the risks?" Impact asked.

"If we do this thing?" Jason asked. Impact nodded.

"Tata has shared enough, albeit perhaps not everything. There is intelligence there, one that guards our destination. But they have only ever once acted to destroy those who arrive there... and that was an aggression which was started by the visitor." Jason said. "The others, they were simply sent on their way."

"That we know of," Crater said. "But the others were sent on their way. Is it not likely that we will face the same, that we will be sent on our way, too? We could just be wasting our time."

"We hope that we can sneak in. We have struggled against stealth tech since we have arrived here. But we have encountered nothing yet, even approaching the capability of ours." Kate added. "Also, whatever else happens, whoever awaits us there, we expect them to be distracted when we get there."

"Why would they be distracted?" Julien asked. The man studying the amulet that Kate was holding now in her hand. It was clearly still vibrating. Jason thought it likely the policeman had guessed the truth of it. Or, if not yet, that he was about to.

"... because there is the other thing." Jason said. Grimacing, as he looked at the room.

"No, I am not even going to ask. Because of course it sodding is... why wouldn't it be? I mean... all I did was find a fucking diary and now... decades later and I am somehow onboard a starship and racing to reach a planet which is going to be destroyed by an enormous rouge star colliding with its own sun... You know, I used to defend coincidences... Hell, they happen all the time and we even have a word for them... To me, this is pushing things a little too far."

"Racing to reach?" Jennifer asked.

Mission Date: Day 348.					We must hurry.

"Where do you think we are all already heading to?" Julien said. Indicating the rainbow again.

"We have already set course. We are already heading there at maximum speed..." Katherine said. Stepping in. A star-map, a holographic 3-D representation of the spiral arm appeared before them all. The two docked ships were clearly marked. So was their destination... So was the approaching star to their destination. The star was far closer than they were. "Our best guess is that we can get to the system between forty-eight and seventy-two hours before it happens."

"Your worst guess? What happens if we get there as it happens, or immediately afterwards?" Hacker asked.

"From here, we know as much as we can. But we can drop out of FTL a light-year away and take better measurements there... we will not risk that." Katherine replied.

"... and, you're sure? Because I watched enough Star-Trek to know that it would make a wonderful episode to show the Enterprise being pulled out of warp by a local nova-event, and then trying to survive the onslaught of ludicrous amounts of radiation as her shield's failed." Hacker added.

"I am sure. I believe I can say, with confidence, that we are ninety-eight percent certain to survive the trip." BOB replied.

"That last two percent. It can be a real bastard," Hacker suggested.

"Can't it though?" BOB replied.

"Shall we have a vote?" Jason asked.

"We are already going there, though, aren't we?" Hacker pointed out. "Is having a vote now, not a little redundant?"

"No, this last piece... as soon as we learned where we would need to go, and the significance of when we would get there, we needed to set course and run hard toward it... immediately. If we hadn't, the last window would have closed already. But we always planned to put this to a vote. We can always stop and go back on our original mission." Jason replied.

Mission Date: Day 348.   We must hurry.

"Our terrible purpose?" Daniel asked.

"That still needs to be done." Jason replied.

"You are not going to simply order this?" Jennifer asked, looking toward both Jason and Katherine.

"No, not this time." Jason replied. "This time, we agree."

\*   \*   \*

## Mission Date: Day 374.

## Forbidden.

Twenty-six days later. After a frantic dash towards the galaxy's edge, and toward the edge of one of the outermost systems there, something began to happen. A section of space, so far out that the star itself shone barely brighter than the others in the sky, it seemed to distort. The distant objects in the background warped further, as if they were being looked at through the rippling surface of a lake. Incredibly localised, impossible to understand and at first it was not even real. Not in the strictest sense of the word. But it became real, and the distortion increased and began to pulse outward from its centre. Moments passed, really just seconds, before a tear opened within the corrupted space. A corrupted ball, with flaring edges of intense Hawking radiation. From within that patch of space surged two starships, one riding on the back of the other. Exploding from nowhere, and finding themselves suddenly somewhere for the first time since yesterday, when they had briefly stopped to ensure they would not die immediately, today. Belting through the vacuum of space at incredible speeds. Heading toward the distant star as its gravitational effect was gradually allowed to exert its influence upon the combined ships, even if only slightly.

As they moved away from the focal point of the event, ahead of them rippled chaotic energies in all directions. Doing so at the speed of light.

They had arrived.

If anyone was watching, to them it would not have been a subtle arrival.

\*   \*   \*

Mission Date: Day 374.     Forbidden.

"Emergence, and split. Thunder-Child separation in five-four-three-two…." Katherine called over the comms.

"One… and separate. Going dark. Pequod, good luck." Jason finished. From the Thunder-Child's stick as he disengaged from the larger vessel.

"Watch over us, and we will watch over you, too." Katherine whispered. But by now, they were not even risking the tight-beam laser comm-link.

"Dani, TT. Remember, we are not hiding. We wait a half-hour, then we reach out with a Sendler-Handshake. Jansen, what are we seeing out there?"

"We have a main-sequence yellow-dwarf star… About 1.08 Solar-Mass. We have the large, extraordinarily obvious, and entirely terrifying elephant, which is barging its way into the room. Loudly. We have one planet and its moon, which is visible. We are seeing nothing else," Jansen replied. Turning away from his station to face his captain. "Katherine, there is nothing else… With the obvious caveat that there could be something else on the other side of the star. There is no equivalence of the Kuiper Belt. There are no other planets visible. We were told to expect this, but… Nothing here computes with any other known star-system."

"The planet?"

"It appears to have a similar mass to Earth's. Its orbit from its star, it is within a fraction of a percent of that of Earth to its sun. It has a moon, again it is a long way out… but it is very close…" Jansen finished.

"Do we have time?"

"If we hurry, bear with me…" Jansen buried himself into his console. Summers moved over to work with him. Standing over him.

"Barely, and only because we believe our destination on the planet itself will be on the other side from that star… when it gets there… we are down to where simple fortuitous events, such as that… matter far more than they should. It is going to be very close, Katherine." Summers said, only seconds later."

"… will the Thunder-Child know this, too?"

Mission Date: Day 374.  Forbidden.

"They will,"

"Jennifer?" Katherine asked. Looking across to where the retired president was standing with her daughter.

"I can sense it now… It is not our moon. But it calls out with a song of its own." Jennifer replied. Moving forwards to stand immediately before the vast transparent dome which encapsulated the bridge. Raising her hand to point dead ahead. To the smaller of the two brightest stars, although Katherine knew she was pointing instead at something close to it. "Similar, but similar does not mean the same… Katherine, it is trying to hide from us… also, its song…. It is not a kind song."

"Mum, I can feel it too. It knows we are here, and it wants us to stay away," Clare said. Standing beside Clare was Alice. The two were inseparable now, and so was Ye. Developmentally, he seemed to be of a similar age to the two children. Larger than both. A little over six-feet tall. His body not yet having developed the ferocity of his father, he looked like the cutest thing in the world. Katherine briefly remembered back to Natalie squealing, and proclaiming that the alien was a Care-Bear. Some sort of toy from her own youth. She had apologised since. To the child and his father. Both had found it amusing.

But whilst his father was on the Thunder-Child, joining in with that mission. They were looking after his kid. Katherine thought about the mission. A moon with wants… perhaps a level of sentience, and if it could detect Jennifer and her daughter, could it not detect the wolves on Jason's team?

…. Perhaps the cloak would hide them from that, too?

"Okay, we keep going for now. I want to hear anything you hear, see, or feel… Please." Katherine said. "Dr Summers?"

"The approaching star, we can all see it… it is easily visible…" Her voice was choked. "Its colour, it is like a blue fire… but the orange that is also there, that is its imminent death. It's coming at an impossible speed, and it is… We must be careful…"

The Pequod's AI took over, highlighting the small, yellow-dwarf-star and, just to its left, the far larger, but still far more distant, star. Burning a fierce blue in

Mission Date: Day 374.            Forbidden.

the sky. Highlighted, with its movement and course marked. Everyone on the bridge could detect its movement, just with their naked eyes.

"We must be careful..." Katherine mused. "Or rather, we should be. It is a damned shame that we can't be. Not and succeed in what we must do here."

"A little piece of wee just came out," Colm said.

"Mission clock updated, and it's on the screen now... We hit zero, and we are dead. We reach the red, and we will probably die. The two stars will pull on each other's orbit to where that planet, and anything on it, are destroyed..." Summers said. "A sliding scale of horrible things, until everything goes boom. Our Chaser-Drives and relativistic shielding are strong. But I would recommend against testing them against what is going to happen here anymore than we need to.... We need to break physics, for our toys to work. What is about to happen here is physics dying."

"Okay, will the Thunder-Child be able to make the same call?" Katherine asked. Looking at the mission clock and not seeing as much time there as they had hoped. Perhaps enough... It should be, providing nothing went too badly wrong.

"They will," Summers replied.

"Good, as soon as we have pushed our active scans out to about one light-hour, I want us heading downhill, faster. One more pulse every half hour after that. Five percent acceleration until we reach eight-hundred thousand knots. We don't want to show any of our hands we don't need to. If something has seen us already, and with our emergence from FTL, we assume they have... let's make sure that we're nice and visible." Katherine leant back in her seat. Sipping from her coffee and staring straight ahead. "Remember people, we are the bait. Here to draw the attention of whoever watches over this system, but not their wrath."

"Aye, Captain." Dani said from the helm.

\*       \*       \*

Mission Date: Day 374.          Sneaking in.

## Sneaking in.

"First EM-ping from the Pequod passing us now, sir," Cleo called from the control room. "We can confirm that our cloak absorbed, and did not reflect, any of the energy. We are hidden."

"Good," Jason replied. Praying that their slightly oblique angle did not throw their shadow toward anything which might notice. They would not reflect a scan, but downrange, and it might be possible for a careful eye to spot the hole they had left in it.

He glanced at the speed rating. Watching it slowly climbing. They had a maximum acceleration profile, and a maximum speed, which they believed would allow them to still trust their cloaks. Hobbled by the need to sneak in. They had the numbers now. A little under thirteen hours to get there, find whatever the magic eight-ball wanted them to find, and to get out. Just getting there, it was going to take too much damned time. Their time on the ground would be all too brief.

At least the planet had been on the right side of the star.

At least their destination would be on the right side of the planet.

... a planet which was uncomfortably familiar.

[Let's be honest with each other. Nothing we are seeing here is a coincidence. Nothing here is much of a surprise.] Alistair said.

[Life, it... damn it my friend... what life we have led that leaves things like this as no surprise to either of us.]

"Fuck's sake," He swore to himself... Dragging himself out of the cockpit to join the others waiting for him in the control-room.

\*     \*     \*

Mission Date: Day 374. Sneaking in.

Mission Date: Day 374.    Sneaking in.

"I hate that I am not surprised," Julien said. Staring at the holographic representation of the distant planet. Jason realising that he was joining in a conversation that was already getting a little heated.

"I am just going with any mad-shit that I run into now… The universe is just screwing with us," Julien finished.

"It is not the Earth," Natalie said, leaning forward.

"It is not the Earth we know. But if you look at this landmass," Capability Brown leant forward and stuck his finger into the floating globe. "This edge here, and here…" He spun the globe around. "Also, the poles."

"Jesus Christ, is that Pangea?" Jason groaned. "BOB, are you able to access any data from Earth about the forming of the separate continents from what was thought to originally have been a singular land-mass?"

"Jason, we are limited. I have some data, but not nearly enough. There is more on the Pequod, but we are running silent and can't risk reaching out. However, I can take Earth and I can push it back through a theoretical timeline and… let's see if our new friend fits, when we model her against…" BOB said, extending out from his tic-tac shape to stand amongst the rest of the crew. Before them all, the globe shifted. Ice caps moved, the luxurious green dying out, replaced by glaciers. Then the land-mass split, with components of it migrating away across the round surface of the planet. The ice ebbing and flowing several more times… before the eerily familiar shape was represented before them.

"Okay, so I took significant liberties to get from there to here. But everything was possible. Most were probable." BOB responded.

"The moon. We had spent long enough recording both now. Do we know how its mass corresponds with Earth's?" Julien asked.

"Identical. Also, it is tidally locked," Brown answered.

"Okay, meaning what?"

"It rotates, but only relative to the Earth, and it takes exactly the same time to rotate as it does to orbit the Earth," Brown answered.

Mission Date: Day 374.                Sneaking in.

"So, either it rotates, or it doesn't?" Julien replied. Frustrated by the complicated reply.

"Relative to you standing on the Earth, then no. Relative to itself, then yes, it does." Doc Brown replied. Shrugging his shoulders and mouthing an apology. "Relative to anything else, and it becomes a little more subjective... Besides, you knew about Pangea?"

"You-Tube, I must have watched something on You-Tube." Julien said. "The approaching star. It is bright blue?"

"The Doppler effect, it is the same as for the sirens in your police cars, old friend." Daniel said.

"Okay, so blue light has a shorter wavelength than the rest of the spectrum..." Julien mumbled something under his breath... "Richard... orange, yellow... indigo... violent... Okay, that makes sense. But isn't shorter-wavelength, EM radiation more dangerous than long? Is that star not firing horrible radiation at us?"

"Jesus, Julien. That was actually a smart question. The answer is yes, but it is nothing we can't survive a short exposure to, and our shields, even our armour, will protect us long past the point its gravitational wrecking ball... It would eventually kill us, but only given more time than we actually have left." Jason answered that one.

"... I came on this mission a little sceptically. I have not been here, not for over a hundred of your years," Tata said. "I didn't like it last time, and I am not feeling a great deal more comfortable hearing that you all recognise it." The massive alien crossed its thick arms over its chest.

"You didn't like it, yet you came back?" Julien asked.

"Not liking something, it does not prevent it from being fascinating."

"Tata, it is time we all laid our cards on the table." Jason said. Wondering quite what the translation matrix would make of that one.

"All?"

Mission Date: Day 374.  Sneaking in.

"Most," Jason shrugged.

"You first, Jason. I think it might prove to be a more interesting tale." Tata said. Grinning at the human's crowding the control room.

"Let's eat." Impact said.

\*     \*     \*

Mission Date: Day 374.          Sneaking in.

Jason did not tell their new friend everything. But he explained the gaps. The earlier promise of 'no-more-lies' was never far from his thoughts. Tata also left gaps. He spoke of his people, but not where they came from.

Tata spoke about a different time in his own life. Long before, he had learned of the looming disaster. An archaeologist, one who specialised in extinct races. In the remnants of those races which could be found, scattered across ancient planets. Leading a team of scientists from his own world.

"We came here, and we saw what you saw. A star, one only three-billion of your years old. But one with so many things missing," Tata said. Taking a massive bite from his food. Crunching it noisily in his massive jaw. "There is a planet, a perfectly normal planet. Albeit one with an unusually large moon… but nothing else, and that should not be possible. So, we decided to take a look at it. Or it would be more correct to say that we tried to."

"The sentinels."

"They shadowed us from mid-system… The legends tell us that they follow any ship that tries to get close. They positioned themselves just off our bow and stayed that way for three orbits. We scanned. But when we started to prepare our lander for atmospheric insertion, we were finally contacted." Tata said.

"A message?" Daniel asked.

"A warning. It just said 'Enough,'" Tata responded. "Let me show you. BOB, you have interfaced with my data-brick?"

"I have," BOB replied.

"Can you show first the sentinel craft?" Tata asked.

"I can," BOB replied. The holographic display flickered, then changed to show a spacecraft. A sphere, with a ring around its circumference. One which protruded out by a good eighth of the sphere's diameter. The entire thing was silver, not reflective, but a matt-silver.

"Do we have a scale?" Jason asked, staring at the holographic image.

# Mission Date: Day 374.    Sneaking in.

"We can." BOB said. Moments later and a holographic representation of the Thunder-Child appeared beside the sphere. The three-hundred-foot-long ship was dwarfed by it.

"It has a diameter of around three-kilometres. The ring itself, it is two-hundred-metres deep and five-hundred wide." BOB qualified.

"Do we know how it works, what it does?" Jason asked.

"No, we don't know for certain that it is crewed, or if it is an autonomous device. We were shadowed by four. We saw none of them coming, not until they appeared a few of your kilometres off our bow. We saw no sign of any FTL jump-energies. Nor did we detect any mechanism of propulsion later."

"Weapons?" Jason asked.

"Honestly, we do not know. But when we continued with our approach, we suddenly found ourselves back out close to our jump-point. One moment we were above the planet in an asynchronous orbit. The next, and we were pretty much exactly where we had arrived. Relatively speaking." Tata replied. Shrugging. "Our sensors, every system on our scientific vessel, were charting every single event in our local space. It was what we were there for. We detected nothing at all which might be considered out of the ordinary. Apart from the extraordinary thing."

"Is this what all other races experienced when they came here?"

"Close, with varying degrees of calamity... those who were only inquisitive, they were treated as we were. Those who responded to the sentinels with any level of anger were destroyed. The Teghra-Dorne empire, they lost two ships who fired upon the sentinels. They sent a fleet of warships. It is said that one ship survived. That the fleet was transported into the corona of the star with only one far enough out to escape. But close enough to watch fifty warships die. I warned you all not to take any aggressive action here." Tata said.

"Okay, well, hopefully the Pequod can keep the sentinels amused without upsetting them. Hopefully, we can slip in. Back to the planet. Can you show us where you are planning to take us?" Jason asked.

# Mission Date: Day 374.     Sneaking in.

"I can, BOB if you please." Tata asked. The image changing again, this time showing a planet's surface.

Jason's eyes zoomed in. Every time he would use the system, he would marvel at the impossible level of microscopic detail in the holographic image. Rolling countryside, littered with ferns across its surface. Small patches of wiry looking grass... and a pyramid. Because of course there was. Tata had described this. But to see it now that BOB had properly processed the alien's files, the reality struck him. Like the ancient structures in Egypt. The proportions were remarkably familiar.

"Were other structures like this found on other planets?" Doc Brown asked.

"Yes, although only in general shape. The Pyramid is a relatively straight-forward and logical structure. Nothing exactly like this, and few of their size." Tata replied. "Do you recognise them?"

"It is hard not to trick ourselves into looking for the familiar, when we have seen so much else here, which is also familiar," Brown replied. Thoughtful. "The stone is effectively granite, and that lies below this eroded limestone... shell... it must have once covered the entire structure. Calcium, carbon and oxygen... This is effectively the same makeup as the pyramids on Earth. Can you zoom in on the arch, here?" The doctor asked. His eyes, albeit more powerful than a regular human, were nothing like the other wolves there. The arch increased in size as the projector zoomed in. Revealing a door, partly hidden by shadow. To its side was a smaller, round-stone protrusion. Moments later, the exposed stone filled the floating image. An emblem. Two dragons, encircling a recess in their middle. A tiny hole.

"That's it." Tata whispered.

Kate pulled out the amulet. The dragons were identical in design. Tata had been correct; he had recognised it. "It has stopped vibrating, finally. It is happy that we know where to go. That is a lock. I believe that this is a key."

"Then this is where we go." Jason said. Murmurs of consent rippling through the small crowd. "This is the only structure on the planet?" Jason asked.

"The only one we detected. Our scans were advanced, but we were only over the planet for around twenty-orbits. We could have missed something.

## Mission Date: Day 374.     Sneaking in.

Obviously, it would prove far harder to find anything below the surface of the ocean." Tata replied.

"Okay... We trust that this is the place. We go there first." Jason said. "You told others about your visit?"

"I did." Tata replied. "I am a scientist. I have always believed that knowledge is for sharing. Others came here, they had before, but more did later. None that I know of got this far, and no one has ever reached the surface and returned to share their tale." The alien shrugged. Again, an oddly human affectation.

"Thank you." Jason approached the image of the planet's surface. Zooming out from the pyramid structure to look at the surrounding countryside. "This is where we start from. We land here," Jason indicated a spot a little over five kilometres from the site. "The ground is heavy granite under a foot of soil... The Thunder-Child can wait there indefinitely. It is also defensible. It would be difficult to approach her, unseen. We make the last few kilometres by bike. Two Tanks deployed, and protecting the ship. Tata, are you happy with your environmental suit?"

"Jason, you know I can breathe that atmosphere. But if it makes you happy, I will wear your suit. It fits wonderfully." Tata replied. His huge smile painted across his enormous face.

The giant bear stood; his modesty protected by underwear, which looked suspiciously like speedos. Jason considered his new friend's structure... but just for a moment.

[If you were a massive killing machine, but you wanted humans to trust you and not worry about you murdering them all... what form would you take?] Alistair mused.

[Alistair...] Jason considered this observation. [... damn you old man. But yes, good point.]

\*     \*     \*

Mission Date: Day 374.     Sneaking in.

Some hours later.

"Why did you bring me along, Jason?" Julien asked.

"I like the way your brain works. The way you think. The way you see things others miss... for you, it must be hard, though. You must wish you had a bigger brain." Jason needled his old friend.

"Your magic benefactors, Jason, my brain has not worked this well, ever... The fog has gone. The clarity..." Julien said. He raised his right hand. Extending his youthful fingers, splaying them wide. Clenching them into a fist, his powerful forearms bunching with thick muscle. "Human perfected, it is not a body-builder... it is an Olympic sprinter, perhaps a gymnast... This reset, I have done little to earn it. I hope I can do so today."

"Julien, you can't let me down, not whilst you do your best... Not whilst you offer me council... and as for what you have done so far in your life..." Jason said. Reaching over and grabbing his friend's shoulder.

"Suit up?" Julien said. Standing, smiling down at Jason.

"Suit up." Jason replied. Finishing his coffee and following his friend from the room.

Mission Date: Day 374.

## Warning.

"You should not be here. It is almost time. It is not safe for you to be here. You should leave."

Katherine almost jumped out of her skin as the unbidden voice echoed across the bridge.

"Team, how is that getting through our systems?" She called.

"It isn't. It is... We have no idea where it is coming from." Jansen answered. Moments later. "Okay, we now have three of the sentinel crafts we were warned about, now off our stern. One more, also matching our course and speed, directly ahead. They are each exactly one-point-ooh-eight kilometres out."

"Who are you?" Katherine asked. Searching the sky before her, and only then seeing the vast craft. "We have spoken with others who have come here before. This is the first time you have spoken with someone who has come here. That we know of."

"If you visit us, how do you not know who we are?" The voice asked.

"We are curious... We know of the event which will take this world in less than a day now. We want to understand what is here. This might be our last chance." Katherine asked. "Also, does anyone know who you are?"

"You are not from those who sought to destroy us. We can tell that. But you are also not where you are meant to be... You carry with you a remnant from a time before this one. A fragment of something that should not be. You come from a time after this. Neither of these things is easily possible."

"Who is it that seeks to destroy you?" Katherine asked. The bridge was listening with rapt attention. She saw Jennifer rushing onto the bridge from the corner of her eye.

Mission Date: Day 374.　　　　　Warning.

"They already have. They don't want us here. They won't want you to be here, either."

"They sent the star?"

"They did."

"That star, it would have needed to be sent toward this sector millions of years ago… The damage, what it will do to this corner of the galaxy… the effects… we know those will push far further. Who would be prepared to wipe out this many civilisations, just to stop you?" Katherine asked.

"They are?"

"Who are they?" Katherine asked. The question hanging there. Unanswered. "Are you trying to tell us that it was aimed with such unerring accuracy from the galaxy, where it was birthed?"

"That star, it did not exist even three hundred of your years ago." The voice replied.

"Impossible…" Katherine answered, but not as a statement… although, it should have been something she was more comfortable with, as a statement… "Also, you are incorrect. We were able to first detect it from tens of thousands of light-years outside of the galaxy."

"Interesting. Then it was somehow hidden from us." The voice replied.

Katherine cocked her head to the side. Thinking. Realising that she was mimicking an affectation she had witnessed in most of the wolves on board. Why was this intelligence surprised that the star might have been hidden from it? Seeing that as being less likely than the star somehow born just centuries earlier…

"You are still here. What are you still protecting… if this planet is about to be destroyed?" Katherine asked.

"The longer the project lasts, the closer we get to the answers we seek."

Mission Date: Day 374.        Warning.

"Forty-two," This was Hacker, under his breath. Earning a dirty look from Katherine and a snigger from Dani.

"What are the questions?" Katherine asked. Only to be met with silence. "Talk to us, we can help... Tell us why you are here?"

Nothing. For long minutes, the Pequod continued to hammer toward the planet. Still shadowed by the sentinels. Just silence...

"Ship, team, I want to know everything," Katherine asked.

"Why talk at all, if they were planning on being this cryptic?" Dani asked, reasonably.

"That, it is a bloody good question..." Katherine replied. "TT, without risking upsetting the sentinels. What options do we have?"

"None of our tactical systems are allowing us to lock on... We can see them on our navigational scopes, but our weapons are refusing to play ball. I can target by eye... But I would be cautious about suggesting that anything works past that." The marine was at her tactical station, just across from where Dani was sitting, and almost directly before Katherine, who was sitting at the captain's position, on the central raised-dais. She spoke with an apologetic earnest.

"Time before we reach the planet?" Katherine asked.

"Eight hours. Give or take." Dani replied. It's ten hours before the collision. Less, before the gravitational forces make everything very difficult." Dani replied.

"Put two counters on screen. I want the timeline before this system is obliterated, front and centre. Increase speed further. I want us at the planet in four hours.

"Aye captain." Dani responded.

\*     \*     \*

Mission Date: Day 374.　　　　　The planet.

## The planet.

Hours later. Onboard the Thunder-Child.

"I am bringing her in. Cleo, I want you paying attention to everything here. You are flying us out." Jason said.

"Aye sir," Cleo responded.

"Team, be ready. I want the Tanks with their feet on the ground as soon as I confirm ready... Everyone, eyes on the prize. Expect funky things. Seeing something funky, even just a little bit funky, and not saying something about that thing... That is what kills us," Jason said.

The Thunder-Child rolled onto its back, dropping toward the planet's surface. Pushing gently into the atmosphere at a little over two-hundred knots. Doing so deliberately slowly, so as not to leave a burning trail of fire through the upper atmosphere. They had orbited the planet first, and quickly, using the overflight to get new scans of its surface. But they had not needed to maintain that speed to stay up. Cheating with their Chaser drives to hang in space and spend just a little while longer studying their target.

Also, their landing site.

"Jason, the atmospheric readings. They're what we thought from the spectrographic analysis on the way in." BOB reported a couple of minutes later.

"BOB, thank you." Jason replied.

Most of the feedback he received from the Thunder-Child's controls was synthetic. Arguably, all. Carefully crafted to increase the feel of flying the thing. But even outside of the additional weight he felt through his feet, his hands, even outside of those, he was always convinced he could feel the airframe moving through the seat itself. She was not aerodynamic at all. She had no real lifting surfaces. But her shields could replicate those, and did. He should not be able to feel anything, yet he was sure that he could.

Mission Date: Day 374.         The planet.

"Like a little bird," he said, just to himself.

The sky blazed with the fire from the two stars. The system's star was still the largest thing in the sky. The other, the supermassive giant, it was also there, too. Visible, easily visible, although if he did not know the threat it posed, would he even have noticed it? It was only by staring at the slightly brighter star, the more distant star, that he could visually track its movement. Although, barely. Also, because it shone blue, with the wavelength of its visible electromagnetic radiation compressed by its speed to morph its light... travelling, as it was, at a not insignificant percentage of the speed of light... Blue-shift. It dropped below the horizon as he brought the Thunder-Child further in, the shelter of the planet shielding their destination from its catastrophic radiation. For a while, anyway.

He felt such tremendous anxiety even allowing his mind to consider the thing. What it meant. What it would go on to mean.

[This much importance, it was never meant to hinge upon me...] Jason reflected. Reaching out to his permanent passenger.

[Jason, I am afraid it always was, my friend...] Alistair replied.

For a moment, both were silent.

"Computer, how long to the ground?" He asked.

"About eight-minutes, Jason."

"Lovely, just enough time. Play Led Zeppelin, Stairway to heaven." Jason said. Feeling Alistair's approval.

"Jason, music found, playing selected track now." The computer replied.

♪♪*There's a lady who's sure all that glitters is gold... And she's buying a stairway to Heaven*♪♪

Soon afterwards, with what he considered being perhaps the most beautiful music track ever laid down, playing over possibly the best audio-system he would ever experience, Jason relaxed into the moment.

Mission Date: Day 374.          The planet.

The planet was old. But far more immediately familiar than any other he had ever seen. Even more so than Epsilon, which was still, by far, the closest Earth analogy that he had ever encountered. Until, of course, today. The plants were not those of the Earth he knew. Rather, they were those which a palaeoecologist would have expected to see on an ancient Earth. Simpler things, cruder things, perhaps. But still life... Wherever there was life found in a cruel universe, it should always be considered magical.

Moving low over the selected landing spot, just minutes later, he dropped the landing gear and allowed the starship to settle upon them. Feeling her sink just a little way into the soil. Her simulated mass was only around three-tonnes. Still, the soil was soft enough for her to sink almost to the granite layer just below its surface.

"Tanks release. Set a permitter. Team, ready yourself. We are leaving."

He saw the alert as two Tanks deployed. Neil and Flaherty. Experience and enthusiasm in equal abundance.

Reaching behind him, he grabbed the intimately familiar grab-rail above his head in the zero-g of the cockpit, and pulled himself through the already opening hatch there.

[Here we go,] Alistair said.

[You always used to say I should cherish the adventure.] Jason replied.

\*          \*          \*

Mission Date: Day 374.    The planet.

"Okay, team. Off we go!" Jason ordered. Bringing his own grav-bike from its resting position and hovering in place. Rocking the machine forward and back with his toes. Testing the recently constructed vehicle's behaviour. Eager to get moving, "Just a moderate pace, a fast-moderate pace. I will take point. Let's move out." Jason said. Immediately moving at an objectively faster pace than he had just suggested and heading directly towards the distant hill. They had set their mission clock, based on what was really little more than an agreed ship-time, before they had even left the twenty-first century and Earth's solar system. Time which had long since lost any external relevance, and had bounced against the local-time on each of the planets they had visited. Its impact was felt more strongly on this one, though.

There was a very real ticking-clock. It was a little before midnight on the planet. But according to their own clocks; it was still midday.

He heard the team following. Pleased that they were finally heading in the right direction. The bikes were graceful, almost silent, and they flowed easily above the tangled bracken and foliage which covered the ground. They were quick. But his anxiety had kicked up a notch, and was doing so with every further perceived unnecessary delay.

He was pleased, though, that whatever familiarity Tata had developed in their frantic race across Darla's capital city, an event weeks ago now, seemed to have stuck with him. Although, in his new armour, his enormous figure looked even more surreal on the thing than it had before.

Julien was solid on the bike. Jason had assumed he would be, even if this was his first time off the ship since the adventure had started. Herrick, an instinctive warrior, and a wise head... he had ridden before. Kate was with them. Hell, she had dragged the amulet which had led them here. Back through time and then, to this very point. Jason's concern, that the magical device had known when they needed to be... but had not known where... It had led them to.

Was there a purpose behind exposing the team to the various alien species in this part of the galaxy's history? Or had the thing simply not known?

He pushed these traitorous thoughts away.

Mission Date: Day 374.     The planet.

Her father, obviously Daniel, was coming along for the ride. Two others, two more of the survivors from Hermentia who had not yet set foot away from the safety of either ship. Doc Brown, and...

"Jason," Natalie called from beside him. The young-woman having increased her speed to easily match his. Her armour, like Julien's, was painted a burnished-orange colour. A metallic terracotta.

"Is this bad?" Jason asked.

"Just that we have flowers here, over there on that meadow. Up ahead, and over beside those trees... flowers with..."

"Damnit... Pollen," Jason replied. "...so, why pollen if there are no... where are the insects?"

"Exactly."

Jason looked over the landscape. Conifers, or some ancient ancestor, marched over the hill to his right and into the distance. Ferns covering what ground which wasn't covered in grass. It looked right. But it wasn't.

"Jason, I have only detected plant-life on the planet. The atmospheric mix has lower levels of oxygen than it should do, with no animal life, not even microbial, and only plants... The mix is off." BOB said. Having floated up to race alongside Jason and Natalie. "We are minutes away. It is almost midnight here. We won't see this system's star, not from here, not for hours. We see the other, the wrong one, far sooner. That star kills everything. It is already doing so on the other side of the planet. We should look to make entry as soon as we arrive. That we are careful, that we take great care to ensure we have as complete scans as possible, first. But that we do not linger, unduly. I recommend just a small team inside, though. The stronger. We will need Kate. She has the amulet and whatever magics have guided us here, they speak through her. Whatever magics might protect this place, they will probably react kindlier to her... possibly."

Because there had been nothing in the universe which could have kept BOB away from this.

Mission Date: Day 374.                    The planet.

"... and who else?"

"... I should also go. The challenges may also be technical. I can react faster, and I am also far stronger than anyone else here."

"I wouldn't say far stronger... You do not want to miss out on this, do you?" Jason asked.

"No, Jason. Whatever chaotic path has led us here. There seems to be a purpose to it all. One which is a little more layered than simply finding the Progenitors and destroying them. I think the mission was always that amulet. Before the Earth was destroyed, and before the first Kate, fled to Epsilon... I think it was always leading us along this path... to this point... do you feel it too?"

"My friend, we are more than pawns in this. But we are also pawns." Jason replied. Glancing around. "You said that the atmosphere here was off. Is it possible that it is artificial?"

"It is unlikely that it isn't artificial."

Looking at his armour's report of the surrounding atmosphere, Jason was rash. "Screw it. Helmet, retract."

"Jason, no," Kate shouted from behind. "The radiation..."

"It's fine, just for a couple of minutes. Try it..." Jason breathed deeply. "Take away the pollution, the crap we have put her through... tell me you don't recognise this damned smell?"

"Jason, I love you... but you are an idiot. I will try it though, providing you do not drop dead in the next few-minutes."

"Hour," the gruff voice came through moments later.

"Dad says an hour," Kate corrected.

Mission Date: Day 374.     The planet.

*   *   *

Mission Date: Day 374.        The Last day on Earth.

## The Last day on Earth.

But of course, it was not Earth.

They reached the pyramid just a few minutes past midnight. Now, with only two hours left to find their way inside, and to find what they were looking for. Whatever the hell that was.

They had seen it earlier, as they had flown over. Images of it, as they had approached in the Thunder-Child. But, as they crested the last of the hills in their approach, as its tip finally revealed itself, and then the rest of the structure, its true scale was revealed.

Enormous.

"Who here has been to Giza?" Julien asked.

"Daniel and Alistair were there in the war. I didn't get there until after the events... until twenty-fifty myself." Jason replied.

"I hadn't." Natalie added. Just moments later.

"They were a lot smaller," Daniel added.

"It is close to nine-hundred metres tall. It is twelve-hundred wide. The triangular sides, they're not quite equilateral." BOB added.

"On Earth, yours were not as big?" Tata asked.

"They were made in a time before machines. Built by hand." Jason replied. "Ancient..."

Their armour filled in the gaps. Presenting measurements, statistics. Information which could prove useful. Some collated by BOB and shared with the team. Jason pulled a dispenser from his rear panier, fumbling to reach behind him to do so, and deployed two drones which could loiter...

Which could loiter for far longer than the planet had left.

Mission Date: Day 374.         The Last day on Earth.

"Team, the opening is up to our right. We will swing wide. Follow my lead and stop when I stop." Jason ordered. Arrowing his bike wide around the structure, bringing their final destination finally into view.

The base of the pyramid was covered in foliage, with long grass and primitive bushes covering the flat expanse of ground they were currently riding across. Jason knew that to the other side, a vast forest abutted the structure. Trees, which were objectively massive themselves, with some being close to eighty-metres high, but which would be dwarfed by the building itself.

Humanity had built taller. During the twenty-first century, emerging nations had competed with the more established to build the tallest. Vanity projects, which had ended in disaster when a building almost a mile high, had collapsed in Belgium.

Jason pushed the horrifying memory from his mind. Looking at the ancient structure, seeing the lime-render where it had flaked away from the stone beneath. Seeing climbing vines which reached high from the grass below. Lying against the stone, but pushing through the old render across much of it. The damage, it seemed that it was only caused by time. It seemed like none of it was structural. He pulled up, Kate stopping right beside him, and they both dismounted their bikes. Staring at the entrance, now only fifty metres away.

Above him was the moon. Not his moon, but that was okay. It was not his sky, either. This moon, though, it was talking to him. Whispering incoherent secrets his soul could not decipher. He looked at it uneasily, and he felt Kate taking his hand, noticing that she was also staring skyward.

"We have not been in Kansas for a very long time," she said.

"We haven't," Jason replied. Squeezing her hand. Turning to face the team.

"Form a perimeter. Tata, stay back for now. Keep weapons stowed. If there is something here guarding this, be it sentient or otherwise, we do not want to cause undue alarm in that something. Kate with me. Let's open that door. BOB, stay back a little, but we will want you with us... remember, this place is likely to be as funky as hell. Seeing something, choosing to say nothing..."

"That is how we die here." Kate said. Finishing his mantra.

Mission Date: Day 374.        The Last day on Earth.

Kate was walking right beside him. The amulet was already in her hand. As they closed to within thirty-feet, it started to glow. An eerie green-light, which threw haunting shadows around them both. For a moment, he was convinced that things lived in those shadows. That the walls ahead were alive, somehow, and with something filled with menace. He pushed those traitorous thoughts away.

The doorway itself, it was in a stone alcove. An arch over the door, which was made from the same stone as the rest of the pyramid. The door, it appeared to be wood. But his armour was not playing ball, it was refusing to tell him what it was. The lock, the two dragons encircling where the amulet would go, shone with its own dim light. It was covered in vegetation, a vine of some-sort, and one which had climbed the door. Jason stepped up to it, drawing his fighting knife from behind the pistol on his hip, and carefully, he cut away at the vine.

As he did, the narrow blade and slender handle felt natural in his armoured hand. Steel, not carbyne, and one he had carried for decades. Its sharp edge, its narrow point, allowing him to pry away the plant matter. Making quick work of the problem. Once he was done, he stepped back.

"Go on then," he said.

"You don't want to do this?" Kate asked.

"No, I don't."

Kate said nothing else. She simply stepped forward and pushed the small amulet into the lock. It fit perfectly, surprising no-one.

Nothing happened. For about five minutes, nothing happened, and they waited. There was no impatience, though, not within any of the team waiting. There was no doubt in any of them that they were not doing the right thing.

Then more time passed. The sky started to shine with an eerie light as something dreadful approached from behind the planet. The atmosphere taking on a hue that spoke only of rapidly approaching doom. Jason monitored his mission clock. They all did. Doubts beginning to make themselves known to everyone. Anxiety...

Mission Date: Day 374.        The Last day on Earth.

Then finally, after an interminable delay, a light glowed from within the door itself. The seams of the wood, the gaps between what appeared to be separate planks, all glowing with a faint-pink light. It intensified, slowly and over more minutes longer. Doing so, until the light was so bright that their armours' visors all dimmed to protect their eyes.

Then the doors swung open. Parting in the middle and swinging outward. Despite that, everyone jumped a little.

Jason peered past the doorway. Seeing a stone corridor beyond it. The same width as the doorway, and without a visible end. Certainly not one that he could see from where he was standing.

"Right, I guess we go inside then." Jason said. Striding forward. His heart in his mouth.

"Do we still have time?" Daniel called.

"Fuck, no," Jason replied. Heading inside anyway.

The entrance was dark. But his eyes, the advanced armour, it all worked together to not make that an issue. There had been some sort of ingress. It looked like water had crept past the door at some point. The floor was damaged, but that was odd to Jason, as it looked to be made from stone. But as he stepped past the damage, the floor lit under his feet, a diffused glow which lit the whole corridor...

"BOB?" Jason asked.

"Jason, there is no detectible technology. The light, I can see it, but my sensors are telling me that it is still dark here." BOB responded.

"Shit," Jason said. "Kate, do you know which way we should go?"

Because they had come to a large room. Fifty feet square, including its height, and with a wide spiral staircase in the middle. One leading upward, disappearing into the ceiling, turning back on itself five times to do so, and also downward into the floor. The staircase looked like marble. The room was ornate. Fully illuminated, with a parquet floor made from what appeared to

Mission Date: Day 374.    The Last day on Earth.

be the same wood as the door. A herringbone pattern. One which was almost identical to the living room in the centre of his apartment in London.

The walls, running around the room's edge, they were covered in murals. There were multiple doorways leading off the room, built into every wall.

"Jason, Kate, did you see the images captured in the crypt back on the Greek island?" Doc Brown asked.

"I haven't, not yet... Should I worry that you are about to tell me that this looks like that?" Jason asked.

"... it is depicting different things. But I would bet an unhealthy amount on it being the same artist." Doc Brown said. "What's written, it's the same language, or some very close derivative of that language. Katherine and I have been researching the data from Hermentia over this last year... Fascinating, but I never dreamed it would be relevant, not anywhere out here."

BOB, I want you to sequester all the drones you need and send them off to record what they can from this place." Jason ordered. "Leave Kate and me with at least two... We might need them,"

"Will do, Jason."

Jason felt the release of two of his. Leaving him with two. Kate, the same. The small swarm heading off quickly through the doorways, up the stairs.

It would all be gone soon; it would be a shame if it were all lost.

More of a shame if they were all lost with it.

"Everyone else. Record what you can. Everything you can. We leave in less than an hour... Hopefully, much less. If we don't die, we can circle back. Everyone, not just drones. Have your armour record everything you get close enough to. But no one goes too far... Kate, where next?" Jason pushed.

"Jason, it is telling me that we should head downwards." Kate replied. Holding the amulet aloft. It was clearly vibrating now. Shaking in her grip.

Mission Date: Day 374.                    The Last day on Earth.

"Brilliant, because good things happen in basements." Daniel called across. Winking to Julien...

"Balls, do they... it is always dreadful." Julien replied.

"Don't worry, you two clowns are staying here." Jason said. "Right, Kate, Doc... BOB, follow me. Everyone else, don't stray too far from this room." Jason ordered. "Daniel, keep everyone alive. Julien, Natalie, make sure he doesn't get everyone killed... and get Cleo here for a pickup. I want us running out of here as if our tails are on fire."

"The Pequod?" Julien called.

"She knows what to do. We cannot risk dropping radio silence. Not until we absolutely have to." Jason replied. Already several flights of stairs away.

\*   \*   \*

Mission Date: Day 374.          The Last day on Earth.

They moved fast, heading downward for a disturbingly long time, relatively. Jason's HUD tracking their descent. In the end, they had climbed over fifty stories and were almost seven hundred feet below ground.

The stairs had been uniform. Mostly, they had been uninterrupted, but they had twice opened into similar rooms to the one through which they had originally entered. Massive rooms. Different murals, that Jason ensured he had recorded himself as he span frantically to focus on each wall.

Then the stairs had finally opened into a vast space that was complete darkness. Jason could sense the space, but even with his suit's sensors, his preternatural eyes, he could not see past the stairway's marble rails.

"BOB?" Jason asked.

"The same Jason. I can tell that there is a space there. But only sound can find it. The atmosphere allows for echo-location, and the space is over a mile wide in every direction. But no EM radiation leaves or enters these stairs."

"Is it possible?" Jason asked.

"It is possible, although I cannot detect any of the tricks which would make it possible. My concern is more about the why than the how," BOB replied.

"How far to the bottom?" Jason asked. Horribly disorientated.

"The next flight."

\*     \*     \*

Mission Date: Day 374.        The Last day on Earth.

Jason stepped away from the last step, and as he did so, he walked out into a room without end. White, the floor was white, and he could see nothing of the floor or the ceiling, apart from simply just white. His suit pinged out EM and Sonar, and he received nothing back but garbled chaos. He felt panic rising and spun around on his heal, hunting for the staircase, which was at least still there. Floating in a sea of white. Kate was stepping off from the last step herself, and looked equally startled.

"BOB, Doc, one of you stays with one foot on that staircase, one foot out here. That thing is terrifying the hell out of me, and I am convinced it might disappear when we are no longer using the sodding thing," Jason ordered.

"I am happy to," Capability Brown said. Sitting on the last step, his feet were on the white floor. It was not exactly what Jason had asked him to do, but it was good enough.

The man was barely a wolf. But it had been more than enough to stop any attempts at enhancing him. He was super-fit. A cross-fit enthusiast. But the descent had been brutal. The man was knackered.

"Where are we going, Jason?" BOB asked.

"We are going to that thing," Jason replied.

Because half a mile away, there was a silver orb, barely visible amongst the shining white... everything. Jason hesitated, then jogged towards it. Kate following hot on his heals and BOB gilding across the floor on skates, on tiny wheels on the end of his slender legs, that Jason had not seen him use since they had left the Ark. Effortlessly wafting across the mirror-smooth surface in such a casual manner, it looked out of place. But it was quick. The time for fucking about had disappeared.

He drew closer, and his armour finally resolved it for him. Fifty-feet in diameter, and made from crystallised marble. Seamless, floating a little over a foot from the floor, it hovered there as they drew closer.

They all drew themselves to a stop. Standing before it. Kate looked over at him and shrugged. BOB wasn't saying anything. Floating now, himself. Just the tic-tac.

Mission Date: Day 374.          The Last day on Earth.

Jason leant forward, hesitated briefly, and then knocked upon it.

                                  \*     \*     \*

Mission Date: Day 374.                The Last day on Earth.

The silver ball opened. First a crack, then there was a blaze of light from within. Too Bright, and as the team watched on, their visors dimming to protect their eyes, slowly the contents of the ball were laid bare. Kate was shocked. The vibrating stone in the amulet seemed to simply go still. Finally, still.

From within the sphere came a voice.

"I have been waiting for so very long. It is good to see you again, my chaotic nightmare. I believe that you have something of mine with you." The lady asked. Stepping out of the light and appearing as if she were coalescing from someplace else.

Jason detected Kate's reaction. Knowing at once that she had also recognised her. He did himself... Although he had only known the woman for a very short while. His attention was drawn to the other person there.

"So, whilst I didn't expect this... I'm now a little surprised that I hadn't." Jason said. "But I would like to say, and not for the first time in this complicated life of mine, but it is not that small a damned galaxy.

James looked up at him. Decades younger in appearance than the last time Jason had seen him. But still practically broken.

"It was Monaco, wasn't it? Tell me it wasn't bloody Monaco..." Jason asked.

*    *    *

Mission Date: Day 374.     The Last day on Earth.

"Incoming. We will be with you in just a minute... There are a lot of stairs..." Jason puffed over the radio. "What's occurring out there?"

"Jason, we have friends... I am afraid that things have become complicated." Julien replied.

The grass looked so impossibly Earth-like, now that he knew what he was looking at. Now that there seemed that there may be some level of deliberate plan behind it all. Fate, but fate that had been somehow manipulated for God-alone knew what sodding purpose.

So, seeing the creature before him... it brought an interesting juxtaposition to the current adventure.

"Cordax, is it?" Julien guessed.

"How do you know my name, human?" the alien replied.

"The description. Really ugly, and missing a leg," Julien replied. "Why the chair? You still have two. A lot of races out here seem happy with just two."

Because he had still never learned to not enjoy poking the bear.

There was a small group before them. Ten soldiers, Cordax's people, he guessed. They were all armoured, and all were wearing environmental protection. He could not see much of them, not beyond that, but they were all standing on three legs, with four arms. With the obvious exception of Cordax.

He had watched the footage; he had later listened to the after-action report. Daniel and Neil had dismissed these creatures as warriors. But Neil had been in a Tank, and Daniel was one. Julien was a brawler; he was not an accomplished fighter. He had overpowered more than one drunken thug in his time. But this, it was not that.

Julien was standing outside the structure. Tata was there. The enormous bugger wearing an armoured suit based on nearly identical technology to his own. Natalie was beside him. She had her firearm at low-ready. She had good instincts. She had already confirmed that she was backing his play. Then there was, of course, Daniel. His chaotic ace up his sleeve.

Mission Date: Day 374.    The Last day on Earth.

But beyond his warriors, Cordax had come with mechanised armour he had likely borrowed from a more worrying friend. Walkers, hugely different from their Tanks, but clearly designed for a very similar purpose. Three legs, but with a singular arm.

He had seen those same machines whilst the Thunder-Child had been rescuing Jason's ground team from the Strenuous, the Teghra-Dorne flagship.

"The chair? I can grow another leg, human. Tell me, can you grow another head?"

"No," Julien replied. Dialling up his suit's shields. "Are there species out here who can?"

It might have been an odd thing to ask, but he was genuinely interested. He didn't get an answer.

"But that is not why you are here, is it? Also, it is not why you're willing to risk sunrise?"

To be fair, his confidence was rising. He had never seen the Thunder-Child operating with her full cloak before. He didn't know if what he was seeing was his armour accentuating the visible distortion that her cloak created. Or, if it was not as convincing to the naked eye, not this close. The starship was hovering about one-hundred metres to their ten-o'clock. Cleo was letting him know that both turrets had a clear field of fire.

So far, and none of the aliens had looked behind them. Julien was not a soldier, but he knew that this was shitty trade-craft.

"No, human... We are not here to find out what you are hoping to achieve this close to the galaxy's death. We are here to find out how you fly so fast... How you do so without detectable thrust. We believe that you have technology, which, if it were shared, might save billions of lives. Yet you came here, to a place where you would almost certainly die. We cannot risk your loss, no matter the cost to ourselves."

Julien took the alien's measure with a more considered eye. Perhaps it wasn't so certain who were the bad-guys.

Mission Date: Day 374.   The Last day on Earth.

\* \* \*

Mission Date: Day 374.    The Pequod.

## The Pequod.

"We have all we need here, human. I believe that your team has now, too. We are leaving. Our work is elsewhere now, and we wish you luck in your own destiny. We are also sorry about the fight you are about to face. We cannot take sides." The sentinel said. Its voice resonating throughout the bridge. "You can have your friends now, too. They are no longer a threat."

"Thank you. Any chance you fancied being a little less cryptic?" Katherine asked. But the line was dead, and she was only mildly surprised when she looked up and saw that the sentinels had departed. "Everyone, eyes open, let's find out if there is anything else out there."

The Pequod's radiation shields had kicked up a notch, warning of the approaching star. The dying star. Warning of how little time they had before the entire system was destroyed. Katherine stared at it for a long second, now almost as large in the sky as the system's sun.

"Science has always wondered what these things look like just before the end..." she mumbled to herself.

"Katherine, our sensors are now up again. We have bogies in our sky and there appears to be a ship of some kind landed on the planet, near to our own team." TT called across.

"Dani, shields to maximum and bring us up to a quarter sub-light maximum. I want a course toward that planet, information about everything that's out there, and a firing solution against anything we do not recognise. We are on a compressed timeline here, and we really didn't need any complications. Summers, Jansen, monitor that star and do your best to raise the team. Everyone, prepare for combat. Everyone, prepare the ship to respond with everything she's got."

"Katherine, we are seeing extraordinary changes to velocities and position now. Of all the bodies out there. The planet is shifting in its orbit, but still seems to be in free-fall. It should be survivable, but only potentially, and not for long. It must be hell. The ocean on the other side of the planet from the

Mission Date: Day 374.      The Pequod.

landmass, the side closer to the stars... Katherine, it's boiling... The atmosphere itself is close to igniting. They need to get the fuck out of there... God help us all. Look at that thing," Summers said. Her voice was layered with stress and swearing.

Jansen, with his precious coffee never far from hand, was speaking frantically into his mic. Katherine had no idea who to.

"Thank you, we can't expect it to continue to follow any predicable models... We cannot rely on something funky not happening... or many funky things happening," Katherine said. Drawing a ragged breath. "Reach out to the team on the ground. Someone who's not swamped. See how they're doing? See what the sentinel meant about us having our friends back?"

"Captain, we have eight warships at the planet. Three of which do not need to maintain orbital velocity. Those that do, they are about two-fifty miles above the ground, and are travelling around eighteen hundred miles an hour around the equator. Wedge-shaped, they are all clearly from the Teghra-Dorne Empire. The three which are just hanging there. They read the same as the flagship back at Darla." TT said. "Two of the three, they are moving toward us. Accelerating away from the planet at... not unimpressive levels. The other, it is taking in what looks like life-rafts... Jesus Christ, I think that they are abandoning the other warships." TT turned to face her captain. "Those ships... they must not have the ability to reach FTL in time. Why would they even come here?"

"If anyone has any ideas about why the sentinels hid these from us, save them for the debrief. Or any idea why the empire would throw starships on a futile mission..." Katherine said. The corner of her eye and the countdown dropped to less than half an hour... and this promised only relative stability. Following that, and it would be a very rapid descent into hell. "Okay, those advanced warships, let's assume that it's possible for them to break away, and enter FTL before that star hits. For them to have got ahead of us, all the ships must have jumped in far closer to the planet... Shit..."

"Boss?" Dani asked.

"Just a general observation... Okay, people, ideas?"

Mission Date: Day 374.     The Pequod.

"Boss, we have seen them. From their position, it does not seem that they were aware of us, either. However, something brought them here, and we should assume that they are now. We are not hiding. I say we break for the planet, attempting to remain a distraction for the ground-team, and if the fleet comes at us, we run and hide behind the..." Dani said. Her voice trailing off.

"Dani?" Katherines asked. Suddenly concerned that her pilot was distracted.

"Someone else needs to check this, because I can't find the moon." Dani finally spoke.

"Well, that is a hell of a thing." Jansen said, moments later.

Katherine stared toward the holographic display, pushing her bio-tech to confirm.

"Everyone. Battle stations. I want targeting solutions against every damned thing out there. Dani, get us down there. We must have their backs. Everyone who is not actively involved in this. Strap in, make yourselves safe. Everyone, things are going to get bumpy, I don't want injuries which could be avoided by wearing your damned seat-belts. We know what to do people. Let's get it done."

\*     \*     \*

Mission Date: Day 374.  The Thunder-Child.

## The Thunder-Child.

"What the fuck just happened? Why did we fly into the planet?" Crater shouted from the starboard turret. Doing so, he thought, perfectly reasonably.

"As far as I can tell, we didn't... The ship is telling me that the planet just flew into us," Cleo responded. Fighting to retain altitude control.

"Shit, the team?" Impact hollered.

Cleo tried to push the noise away... this was different, vastly different from her training. The Royal Navy Air Wing, the Fleet Air Arm, had prepared her for war. It has not prepared her for this...

"Computer, damage report?"

"Maverik, the Thunder-Child suffered no damage to any critical or tertiary systems. We have no injuries reported."

"Computer, thank you. I want you to connect with BOB, and I want you to tell me what just happened. There was clearly a gravitational event which shifted this entire planet. I want a report on the health of every member of our ground-team, let me know if any of them are non-operational." Cleo ordered. Looking ahead at the four figures who were pulling themselves to their feet. Still facing the enemy troops, who, if anything, they had fared even worse.

"Impact, Crater. Confirm target selection against the enemy armour. I am about to make ourselves known. If they react aggressively, just fucking kill them. Then take out the soldiers who have not laid down their weapons. The time for any more fucking about... it is gone."

Selecting the Sendler Protocol. Cleo took a breath. Switched off the cloak, and ramped up the shields to maximum. Idly wondering why there were lower settings as she did so.

Mission Date: Day 374.          The Thunder-Child.

"Enemy forces currently threatening our team. Stand-down, and allow us to leave unmolested and I will not take any lethal action against you."

Because it was always good to live in hope.

Then the sun came up. A little earlier than they had expected.

Only, this was very much the wrong sun.

\*       \*       \*

Mission Date: Day 374.              The Thunder-Child.

[Localised gravitational event. Caution, localised solar-radiation event. Armour holding. Shields holding. Advise seeking cover.]

What the fuck?

Julien struggled to first his knees, and then he stood unsteadily on the ground. Staring around him and watching in horror as the grass burned around them. Catching fire, as the planet died. Natalie was already on her feet, her railgun to her shoulder, and staring at the chaos ahead. Around him, the air flared with an almost unbearable heat. His armour flagging warnings, the shimmer of sudden heat-distortion, pouring from the scorched earth in waves.

How had beings, ones who had mastered the travel between stars, not also known this was coming... Why the hell were they getting in their way?

Then the world plummeted away from him again. A second later, and he was forty feet in the air. His neural interface offering him limited flight options, which allowed him a more graceful landing. Cordax had fared far worse and was being helped from his chair by two of his warriors who were still capable of movement. Tata was okay, or he appeared okay when Julien's armour automatically queried his. Daniel was moving, checking on Natalie, who was struggling to her feet.

"Team, we need to get on board the Thunder-Child, and we need to get the fuck out of here." Natalie called.

She wasn't wrong.

The walker units from the empire turned in unison to fire towards the Thunder-Child, which Julien was only now realising wasn't cloaked any longer. Her shields blazing instead.

Their hubris had been tested out here. They had seen technology frighteningly powerful, and more than capable of challenging their own. These machines, against their warbird, they weren't that. Plasma-fire hammered against her shields, enveloping the starship in chaotic fire. But they didn't make a dent. Julien could see Crater and Impact, as their weapon-turrets moved on the dedicated track, already locking onto the machines, and fired only a heartbeat later.

Mission Date: Day 374.             The Thunder-Child.

Designed to battle starships, the inevitable result was brutal and quick.

His armour screamed new things. Previous warnings, ignored warnings, suddenly made real. Telling him about improbable things. About imminent atmospheric-ignition. The outside temperature surged past eighty-degrees.

He could see those who had survived the Thunder-Child's fury Cordax amongst them, highlighted through the smoke and carnage by his armour. Ghosts in the flames.

"Cordax. We are leaving," Julien forced a Sendler Handshake on the dazed alien. "Fuck about, and you die. Behave, and just run."

"... Thank you human... good luck."

The sentiment seemed genuine and surprised Julien.

"Jason... Things are getting very real out here. We must go. Now," Cleo shouted. Dominating the channels. Julien was pretty sure the young woman would wait. But only pretty sure.

"Coming now, we were a little banged up when the world shifted. But we are running. We have two additional people with us... They don't have protective clothing. Cleo, get the Thunder-Child over the doorway. Extend the shields, if it is possible. We will need to get them inside and to the med-bay asap."

"Will do, boss." Cleo responded. The Thunder-Child swinging through the sky to position itself just where she was needed to be.

Julien sprinted toward the descending ramp himself. The fire thankfully subsiding within the shield's influence. Christ knew what state the air was in. Natalie, Daniel, and Tata were only a few strides behind him. Even as he sprinted over the burning grass, struggling to keep his footing on the undulating ground, he marvelled at how wonderful it was to even be able to run in this way. Then the old man remembered the gigantic dying star which was about to collide with the planet's sun, and all feelings of wonderment were replaced once more with impending catastrophe. Had the world not been literally on fire, he might have considered Jason's last update in a little more detail. But instead of that, he was terrified. Taking one last look at a sky

Mission Date: Day 374.  The Thunder-Child.

on fire, and through the flames seeing the two suns. One far larger than the other.

He got inside the ship, just as Jason erupted from the entrance of the pyramid; a middle-aged man held in his arms. Kate following just a heartbeat later, with a woman over her shoulder. With Doc Brown, and then last, BOB.

As he clambered deeper into the ship, moving first through the tiny-hangar, he used his bio-tech to hunt for any sign in the system, which might tell him how Cordax had arrived. The unusually powerful shuttle was about ten-clicks out. Wedge-Shaped, its design familiar enough by now. The image had been captured by the long dead-drones they had sent skyward just a short while ago. He paused, called on his interface to unlock the grav-bikes and sent a Sendler message to the mercenary, letting him know they were available.

Pleased that he had taken a moment to not be a dick. He hammered into the Thunder-Child's control room, pulled an acceleration couch out of the wall, and strapped himself in.

Others would know what to do now. Certainly far better than he did. If he were needed, he would get involved. Until then, he would not get in the way. Natalie was strapped to the command console. The large table, in the centre of the room. Disturbing holograms showing local space hanging before her. Jason sprinted past them both, the man he had been carrying, no longer in his arms, and jumped, feet first, through the opening hatch into the cockpit.

As the hatch closed, Julien reflected that it was odd that their end goal had been to collect two people. He thought it a little odder that he could swear he had recognised them both.

\*   \*   \*

Mission Date: Day 374.               The Thunder-Child.


The Thunder-Child's cockpit had always been configurable for two pilots. Jason did not need Cleo to exit, he just needed to take the stick himself. The cradle extended from behind him, enveloping him and connecting with his armour. Her own cradle, only needing to move to the left. Her controls following her.

"Cleo, thank you. I want you to monitor the sky, and feed the local threats to me," Jason ordered, as he took control. Finding himself immediately fighting the broken influence of the planetary mass below them. The entire ship shaking in the chaos as he stood her on her tail, and sent her blasting into the sky.

"Jesus Christ," Cleo exclaimed.

Jason felt himself completely lost for words as the Thunder-Child found herself in what appeared to be an enormous explosion. An orange-yellow fire that surrounded the starship and bulged against the protesting shields. It took a moment for him to realise that it was the atmosphere itself that was on fire. The initial fury subsiding, but continuing to burn. Dancing around the edge of the shields. Chaotic lightning cutting sheets of white plasma through the flames.

He reached forward and briefly rubbed the tiny marble. The one containing the beautiful depiction of his Earth. Still mounted on the console-pod, now shared between him and... fuck it. She got there first. Between him and Maverick.

The old keepsake would bring them all luck today.

"Cleo, this can't hurt us. What else is happening out there?" Jason asked again.

"On it. We have the Pequod online. They were approached by the sentinels Tata warned us about. The current consensus is that it was the sentinels who hid the empire's approach." Cleo replied. "We have warships which are abandoned in orbit. Ships who would not be fast enough to get free. At least five. Three others, each of a similar class to the one we nuked above Darla. One is picking up life-rafts from the abandoned warships, or rather, it is trying

Mission Date: Day 374.  The Thunder-Child.

to. The others are pursuing Katherine... and we have a metric shit-tonne of fighters... and above that, we have..."

As if to underline her point, the Thunder-Child seemed to stagger in space, to fall outside of any expectation of control, as local space-time struggled to cope.

"What the hell is causing this?" He shouted as the ship bucked around them.

"The moon... it is gone, but not all its effect is gone. We are seeing gravitational waves pulsing from where it used to be... The supermassive star, the impending collision, it's making things rather complicated... but until the moon buggered off, things were a little more predictable." Cleo replied.

"Jesus, okay... right everyone? Everything bad is happening. Pequod. If we cannot dock, we run to the prearranged point and we meet there...Do not wait for us. Go as hard as you can," Jason called out. "Cleo, dial up the chasers to minimise our relative virtual mass as far as possible to still allow us to manoeuvre... and... oh my god."

The Thunder-Child continued to arrow through the burning sky. It took a few moments to recognise the debris, which were falling past the ship, for what they were. The air, the atmosphere, everything was on fire. The fragments were displayed holographically into his line of sight, and he watched in horror as through the chaos fell the brutalised remnants of what must once have been escape pods. The crew of the abandoned warships killed as they had found themselves dragged instead into the planet's influence. Dozens of them, even in their tiny patch of sky, and each filled with so many dead spacers.

The surrounding fire began to finally lessen, and Jason pushed harder as the atmosphere thinned and the corrupted gravity of the planet fell further behind them. Still only by a few percentage points... but he was convinced that he could feel it.

Then, out of the clearing sky, the shattered hull of a dying warship erupted toward him. Balls of fire tearing into the vacuum of space. In free-fall they burned as... It was dreadful. The rupturing hull was skipping through the outer edges of the atmosphere, and Jason was forced to bank hard to avoid it.

Mission Date: Day 374.    The Thunder-Child.

Flying briefly across its dead, wedge-shaped hull. Forgetting it moments later, when...

"Jason, we have multiple missiles fired from that ship. Many aren't making it. Christ, they're struggling, but they have acceleration profiles which suggest they can work outside of... I will handle close defence. Impact, Crater, position and fire on approaching ordinance." Cleo reported calmly.

"Thank you. Tell me if we have an issue I need to respond to, otherwise I am getting us directly to the Pequod." Jason replied. Moving the chasers to... The Thunder-Child shuddered, then fell backwards. Plummeting toward the planet as if some mad god had simply erased their forward momentum with the snap of its fingers. "Damn, the chasers can't maintain a coherent field this close to the planet. Moving over to solid-fuel until we can get far enough out. Relative mass to one-kg..." Jason raced through the control selection and unleashed the full power of her physical engines.

That the Thunder-Child could manage flight at all, her shielding barely still capable of fooling local space about her own weight, had been, by no means, a certain thing. The solid fuel rockets providing millions of pounds of thrust. Jason, needing to fight the controls as to keep her on course. Inexorably, she climbed skyward again, clawing her way back into space, doing so again as the supergiant came again over her new horizon. The shields dimmed, as Jason watched in horror as the two colliding stars seemed to only be moments from touching. The sight was breath-taking, even distracting him from the frantic firing of the close-defence systems and the two turrets, which were fighting off whatever missiles, whatever fighters, had managed to stay with them.

The thrust engines, those that saved them, they had been added almost as an afterthought by a human crew, one not yet ready to fully trust the technology of their benefactors.

A moment later, just a traitorous thought, and he briefly considered what might happen if the shielding around the captured primordial black-hole, which was his ship's heart, failed, or was disrupted at all in the same way... That, at least, would be quick.

"Ten minutes until the end, captain. We need to get further out to help the Pequod... She is being pursued by dozens of fighter craft... and two of the

Mission Date: Day 374. The Thunder-Child.

most powerful warships." Cleo said. "Like us, she seems to be struggling to get power through her Chasers...

"The third warship?"

"She didn't make it clear of the planet."

"Fuck me, all-right. Get the Chasers back online. We are getting stuck in." Jason said.

\*   \*   \*

Mission Date: Day 374.     The Thunder-Child.

"TT, tell me about the fighters?" Katherine shouted.

"They can hurt us, but right now and they are only weakening our shields. But eventually they will hurt us. I am tracking and killing what I can with the turrets... there are just so damned many of them."

The Pequod shuddered as her Chaser drives fought to maintain their coalesced fields, as the starship fought to break free of the chaotic gravitational mayhem.

"Katherine, I am accelerating as fast as we can... but we are not moving fast enough, not yet. We are down to only minutes... and then, only possibly. We need to be pushing hard for FTL, right now, or we will not outrun that thing," Dani shouted out her update as the Pequod was sent on an even more intensive rollercoaster. Tumbling briefly, end over end, her engines were at least capable of compensating for that, and she kept charging forward as best she could. Able to keep the effect of her Chasers facing in the right direction, regardless of the orientation of the ship.

"Captain, the Thunder-Child is clear of the planet... she is moving faster than us, but she will not get past those warships." Jansen followed up.

Katherine stared toward the clear-dome. Her fingers, gripping her bucking chair, white against the straining material. The restraints were enough to keep her pinned there. More than enough. The Pequod could disintegrate around her, and she would still likely be locked into her damned chair.

The holographic images of both the colliding stars, and the warships chasing her ship, meaning to kill them, dominated her view. It made no sense. In engaging in a fight, the empire's forces were killing themselves, too. The stars... Christ, the stars... indecision wracked through her. Determination following in its wake a moment later.

"TT, arm four anti-matter warheads. Target both warships with one each, and have the other two detonate amongst those fighters. Be ready on my go."

"Will do, boss. Ready on your command," TT replied.

"Will they work?" Katherine asked.

Mission Date: Day 374.  The Thunder-Child.

"They will absolutely detonate. Will they fly?... all I have as an answer to that question is 'probably', sorry, boss." TT shrugged.

"Thunder-Child, did you get that?" Katherine asked.

"Katherine... that's insane, but there is nothing else. We are ready," Jason replied.

"Dani, rotate us around and TT fire when everything is pointing in the right direction." Katherine ordered.

A moment later, the star field swung around them, and she stared into chaos. Watching as the saturating weapon fire was only barely visible against the light given off by the super-massive star... She could see tendrils reaching out between the two massive stellar giants now. Arching plasma, which meant nothing good whatsoever. Then she saw the reports of the multiple weapons firing. Then, just seconds later, she saw the sky split asunder by explosions amongst the pursuing fleet.

Before, she would have considered the detonation of the antimatter warheads as unimaginably violent. Today, they were less than an insipid child's toy.

"Captain, we have annihilated the warships. If any of the fighters are still capable of moving under their own power, none are doing so that we can detect." TT reported.

"Dani, bring us around and maintain the charge. Let us see if we can survive this bastard. Thunder-Child, get to us, dock, we are going to need everything either of us still has left to give. Can you make that work in the next two-minutes?"

Because they had less than three.

\*   \*   \*

Mission Date: Day 374.                The Thunder-Child.

"Probably," Jason replied. Dropping the hammer all the way home. "BOB, I want you rationalising any choices I make. Let me know if I am fucking up... Everyone else, hang on."

The Thunder-Child pushed through the wreckage of the destroyed fleet. Shields to maximum, and only barely avoiding the big chunks. Battering the rest out of their way. Speed was all that mattered now. Jason was briefly horrified at the loss of life. Confused why it had been necessary at all.

The thrust-engines had been working flat out for minutes now. Their fuel reserves were burning through horrifyingly fast. But they were gaining on the Pequod, and the Chasers' influence was ramping up as the fields finally bound and started to do their thing properly. As the localised corruption of space-time was better managed, and the engines proved themselves better able to sustain the lie that they were the most powerful gravitational event in the area. The shaking, it had not gone away, and he could easily see the Pequod struggling with the same distortion effects through his sensors. It was distracting. But the Pequod was drawing closer. Not yet visible to his own eyes, she was accelerating hard herself, and the holographic display painted her against his sky.

"Jason, I am sorry. But I must do this," BOB answered seconds later. "Comms down, playing St Elmo's fire."

♪♪*Growing up, you don't see the writing on the wall... Passing by, moving straight ahead, you knew it all,* ♪♪

What the hell?

Jason had watched in horror as his controls first went limp, then retracted away behind him... as did Cleo's. The music surging through his armour, overwhelming with its nineteen-eighties synth urgency. The shuddering lessened, and he heard the Chasers winding up their power again. But now, they were doing so far too fast... Two loud bangs came from deep within the ship behind him. One had been an explosion. At least one. There was a screaming, mechanical roar that wanted to shake his very soul from his body. Nothing could make that sound, not for long, not and continue to function. It didn't lessen, and the ship vibrated violently. A vibration which increased in frequency until it was almost a wall of sound. He could barely move past the

Mission Date: Day 374.     The Thunder-Child.

sheer physical onslaught. There were several more explosions from behind him, although they seemed lesser than the first two. Perhaps it was simply harder to hear over his own screaming.

♪♪*St. Elmo's fire (Ooh, oooh, oooh),* ♪♪... and, of course, over that.

The Pequod, once thousands of kilometres away, grew horrifyingly quickly before him. His tattered mind assumed that BOB had taken over that ship, too. Their velocities seemed to match in the last split second, the Pequod flaring in space, as her hull reared up before them. His warbird presenting her belly to the docking point, and both ships slammed into each other with a terrific force. Jason was bounced around inside the cockpit, only his armour and the strength of the cradle, preventing him from being seriously injured. Cleo was still locked beside him, and he could see her cursing as she held on for dear life herself. He could not hear her. The starships were tumbling through space, but they appeared to be docked. Although sirens, warning of catastrophic damage, wailed through the ship. Those were still audible within the cockpit.

♪♪ *I can climb the highest mountain, cross the wildest sea... I can feel St. Elmo's fire burning in me, burning in me... You don't see the writing on the wall...* ♪♪

That made little sense.

Jason watched the most terrifying event in the universe unfolding before him as the ships spun through space and... was BOB deliberately flying backwards so that Jason could watch his own death?

He watched in utter horror as the stars finally collided. Knowing that he was watching something which had already happened minutes earlier. Entirely unable to turn away, close his eyes, or even blink. The plasma of both folded together through a blaze of impossible energies as the two behemoths slammed together with forces almost incalculable. Certainly, entirely unimaginable. He watched in terrible fascination, hypnotised as something so utterly insane happened before his very eyes. Stella giants. Amongst the largest possible forms of structured matter in the universe, annihilating each other in a blaze of utter...

Mission Date: Day 374.        The Thunder-Child.

♪♪*St. Elmo's fire, St. Elmo's fire,* ♪♪

Perfectly timed.

Because it was beauty. It was that, too. So beautiful. Although he thought it possible, that it might cost him his soul to think so.

The smaller star bulged as it was forced into the larger, disappearing into a star which immediately seemed to shrink away... Too small to be there, anymore... snuffed out, gone. Its matter compressed into a single... its corona, the ejected matter... That was there in insane tatters. Then something grew from the blackness with such immediate terrible burning fury... The Thunder-Child's canopy darkened, the shields flared as the radiation intensified and the ball of almost infinite power grew horrifyingly fast... first, the size of a soccer-ball, then, less than a heartbeat later, it was immediately vast enough to fill the sky... Still a ball, but one whose outside edge was rushing toward them at... He was seconds away from an explosion, bare minutes away from its epicentre, and one which would continue to kill everything in its path for centuries. Blasting death at the speed of light... seconds away and... his last thoughts turned to Kate.

Jason reflected that it was happening too slowly, that all of it was happening far too slowly. That he should already be dead.

Time dilation? How fast were they moving?

... and he continued to watch in fascinated horror, as the edge of the radiation bubble, of chaotic energy, slowed further and then seemed to instead hang there... blazing fire that was suddenly everything. His armour was still feeding him some information, and it was telling him that the event's edge was creeping toward them... that it was less than one-hundred thousand miles away... He had no breath left; he had forgotten how to take the next. He had nothing left in his fractured mind that would allow him to order his armour to stop telling him things he really did not want to know.

Then it fell backwards... dropping back. Which was impossible. Which should have been impossible.

Mission Date: Day 374.                 The Thunder-Child.

He heard Alistair swearing enthusiastically with a maniacal glee. Suddenly aware that he had been doing so for a while now.

Out there, Jason barely processed, was now a singularity, one which would have shed some of its huge velocity as it smashed into the smaller star... but far from all. One which would continue onward upon its terrible journey. Killing everything, after it had killed... him. Which would happen right now...

Then the rainbow came. Brutalised, corrupted at first, and he didn't know if this was his brain failing to cope. Or, if something very funky was happening. Then he remembered that everything funky had already happened. Then it simply smoothed out.

Then the music finally finished.

♪♪*Burning, burning in me, I can feel it burning...* ♪♪

Then he passed out.

Which was fair enough. With all said and done, it had been an eventful day....

\*      \*      \*

Mission Date: Day 374.                    Aftermath.

## Aftermath.

"Where are we?" Jason got out. "Is anyone else alive?"

All he was met by was silence.

He felt a knocking against his armoured chest, and he looked over to see Natalie. Her face was as white as a sheet behind her visor. She leant towards him, pushing her helmet against his.

"Comms are down. I can't get power over to anything at all in the cockpit. Do you know how to open this hatch manually?"

Her voice was faint. She was deliberately transmitting through their hard armour so that he could hear her. Hard carbyne armour, insulated to protect the wearer. It was only by touching visors and screaming at the top of her voice that he had heard her at all.

"Why are the suits comms down?" Jason replied. Shouting himself. Seeing the woman's frustrated face, as she simply shrugged her shoulders.

He forced his restraints free, and untethered his armour. It was just the comms that were not working. The armour's power was reading fine. The starship was another matter altogether. He turned around, grabbed the emergency panel, and popped it open. Inside was a wheel. He grabbed it and wound it. It was not quick. The door was incredibly strong, and the gearing on the manual opening was horrendous. Once he had the thing open, Jason pulled himself through first. Chivalry was not dead. He was simply a massive bastard, and Cleo would have needed to squeeze past him. He got through to the Control centre. Seeing Natalie crouched in the far corner, her head in her hands. Seeing Julien pinned to a seat. Watching events with a crazed eye. The other closed... fluttering on a face which suddenly looked as old as the dying man he had pulled free from the Greek island. A lifetime ago.

BOB was there, looking toward a console. Jason strode toward him and tapped him on the top of his head. The pixilated face turned toward him, and Jason tapped his helmet and mimed a phone. Puzzlement flickered across

Mission Date: Day 374.                    Aftermath.

BOB's face, replaced immediately afterwards by understanding, and suddenly his comms burst into life. Angry voices filled the space. Questions, accusations... general levels of fractured minds recovering from an extraordinarily high-stress situation.

"Right, this is Jason. Private feeds only, or stay off the comms. Anyone not responsible for keeping either starship flying, and who can still move under their own power, I want you to find and treat any injured. I am with BOB, and I will report back shortly." Jason ordered. He checked his armour's readout. The atmosphere was solid, relatively, so he stowed his helmet. Finally, drawing a ragged breath. Finally, free to. Coughing on the acrid fumes.

"BOB, what the fuck happened?" Jason asked. His own voice cracked as he attempted to process quite a lot. "Why did you turn the ship? What the hell was the music for?"

"We were not going to make it. Not unless I took control, myself. I didn't have time to ask permission." BOB replied. "I needed to concentrate. Too many people were speaking. So, I disabled comms. Turning the ship, would you ever have forgiven me had you missed that? I piped the images to anyone still wearing armour. Those with augments, too. The music? I thought that might help calm people."

"Okay, bold choice and the music was so disturbingly fitting a choice that I don't even know where to start peeling back those layers. Not yet, not even close. I think I watched the nova almost touching us, just before we hit FTL.... I watched it slow down as we hit light-speed in real space... That is not meant to be possible... my friend, I do not doubt that if you had waited for another second..."

"Less than a second... so far less than a second, that I don't think you are even close to being ready to hear the full truth of it... and yes, it was not possible until I made it possible. We didn't hit light speed, not in real-space. That remains something that matter cannot ever achieve. But we got close enough to... Jason, before I did this, I had calculated only a little over an eighteen percent chance we would survive at all... I soon discovered I had been wildly optimistic. I may ask you more about those gods that watch over you, but perhaps a little later. I had no other choice, but I still thought I was killing us all. We have damage to both ships. Catastrophic damage that will take

Mission Date: Day 374.          Aftermath.

months to repair. My docking manoeuvre was... enthusiastic and what I asked of the engines, of both ships, both before and immediately after, was... a lot. But we are a little over two light-years from the Pangea system. We have time to repair ourselves and to leave before we are in any further danger."

Jason was a little concerned that BOB was now referring to the system as that.

"Where are we, BOB?" Natalie asked. Her own helmet now stowed, too. Her face wan.

"We are lost in the space between stars." BOB answered. "We are safe. No one can find us here. The closest system is gone now. The next nearest is four-light-years away..."

"Okay, good." The young woman replied.

Jason watched the text-only update. The casualty report. Colm was critically injured. But should recover. The scientist, Summers, she had a broken arm and hip. Both were in the infirmary. There were no other significant injuries. Although few had escaped entirely unscathed. They had been damned lucky.

"Good news team. The ships are repairable... We are going to be okay." He broadcast to both ships. "Not for a little while, and there is a lot of work to do. Quite a lot to do, before we can even consider transferring between the Pequod and the Thunder-Child... the transition room did not survive the docking manoeuvre. But we should be safe where we are for now."

\*     \*     \*

Mission Date: Day 374.    Aftermath.

He made his way deeper into the Thunder-Child. There was someone he wanted to speak to.

Looking around, as walked through his ship, seeing evidence of overloaded systems everywhere. Fire-damage, where there was nothing present that should have been able to catch fire. Even one section of the corridor which curved around the singularity on the top deck, the walls of which had blown out entirely. Power trunking, as thick as his waist, which had apparently been super-heated to where the surrounding material had exploded. The stench of ozone pervaded the entire ship. There was also the stench of burned plastic, almost everywhere. Acrid, catching in his throat. Which was odd. As far as he was aware, there was no plastic onboard the ship.

It would be nice to finish a mission, just once, without breaking his damned ship. Without being unconscious, himself.

He had looked in at the mess-room on his way past, seeing Impact and Crater sitting there. Both men looking like they would need a minute. Both men staring at an unopened bottle of whisky on the table between them. Neither drinking, not just yet. Two men who would have been sitting in the turrets as the stars collided.

Two men, who would have been front and centre to the most savage event that it was likely that any considered mind had ever looked at before, and survived to tell the tale.

"Save me a glass," He grunted. Crater raised the bird, then changed that to a thumbs up. Good enough.

He might join them later.

He pushed this thought to the back of his mind for now.

He had people to speak to first.

*   *   *

Mission Date: Day 374.        Anger.

## Anger.

Before all of that. He made a quick stop in his quarters first.

Jason had picked up his railgun again, but had shuck off his armour. Pushing it into his locker for servicing and cleaning. After a quick shower, a longer cry, and pausing only to grab his weapon, he had stormed into the infirmary.

Daniel was already there, so was Kate. Only Kate was still in her armour. Both looked pissed. Both were likely battling a hell of a lot of emotions following the last year and the sheer scale of events they had just barely survived.

Tempers were fraught. His own? He thought it likely that his last nerve was hanging there by the slenderest of threads. The wolf was literally howling in fury just below the surface. Its rage masking its terror. He was barely able to control it. Barely wanting to. James looked at him. Saw his anger, wincing. Jason raised his weapon and drew a bead on the man's face. Shocking himself that he had done so. He was possibly a little more surprised that he didn't immediately shoot the man.

Doc Brown was there, raising his hands and looking like he might try to deescalate things.

[Calm,] Alistair advised. [If you are going to shoot him, do so in his leg...]

"Alistair says hello, James." Jason growled. Before turning to Kate. "You good?"

"Not in the slightest bit. But far better than I have any right to be. I spoke with Katherine. She is pretending to not be as excited, as she so bloody obviously is, about the data we were able to capture from the... from that sodding event. She will wait, I hope, for everyone to calm down a little bit first." Kate replied. Smiling wanly. Then she screamed... smiled a crazy smile and cried a little bit. Jason gave her a minute. "No one sees what we just saw... not and lives." She finally said.

Jason had no idea what to say about any of that.

Mission Date: Day 374.        Anger.

He looked over at Daniel. The man merely raised his middle finger, giving Jason the bird. Jason ignored him. Turned to the two rescued from the planet. Closed his eyes and counted. He reached higher than he might have otherwise thought he might, before he could open his eyes again.

"Now, which one of you two is going to speak first?" Jason growled. Looking back at James, then across the small room to the other medical bed. Staring at the lady sitting there. "I would caution you both first against any thoughts you might have about lying to me..."

"I am so sorry to have put you through so much," the lady started.

"Kate, you know her. What is her actual name?" Jason asked. "Not that name she gave me when we last met... What is her actual name?"

"Emma Urien." She ran another department back in London.

"Witchy stuff?" Jason asked.

"Witchy stuff." Kate confirmed.

[ask the woman if she is related to Urien Rheged...] Alistair advised. His thoughts becoming Jason's a moment later.

"You have, I think, been known by many names. Miss Le Fay?" Jason asked. His heart sinking.

"Many names," she replied. Sighing. "Although, you know as well as anyone that legends become myths and so much is lost in history that the truth is sometimes perhaps close, but rarely what you might guess it to be."

"You sent a woman to meet with me. She found me in Bordeaux. Yet, when I saw you a few years later, you carried then the amulet Kate has now..."

"I did. For you, it was still your future then, although now your past. But then, it was still my future, too... I, we were both caught and held and my abilities, they were damped. But I could still cast my stone into the aether... I could instil within it an intent which would hopefully find you, and guide you all to hopefully find us."

Mission Date: Day 374.           Anger.

"It would have been useful to start with where you actually were." Jason said. He thought perfectly reasonably.

"If only we had known ourselves," she smiled. "Breadcrumbs. I am sorry that we could not do any better."

"Because, even arriving a few hours earlier, and that would have been a lot less exciting." Jason said. Again, he thought, doing so perfectly reasonably.

"Just a few hours earlier, and the sentinels might not have been so happy for you to become involved. Timing, Lord Connaught, in life, as it is in comedy... it is far too often, everything." The woman replied. "Also, don't consider me the architect of all your more recent troubles, young man... There are other things afoot."

"I have not gone by that name, not in a long time..." Jason replied angrily. "James, what was your place in this... what happened to you?" Jason asked. Turning his attention to the other. Sniffing him... "Christ, was this Monaco?"

"It was Monaco, yes. Daniel's old friend."

"Alistair's, too."

James just nodded. Slowly.

"Okay, Morgan Pendragon... It is time that you tell us a story which will not have me blasting you out of the nearest airlock. You have taken us away from our mission, doing so with cold manipulation. You bring us to a world based on an ancient Earth, with a moon crafted from a bastardisation of Theia and... Christ knows what else..."

"... and your payment for your services was Kate's father... I wove such a tangled web, but it was not one with only selfish ends."

"Talk," Jason ordered. Bringing the weapon to his shoulder.

"Okay, you will not be entirely happy with what I must tell you. But I should start with a warning." She said.

"Go on."

Mission Date: Day 374.  Anger.

"Because this is where things get a little more complicated."

\* \* \*

# THE END!

## For now.

# Authors Note.

## Book Five: Their terrible purpose.
## Originally, 'The longest patrol.'

The title changed. In the last weeks of editing the final run-though.

The original title, 'The longest patrol,' this came from an old Battlestar Galactica episode from the seventies. To me, it spoke of the team losing themselves in the far past. But then I wrote 'Their terrible purpose,' for the first time as a phrase… and it became that, instead.

It fits the narrative better than the other. Also, the intrepid crews have further to go in the next instalment. That first title, it has a new home there.

As an author, my life is simpler than the days of paper manuscripts. Far simpler. Changing a title, a matter of moments.

'All they can do is hope that they have prepared enough.'

This phrase it kept coming back to me as I worked through book four. The Fracture.

The Progenitors, they attacked a galaxy which had been teaming with life. Working to exterminate all others. If the team travels back in time to before that, they will therefore find themselves in a galaxy which could well be teaming with life.

This was a galaxy that they would need to navigate carefully.

Also, they had not been masters of their own destiny so far, so why start down that path now?

Authors Note.   Originally, 'The longest patrol.'

The amulet. They had this thing. We first encountered it when we met the Lady in the bar in London. As Daniel hunted his monster in 'Songs to dance to'. It was then gifted to Jason in Bordeaux.

It tied back to Theia; I knew that already. But there was also power there which was far more nuanced than simply moon rock. That became a little more obvious when I considered its influence in Hermentia, during the Fracture.

Could it have intent, too?

So, where do they go?

We found out.

Where do they go next?

There are two stories. The Longest Patrol and Monaco. These will be told in one book. If they have a long way to go, stories of the past should be shared to pass the time.

Because someone built Pangea. Because it was not Earth. The moon there, that came from somewhere else, too. It has a purpose, but what purpose? Someone else is out there, who is powerful enough to destroy that project by throwing a star at it.

We really need to meet them.

Also, James, Jason... something happened in Monaco.

The Sendler Protocol.

A handshake shared between spacefaring races. The first voyager probes explained humanity on a golden record. Carved into that record were depictions of the simplest atom. The first element. Hydrogen. It was deliberately displayed in its two lowest states. Something which should be instantly recognisable to another race. The shared knowledge, from which understanding of one-another, might someday grow.

Authors Note.                Originally, 'The longest patrol.'

We could do more today. Better. Just in a few decades and a probe the size could carry the entire history of our species. Far more, by the time we reach out into the stars ourselves...

I like to think that BOB made shorter work deciphering it than most would have. But I enjoyed the thought that such a thing would exist.

Thank you, once more, kind reader.

Aiden.

Printed in Great Britain
by Amazon